The Tigress Caged

Helen Rayson-Hill

Glass House Books
Brisbane

Glass House Books
an imprint of IP (Interactive Publications Pty Ltd)
Treetop Studio • 9 Kuhler Court
Carindale, Queensland, Australia 4152
ipoz.biz/glass-house-books/
ipoz.biz/ipstore

First published by IP in 2023

© 2023 Helen Rayson-Hill, and IP

Printed in 12 pt Book Antiqua on 14 pt Avenir Book

ISBN 9781922830371 (PB); ISBN 9781922830388 (eBook)

A catalogue record for this book is available from the National Library of Australia

Glass House Books
The Tigress Caged

Helen Rayson-Hill trained as an infant teacher, and taught in country Victoria, Melbourne and the UK. Later, she became a drama teacher following a long interest in the theatre.

After a family transfer to Brisbane, she was appointed Queensland Manager of the Australian Elizabethan Theatre Trust. For two years she co-ordinated National Arts Week in Brisbane, working closely with the Queensland Government's Ministry of the Arts and Brisbane City Council.

On returning to Melbourne, Helen held a position at the Victorian Arts Centre in the Membership and Fundraising and Development Department. For two years she was an adjudicator for the Victorian Drama League.

Helen has performed on the stage in Melbourne and Brisbane and on television in *Neighbours* on Channel 10 and *Something's in the Air* on the Australian ABC network.

Writing has always been an interest of Helen's and she is a member of the Writers' Circle at Melbourne's Lyceum Club. She has written plays for her drama students as well as sketches for amateur theatre. Also an artist specialising in oils, Helen has held successful exhibitions at several Victorian galleries.

Helen's short stories and memoir pieces have been published in anthologies, and she has written a children's book, *Kid Detectives*. The story was inspired by her grandson who wanted to know how children entertained themselves before electronic devices filled their lives.

Helen has long been interested in Medieval history, especially in the life of Eleanor of Aquitaine. After many years of research, inspired originally by the play *The Lion in Winter* by James Goldman, Helen was motivated to write about Eleanor's amazing life. *Eleanor, the Firebrand Queen* became the first in a series of historical novels about this Medieval feminist, followed by *The Lion and the Tigress* and now this, the third volume.

Glass House Books
Brisbane

for my family

Contents

Genealogy   viii

Chapter 1 The Young King   1

Chapter 2 The Truth Will Out   7

Chapter 3 Prophesy and Death   45

Chapter 4 A Blessed Relief   60

Chapter 5 Aftermath   71

Chapter 6 Conflict   82

Chapter 7 Geoffrey's Wedding   91

Chapter 8 The Death of Pendragon   96

Chapter 9 Henry Cornered   107

Chapter 10 Festering Rebellion   111

Chapter 11 Incarceration   123

Chapter 12 A Loosening of the Shackles   137

Chapter 13 A Stolen Inheritance   151

Chapter 14 Grief and a Joyous Reunion   160

Chapter 15 Matilda, Queen of Saxony   165

Chapter 16 Amaris   179

Chapter 17 The Christmas from Hell   209

Chapter 18 The End of An Era   235

Genealogy

Eleanor: 1122/23-1204 (Birthdate sometimes disputed) Queen of England, Duchess of Aquitaine and Gascony, Countess of Poitou

Mother: Aenor de Rochefoucault married William X of Aquitaine

Grandmother: Dangerosa de Rochefoucault

Grandfather: Aimery de Rochefoucault Viscount of Châtellerault

Uncle: Lord Ralph de Faye, mother's brother

Father: Duke William X of Aquitaine

Uncle: Prince Raymond of Antioch, father's youngest brother six years older than Eleanor

Grandfather: Duke William IX of Aquitaine

Grandmother: Phillipa, Countess of Toulouse, Eleanor was rightfully Countess of Toulouse by inheritance

(Dangerosa and William IX were lovers and lived openly together in the Maubergeonne Tower in the Palace of Poitiers.)

Eleanor's sister Petronilla (also known as Nilla): Countess of Vermandois, husband Raoul, Count of Vermandois

Eleanor's brother: William Aigret (Died as a baby or toddler)

***

Henry II (Plantagenet): King of England, Duke of Normandy, Count of Anjou 1133-1189

Mother: Empress Matilda, Dowager Duchess of Normandy (Cousin of Stephen of Blois, Stephen's son Eustace)

Father: Geoffrey Plantagenet, Duke of Normandy, Count of Anjou

Brothers: Geoffrey and William, half-brother Hamelin (Illegitimate) Mother said to be Adelaide of Anjou

***

Children to Eleanor and Henry:

William, Count of Poitiers 1153-1156

Henry (Hal) the Young King 1155-1183, married Princess Margaret of France

Matilda, Queen of Saxony 1156-1189, married King Henry, the Lion of Saxony

Richard I (the Lion Heart) King of England 1157-1199, married Berengaria of Navarre

Geoffrey, Duke of Brittany 1158-1186, married Constance of Brittany

Phillip (Date of birth not recorded. Probably died shortly after birth)

Eleanor (Lenore) 1161-1214 Queen of Castile, married King Alphonso of Castile

Joanna 1165-1199 Queen of Sicily, married King William of Sicily, second husband Raymond VII of Toulouse

John 1166-1216 King of England, married Hawise daughter of William, Earl of Gloucester (marriage annulled), married Isabella of Angoulême

Other Historical Figures:

Geoffrey (the Bastard) 1152-1212 Henry's illegitimate son, before marriage to Eleanor, became Archbishop of York, mother possibly Ykenai

Otto Duke of Brunswick, Eleanor's grandson (son of Matilda and Henry of Saxony), became Holy Roman Emperor, considered once to become Duke of Aquitaine

Eleanor's 1st husband King Louis VII of France, their daughters Marie and Alix

Thomas Becket, became Archbishop of Canterbury, succeeded by Archbishop Baldwin

Saldebreuil de Sanzay, Constable of Aquitaine

English Chancellor Geoffrey Ridel

Hugh de Saint-Maure, a powerful Poitivin noble

Princess Alais of France, Louis VII's second daughter to second wife Constance, sister Margaret, wife of Young King of England, Hal (Henry III)

King Phillip Augustus, Louis VII's son to third wife Adela

Count Raymond V of Toulouse

Chapter 1 The Young King

Papa's old library was my sanctuary. I slumped into the chair at my desk and turned the pages of my journal. So much had happened.

Henry had arrived at the Palace of L'Ombrière to collect Hal. The time had come for him to be crowned the Young King of England in Westminster Abbey, but he balked at the prospect.

'Darling, your crowning is a great honour. It is your father's tradition. Not only that, it is your duty.'

'I do not care! I do not want the damn title, two meaningless words. And I am not going back to England, so there!' He stomped to the door.

I raised my voice. 'I am sorry, Hal, but you must obey. As I have said, you are duty-bound. Furthermore, this is your destiny. It is ordained...'

'No!' The door slammed.

But I was certain it was his suspicions regarding the state of Henry's and my marriage that was behind his reluctance. His father and I were estranged. I had walked out, bolted to the Aquitaine after discovering his affair with Rosamund Clifford, which was at its height when John was born. Amidst the hurt and humiliation, though, I think I still loved Henry, desired him...but?

When Henry arrived, he begged my forgiveness. He kissed me and tried to unlace my gown, but the braided cords knotted in his haste. Frustrated, he tried to rip the sumptuous robe from my body. We ended in a tangled heap on my bed fully clothed, boots and all. Henry tore at his braies with one hand, with the other, he tried to hoist the twisted silk above my knees. My passion for him almost over-ruled common sense. But, at the last moment, I could not bring myself to lie with a husband I no longer trusted. I struggled from his groping and pushed him away.

Hell was about to break lose between us when Jerome banged on my chamber door.

'Lord Henry! Lord Henry!' His voice was insistent. 'A courier has just delivered a missive for you, Milord. He said it is most urgent and must be placed in your hands immediately.'

Henry stormed to the door, wrenched it open and snatched the letter from my dear childhood companion, now a Benedictine monk. I dashed towards my dressing room, but an animal howl halted me. The letter was from Henry's brother William. Their mother, Empress Matilda, had died.

Within days, the family sailed to Barfleur and galloped to Rouen. Matilda had been interred in her beloved Abbey of Bec by the time we arrived. We attended memorial services and prayers for her immortal soul in Rouen Cathedral.

Henry readied himself to sail to England after the ceremonies were over. But Hal was still stubbornly protesting.

'I am not going! I do not want to be crowned.'

I tried to calm him. 'Hal, please, listen. I have told you; you have no choice. You are your father's heir—by the Grace of God, the Young King of England.'

Hal was about to bolt. I barred the door.

'Hal, please…please…do it for me.'

We stood eyeball to eyeball.

'I am not going without you, Maman. I do not care what you say!'

I took Hal's face in my hands. 'I promise I will accompany you. I want to, and it is my duty.' I kissed his forehead and left to inform Henry of my decision.

I steadied myself and entered Henry's chamber.

'Henry, I am sorry to interrupt, but I must speak to you.' Icicles hung in the air. 'I will be returning to England with you to attend Hal's crowning as the Young King.'

'And so you should, Eleanor. It is your duty, as my queen as well as to Hal.'

'I am aware of my duties to Hal, Henry.'

His tone of voice had me gritting my teeth, so I turned to leave, muttering, 'It is a pity you do not.'

'So that is it, Eleanor?' Henry shouted after me, 'Why not just send a courier?'

***

We arrived in London. Preparations for the crowning were finalised. Richard, Geoffrey and the three girls were excited as was our youngest son John, who was with us from Fontevrault Abbey.

The ceremony proclaiming Hal as the Young King was deeply spiritual. The pride I had in my beloved son was immeasurable when the crown was placed on his head.

But Thomas Becket's bitterness hovered. Henry had forbidden him from crowning Hal, although it was his right as Archbishop of Canterbury. Instead, Archbishop Roger of York officiated. Becket was out for vengeance. He had refused to obey the Common Laws of England like his predecessor, and his defiance led to a schism between him and his king. Becket insisted unordained clerks who committed crimes while employed by the church should be judged by Canon Law, rather than within England's legal system. Thomas Becket then exiled himself in Paris and endeared himself to no-one other than like-minded clerics.

***

We returned to the Palace at Westminster after the ceremomy for a sumptuous banquet in the Great Hall, now as bare as a monastery refectory. After I discovered Henry's affair, I stripped our royal residences of all adornment that came from my dowry. I started at Woodstock and worked my way through Windsor, Westminster and Winchester, our major royal residences. Henry was lucky to be left with a bed to sleep in, let alone a feather mattress.

As far as I was concerned, Henry deserved the austerity with no rich décor to impress his barons or another woman. Luckily, the weather was balmy or the elaborate tapestries that had kept out the draughts would be missed. I wondered what excuses Henry used to explain their disappearance. Sir Robert whispered he was having a war against extravagance.

After the celebrations were over, the rest of the children and I prepared to return to the Aquitaine. Hal had to remain with his father. He was miserable. I took him to the library, the only place I had not torn asunder, and sat him down.

He begged. 'Maman, please, please stay. It is going to be hell without you.'

'Do not despair, darling…'

'But, Maman, what will I do? Papa barely talks to me. I will be twiddling my thumbs.'

'I will speak to your father, make him realise he must give you duties to train you for your regal responsibilities.'

'That will be the day. You are the one who teaches us; Papa just yells.'

'I will do my best to make him understand.'

Hal thumped his fist on my desk.

'Why will you not tell me what is really going on between you and Papa?'

'It is better we live apart to give us time to heal our differences,' I muttered.

I knew it was a lame excuse. Hal was on the cusp of manhood. I had no idea what he knew about laying with a woman. It was something I could not discuss as his mother, nor could I reveal the gruesome facts as to why I could not stay in England as Henry's wife. I believed Hal was still too young to understand the causes of his parent's marital problems.

***

I had discovered other infidelities on Henry's part while in London. These were women of noble birth, not just a couple of milkmaids or tavern strumpets, but women who no doubt were attracted to the king by his title. Some had borne him children.

I confronted him. 'What is your explanation, Henry?'

'It is a pack of lies by those who want to discredit me and come between us. Was it Owain Pendragon, or Brynn, that Welsh witch?'

I ignored his insinuations and handed him a list.

'Anyone could have written that!'

'The proof comes from a convent where at least one of your bastard daughters is housed.'

He went pale, but I remained calm. 'I will be leaving within the week for Bordeaux with the rest of the children. It is also time you fulfilled your promise to Geoffrey by bestowing on him the title of Duke of Brittany. Try to get on with Hal, and for God's sake, Henry, give him duties! Teach him about the governance and laws of his kingdom. I have started the process. It is time for you to continue it. Now I must prepare for my departure.'

Henry put his hand on my arm.

'Take your hand off me,' I demanded.

When he did not, I slapped it away and walked with as much dignity as I could.

'We have a political alliance, Eleanor. You are still my queen.'

With my hand on the doorknob, I paused.

'Mop up your own mess, 'enri Plantagenet-a. I broker peace then you destroy it. As I was trained by my father, I will govern the Aquitaine. I will work to repair the damage you caused in my County of Poitou by sending your mercenaries to pillage the land and rape innocent villagers. I will endeavour to regain the trust of my vassals by applying the laws of my duchy, not the Anglo-Norman tyranny you live by. Now I will take my leave.'

***

The day before my departure, Hal again begged me not to leave him with his father. I hugged him and reminded him I would see him in Normandy when he was to marry Princess Margaret of France. Hal ranted and raved, sounding horribly like Henry.

'It is bad enough that I must wear a hollow crown. Now I must marry a baby.'

Hal's indignation made me laugh. 'Darling, Princess Margaret is about your age.'

'Really?' Hal then smiled. 'Yes, I suppose she would have grown. What does Margaret look like? She could be ugly?'

'I have never seen her. King Louis prevented that. But Louis was good looking when I knew him. Margaret's mother, the late Queen Constance, was said to be attractive, dark-haired, Spanish looking.'

'What if Margaret is narrow-minded like King Louis?'

'That I cannot answer, but as she has not been reared in the French court, she may have had a wider upbringing.'

'Will I have to go to bed with her?' Hal blushed.

'Ah… well now… that is something you will have to ask your father or Sir Robert. But I am sure if she is attractive, that is… um… something you will want to do.'

Hal shuffled his feet as I cleared my throat.

'Darling, try to get along with your father. We are duty-bound to follow the destinies that God and our births have placed on us. We cannot do otherwise.'

'I am never going to forgive Papa. I know he has done something bad to you and I do not want to stay in England. My life is going to be wretched.'

'Darling, you are not entirely alone. You have Millicent and Agnes with you, and all the members of your court from the day you were born. Sir Robert will always be a mentor, too, and friend if you need advice.' I had to keep a brave face.

Dear God, I prayed, *please help Henry to be a father to his son and heir.*

It was a wrenching goodbye. Henry came to Queenhithe Dock on the Thames but stood aloof. I did not acknowledge him. We had nothing more to say to each other. Robert escorted me and the other children onto the barque. They, too, were sad saying good-bye to their brother. I begged Robert to look after Hal, to keep me informed of his progress, and to try to get father and son to respect each other if nothing else.

Chapter 2 The Truth Will Out

When I returned to Poitiers, I summoned my justiciars for a report about what had transpired in the Aquitaine while I was in England. Uncle Ralph said there were still some disgruntled Poitivins after Henry's rampage through the County. A diplomatic discourse would have been far more judicious than sending in his troops. It would remain a festering sore for years. I said I would write again to the complainants to see if I could calm them. Some of the nobles, though, were going to have to be patient. I had pacified most, but one or two held a grudge, Hugh de Saint-Maure being the most outspoken. By now, the reparation I put in place in the affected villages should be helping.

Apart from Poitou's grumbles, there were few disputes to consider; just the usual charters and petitions. We moved on to the exchequer, which was healthy. But we had scarcely finished treasury matters when a courier slid off his horse with epistles from the Limousin where pockets of discontent flared occasionally.

I would have to ride there to deal with these cantankerous vassals—a week in the saddle that I did not need. I decided to take Richard. He would encounter problems of this nature in the future, and the experience would be beneficial.

After we arrived, we met with the local justiciars. A list of grievances was thrust under my nose from the same families around Limoges and Châlus. I read documents going back many years, old charters that should prove or disprove ongoing claims over estate boundaries. Dowries were also disputed. Was it ever thus?

These same nobles had been bickering for generations, at times aggressively with sieges and destruction. They drove my mild-tempered father mad. Although they were becoming belligerent again, so far, they had not come to blows. I intended to end their stupidity. My forbearance, especially in my present mood, was exhausted. If they thought they could intimidate me, they were wrong. I summoned them.

'Gentlemen, unless you can come to peaceful agreements to abide by the judgements put in place by my father, you will face more than my wrath.'

Their defiant looks provoked my ire.

'I refuse to put up with your frivolous disputes. Furthermore, let me impress on you, if you think Lord King Henry's methods of law enforcement are bad, they are nothing to what I can inflict on you. The choice is yours. Stop your petty disagreements and stop wasting my time.'

I glared down at them from the dais where I and the panel were assembled. 'You live on estates bestowed on your forebears through generous charters afforded to them by my Great Grandfather, Duke William VIII of Aquitaine, for loyal service. Those, I can cancel with a stroke of my quill. You will be stripped of your titles, and with your heirs you will be tilling the earth with your serfs. Moreover, your castles will be levelled to the ground if I do not throw you into dungeons of hell in the meantime.'

Before they could utter a word, I turned on my heel and stormed out. I was tired of their discontent. When Henry was around, they kept their heads down till he was back in Normandy or England. They would then don their rusty mail, wave broad swords, and threaten each other's lands—enough was enough!

To prove my point, I took hostages from their families and told the lords of Limoges and Châlus their children would be returned when they peacefully settled their strife. I gave them four weeks.

Their wives screamed and wailed as I rode away at the head of my guard. It was most unpleasant. Once I would never have acted so severely, but I was in no mood for their pathetic squabbles. It was time to make an example of what could befall others if they stretched the laws of the Aquitaine to build petty fiefdoms!

***

Richard was quiet during our return to Poitiers. I could see something was troubling him but waited till we threw off our capes before questioning him. I was weary and not happy with myself.

'Well, Richard, what is on your mind? You have hardly said a word since we left the Limousin.'

He mumbled something.

'For God's sake, spit it out. I do not have all day.'

'Maman, um...'

'Well?'

'You have always stressed it is better to be diplomatic when dealing with our nobles. Even when they are being a nuisance you have emphasised that we should listen to their arguments to get the facts, to look at both sides of the debate. But you behaved like Papa in the Limousin. You charged in yelling and screaming, and now we have six little hostages sobbing in the garrison.' It came out in a rush.

Before I could get a word in, Richard went on.

'What happened to consensus, Maman? You have always said threats were counterproductive.'

'I, well...'

The weir burst and Richard was in full flow.

'What has happened to you? You have become like a... winter's day, cold and horrible. You bite every one's heads off. You are more impatient than usual. We want our smiling, loveable Maman back!'

'Oh... I.' To be honest I was at a loss for words.

'Why not say what is going on?' Richard had gone red in the face.

'I have a few worries I am trying to overcome. They are more concerning than I thought they would be, and I am sorry if they are affecting my temperament and judgement.'

'I know that is not the full story, Maman. Just wait. I will be back.' Richard harrumphed.

I sat with my head in my hands. My life was now burdened with sadness, which dragged me down. Furthermore, I had not told the children why I was really in the Aquitaine.

Richard reappeared, puffing. He thrust a letter into my hands. I recognised Hal's scrawly writing, thinking it was good the brothers corresponded till I read the contents. Hal's letter was full of invective. He called his father a faithless despicable rat who had broken my heart and had given me no choice but to leave.

*Rich, I hate Papa. There are more bastards than
hairs on a cat's back. One day, I will kill our father
for what he has done to Maman—to us. I am miserable and lonely here. I miss you all. As you know I
did not want to be crowned the Young King. It is a
burden and Papa teaches me nothing. Sir Robert tries
to keep me cheerful but often he is away serving Papa.*

Rich, keep Maman safe and try to make her happy.

*Your brother,
Hal*

My icy resolve melted. Poor Richard had to mop up the deluge.
He was a big boy, fast becoming a man. He gave me a clumsy,
loving hug, not really knowing what he should do.

'I am sorry, darling. Can you order me a drink?'

Richard knelt by my chair. His earnest blue eyes stared into
mine. He then stood, strode to the door, and wrenched it open.
He turned with a face like a storm cloud.

'If Hal does not kill him, I will!' The foundations shook as
he exited.

My thoughts bounced around my brain. How could I
explain? Richard would tell Geoffrey, who would analyse Henry
and me with calculated curiosity and cause more anger from
Richard. Matilda, who adored her father, would be distraught
that he was not the paragon she believed he was. Lenore and
Joanna hardly knew him, and John was back at Fontevrault.

Richard returned with wine, which I did not really want at
that time of day but accepted graciously, because he did not know
otherwise. He picked up Hal's letter from the floor, crushing the
parchment in an iron fist. I thanked him for the wine while
Henry-like he stormed around the room.

'Richard, stop! Slamming doors and threatening your father
does not help.'

He pouted but stopped pacing in circles. I could not avoid
the issue any longer. It was time for a family conference.

'I need to talk to your brother and sisters. Come.'

I strode to the school room where the others were attending
their lessons. I dismissed the tutors except for Jerome, whose

support I needed. Matilda and Geoffrey glanced at each other.

On second thought, I told Lenore and Joanna to go and play. They were too young for the canon ball with which I was about to shatter their lives. Jerome sensed something was amiss. I told Richard to sit and hissed at him to keep his mouth shut. Jerome sat beside him, for which I was grateful.

'Maman...'

I cut Geoffrey off.

'I know the three of you are aware your father and I are not happy. I am still Queen of England... but as far as I am concerned, my marriage to your father is over.'

None of them uttered a sound. Richard sat with his head down. Geoffrey's eyes were boring through me, for once unable to read my mind. The silence was shattered by Matilda shrieking.

'Why are you being so cruel to Papa?'

Richard's voice was strident. 'Because he is sleeping with every bitch on heat in England and God knows where else. We all know about our half-brother, Geoffrey the Bastard, well there are others.' He flattened out the screwed-up epistle.

'Read this.'

Silence fell while Matilda scanned Hal's letter, before sweeping it away. 'I do not believe this. Hal is making it up. Papa loves Maman.'

Then they all started yelling at once.

'Stop! All of you!' I barked.

Jerome put his hand on my arm. I had not told him about Henry's other indiscretions, but he realised there was truth in what Richard said. He asked to read Hal's letter. His heavy sigh filled the schoolroom.

'This is a shock. I knew about Rosamund Clifford...'

'Who is Rosamund Clifford?' Geoffrey's voice rose above Jerome's.

Jerome looked me in the eye, but I answered. 'Your father's first affair—as far as I know.'

The children looked from one to the other, stunned into silence.

I was shaking.

Jerome continued; his voice was flat. 'As I said, I knew... from your mother... but I did not know about these others. Matilda,

I know you love your father, but he has given into temptation in Lady Eleanor's absence. You cannot imagine how hurtful that is. Your mother loves your father and thought he loved her. The first infidelity was devastating. Now Hal says there are others. Should these not have occurred, there might have been a small chance of a resolution.'

I stopped Jerome. Matilda was crying piteously. Geoffrey was stunned, speechless for once. Richard's clenched knuckles were white.

I stood and put my arms around Matilda's shoulders, whispering, 'Matilda, you do not have to judge your father, nor do you have to stop loving him. It is my problem, not yours.'

Geoffrey was crying too. Deep down, I cursed Hal for his revelation.

'I want to kill him too for what he has done to you.' Geoffrey sniffed into his arms, no longer the garrulous smart ass.

'Enough is enough! If any of you touch one hair of your father's head, it will be over my dead body, Hal, too.'

I screwed my pride to the "sticking post".

'Richard, Matilda and Geoffrey, I had difficulty coming to terms with the first affair. It was known, it seems, to the whole of Christendom, even my maids, but not to me. After discovering there were more, any chance of my forgiving your father became impossible.'

I took a deep breath. 'I feel not only smouldering rage, but deep humiliation and unbelievable anguish. Do I love your father? I am not sure—I think so, probably… But the man I married I no longer know; he is a stranger to me. Worst of all, I can no longer trust him. Nor can I forgive him not just for myself, but for the pain he has inflicted on you, his legitimate children.'

I did not want my sadness to distress my children, or to drag them to where I was struggling. I begged them, especially Geoffrey, not to tell their little sisters. I dreaded their fate. Matilda was to wed the young Duke of Saxony. I had been told he was a good conscientious young man, but who was to know if these were the facts. Renée described Louis thus when I learnt I was to marry him. How wrong that was. He was weak and easily manipulated. I prayed the young Duke of Saxony would be good and kind to Matilda and that his father's court would treat her with the honour and respect she deserved. Hal was battling his own worries regarding Princess Margaret. Then what sort of example were their parents setting?

***

Henry's reign over his people was becoming tyrannous—another worry. Barons, bishops, Reverend Mother Joan, and others, who over the years had become my friends, reported smouldering discontent in counties and shires throughout England. They begged me to return. They believed it was only Queen Eleanor who could restore equilibrium.

And what of my own behaviour? Richard's observation was right; I had not handled the nobles of the Limousin well. I recognised the tone of my meeting with them and their justiciars was no better than Henry's. I had allowed my personal problems to impact on my judgement. I should have appraised my nobles' grievances on their merits. Instead, I was influenced by my emotional state of mind. Now, I had six young hostages to deal with and a group of very disgruntled families fuming in the Limousin.

I collected my sad and sulky brood. I reminded Richard about the hostages. I admitted I had made a rash mistake, but I had to keep them for the four weeks I had stipulated. I told him we would treat them kindly, place them in decent accommodation, and look after them. I put him in charge of their wellbeing because I terrified them. I asked him to enlist Matilda's aid. She was refusing to speak to me, except to call me a witch. She was in denial that her beloved Papa could behave the way he did.

Next, I gave my report to Uncle Ralph about the episode in the Limousin. He listened and replied, 'Eleanor it is time the nobles of Châlus and Limousin were reprimanded. Their petty squabbles have been festering for too long. We do not want to draw Lord Henry's attention to these miscreants and end up with another attack like Poitou.'

'True, but I could have managed the situation better. I need to have a good hard look at myself.'

'My dear, those nobles needed to be brought into line. Let us hope they have learned their lesson.'

I sighed. 'Uncle Ralph, I must improve my disposition and general humour and try to find a new path from the vindictive one I am treading. I am failing to instruct myself and wallowing in self-pity.'

'I am not sure I understand.'

'I went to the Limousin and made errors of judgement. The problem might have escalated had I not intervened, but I overreacted. Worse, I did not listen or consult but came away with six terrified children whom I am holding hostage to force their kin to comply with my will, instead of the laws of the land. I allowed my personal situation to overwhelm my objectivity.'

'Hmm! And you and Lord Henry are no closer to a reconciliation? You have not considered returning to England?'

'No! Definitely not!'

'I am saddened to hear that. We have been hoping...'

I interrupted. 'Returning to Henry is not going to help because I will probably help my sons to... let alone what I would really like to do to him!'

Uncle Ralph sighed. 'Well, so be it. As for your actions in the Limousin, by the sound of your "eloquent" speech you have already recognised what you should do. Therefore, your problem is solved. In the future, you will listen before acting hastily. But I am sorry you cannot see your way to resolve your problems with the king and try again.'

I exploded. 'It is not just me; it is the children. I cannot forgive Henry even if he crawls all the way to the Aquitaine on his hands and knees, wears a hair shirt, and flogs himself!'

'The Lord forgave sinners, Eleanor, even Judas.'

'Uncle Ralph, that is why he is the Son of God, and I am a mere mortal. I seem to remember He also asked why His Heavenly Father had forsaken him? Now I have duties to perform. Thank you for your time.'

I knew I was abrupt with my dear uncle, but my patience had run out. That was something else I needed to work on. I made my way to the school room where I could hear the peals of laughter of children having fun. The girls were playing blind-man's-buff, supervised by Matilda. Geoffrey and Richard had the boys outside making bows and arrows from branches of one of my favourite shrubs, which looked bedraggled. Agatha and

Cecelia, their nurses, were having a lovely time watching the chaos within and without. The Latin tutors, Father Matthew, and Brother Alain, were joining in with gusto. Cecelia saw me and suggested I join the game. Matilda gave me a vigorous shove into the fray, deliberately I suspected. There was a hush while she tied the blindfold around my head—tightly! She spun me around three times and left me giddily groping, as I tried to grab some very agile children.

The boys joined in the cacophony of shrieks and squeals of delight. I made a desperate lunge at someone whom I grabbed, but it was not a child. His manly odour was all too familiar. Henry! I tore the blindfold from my face. I was speechless. Nurses and tutors herded the now silent children outside and galloped them towards the archery range.

Before I could draw breath, Henry tried to envelop me in his arms. I shoved him away. I tried to push past him to get through the door, but he barred my exit. I backed away from him. My anger rose but I did not want a scene in such a public.

'Will you let me pass, please?'

'I wish to speak to you, Eleanor.'

'Then make an appointment for an audience and I, as Duchess of Aquitaine, will consider your request amongst other petitioners.'

My formality so surprised him, I was able to side-step him and bolt to the library.

What in God's name was he doing here? I guessed he must have arrived before I returned from the Limousin and was staying outside the palace? Did Geoffrey or Matilda know he was here, or the little ones? I assumed no, because one of them would have blurted.

Henry, of course, knew where to find me. Palace staff ran for cover as he stormed towards the library. I bolted the door, but he attacked it like a battering ram and bellowed at me to let him in before he broke it down. I did. Henry catapulted into my desk, sending documents and quills to the floor. I avoided smirking at his ungainly entry, but now I was alone with a raging bull.

I wrapped my hand around the hilt of my trusty stiletto.

Henry roared, 'How dare you treat me like one of your vassals.'

'Lord Henry, I now consider myself your wife in name only and as Queen of England by political alliance. My priority is to the people I serve as Duchess of Aquitaine and Gascony, Countess of Poitou, and other lands of my realm. As you fall into none of these categories, you can take your turn or your leave.'

I stood by the door, my blood pounding.

When Henry found his voice, it was low and threatening.

'Do I presume by your answer you do not wish to attend Young King Henry's wedding in Rouen or say farewell to Princess Matilda and Princess Lenore when they leave for the courts of their betrothed?'

Henry had to fetch Amaris to help me to my bed chamber. I had collapsed as the horror of his proclamation hit me. My two daughters, the ones closest to me, would be leaving. Only Geoffrey and Richard would remain in my care with Joanna, who was safe for now because she was only three. Lenore, however, at seven, was far too young to send to an unknown household to be brought up by strangers. Worse, Henry had not told me to whom he had betrothed the child. What of her education? She was a bright little girl. Matilda at least had known of her plight for two years, and I was preparing her though she was only twelve.

No wonder Henry arrived secretly, followed by his attempt to soften me up in the schoolroom. My poor innocent children were hoping for me and their father to be reconciled.

***

I spent the night in my chapel. Peter, my confessor, and Jerome were with me as, prostrate, I begged God to tell me why I must live in this hell on earth. He took my eldest son, my beloved William, and wee baby Phillip. Were their deaths at only three years and at birth not enough punishment?

'Peter, why do my daughters have to be sacrificed like pawns on a giant chessboard? Lenore at seven should be with her mother regardless of the political alliances or regal expectations of her status. If she and Matilda were older, I would understand, but they are too young, even Hal! Dear God, Henry had him crowned a reluctant Young King, and now he must wed at only thirteen. I remembered how immature Louis was at fifteen.'

'Lady Eleanor, it is a dilemma. But you have given the Young King a good grounding in what is expected of him. He is mature beyond his years.'

I massaged my forehead to ease my headache. 'I know Hal's education is better, and he is certainly more intelligent than my first husband, but he is still a boy.'

'Your concerns as his mother are admirable, but his destiny has placed him above others. I am sure your influence throughout his young life will hold him in good stead. You can take courage from that.'

I took a breath. 'Peter, I have never met Princess Margaret. I hope she has a pleasant disposition. How will Hal manage if she is uneducated? Will he respect her? I have surrounded him with knowledge and employed the best tutors. I have emphasised women of rank should learn, to enquire, and to be forthright. He knows I have been blessed with high intelligence. I have made Hal think and question.'

Peter nodded as I continued, 'He needs a wife with nous. When he inherits his father's kingdom, she as queen could be regent. She has to be familiar with England's laws and gain the respect of her people.'

'Milady, I agree. I suggest you and Lord Henry calm yourselves and try to discuss your concerns. In the meantime, I will pray for you all.'

***

We had to make a formal announcement. I insisted Henry speak to his children first. I knew not if I could stand before them to declare Lenore's fate and repeat Matilda's. As it happened, it became a right regal occasion. Its pomp kept us civilised. John, too, had travelled from Fontevrault with the nuns who cared for him to be part of the occasion with his family.

The children were summoned to the Great Hall. Matilda, as the eldest present, led them into their formally throned parents. In attendance were Uncle Ralph, Sir Robert, the Bishop of Poitiers, my justiciars, and the hierarchy of my household. As if that were not enough to alert the six of them something was afoot, my harrowed expression and pallid complexion said it was dire.

A silence hung in the air greater than waiting for prayer. As Henry stood, I thought, *I hope you are riddled with guilt for trading our daughters off to advance your empire.*

He cleared his throat. 'Lady Eleanor, eminent guests, children. In two months' time we will be attending Young King Henry III's wedding to Princess Margaret of France in Rouen. From there, Princess Matilda will be moving to the court of her betrothed, Prince Henry, Duke of Saxony. Princess Lenore is aligned to Prince Alphonso of Castile. Likewise, she will be leaving for her new court where she will live until old enough to marry. Prince Geoffrey is destined to become Duke of Brittany through his betrothal to Duke Conan's daughter Lady Constance. Princess Joanna and Prince John, your turns will come when you are older. Lady Eleanor, Queen of England, your mother, will now address you.'

I stood, blood thumping in my temples.

'Lord King Henry, assembled guests. Dear Geoffrey, may I congratulate you on becoming Duke of Brittany. I am proud of you. I wish you well and hope you and young Lady Constance will like and learn to love one another. I must stress the duke's family is fortunate in getting as the future Lord of Brittany one of the most brilliant minds in Christendom.'

Never known to keep his mouth shut, Geoffrey piped up, 'Just like yours, Maman'.

At least some tension was released with a little mirth. I then had to find courage to continue, to calm my galloping emotions. Within the pause, Papa's voice came to me—*do your duty.* I took a deep breath and managed to ignore the crowded gentry.

'Matilda and Lenore, as you know, when I was barely thirteen, my beloved Papa passed from this world. He had not betrothed either your late aunt Lady Petronilla or me to anyone. But his sudden death on his pilgrimage to Compostela in Spain left us alone, defenceless, and open to adventurers, especially me as his heir to the Aquitaine. On his death bed, he placed me under the guardianship of the late King of France, Louis VI, who married me to his son, now King Louis VII. You all know the marriage was annulled.

'Although it pains me that you must leave me, your mother, for the courts of your betrothed, at least your futures are secure. For that, I must be grateful. Nevertheless, not a day will pass when I do not think of you and have you in my prayers. I hope you will both have successful and happy lives in your coming marriages. I pray you will be loved as deeply as I love and cherish all of you, my children.'

With that I had to sit. I heard the strangled sobs as both girls clutched each other. The atmosphere was one of heavy sadness.

Richard, though, leapt from his chair crashing it backwards and shouted at Henry, 'I will never forgive you for betraying our mother, or for planning to send my sisters away. I hate you! When I am older, I will avenge my mother.'

He raced from the Great Hall, shouldering through the heavy doors. Jerome rushed after him. Henry, furious and red-faced, was unable to move because of the surrounding nobles and clergy. What a debacle! Silence surrounded the Great Hall. I stood and hauled my royally decked body to where my older daughters were clinging to each other, sobbing. Joanna started bawling in sympathy. Meg, her nurse, tried to comfort her. John shrieked in bewilderment. Sister Marie from Fontevrault picked him up.

I steered Matilda and Lenore to one side and tried to comfort them. Their maids flustered about with tears in their eyes. I heard Uncle Ralph loudly inform Henry he was not going anywhere. There was scuffling in the background with the Bishop of Poitier's baritone calming Henry. There was a tug on my gown. Geoffrey wormed his way into my embrace as well.

***

Everyone flocked around me and the children. My address had touched them. Henry was left on the outskirts. Robert, too, showed little sympathy for him.

After I had calmed the older girls and Geoffrey, I had their maids and Sister Marie take all of them to the nursery. I told Matilda and Lenore I would come to them after I had disrobed from my regal attire and had found Richard. There was no sign of Jerome.

Before I made my way to my chambers, I asked Robert to bring Henry to the library. Celeste and Amaris were all thumbs undressing me.

'For God's sake, cannot you hurry? Get me out of this damn gown.' I shoved the hilt of my blade into Celeste's hand. 'Just cut the cords if you cannot unlace them.'

I entered the library breathing like a dragon. Henry stood, a pillar of stone and icy bravado.

'Now you know what it feels like to be alone. The sentence you have bestowed on our daughters is exactly what you are experiencing now—misery.'

No answer.

'This is how I feel daily. My pillow at night is soaked with tears. You have just made things worse. Not only will I now be weeping for the love with which you once cherished me, but also for Matilda and Lenore.'

I took a deep breath. 'Henry, I have lived through the loneliness and home-sickness Matilda and Lenore are going to experience even though I was lucky enough to have Nilla and Renée. But they, too, were surrounded by strangers unable to speak the language. We cried ourselves to sleep, we mourned Papa and received no sympathy whatsoever from the French court. I do not want that crushing wretchedness to be suffered by our daughters. If you wait until they are more mature, they will be better able to manage.'

Henry's silence only enraged me further.

'You knew this was how I would react; therefore, I can only presume you have decided to take them away to spite me. You are nothing but a cruel, unfeeling, cunt-sniffing tyrant.'

I turned on my heels and left.

'How dare you walk out on me!' Henry's booming voice followed me.

I ignored him. I had to calm Richard if I could find him.

It saddened me. Richard was still a young boy, just a little older than Henry was when he had to fight at his mother's side in England's civil war. Was this what I was forcing on him? I did not want my boys warring against their father, but I feared it could happen. Henry had created his own monster by becoming distant, impatient, and finding them irritating when all they wanted was their Papa's attention. As much as I had loved him, I knew Lord Geoffrey, Henry's father, had scant time for his sons. Henry's mother was not interested in them either, except for Henry as fodder for her campaigns in England. Whereas Nilla and I were brought up by a loving father who wanted his daughters by his side.

***

A churl told me Prince Richard had headed for the stables followed by Brother Jerome. Thank God, it was not the armoury! I found both in a far stall with Richard's beautiful black destrier. The horse was bridled, which was all he had managed before Jerome found him. Richard had been crying and his face was streaked and dirty. Jerome was talking to him in an earnest but calm voice.

Richard was leaning against his horse, which was standing passively as they did when they sensed their owner needed comfort, its body warmth giving Richard a metaphorical hug. Jerome sighed. I went to Richard, so tall, so handsome, and more mature than his years. I brushed his russet curls from his face. He wrapped his arms around me, and I held him tightly. I let him cry.

Jerome asked, 'Do you want me to go?'

I shook my head. 'We must talk. I suggest the fairy dell?'

Jerome nodded and we walked past the stables along the cobbled path used to enter and exit the Palace grounds by horse-back. Through the courtyard there was a secluded copse of ancient oaks with branches spreading wide to the ground, our fairy dell, so named when we were children. To one side there was a large log, a place for rest, for secrets and escape.

We sat down, and I chose my words carefully. 'Richard, darling, I understand your anger... I, too, am furious with your Papa, but you must not allow the differences between us to prejudice your feelings. Your father was... is the love of my life and the last thing I want is for you or your brothers to harm him.' Richard sniffed, and I emphasised, 'Just think, if any of you hurt your father, how could you live with yourselves.'

Silence.

'Do you understand?'

Richard murmured, 'Yes, Maman.'

'Good. Regarding your sisters…as sorrowful as it is, Matilda will have to go to the household of the young Duke of Saxony. At Hal's wedding, I will meet with the young man and his father the king, who will be present. Should I find the prince unworthy, regardless of the furore, I will annul the betrothal. Lenore, I hope I can prevent from leaving my care till she is older. I pray your father has not gone too far with the arrangements to have her taken to Castile.'

A breeze ruffled the trees. Distant bells rang out. Richard was silent.

'Talk to me, Richard—I need to know what you are thinking,'

'Papa has never liked me. He just shouts and criticises… I hate watching you and Papa tear each other apart… I try not to take sides, but I cannot help it. All of us, even Matilda deep down, know it is Papa's fault. He should be punished, not you, Maman.'

Richard stifled a sob and wiped his nose on his sleeve. I handed him my handkerchief.

'I am still young, I know, but one day, Maman, I will be a man, so will Hal and Geoffrey, and even peevish John. I swear I will not touch our father for now, but I do not know what the future holds or if I can keep that promise. My loyalty will always be to you. I am your Liege Man of Life and Limb.'

I was nonplussed, honoured, and amazed at the seriousness of my son. Jerome too was impressed by the depth of Richard's words vowing, as a knight would, to be my protector for life, a boy!

We trod our way back at the palace. I sent Richard to his quarters. There was much I had to do. I told Jerome we would speak later.

I found two sorry souls by the time I arrived in Matilda and Lenore's bedchamber. Neither had eaten a morsel of their repast. Their maids had prepared them for bed.

'I am sorry I have kept you waiting, my darlings. I did not realise how much time was taken up with Richard.'

Matilda rubbed her eyes and said, 'It is all right, Maman, we understand.'

'Matilda, my precious, I will be having a serious conversation with the King of Saxony and his son in Rouen. If I find them unsatisfactory in any way, I will dissolve your betrothal regardless of your father's pledges and alliances. Lenore, sweetheart, I will do everything in my power to have the day you must leave my household postponed, even if I must grovel to your Papa on my hands and knees.'

'I want a cuddle.' Poor little Lenore was exhausted and nestled on my lap.

Matilda gave us tender kisses and a quick hug before she climbed into her bed.

Joanna whispered, 'Me want cuddle, too.'

Both little ones snuggled up. Joanna fell asleep. Meg took her to her cot whilst I did my best to comfort Lenore. I held her tightly to my chest, rocking and kissing her. Although seven, she still sucked her thumb. She entwined a lock of my hair around her fingers, another habit from babyhood.

I would obtain further information regarding the suitability of her betrothal for a girl of her status. Henry, as usual, had made the alliance without consulting me. Papa knew the old King of Castile, but he would be years gone. I remembered Papa laughing that he was an old scoundrel. I did not want my daughter in a family whose men were untrustworthy. My situation was bad enough.

I knew not what time it was when I was awoken by someone relighting the guttered candles. Lenore was asleep in my arms which were now numb from her weight. It was Henry. He lifted the sleeping child out of my arms. He was confused, not knowing which was her bed. In the end he tucked her in next to Matilda. If Lenore awoke in the night, at least she would have her sister for comfort.

It had been a long draining day. Henry accompanied me to my chamber. All I wanted was my bed, so I wished him goodnight. He had moved back into the palace from wherever he had been hiding. With speed I bolted the adjoining door between his bed chamber and mine. The man certainly had a cheek if he imagined I would want to lay with him.

It was a terrible night. I tossed and turned, my mind running in circles. Henry rattled my door but gave up after no response.

Judging by the noise next door, he and Robert had a few ales with whomever else was around from his entourage. Not that they were keeping me awake, but I did wonder how they could enjoy themselves considering the drama of the day.

I had to work out what I was going to say to Henry regarding Lenore. I was determined she would not be leaving for Castile. I toyed with the idea of hiding her in a convent somewhere, but I knew she would be just as lonely and miserable there as she would be under Alphonso's roof. The sun eventually crept in, illuminating the night as the cocks crowed.

My morning prayers were fervent. I begged for guidance. I bathed my tired eyes and blotchy face. It was time to speak to Henry regardless of how he hated being disturbed in the morning.

I entered the lion's den. 'I am sorry to interrupt, but I cannot wait another minute to discuss Lenore's fate. It is too important.'

Henry grunted but stood and pulled up another chair to his table. I perched on the edge with nerves galloping. He offered to share his breakfast. I shook my head. There was no use dithering, but my rehearsed speech came out as a garble of anger and frustration.

'Henry, Lenore is too young to leave her home and all that is familiar. She will be unhappy and lonely. What is more, she does not want to go.'

Henry pushed his plate away and wiped his mouth.

'Her education will be jeopardised,' I said. 'She is intelligent. What of her languages? She speaks all I am teaching her well, but she does not know Castellan or Spanish and nor do I. Not only will she be among strangers, she will be unable to communicate with them. If she can spend more time with me, I will employ tutors to make certain she learns the tongues of her betrothed so she will not be isolated within his court.'

By now my ire was dancing on my lips.

'Who is this young man? I know nothing of him because you have neglected to inform me what sort of person he is; what his family is like. Are they respected? My father knew the old king whom he described as a rake and a womaniser. What if that boy Alphonso has the same morals? I do not want my daughters to suffer the same humiliation and unhappiness I have had with you.'

By now I was thumping the table, spilling Henry's ale and attracting the attention of Robert, who blundered in, bleary-eyed before beating a retreat.

Henry's voice hit a crescendo. 'If I can get a word in edgewise, I will answer your questions. I agree that some of what you say, Eleanor, makes sense. The timing of her departure can be negotiated. The boy's father is an amicable man, and his wife a loyal, honourable woman.'

Was that a dig? I decided to ignore the implication.

'It is all very well for you to carry on, and expect me to go back to the King of Castile with new proposals,' Henry continued. 'But what are you going to do in the meantime to facilitate the agreement? This alliance will strengthen your borders with Gascony, Eleanor.'

'I will make sure Lenore is readied for her role as the future Queen of Castile. As her mother, I will educate her for the responsibility awaiting her. But she is nowhere near prepared. She is a little girl, who still takes her dolls to bed, for God's sake!'

'You will do anything?'

'Of course.'

'Then maybe you should set her an example.'

'I do.'

'By leaving your husband and abandoning your role as Queen of England? What sort of example is that, my dear Eleanor?'

God's Teeth! The colour drained from my face.

'If you want Lenore to continue around your skirts,' he went on, 'you will return with me to England after Hal's wedding as my queen, which is your dutiful role. Moreover, you will oblige me as your husband by not locking the doors of your bed chamber.'

I had no choice. Lenore's happiness was paramount, her education imperative. I promised her I would intervene even if I had to crawl on my knees. I now had to swallow my pride and crawl.

Henry looked at me with that familiar gleam of lust in his eye. I tried to keep my face impassive. He knew he had snared me.

'But I do not want another child. I do not think I have the… the strength to give birth again,' I whispered.

Henry looked stunned. 'You are still—um able to conceive?'

'So far…I believe so.' My monthly cycle had yet to cease.

The silly grin on Henry's face made me want to slap him.

'Then how about you set an example to your legitimate children by being faithful to your wife. We would not be in this unhappy situation if you had kept out of the beds of the whores you have impregnated. Nor would your sons want to rebel against you to protect their mother,' I snapped.

'They will get over it.'

'Do not be so sure. One day they will be grown men.'

I then excused myself, not being able to stand another second looking at Henry's smug face.

I needed to talk to Lenore, calm Matilda, and tell the boys what had transpired between us. The children looked suspicious. I did not mince words. 'Lenore has been given a reprieve and will not have to leave home for another five years.'

Matilda burst into tears. 'It is not fair!'

So, I had one happy girl and the other miserable.

'We are all leaving for Rouen in two weeks. I will be returning to England. My services and duties are needed. I will reside with your father.'

I enveloped Matilda in my arms. 'Matilda, darling, please do not cry. As I have promised, if I find young Henry of Saxony unworthy, I will have your betrothal annulled. In the meantime, I suggest you talk to Sir Robert who has met him and whose honesty I value.'

I recalled the tutors and told them to continue the children's lessons. I glared at Geoffrey to hold his tongue, Richard likewise. Jerome accompanied me back to my quarters.

'Dare I ask?'

'I must do Henry's bidding, or Lenore would be on a horse to Castile. I must put her happiness before mine. I might as well be wretched in England as here. You will come with me, will you not?'

'Of course.'

I then broke the news to my maids, who were flabbergasted. I had to swallow my pride and have my churls drag all the carpets and tapestries out of storage to return to the English palaces. I received some sympathetic glances. There are no secrets below stairs.

I arranged for my six little hostages to be returned to the Limousin with Uncle Ralph as diplomatic envoy. I hoped he could placate their smarting parents and excuse their duchess. I was sure the children thought I was mad. Uncle Ralph said he hoped their noble parents had learned a lesson. He did not query my decision to return to England.

Last-minute duties were achieved amidst a whirlwind of errands. I requested that we travel by ship to Barfleur then by horse to Rouen. I wanted to see Renée and Clotilde; I also had the remainder of the English furnishings stored at L'Ombrière that I could dispatch directly from Bordeaux to England.

Henry did not break down my bed chamber door, which was surprising. Maybe he did not want another child either. Or was he observing my bodily workings from a distance, not believing I was still getting my monthly cycle. Another reason I wanted to visit L'Ombrière was for a supply of those heart-shaped Silphium seeds to grind and mix with beeswax, which, when inserted in one's female parts prevented conception.

***

We were ready for Rouen after frantic days of organisation from palace to palace. I could not remember the number of farewells made, with Renée thinking each one was going to be my last.

Her advice was sensible as usual. 'Darling child, you must curb your temper. Behave with dignity and remember your ordained position.'

She had stern words for Henry too, not mincing a syllable.

'Lord Henry, take a good look at yourself. You might think you are above earthly law, but you are not above the laws of God. Moreover, show some decency. Respect your wife and queen, or you will rue the day when your sons are grown.'

The voyage to Barfleur was pleasant. Matilda enjoyed the balmy breezes and gentle sea, which took her mind off her destiny. Henry took a different galley. He did not object to me travelling with the children. Maybe he thought if there was a catastrophe, he would be rid of the troublemakers altogether, including John, brought from Fontevrault to become part of the family. After we disembarked, our vast entourage stretched for leagues as we rode towards Rouen.

***

It was an odd feeling, not to be met by Empress Matilda. The castle felt empty without her powerful presence. But there was Hal, taller than me now. He flew into my arms for an embrace followed by an especially lovable reunion with his sister. They had always been close. I wondered if they would see each other again after Hal was wed and Matilda left for Saxony. Hal and his father greeted each other with stiff formality.

We settled into our quarters. There were several formal gatherings organised before the wedding ceremony was to take place. Princess Margaret was brought from the estate of Lord Mortimer of Rouen, a cousin of Henry's, where she had been living since a tot, though I found out she was older than I thought. A relief in some respects.

Margaret was to be introduced to Hal at a ceremonial banquet to be presided over by Henry and me. These arrangements were organised before our arrival in Rouen, so all was in readiness.

But the meticulous planning was undermined. Louis, who had arrived for his daughter's wedding, refused to be within my presence and demanded I absent myself. It was unbelievable. My ex-husband was still holding a grudge against me for marrying Henry. You would have thought after more than fifteen years he would have accepted the status quo. Of course, it was really the loss of the Aquitaine that stuck in his craw. Well, be damned if I was going to desert my son on such a ceremonious occasion. Henry would have to sort it out. He and Louis had betrothed the two, so it was up to them to come to a civilised agreement.

Hal felt indignant as the Young King of England at Louis' behaviour. He told his father he would not marry Margaret unless his mother was present at the wedding ceremony and all official functions leading up to it. Henry agreed, probably because Louis now had a son, which made it unlikely that Hal would become King of France. The only sticking point was the Vexin, Margaret's dowry, which Henry prized. But foolish Louis had more to lose. His daughter would not be Queen of England.

I was quite enjoying myself and proud of Hal's stance. He had nothing to lose after all. Henry was relishing taunting Louis. I cared not for his presence either. As for the Vexin, the Normans had survived without that sliver of land between them and the French Kingdom in the past. Furthermore, Henry's army was far more capable than the French under Louis.

I spoke to Henry. 'I have a couple of ideas. Why do we not send messengers to all our guests and dignitaries informing them that, because of King Louis' irrational demands, the betrothal will be declared null and void. Or have Hal and Margaret meet and they can decide their own futures. Should they wish to go ahead with their marriage, we have the Bishop of Rouen who will be officiating anyhow, or Jerome could conduct the service. We and the rest of the children can be witnesses. Louis can go to hell.'

'I like your ideas, but what if Louis calls our bluff.'

'What if he does? Hal does not care one way or the other regarding his marriage to Margaret. Louis will have the humiliation of having to take her back to France, a girl whom he does not know and has had no contact with since she was a baby.'

'Eleanor, I am not sure.'

'Well, do not dilly-dally in case Louis tries a similar tactic, though I doubt he is that smart, and he has too much to lose.'

'All right, let us have Margaret and Hal meet. She is a friendly, pleasant young girl not unlike Matilda in temperament. The young couple can decide for themselves.'

I put this to Hal who shrugged, but conceded he was curious. Margaret was being housed for the wedding with her guardians in Henry's mother's old palace, which had been refurbished for the occasion. Louis was a guest at a local monastery, still happy with austerity.

Around the late Empress Matilda's palace were magnificent gardens. To the south, they opened onto a small wood leading to the castle. Hal knew the place from when we used to visit his grandmother. I arranged for him to wander down there with Matilda and Lenore whom I thought would be suitable chaperones, Richard being too aggressive and Geoffrey too garrulous. We intended to follow.

Henry sent a message to Margaret's guardian and entourage, inviting them to make use of the late Empress Matilda's grounds with her maids. They accepted.

There must have been an introduction of sorts between Hal and Margaret, because the members of her retinue were a little flustered when we strolled into view. The women bobbed up and down like apples in a barrel. Hal wore a silly grin and muttered that he would explain later.

Henry soon disarmed them with Plantagenet charm. 'I hope you are enjoying my late mother's beautiful gardens, and I trust, Princess Margaret, you are not offended by the unexpected arrival of the Young King and his sisters.'

She blushed and shook her head.

Hal remembered his manners. 'Um, allow me to introduce you to my father, Lord King Henry, and my mother, Lady Queen Eleanor.'

Margaret curtsied while Matilda and Lenore sidled up to me. Lenore snuggled herself among the folds of my gown. I ruffled her tousled head of honey tresses as she smiled up at me. This was not missed by the princess who looked at me with curiosity.

'Lady Margaret, I am honoured to meet you at last. Would you like a few words with the Young King?' She gave Hal a quick glance and nodded. 'Good. Now Lord Henry and I must return to the castle. It was lovely to meet you.'

Margaret bowed again and we left. Lenore and Matilda remained for decorum's sake.

***

Henry and I for once were in absolute agreement. Whatever Hal decided regarding Margaret we would support his decision. I had tutored him on a few things to talk about to break the ice as I recalled my disastrous introduction to Louis. I suggested he ask if she liked books, then he would discover if she had been taught to read. If she was shy, he should try to bring her out of herself. I looked for Louis in Margaret, but her dark Spanish eyes and hair were all from below my Aquitaine border—a relief.

Henry and I agreed it was up to Louis to show some flexibility regarding my presence. After all, he was our guest. If he expected us to pay him homage as King of France because he was overlord in Normandy, he was wrong. As King and Queen of England we were his equals. What was more, his daughter was brought up in Normandy and was betrothed to the Young King of England. All this had precedence over whether he wanted to be in the same room with his ex-wife. Henry said he would wait for Hal and the girls to return, then ask Hal for his opinion.

I was impatient awaiting. At last, we heard them galloping up the circular staircase. They puffed into our chamber. I leant forward in my chair and asked, 'Well, Hal, we cannot wait to hear what happened.'

'Hal grinned. 'Maman and Papa, we had great fun...'

Matilda beamed and interrupted. 'Yes, Maman, Lenore and I raced off. Hal had to try to catch us...'

'Shush Matilda! Do not butt in... It was not easy. They ran all over the place yelling and shrieking. I eventually caught them as they tore through the palace gates. I grabbed Lenore and whirled her around. She was squealing her head off. It was hilarious.'

'Oh, dear... I hope you... calmed down.' It was hard keeping a straight face.

'Well, Matilda yelled at us to stop because we almost bowled over the princess and her maids. They looked a bit stunned. Then Lenore blurted "Who are you?"'

'Yes, they looked aghast, as if I was some sort of freak— Matilda, too.'

'The nurse was a bit uppity, was she not, Lenore? She said in this haughty voice, "Might I ask the same question? Can you please introduce yourselves?" She was très hoity-toity...'

Hal interjected, 'Matilda, she was not! Then Lenore started tittering, so I pushed her behind me and said I am Hal, and these are my sisters, Princesses Matilda and Eleanor of England.'

'Maman, the nurse went as red as a raspberry like this.' Matilda puffed up her cheeks.

'Matilda, really! Go on, Hal.'

'Oh,' she then replied, 'this is Princess Margaret.'

'Of France!' was Matilda's fruity imitation.

'Matilda, you are exaggerating.'

'I am not, Hal! Then Lenore had this look on her face as if she was going to say something silly, so I clamped my hand over her mouth. But we got the giggles, and Margaret and her entourage stood gaping like gargoyles while Hal eyed her off.'

'I did not, Matilda.'

'Hal, You did so.'

'I just told them I was pleased to meet them and apologised for my rowdy sisters.'

'Ouch!'

Hal rubbed his ankle and glared at Matilda. 'I explained that we did not mean to blunder in with our game. Then you and Papa turned up.'

Henry and I glanced at each other, trying to keep our faces expressionless. 'It sounds like you enjoyed yourselves and Margaret did seem pleased to meet you, Hal.'

'Ah, I suppose so.'

Lenore, not to be outdone, smirked and said, 'Margaret was really giving Hal the once over, too.'

Hal scowled. 'Keep your mouth shut, Lenore.'

'All right, all right, enough,' I said, calming the excitement. 'Now, girls, off you go. You must get ready for tonight's festivities.'

'But I reckon Margaret is a bit soppy.'

'Matilda, mind your own business.' Hal took a swing at his sister.

'Hal!' I interrupted, 'Quieten down, and you two as well... Lenore and Matilda, go!'

Matilda sidestepped Hal's cuff as she and Lenore raced out the door. Peals of laughter echoed along the gallery.

Hal muttered, 'Girls,' and shuffled from one foot to the other.

'Well, Hal what do you think?'

'Maman, I think she is a bit shy. She did not say much because I did most of the talking. She probably thinks I am a garrulous know-it-all.'

'My priority, Hal, is whether she has been educated.

'I think so. She knows Langue d'Oeil and Latin and has a smattering of English. She knows her scriptures, but she has not read many books. She likes music and can play the lute and harp. And she can do all that womanly stuff like weaving and embroidery.'

I was amazed he had covered so many topics.

Henry asked, 'What do you think of her, Hal, as a future wife?'

'I have no idea, Papa. She is pretty. I like her dark hair and eyes.'

He looked at me and asked, blushing, 'Maman, does she resemble King Louis?'

I shook my head. 'From what I recall, he had fair curly hair, blue eyes, and a bit of a beaky nose. Your father has seen him more recently.'

'Yes, but he is going grey and a bit thin on top.'

Hal went quiet and peered at me as if examining something peculiar he had never seen before, which was odd.

'Oh, Margaret thinks you are beautiful, Maman,' he paused, still frowning. 'Um...er... suppose you are...Oh, she was impressed Matilda and Lenore were allowed to run and play, and she likes puppies and kittens.'

We let him go. Hal, too, needed to bathe and change into regal regalia.

Henry, with his Plantagenet wit, could not resist imitating Hal. 'Um—er I suppose you are.'

'Do not push your luck, Henry.'

Henry grinned. We looked at each other, none the wiser really regarding Hal's observations.

'She sounds like she is not as mature as our daughters, but kindly if she likes little animals.'

Henry shrugged.

'I wonder if she will be flexible enough to learn?'

'No doubt, my dear Eleanor, once you get your talons into her, she will be able to quote *The Aeneid* word for word in no time.'

'Thank you, Henry, for your vote of confidence. At least Hal shows no signs of disliking her.'

'But,' Henry went on, 'we have no idea of what Margaret thinks of him.'

'No,' I smiled, 'But it is amusing to know that, should they marry, she will be within our household despite Louis not wanting her exposed to my influence.'

'Well, Eleanor, I am sure you will be able to mould her into a suitable queen. By the way, I have written to Louis.'

Henry showed me a missive he had scribed formally, inviting Louis to attend a banquet to welcome Princess Margaret and to meet her future husband, his family, and nobles.

'A lot will depend on Louis' reply as to whether the marriage goes ahead. Should he refuse to attend gatherings including you, the betrothal between the Young King and Princess Margaret will be null and void as I have penned in this second epistle. You can see I have emphasised his daughter will never be Queen of England and the princess will be conducted to his accommodation from where he and his daughter will be escorted out of Normandy.'

'I see, Henry, you are allowing the Vexin to be returned?'

'That will prove we are deadly serious, Eleanor.'

He asked me to co-sign both letters. Robert was to deliver them, to add to the formality. Copies would be sent to Lord Mortimer should Louis refuse the invitation.

I believed Robert was hoping Louis would get his comeuppance as he loped out the door wearing a conspiratorial grin. Despite this possibility, I was concerned for Hal, because I think he was prepared to accept Margaret. Before I was readied for the banquet, I told Henry I had better warn Hal. I knew full well that Louis was capable of "cutting off his nose to spite his face".

Hal was half-dressed when I arrived. Geoffrey and Richard were teasing him, which was not helpful.

'Hal, darling, I hope I am not embarrassing you.'

Geoffrey guffawed lasciviously.

'And you two could at least try to cooperate. Hal, your father has officially invited King Louis to all our functions, emphasising the consequences should he refuse to be in attendance with me.'

'Maman, I am prepared to marry Margaret. She is not that bad.'

'Oooh!'

'Geoffrey, you have been warned. And you, Richard, can stop smirking.'

Ignoring his brothers, Hal said, 'But I do not want to have anything to do with the House of Capet if King Louis will not accept you, Maman.'

I gave him a quick hug and left to talk to the girls. I shook my head as the ribaldry continued as I shut the door. Boys!

Matilda, Lenore and Joanna were in a far more advanced state. Lenore just needed the finishing touches to her hair. She had inherited my wild locks, which took a lot of brushing to remove the knots. Lenore was howling and ouching. John was with them. Matilda, always the little mother, was entertaining him with Joanna. I told them what might occur.

Lenore piped up, 'That would be a shame. Margaret was all right even if Matilda says she is soppy, and I reckon she liked Hal.'

Matilda nodded. 'Maman, Lenore and I think King Louis is a miserable mean-spirited idiot if he will not honour your presence at all the formalities.'

Bless my loyal outspoken children.

Louis yielded. Robert grinned as he told me.

'It was most amusing watching him trying not to lose his temper. At first, he refused the invitation in a very high-handed manner. So, I handed the fool the second epistle for him to peruse at his leisure and apologised that I had to leave at once to inform Lord Mortimer to prepare the princess for departure. As I walked to the door, I heard this sort of strangled gasp when he realised the consequences of his actions and called me back. His face had turned purple with rage, and he was striding up and down. He yelled, "Plantagenet and his whore would pay for their actions." I apologise Milady for what Capet called you.'

'That French bastard will regret his rudeness,' Henry growled.

***

Henry and I were dressed in our regal regalia. Girdled around Henry's pristine white gown was a belt of gold. Over the gown he wore his sweeping, scarlet ceremonial cape embroidered with rampant lions. His crown gleamed on his temples. It had been a long time since I felt overwhelming pride in him. I too wore scarlet. My gown was of rustling silk, heavily embroidered in precious jewels and gold. I eschewed a veil. My hair was elaborately plaited and enmeshed in a filigree nest of gold thread, studded with gems and pearls. I loved this style because it enhanced my neck and displayed my earrings. Henry's simple cross was about my throat. My chamois slippers matched my gown.

Together we assembled outside the Great Hall. Our guests waited within for the doors to open. The children were ready to walk the distance to the dais. My pride when I saw them beamed like a beacon. The oldest boys, so tall and handsome, stood alongside our beautiful daughters. Matilda and Lenore took Joanna and John by their hands. My seven surviving children were magnificently dressed like their parents for this royal occasion.

There were gasps as the children preceded Henry and me to their own trumpet flourish. The doors closed till the children stepped onto the dais and were seated then flung open for our entry. The royal fanfare echoed through the Romanesque arches of the old Rouen castle, the seat of the Plantagenet dynasty. How proud Empress Matilda would have been of her son, Duke Geoffrey also. Slowly we made our way thronged by homage on either side. Vivat Rex and Vivat Regina reverberated from our noble's throats around the Great Hall. What Louis made of this pageantry I could only guess. The pious House of Capet was never disposed to regal ceremony unless it was religious.

I hoped Louis squirmed with envy, being surrounded by the offspring I had borne Henry. None of these were five years apart. Each followed the other, an almost annual procession. Henry and I put our differences behind us for the sake of Hal and Margaret. It gave me comfort she was not brought up under Louis' sanctimonious roof. She looked shy when she was seated in prominence next to Hal, who gave her an encouraging smile and whispered something to her. Her dark Spanish eyes sparkled. I wished them well with all my being.

Louis was forced to acknowledge me as Queen of England, which must have galled him. He had aged and was stooped and still resembled a monk. Amaris said Louis could not take his eyes off me, Henry neither.

***

The ceremony for Hal's wedding was beautiful. Louis had to suffer my proximity. He uttered not a word to me. But he hardly spoke to me in our fifteen years of marriage either. I thought it was interesting that he was unaccompanied by his latest wife, Queen Adela.

Robert commented, 'Milady, I think the poor fool is still in love with you.'

My tongue could not resist. 'Which one, Louis or Henry?'

'Both, by the looks on their faces.'

I shook my head. An empty sadness haunted me. After the formalities were over, I had to return to England with a man I no longer trusted and to live in an atmosphere I knew would be difficult. Nor was I looking forward to farewelling Matilda.

I met with King Henry of Saxony and his son, another Henry. It was a relief. The king was a lively intelligent man with a sense of joy about life. But he also had a serious side, and a rounded sensible grip on his world. His son was well educated. I had a lengthy conversation with the young duke. (Henry Plantagenet said I cross-examined him.) I found a kind, down-to-earth young man aware of his responsibilities. To my relief, Matilda liked him.

'He is nice, Maman. A bit like Hal. We laugh at the same things. I think we will be able to get along.'

'Darling, I am relieved. Your happiness is all I pray for, but I will miss you. Young Henry's Papa also told me his wife, Queen Gertrude, is looking forward to welcoming you. The king has promised you will be well looked after and welcomed into their household.'

Matilda smiled. It was a weight off my mind regardless of the sadness I was feeling. There were many hugs and kisses as we said our goodbyes to our eldest daughter. She and I clung together and tried to keep our tears in check.

It was not such a happy farewell between Margaret and Louis. God knows what he said to her, but I saw her face fall when we set off for Barfleur.

Hal also noticed something was amiss and said, 'Maman, um...can I say something?'

'Of course.'

'Please, can you and Papa call a truce? I do not want to bring Margaret into a battleground. I want her to be happy.'

'Have you spoken to your father about this?'

'Yes, but Papa said it was up to you.'

'What!'

'Maman, please...'

I was furious. As far as I was concerned Henry should take responsibility for our marriage too. After all, he was the adulterer.

Hal and Margaret had their own quarters at Westminster, separate from the royal wing for their privacy and peace. It would lessen my influence on the girl, but it was for the best. I knew Henry as I knew myself; the merest spark could ignite a cauldron, not particularly welcoming for the young bride and groom.

***

It was a bitter-sweet arrival in London for us. Hal and Margaret had to get to know each other. And after my outrage that stripped the palace, much refurbishing had to be done. Piled in heaps were the carpets, tapestries, and furniture that had made Westminster habitable. At least this time I could refurnish its many rooms without 'Master' Becket's interference. This was many years before his rise to Archbishop of Canterbury. Henry had appointed him to oversee the repair of the damaged palace after England's civil war. The décor was supposed to be my responsibility, but Becket tried to overrule me—a mistake!

The project kept me out of Henry's hair. He had many administrative duties to perform, spending his days surrounded by justiciars, the chancellor, bishops and barons. Becket, although exiled in France, continued to make Henry's life difficult with his rancorous and vigorous dissension against English law.

Henry kept me ignorant of affairs of state. I had to glean what was happening within the kingdom from Jerome and Robert, experts at sorting fact from gossip. I met the new chancellor Geoffrey Ridel, a charming erudite man, at a recent banquet.

'Lady Eleanor, I am delighted to meet you at last. Your court has a most civilising effect on King Henry's entourage.'

'Thank you.'

'The palace is no longer a cross between a bear pit and a tavern. It is delightful to have ladies' company and sweet perfume instead of the odours of the stable. Your tinkling laughter is like a springtime brook,' he whispered.

I enjoyed his company, but I knew if I paid him too much attention, I would be getting black looks from Henry.

At the same event, seated on my right, was the rather dour Bishop of London, another who wanted Canon Law meted out to the unordained employed by the church. His whining voice drilled into my ear.

'Surely, Milady you can make the Lord King see sense. The small misdemeanours occasionally committed by our clerks are choking the judiciary, which should be deciding on more serious crimes. Canon Law is far more suitable in these minor cases to bring these men to justice.'

'What about the crimes that are not minor?'

His puffed-up reply inferred, 'That is impossible.'

'Indeed. So, tell me, what is the difference between a baker stealing a candle from the church and a lay clerk committing the same crime. They are identical offences, so why should one be tried in one court and one in the other? The clerk would probably be told to say a few Hail Marys when the other would be more severely judged though both are civilians in the eye of the law.'

I did not think the bishop was as pleased to see me as was the chancellor.

***

I helped Hal and Margaret make their quarters attractive and comfortable. It gave me an opportunity to ask Hal, 'How are you and Margaret getting along?'

'All right…' Hal blushed.

'Hal, I do not want to embarrass you. It is just a general question.'

'Oh! Um…well, she is shy and prefers to keep with her maids where she is comfortable. She struggles with English. Do you think she could join Lenore, Richard and Geoffrey with their lessons?'

I nodded. 'Of course. Can I help? I have time on my hands. I have almost forgotten what a panel of justiciars looks like. England's affairs of state are as mysterious as interpreting runes these days.'

Hal caught the tone of my sarcasm and frowned. 'I hope Papa is treating you with respect, Maman.'

'I keep out of his way, and he avoids me. We meet on official occasions when necessary, and I perform my duties as regal decoration. This way we are not fighting. Anyway, I am quite happy to help with Margaret's English.' I patted Hal's arm.

He was silent. I suspected there was something he was not telling me.

'Hal, instead of standing there looking like you are protecting state secrets, what is on your mind, for God's sake?'

'Maman, I think Margaret finds you intimidating. You are too clever for her, I believe.'

I was aghast. I had hardly spoken to her except in general terms. I looked at Hal with suspicion. I detected there was something behind Margaret's imaginings other than my intellect. I wracked my brains to put my finger on it, going back to Normandy. Margaret was shy, yes, but I had treated her warmly and she seemed to respond. She had seen us as a family. Henry and I had been civil to one another. Then I remembered her farewell from Louis when her happy face fell, and she looked at me wide-eyed and fearful.

'Louis said something to her when we were leaving Rouen. I noticed she seemed distressed after that. Do you know what it was?'

'I have no idea, Maman. She was a bit quiet, but I put it down to her leaving Normandy.'

Nevertheless, I was suspicious. I knew Louis resented the loss of my wealth and was jealous of Henry, but...

'Perhaps you should find out,' I suggested. 'In the meantime, I will arrange for Margaret to join your brothers' and sister's lessons if I cannot help.'

'At least she will not end up with a funny accent,' Hal grinned.

'Really, Hal! At least, I can speak and understand the language, regardless of my funny accent.'

***

Several weeks passed, and our lives plodded along. Henry and I travelled to Oxford. It was uncomfortable being close to Woodstock. It had too many painful memories. I did not want to be reminded that Henry's extra-marital affair with Rosamund Clifford took place nearby. After I had walked out, I heard he flaunted her at some banquets within the palace.

Then I discovered, much to my disgust, she was still residing in the tower Henry built for her there. I said naught, but I was determined to put an end to that strumpet residing in one of my royal residences. I cornered Robert to make sure it was true.

'Lady Eleanor, he is only keeping her there because she is gravely ill.' He blushed with embarrassment.

'Robert, I was gravely ill after John was born at Woodstock, but that did not keep Henry out of her bed!'

Robert hung his head. I stormed off. I had a dilemma. Henry was due to travel to Warwick. He would be away for two or more weeks. So far, I had not let him out of my sight, but I was determined to oust Rosamund Clifford from Woodstock. Henry did not ask why I decided not to accompany him. After he left for Warwick, I planned to avenge myself even though vengeance does not carry much common sense.

I rode the short distance to Woodstock at the first opportunity. I went alone except for Antoine, who did not question why my usual guard was absent. My arrival sent the household into a panic. I was the last person they expected. The new tower was obvious. The constable and steward flapped about apologising for the lack of fires in the grates. I reassured them that I was only passing through and ordered them back to their duties. I instructed Antoine to have a carriage and driver waiting in the courtyard ready to leave at speed.

My fury mounted. I hitched my gown and stormed up the tower's circular staircase two at a time to a bed chamber and flung open the door. My nostrils were overwhelmed by a sour odour. Propped on pillows was a woman wracked with decay. If she had been pretty, she was not now. Her maids had no idea who I was and looked stunned. Nevertheless, power and position loomed in front of them.

'This is an order. You have until the next bells to pack up that putrid pustule and leave.' My voice commanded authority.

The women gasped.

I towered over them menacingly. 'How dare you. Who are you?'

'On whose authority?' a voice croaked from the bed.

'Mine! Eleanor, Queen of England, and Duchess of Aquitaine. I suggest you vacate unless you wish to be incinerated when I burn this tower to the ground! Let me help you!'

I hoisted a stool, strode to the window, and smashed the glass. I then grabbed linens and anything else I could lay my hands on and shoved them through. Shrieks and screams issued from the horrified attendants.

I wrenched one of the large candles out of the iron candelabra and held it aloft and spat, 'I suggest you move unless you want to be engulfed when I throw this onto the bed.'

'You cannot surely expect us to remove Lady Rosamund from her bed. Her health is dire.'

'LADY! Since when?'

My stiletto glinted in my right hand; the candle flared in my left.

'And it depends on whether you wish to be tried for treason or how much you value your lives! I demand you obey your queen NOW!'

The putain whined from the pillows, 'Henry will hear of this outrage.'

So familiar, how dare she!

'If you mean MY husband, the Lord King of England, indeed, he will!'

They heaved Rosamund Clifford from the bed, dragging and half-carrying her moaning down the stairs. I held the flame to the furs and feather-filled covers and watched them catch and flare, then I threw the candle onto the bed. Lastly, I kicked over the iron candelabra and slammed the door as the rancid smell of burning assailed my nostrils. The carriage and its driver waited. He was ordered to take the occupants at speed to Godstow Abbey. I hoped they hit every pothole in the road.

Before I returned to Oxford, I threatened our Woodstock retainers that should they reveal my visit, they would end up in irons. The constable bowed and eyed me in a knowing manner. I believed he was on my side.

Henry returned from Warwick. The fire at Woodstock was discussed. An 'accident' with a candelabra, apparently. Only the tower suffered damage. I heard our many churls and other servants put all their efforts into preventing its spread to the main structure. I would not have cared if the whole of Woodstock had burnt to the ground. I hated the place. It surprised me that Henry showed no interest in inspecting the damage, and I have no idea if he inquired about the location of his whore.

We were preparing to travel back to London from Oxford in

two days' time. Henry suggested I go on ahead if I was missing the children. Firmly, I said no. Rosamund Clifford might be out of nearby Woodstock, but I was going to make sure Henry did not sneak off to find her.

I was not missed on the day of the blaze. My maids thought I had gone riding and never assumed otherwise. Antoine would never utter a word, even on the rack. I was certain none of our Woodstock retainers would reveal they had seen me, but that woman's maids could. It depended on how much they feared my wrath.

***

Brynn was back. She reappeared in her usual mysterious manner just before Henry returned from Warwick. I worried the Welsh King might be nearby; well inside English territory if he was. I had deliberately not asked about the affairs of state on Owain Pendragon's border. I wanted to preserve the tentative peace between Henry and me and not provoke a jealous outburst. Henry's obsession about my so-called liaisons with the Welsh leader were a figment of his imagination. Yes, I found Owain attractive but that was all.

My suspicions were correct. Pendragon had made incursions across the border and was sighted between Shrewsbury and Warwick. Our return to London was postponed while Henry prepared his men to chase him down.

I had a problem. I did not want Henry galloping within the vicinity of Godstow Abbey on his way to confront the Welsh King without me as chaperone. But I knew if I insisted on travelling with him, he would imagine I wanted to contact him.

I was edgy. I decided, though it was risky, to write to Lord Owain to beg him to return to his side of the border and to keep our unwritten treaty. I signed it, The Queen of the Wood Sprites, his endearing address to me.

How to send it to him without Henry's knowledge was going to be a challenge. Before I attached my seal and employed a courier, I consulted Brynn. It was awkward. What reason would I have to follow this plan? It looked like I was warning Pendragon of danger when my real reason was to keep Henry within my reach. By now, he would know where Clifford was.

'Brynn, I have good reasons to write to King Owain. I want to prevent a confrontation, and… I need to keep King Henry close at hand.'

Sibyl-like, she replied, 'I can foresee your concerns, Lady Eleanor.'

'Furthermore, I am sure King Owain will know of my whereabouts.'

Brynn then surprised me. 'Milady, can I please read your letter?'

'Yeees!' I handed it to her.

Brynn scanned the page. 'I do not want to be presumptuous, but may I suggest I scribe it into Welsh? At present, no-one in England can read it.'

I was hesitant but agreed. As I read the Latin, she took my quill and rewrote it in her native tongue. I had no choice but to trust her and to rely on her courier.

Henry huffed and fumed, getting his men together and wanting to leave at the speed of a meteor. I feared he would be prepared before Owain received my begging letter. Thank God, two days before Henry was ready to leave an exhausted rider appeared carrying scrolls from informants near Shrewsbury. Owain Pendragon had retreated behind his border. I uttered a prayer of thanks that the old verbal treaty held and congratulated Henry on thwarting the Welsh ruler.

Henry and I rode out of Oxford. I kept aloof for most of the ride to London and the Palace of Westminster. I was pondering over a message the Queen of the Wood Sprites received. It informed me that Henry's strumpet was not expected to live much longer. If Henry knew of her fate, he said naught, but then he would not in my hearing. I expected an excuse for him to ride to Godstow, which was the last thing I wanted. If he discovered my visit to Woodstock I would be in a mighty mess. I made a point of keeping Henry fulfilled.

Chapter 3 Prophesy and Death

We stopped at a manor before London where I took Brynn aside.

'Thank you for contributing to the peace between England and Wales.'

She smiled in that enigmatic way of hers. 'Milady you are held in high esteem on the Welsh side of the border.'

I smiled. 'Perhaps.'

'And I have something for you.' Brynn handed me a scroll. The seal was beautiful, but it was not the Welsh King's. I broke it and unrolled the velum. It carried one line. "The eagle of the broken covenant shall rejoice in her third nesting."

'God in Heaven, Brynn, what is that supposed to mean?'

She shrugged. 'I have no idea, Milady, but it is the prophesy of Merlin.'

'Merlin!' I frowned. 'Was he not a wizard from an ancient Celtic saga, like a Greek oracle?'

'Yes Milady. He had amazing foresight and could predict the future.'

'You might believe that, but I find it disturbing. The only prophesy I have been given was unsettling and continues to create angst.'

Her eyes seemed to bore into mine. They disturbed my equilibrium.

'Brynn, you must excuse me; I have duties to perform.'

I knew I was avoiding the issue. I flung Merlin's so-called prophesy amongst my belongings.

***

At Westminster there was a pile of letters on my desk. Most were from Uncle Ralph, one from Clotilde and another from my dear friend and cousin, Faydide. I decided to read Faydide's letter last and broke the seal of The House of Aquitaine.

I flew out the door of the library into the arms of Jerome, who was running towards me. Renée, my petite Maman had died in her bed. She used to joke she would be found face down amongst her favourite herbs. Jerome and I clung together entwined in grief. Apart from Papa, she was the most important person in my life. Love was her scripture writ in capital letters. With love she protected, scolded, and taught. As Duchess of Aquitaine, I was her vassal. I bent to her philosophy and gave her homage above all others. If she gave me a slap, I deserved it. She could sooth a heartbreaking pain that no-one else could with a tight embrace. Like when Papa died…Who would look after me now?

I instructed Jerome to inform the children. Renée was far more a granddame to them than Empress Matilda. I had to tell Henry. I interrupted a meeting he was having with his panel of justiciars. He knew something was amiss by the expression on my kohl-streaked face. He accompanied me back into the gallery. I only had to utter 'Renée' when he knew. Henry held me close. He told me he would dismiss the panel and return. I said I had to go to the children and began walking. Henry called out after me.

'Darling, you are going the wrong way.'

I turned, but a trance overwhelmed me. My feet just walked, guided by…something out of my ken.

I was found sitting on the bridge that crossed the Thames near Westminster amongst London's litter. Henry had sent a search party of guards to find me. A cavalcade came careening towards me, flaming torches held aloft. I remembered a shout. 'Milady?'

Antoine leapt from his mount. He looked at me in disbelief. My men were all around, relief written on their faces.

'Thank God! he cried, 'Are you all, right? What are you doing here?'

I had no idea. Bewilderment had swallowed me up. Antoine lifted me to my feet and peered at me.

'Come, Lady Eleanor, let us take you home.'

Antoine boosted me onto his horse, apologising I had to ride astride. With agility he re-mounted behind me. We rode back to Westminster to the relief of my children, Jerome, my maids, and retainers. Henry stood with them, nonplussed, and angered by my disappearance.

Antoine related, with a distasteful look on his face, how he had found me in the dirt. He said I probably had fleas, lice, and other pests. My maids prepared a tub of steaming water in which to bathe me. My hair was scrutinised, lathered and scrubbed till I thought my scalp would detach from my skull. No matter how much I yelled and complained my maids took it in turns to torture my head. They burned my clothes.

As I sat by the fire, my hair was dried and examined again. I believe I shone all over like a newly minted coin. All the physical pain of the fine-toothed comb snagging through my waist-length mane kept my thoughts off Renée.

Brynn stood beside me. She handed me an evil-looking physic.

'Milady, drink this—all of it,' she ordered.

I took a tentative sniff. 'Ugh! it smells foul!'

'It will calm you and help you sleep,' Brynn said.

I took a sip, gagged and pushed Brynn's hand away.

'Dear God in heaven, are you trying to poison me?'

'Drink it, or I will hold your nose and pour it down your throat, Milady. You will thank me on the morrow.'

My maids echoed Brynn. Outnumbered, I drained the mug. Brynn gave me a spoon of honey, which did little to disguise the bitterness in my mouth.

I was then tucked up into my bed. Whatever was in that physic knocked me out. When I awoke, Henry was beside me. The old whalebone talisman was around my neck with its Celtic words of protection warming my chest. What he made of that I knew not. Perhaps Brynn charmed him in some way. At times I was sure I had a strange being in my midst, a Welsh Faerie from another sphere.

When I stirred, Henry began questioning. 'What in God's Name did you think you were doing, disappearing like that, throwing the whole household into turmoil and fear for your safety?'

I shook my head. 'I do not know, Henry. I felt numb... in mind and body. Every time I bid her farewell; I pushed away the thought that one day Renée would be no more. But she went on and on.'

Henry sighed. 'Yes, I know. That is how I felt when Maud died.'

Maud, Henry's nurse, had been more mother to him than Empress Matilda ever was. Henry's next words brought us both to tears.

'You know I loved Renée too... except I do not think the feeling was always mutual, like when she behaved as viciously as a goose defending one gosling. You are much the same with ours,' he said.

'Are you calling our children geese?'

By now we were crying and laughing because the analogy regarding Renée was so true. It was a brave person who came between Renée and her charges. She may have been small in stature, but like a goose she would rise on her toes, spread her wings and hiss and honk towards whomever she thought threatened her brood.

Henry and I relaxed a little remembering Renée. It brought us closer than we had been since Hal's wedding.

'It is hard to fathom my reaction, Henry. In situations where I have no control, I find I cannot think logically. Like when Marie and Alix were born, and Louis took them away, I felt impotent. It was the same when William died. I carry the grief and guilt to this day because I could not save him. You did your best to console me, but I felt useless as William's mother.'

We were quiet. I shuddered. My mind flashed back to after the Second Crusade when anxiety consumed me like a nightmare. During my marriage to Henry, I had mostly overcome the panic, but his recent behaviour had undermined my equilibrium.

I broke our silence. 'Henry, you have enabled me to use my skills, given me responsibilities and allowed me to use my wits for which I thank you. Yet, I can see you are conflicted when I succeed easily at times you cannot. I fear I have forced you to find flattery elsewhere by appearing critical or over meticulous when reading a document, for instance.'

'Eleanor, I have spoken Latin since childhood. I had the best of tutors, but you sniff out grammatical errors like a dog digging up a putrid bone.'

'Henry, I think and dream in Latin. It is that easy.'

'So do I, but I am not pedantic like you are.'

'I was trained to be meticulous, Henry. It hurts when you think I rule by batting my eyelids at recalcitrant nobles. I do not! I find ruling a duchy or a kingdom challenging but stimulating. I only use charm when necessary. In truth, I am as cunning as a vixen. I achieve consensus amongst diverging barons when you cannot by using diplomacy, not threats.'

'I do not have time to flirt and talk Eleanor. You can protest, but I have seen you in action—Circe and the sirens.'

I ignored the insult as much as it annoyed me.

'Look at Geoffrey. See how learning comes naturally to him, how his curiosity and his precociousness are like a second skin. Nobody taught Geoffrey to read, he just did. Our chess games are getting more difficult for me to win.'

My voice was getting louder.

'Jerome says I was the same as a child. But as a woman I am considered a freak, a witch, and an abomination, for supposedly trying to emulate men. You know I am no man. I am all woman!'

I took a deep breath to control my temper.

'Henry, I want control of my life. I do not want to compete with other women for your love. Nor should our legitimate children have to battle for acceptance with those born as bastards. I have never been unfaithful to you because I have had no need, believing I was loved as I love you.'

Henry was fidgeting. I had hit a sore point.

'Thank you for your sympathy and kindness regarding Renée,' I went on. 'I am sorry I caused you concern by my lapse yester-morn. Now I need to dress. I must speak to our children.' I paused at the door. 'I hope you will heed my words, Henry. After all, I am who I am, my father's daughter.'

We all mourned beloved Renée, Jerome and I especially. I organised prayers for her immortal soul and held vigils. She was buried as instructed in our family crypt at L'Ombrière next to my mother Aenor.

***

In the meantime, Becket was still worrying Henry. Hal was agitating for responsibility as the Young King. But would Henry loosen his grip on counties, shires, or a small estate? No! Their arguments were becoming more intense, urged on with gusto by his younger brothers except for John, who was under three. It infuriated Hal that Richard and Geoffrey had future lands to rule. Furthermore, I was training Richard. I assigned him duties as the future Duke of Aquitaine and let him read correspondence from my uncle and my justiciars, which annoyed Hal further. I planned to have Richard return to Poitiers to sit with my panel and be tutored by Uncle Ralph.

Hal was on edge. 'Surely you can do more, Maman, to persuade Papa on my behalf.'

'Hal, I beg you to be patient.'

Hal's reply was strident. 'Maman, I am running out of patience.'

'All right! Mine, too, is stretched. I will try again! Though I have lost count of how many times I have broached the subject. My last attempt almost ended in another spectacular argument. I am on my limits, Hal. And I am trying to remain calm and civil with him for the sake of you and Margaret.'

'The trouble is, Maman, you are giving in to Papa in your old age.'

'My what?'

Hal bolted from my quarters with my voice echoing behind him.

Well, that put me in a foul mood for the rest of the day. I took my glass to the brightest window in my chamber looking for wrinkles. I made Marion search my hair for any grey, which she thought was amusing, so I bit her head off.

I sulked in the library. Henry had been laying with other woman; I was nine, nearly ten years older even if he did look weather-worn these days. I had taken my looks for granted, but I was nearly fifty years old. Were people being polite when they said I was still beautiful? Why was I becoming so vain?

That evening, I went to more trouble with my preparations. I had my hair braided in Henry's favourite style. I wore the perfume he loved. Renée did not want me to wear white when she died, so I wore a gown of pink damask. We were to dine with just the children and our retinues. Hal and Margaret were eating within their household. Geoffrey sniffed the air with exaggeration. 'Ah, Maman, trying to asphyxiate us, are you? Who are you trying to impress?'

'Geoffrey do not be rude,' Henry grunted.

Richard gave his brother a shove. 'Shut your mouth, Geoff. You look lovely, Maman. Does she not Lenore?'

'Yes, I love your gown.'

'Me, too,' piped up Joanna.

John sucked his thumb.

Robert was complimentary. 'As glamourous as usual, Milady.'

Henry had lust in his eyes, so my efforts were noticed by him in a lascivious sort of way. The two girls retired after dinner to one end of the room to play a game Lenore was teaching her young sister. John was taken to his cot. Richard strummed his lute. He was becoming quite a composer and was working on a new piece that was very pretty. He said it was in honour of Renée, which brought tears to my eyes.

Geoffrey started nagging. 'Come on, Maman, how about a game of chess?'

'Not tonight, Geoffrey.'

'Come on, or are you afraid of being beaten?'

'Huh!'

'Well, come on then. Got you scared, have I?'

Geoffrey pestered me till I gave in. What I really wanted to do was talk to Henry about Hal. It would not be a short game and I would have to concentrate with all my might. Henry filled up my goblet. A new shipment had arrived from Bordeaux.

'Do you want to fuzzy my wits?' I snapped.

'Maybe the game will be over more quickly if I do,' was Henry's retort.

'You play him, then. He has been dying to whip you since he was four years old. I could then play the loser.'

Henry quickly absented himself. He challenged Robert to a game of Latrunculi, an old Roman game of military tactics more suited to his temperament. My women watched on, quietly gossiping.

The candles were spluttering. Everyone had either taken themselves to their beds or were dozing in chairs. Geoffrey was the only child left in the room.

'Geoffrey, bed. We can finish the game on the morrow,' I said.

'Not yet, I have tactics to follow!'

'No, Geoffrey. We will finish tomorrow.'

'And if you do not move you will get a clip around the ears,' Henry threatened.

'Are you going to let him touch me?'

'If you do not move, Geoffrey, I will be the one slapping you, so go.'

He looked from one parent to the other with basilisk eyes. Before Henry had time to retaliate, I stood fuming over my double, my duplici, ordering him to leave.

'Geoffrey, do as you are told, or I will tip the board over.'

'Only because I am winning and have you on the run.' He ducked my right hand. 'You are avoiding the inevitable, Maman.'

He side-stepped Henry's well-aimed foot with a final parting shot.

'And I know where every piece is should you think of touching the board.'

'Bastard!' Henry yelled.

'Not if you put me there. I know how babies get into mothers now.' The door slammed as Geoffrey sped out of the chamber.

Henry and I looked at each other. Robert was laughing in his goblet. My maids thought it a good time to leave. I gave Jerome a look that said, 'Do not you dare.'

But Henry needled instead. 'Like mother, like son!'

***

Later, Henry came to my bed. When he was relaxed from our love making I said, 'Henry, I really must talk to you about Hal. He needs greater responsibility in the ruling of our kingdom. You must give him lands to govern, Normandy, for instance. If you do not stop overlooking him, he will rebel.'

My timing was ill-conceived.

Henry hitched himself on one elbow and stared at me, sneering. 'So, that is what tonight's primping was all about. Hal! And I foolishly thought your gown, perfume, and hair were all for me. But no, Mother Goose's goslings are paramount as usual.'

My patience evaporated. 'No, Henry. As a matter of fact, I

did it for me and Renée, the gown especially.'

I turned my back on him. 'Thank you for spoiling my night.'
What was the point? I thought.

If I told Henry the truth that I was afraid my looks were waning, he would not believe me, or he would twist the knowledge to suit himself. My anger boiled over as I flung back the bedclothes and let the chilled air into the bed. I grabbed my shift from the floor, dragged it over my head and stormed out the door.

My feet were freezing, and the thin silk shift did little to keep out the cold as I trod along gallery after gallery through the eerie silence of Westminster. A back stairway took me down to the kitchens. I tiptoed past nodding churls in the shadows, heading for warmth. Tiredness overcame me as I crawled into a corner near a few glowing embers in the huge range.

What was I to do? I knew I could not continue tippytoeing around Henry, avoiding what might cause an uproar to keep Lenore from the House of Castile for a few years. Like Hal, I was given no role in the ruling of England, my duties were purely ceremonial. Then I had to act as handmaiden for his sexual appetite—once a pleasure now a duty followed by the fear of another pregnancy, regardless of the steps I took to prevent it. Our children were growing, no longer needing me. Hal had his own household. Richard would return to the Aquitaine. Geoffrey was soon to leave for Brittany to marry. Matilda, thank God, was happy, living joyously with her new husband. All her letters were full of love for her Henry. Pointedly, she wrote, 'no-one argues, Maman'.

I had slept a little, woken by the sounds of the kitchens being readied for the day to come and food to be prepared. Undetected, I slipped away. The morning air was icy. The bells of the abbey rang out in the distance. I made my way to the library. It was not warm either, but there were a few coals in the grate. I threw on some kindling then almost asphyxiated myself blowing on the embers so they would catch. The fire flared. I added some larger pieces of wood and was huddling as close as possible to the warmth when the door opened. Amaris rushed to me, pulling off her cape and draping the warm woollen garment around my shoulders.

'Milady, I have been looking for you. What on earth are you doing in here in only your shift? You look chilled to the bone.'

'Amaris, I cannot go on. I am at my wits' end. I can no longer remain under the Lord King's roof—even for Lenore. I plan to return to the Aquitaine. After I am dressed, will you send for Jerome, please?'

During the night, I planned my strategy. My intentions for Richard I would bring forward. I would smuggle Lenore out with him along with Joanna and John. The three could go to Fontevrault where Lenore would be protected until she turned twelve. Henry had enough scruples not to invade the abbey. Hal and Margaret could house themselves in Normandy with his Uncle William, where Hal could continue his preparations for knighthood. I would escort Geoffrey to Brittany to meet his betrothed. They were too young to marry, though Geoffrey was mature beyond his years intellectually. Constance could be brought to live in our court in Poitiers while Geoffrey continued his studies, though I did not like removing young girls from their households. Later, they could return to Brittany to wed.

Amaris was not surprised my resolve had collapsed.

'Milady, his Lordship might stray again should you leave.'

False bravado answered. 'I no longer care.'

'Hmm!' Amaris was sceptical.

Nevertheless, I needed to be in control of my life rather than being Henry's puppet. He was to go to Winchester in two weeks' time. I was expected to accompany him. It gave me a week to prepare the children. I was placing a huge onus on Richard. It would be necessary to assign some of my Praetorian guard to escort them to bolster Richard's Aquitainean troops. They would sail to Bordeaux then ride to Poitiers.

***

Henry never asked where I had disappeared to during the night. When I returned to my bed chamber, he was up and dressed. I was eating my repast when Jerome entered. After I related my intentions, he looked at me sadly.

'I thought, Elly, you and Lord Henry were making progress in your marriage.'

'Henry might be fooling himself, but I can no longer take the sarcastic gibes. The pressure of having to buckle to his every whim is becoming unbearable, Jerome. I watch him make errors in judgement unable to say a word. And his unwillingness to trust Hal's abilities or to make any attempt to prepare him for his future role is not only distressing but lacking in vision. If I step in, he accuses me of trying to undermine his authority.'

Jerome recognised I had made up my mind. I pondered over whether to plead I was unwell to avoid Winchester or leave with Henry and let Jerome send the children to safety. I decided to feign illness; then I too could travel out of England. I would accompany Hal, Margaret, and Geoffrey. All the other arrangements were in place. Richard, although not fully aware of my reasons, was prepared to look after his little sisters and brother. Brynn insisted I wear the talisman—always.

Only my most trusted retainers knew of my plans. Jerome warned me of how Henry would react, but I calculated by the time he could rally his troops to halt my flight, I would be across the channel.

***

We successfully left England. I travelled with Hal, Margaret and Geoffrey to Barfleur. My beautiful hispano, Beelzebub, was already in Rouen and brought at my request to Barfleur. We were met by Henry's brother William, who took Hal and Margaret to his estates. I rode to Brittany with Geoffrey, my entourage, and the remainder of my Praetorian guard, where we were accommodated with Duke Conan. Geoffrey met Constance. She seemed a pleasant enough girl, although there was something about her that I found uncomfortable. Not that it mattered. I was not the one marrying her.

Duke Conan and his wife, Marguerite, were most courteous. After several days of discussion, it was decided the young couple should wait a few more years before marrying. I proposed Constance remain at home. The Duke and Duchess of Brittany were delighted with the idea and readily agreed.

We left Brittany, retracing our route back to William's chateau where we enjoyed a few pleasant days with his family.

One evening, William asked to speak to me alone.

'Eleanor, Henry is ranting that you have broken your promise to remain with him as dutiful queen and wife.'

I exhaled and tried to calm the edge in my voice.

'I expected as much, but I am just a pawn on Henry's chessboard, William. I feel diminished as a person as well as constantly having to be wall and moat between Henry and the boys, particularly Hal.'

'Well,' William replied, 'I am not surprised he is dithering. That is how Maman operated. Our brother Geoffrey was affected badly by her ignoring him, which turned him into a rebel, and, as you know, at times an untrustworthy one. I was lucky. I was sent to Papa's sister, Aunt Sybilla.'

'Please, William, give Hal responsibilities other than the ones he will have training as a young knight.'

'I will do my best, Eleanor.' He took my hand and gave it a squeeze. 'You know Henry is on his way to Barfleur?'

'Yes, I have heard. I think it best if I to ride on as quickly as possible across the Norman border.'

'Indeed. I love my brother, but I would not want to face his fury if I were you.'

'I am not afraid of him, William, but I...I just cannot go on.'

***

Our journey was uneventful through Maine and most of Anjou. I had risked staying overnight in the Plantagenet Castle at Angers but was treated kindly as their Countess. We left Angers and rode towards Fontevrault where I wanted to spend some time with Joanna, Lenore, and John, as well as delighting in Isabella's company.

Our final ride to Fontevrault Abbey was through lightly forested, gentle terrain before it opened onto the wide river valley of the Loire. There pandemonium exploded like cannon balls around us.

We were ambushed. I was riding amid my Praetorian guard with Jerome, Peter, Geoffrey and Lucille. Where our attackers came from or who they were we knew not. My men immediately tightened a cordon around us. Luckily, my maids in the carriages were well behind.

A furious melee took place. I remembered shrieking 'Geoffrey' as terrified horses reared and screamed. Arrows flew, broad swords flailed and clanged. I saw Simeon felled in front of me, crashing from his horse in a bloodied heap. My horse reared as Simeon's destrier bolted in fear. I was not expecting his animal to move the way it did, so I was thrown from shying Beelzebub into a maelstrom of thrashing hooves. How I was not trampled I knew not. In front of me lay a strange archer, obviously dead. Instinct drove me to grab his bow and quiver. Combined with the speed of all those years of practice on archery ranges, I fired the first arrow at an on-coming horse, shooting it through the neck. The wounded animal went down, tossing its rider in front of me. Before he rose to his feet, my next arrow was through his leg. I continued in this manner till I had emptied the quiver.

I was on my knees between kicking legs, grinding sod, and bellowing men when I was grabbed from behind. I fought with all fury till I realised it was Peter. He threw me towards someone as a sword felled him.

My confessor was unarmed. I staggered upright hoisting my ripped gown ready to run, only to see my eleven-year-old son charging through the throng firing arrow after arrow, his young thighs gripping the animal, its reins loose, a golden-haired angel. Another body threw itself over me. I writhed and fought to stand but was pinned down.

Amongst the mayhem, a second army arrived out of nowhere, scattering those who had attacked. Then the tumult stopped as swiftly as it had started, an eeriness descended, except for the moans and cries from dying horses and men. The terror of the crusade flooded back as I disentangled myself from the weight above me. It was then I realised to my horror it was Jerome.

He was not dead, but his life was ebbing from a gash on his chest. Hysterically, I pleaded with him not to die as I cradled him in my arms. His warm blood soaked my gown, already wet from Peter's life force.

Jerome looked at me through his dimming dark eyes. I kissed him with all my might, rocking him, begging, pledging God I would do anything but to please save my darling Jerome.

Somehow with his last ounce of strength, he whispered, 'I love you, wild child. My love, my life, my unattainable Elly.'

I was hysterical, having to be dragged away from Jerome's body. Geoffrey, little darling, was yelling, 'Maman, Maman,' because my gown was drenched in blood with him not knowing whose. Praise God, he seemed unhurt.

The man who carried me was Guillaume le Marechal. Guillaume was a roving knight in the service of the Aquitaine and others on and off for years. He was travelling towards Anjou when by happenstance he heard the battle ahead. He and his men galloped to the scene. They saved many lives.

Guillaume took charge. They carried my darling Jerome's body to Fontevrault where Isabella and her sweet nuns took over. I was inconsolable. Peter was brought too, and Simeon. Then we realised Lucille was badly hurt. Two days later, she died. Lucille had served me as a beloved maid for over ten years. She came into my service after I divorced Louis. She rode like I did, at one with the horse which was why she was by my side and not in the carriages with Amaris, Celeste, and Marion.

Unhurt, praise God and safe, Geoffrey wept, clinging to me, not wanting to let me go, my brave little duplici. It took several nuns begging me before I removed my torn, blood-soaked gown, and my body examined for injuries—a gash on one arm, abrasions, and bruises but nothing too serious. My three little ones were distraught.

If I had stayed in England. Had I obeyed Henry's wishes… if, if, if… "a game for scholars"! But, no, I am arrogant Eleanor, wanting her own way at all costs. Always the superior 'know-it-all.' How could I ever forgive myself for putting the lives of my beautiful Jerome, my gentle confessor Peter, loyal Lucille, Simeon, a long-serving knight and so many others that day at risk? They gave their lives to protect me. Worse, I endangered Geoffrey, all for my overgrown self-worth of having to be in control, always impatient, and always impetuous.

Dear little Lenore, Joanna, and John calmed eventually and did their best to cuddle Geoffrey and me, to help in their sweet childlike ways to comfort us. It took all my strength to leave them at Fontevrault, but I was terrified of what could befall them.

Two weeks later, I arrived in Poitiers, guilt-ridden, battered, and lucky to be alive. I wished I could obliterate what had occurred. My memories haunted me day and night.

Antoine took Geoffrey and me to one side. He emphasised the carnage would have been far worse had it not been for our archery skills. I sobbed. I loved horses, and loathed hurting one. Brave Antoine, like Simeon, had been at my side since I was the young Queen of France and knew I had honed my archery skills over many years. He knew I had witnessed how, during the Second Crusade, horses were shot to dislodge the heavily armoured knights, making them vulnerable on the ground. Geoffrey said he learned from my stories about Saracen archers attacking from horseback, and how they fired their arrows while gripping the galloping animal with their thighs.

It was discovered that the men who ambushed us were a group of mercenaries who had been following our movements, thinking they could capture the Queen of England for ransom. I was relieved because I had wondered if Henry could have been behind it. I learned later from Robert that Henry was sick when he found out Geoffrey and I were attacked, and deeply saddened by the deaths of those so close to us.

I toyed with the idea of going back to Henry with my tail between my legs. But Amaris' common sense prevailed.

'Milady, how long would you last? This is part of your destiny, as painful as it is. What is more, Lucille would come back to haunt you if you returned to England. You have made your choice. Stick to it, or all their lives are for nothing. More importantly, do it for Jerome; for his love.'

So, I had to suffer God's wrath with no confessor. The truth that Jerome was in love with me, confirming my suspicions, was the hardest to accept. I missed my childhood companion. As an adult, he had become my mentor, a sensible calming influence. I yearned for his wicked sense of humour, good judgement, intelligence, and an earthiness that anchored him to the world. I could hear his voice. *Come on, wild child, that is unrealistic.* In other words, keep your feet on the ground, Eleanor, and follow your ordained path. But God, why, oh why?

Chapter 4 A Blessed Relief

For a distraction, I took Richard and Geoffrey to inspect the Cathedral of Saint-Pierre in Poitiers. It had undergone a huge rebuilding programme. Henry and I had provided funds. The huge stained-glass, crucifixion window had not long been installed. It was magnificent and glowed with colour. Richard and Geoffrey were impressed, too, by its splendour.

Also, I wished to speak to Jean des Bellesmains, Bishop of the Cathedral, not something I was looking forward to, seeing he was an ally of Becket's. But I needed a replacement for dear Peter. We were escorted to Bishop Jean's palace.

He was courteous and offered us wine with a tasty repast.

'Your Ladyship, please accept my deepest sympathy for your recent travails. A most sorry episode. If I can be of any help, it will give me the greatest honour.'

'Thank you, Your Grace. I am the most afflicted. I have lost my two closest clerics in Brother Peter, my confessor, and Brother Jerome, and am sorely without succour. I need someone to fill Peter's position.'

The bishop nodded wisely. 'I will give the matter my deepest consideration. I presume you would prefer another monk from Brother Peter's order?'

'I care not from which order the priest comes, Your Grace, as long as he is sympathetic to a woman of my learning and is as well read.'

'Mmm. Yes.'

I could see he was mulling over my wishes, perhaps not saying what was on his mind because of the presence of Richard and Geoffrey.

'And when will the Lord King be gracing our duchy? It is some time since he was in Poitiers.'

Out of the corner of my eye, I saw quick glances between my two sons, hoping above hope neither, especially Geoffrey, was going to say something inappropriate. What the bishop understood about the state of my marriage, I knew not.

I answered, 'Lord King Henry is far too involved in the affairs of state in England and Normandy and has entrusted me with the governance of the Aquitaine.'

'Ah yes,' Jean pontificated, 'he is in conflict with the Archbishop of Canterbury. I hear Thomas Becket is still in France. A sorry case. It is a shame, Milady, you cannot influence the Lord King on the value and practice of Canon Law within the clergy.'

I took a steadying breath, 'Within the clergy, Canon Law is still practised, Your Grace. It is only from without the church that it is not. The civilian population is judged by the Laws of England with no prejudice as to trade, profession, or status, including all citizens who are not ordained members of the church. If employed in a clerical position by a bishop or archdeacon, that does not make them an officer of the church unless they have taken holy orders.'

Bishop Jean stared at me agog. I might be estranged from Henry, but it did not make me a traitor to his rule of law in England. I was still his queen. Moreover, Becket was a conniving beast. He ingratiated himself into Henry's bosom when it suited him, then after being ordained and given his honours, turned and placed himself above his king. To change his long-held opinions as chancellor was low to say the least. Canon Law was biased against the common man for the privilege of petty clerks. It was an affront to England's legal system.

Of course, Monsieur Sabots Intelligents could not keep his mouth shut, and I was too distant from his chair to poke him into submission. I held my breath.

'Maman, ah Lady Eleanor, is correct, Your Grace. The laws of England were good enough for the previous Archbishops of Canterbury like Becket's predecessor, the late Archbishop Theodore, a most learned and erudite man. But now we have controversy all because members of the clergy want to protect the villains in their midst by giving them lighter sentences through Canon Law for crimes committed within the general community. That, Your Grace, is unfair. If that layperson is a criminal, he must be tried as a criminal. What if one had committed sodomy, for instance?'

I nearly choked on my wine. Worse, I could see by the glint in Richard's eye he was enjoying Geoffrey's "sermon". The bishop was turning purple in front of the Houses of Aquitaine and Plantagenet.

Before anyone could utter another word, I stood.

'Well now, thank you Your Grace, for the delicious repast and your kind words, but it is time for the princes to return to their studies. My congratulations on the refurbishment of the Cathedral. The stained glass is awe-inspiring.'

I hoped I charmed my way out of Geoffrey's none too helpful "opinion". His Grace, I thought, was as happy to see the end of us as I was to leave. Outside, before mounting to return to the palace, I glared at them.

'You two can stop snickering. Neither of you are too tall to have your ears slapped. Geoffrey, if I end up with a confessor the likes of the late Abbé Suger of St Denis, you will be on the next ship to Portsmouth. And Richard, you do not need to encourage your garrulous, know-it-all brother by grinning like a gargoyle.'

I dared not ask what they knew about sodomy.

***

Henry wrote requesting I attend the Christmas court in Rouen. Despite reservations, I agreed, regardless of how fraught it could be. I was desperate for a change of scenery, and I hoped, a little comfort. Of course, he wanted the children to attend as well, but did I trust him not to whisk Lenore out from under my nose? No! But I did not want her to miss family festivities, either. I would cross that moat if it happened.

The Christmas court in Rouen started as a happy event, more so than I expected. My flight from England was not mentioned, more because Becket loomed large in Henry's mind. Hal's crowning, undertaken by the Archbishop of York, was extracting ongoing revenge from the vindictive man. He had placed interdicts on parts of England with Pope Alexander III's permission. He, too, believed only the Archbishop of Canterbury should crown an English king. Henry was therefore forced to negotiate with Becket, who had returned from exile, probably strutting like a bantam cock. Then he tried to excommunicate members of the clergy who favoured Henry. There were several vacant Bishoprics pending after Becket took himself to France. Those of the clerical hierarchy who had legitimately elected members to fill these vacancies were the ones suffering Becket's edicts. No wonder Henry was a bundle of nerves.

After the Christmas services, we sat down together for a fine feast. It was wonderful seeing Hal and Margaret. They were happy together, which was a pleasure to see. William and his family were there too. Richard was a little quiet, holding his temper in place with his father. The boys were becoming young men with deepening voices. Slender Geoffrey, too, was developing. Lenore, whose attendance I risked, was becoming more beautiful each day. I noticed Henry looking at her with a wistful expression. What he was seeing in his middle daughter I knew not. Joanna was more like Henry's mother. She would be a handsome woman. I still had no idea who John looked like. He was a puzzle. But he and Henry had bonded. Henry wanted John to return with him to England. That could be interesting.

Robert came and sat beside me and said, 'I was horrified when I heard about the ambush and saddened to hear about Brothers Peter, Jerome, and lovely Lucille's deaths. Thank God you were unharmed.'

'I may not have any physical scars, and my bruises have faded, but, in my head, I battle daily with the horror and guilt. Robert, if I had not left England the way I did, they would still be alive.'

Robert shook his head. He was about to say something when Henry wandered over carrying two goblets. Robert stood.

'Milord, take my chair. I will excuse myself if you do not mind.'

Henry sat and handed me mulled wine.

'Thank you.' I took a sip and said, 'Henry, I have made a grievous error of judgement that resulted in the deaths of Jerome, Peter and all the others.'

'Did you know you were going to be ambushed?'

'No! Of course not. It came out of nowhere. One minute we were riding along peacefully, then these mercenaries and roustiers attacked.' I swallowed my wine.

'Then how can it be your fault?' He signalled to a page to top up my goblet.

'If I had not left… Henry, I have no confessor. I have lost my childhood friend and mentor, and Lucille as well. She rode like the wind through the night with us, remember, and with me alone often. She put her life on the line for me. When that pipsqueak Scot, David, usurped his uncle, King Malcolm's crown, she was at my side. Lucile rode like I do—did, she was part of the horse. That was why she was there though I did not see her injured. I was too busy fighting for my life.'

'I heard you fought like a knight and saved many lives.'

'But not the ones I cherished most. Jerome died in my arms.' My voice caught as tears welled. Henry took the goblet from my hands and called to Robert that we would be back soon. Away from family and guests we sat in Henry's chamber. He let me cry, mopping the kohl from my cheeks with his handkerchief.

'Geoffrey was like a golden angel, Henry, flying through the fray. He reminded me of a Saracen archer. I had no idea he could ride like that.'

'Like mother like son, methinks.'

'Like his Papa, too, Henry.'

Henry grunted, then spoke. His voice had an edge.

'Although I am relieved you and Geoffrey were not hurt or abducted, it angers me because you broke your promise. You preach honour when it suits you. Then…' He balled his fist.

I bit my tongue and held my breath, then whispered, 'I think I have paid for it Henry.'

'Indeed.'

We sat in silence, except for the thumping of my heart, staring at the flames in the grate. Then Henry said, 'I do not expect you to return. You are better employed where you are. I have too many problems in England and have no time for discontent to break out in your lands. Your hot heads are more inclined to obey their duchess.'

In the dim light, Henry would not have registered my surprise. But I was pleased he seemed to be learning on that front, especially as I knew of a few nobles in Poitou who would like to run him through. I continued to placate them where possible.

'You can take Lenore back to Poitiers too. She is too beautiful to be ravished yet.'

I must admit I had not taken in her features like that. I only saw a little girl who enjoyed playing jacks.

'No wonder your father was tardy betrothing you, Eleanor. If you looked like Lenore at the same age, he would not have wanted to lose the joy of his life, his beautiful, beautiful daughter.'

All I could do was breathe 'thank you'.

The tension relaxed between us. We had avoided a skirmish for which I was thankful. His hand closed over mine, and he rubbed his thumb back and forth across it. He said nothing nor made any overtures, but through loneliness and sadness I needed him. But how would Henry react to my desire. I glanced at him sideways. He was staring into the fire, deep in thought. So, I loosened his grip, stood, and started massaging his shoulders. They felt tense; knotted. He said nothing but did not pull away. Slowly, his head rested back against my breasts. Gently, I continued. His eyes closed. I thought, *Damnation Henry, do not fall asleep*. I kissed the top of his woolly grey head. I was arousing myself, but Henry seemed to be dreaming and I was on the wrong side of his body to stimulate what needed to be stimulated. Instead, I worked my fingers up his neck to his ears where I started to fondle his ear lobes. Henry exhaled, followed by a deep moan. Ah! At last, I was getting a reaction.

'Are you trying to tell me something, Eleanor?'

'Wanting something, yearning would be closer to the point.'

'Well, you had better come around here.'

We undressed each other in front of the fire, then flew into the chilly bed. We snuggled into each other as much for warmth as for desire, and progressed with practised precision to caress, and continue to arouse. How attuned we were to each other's bodies. Henry's member was hard in my hand. As I felt it begin to pulse, I guided it within. All the pain and horror of my recent travail vanished in a simultaneous throb of passion.

I got what I needed, even if I knew my satisfaction would be short-lived. I asked myself why, as husband and wife, we could not find accord in our lives when we were so sensually in harmony. But I knew I could not forgive Henry's brutality to my people or for neglecting the boys no matter how I satisfied my short-term longing. When we reappeared, I did not think too many people missed us. Robert guessed, though, and imperceptibly shook his head as much to say, will you never learn?

Good cheer was all around with people merrily imbibing. Minstrels were playing, and the children were delighting in their little gifts and trinkets. Goose, duck, and other fowls had been consumed followed by spicy sweetmeats. Henry and I returned to our roles as king and queen, circulating throughout the Great Hall.

But, at the height of our family celebrations, the tendrils of Becket's discontent tightened around Henry. A courier arrived, stomping his freezing feet and blowing on his chilblained fingertips. He handed an epistle to Henry, who took it to one side to read. A howl issued from Henry's throat, his benign humour turning to one of fury in a heartbeat. Our merriment came to a halt. I rushed to his side. Henry crushed the epistle in his fist; threw up his arms in frustration, and roared to the vaulted arches, "Will no one rid me of this turbulent priest!"

Henry thrust the crumpled letter into my hand. While I scanned the page, through the mighty oak doors burst Roger of York, Joscelin of Salisbury, Bishop Foliot of London and what seemed like an abbey of eminent churchmen stamping the snow off their boots. The Great Hall was in pandemonium. The men's faces registered despair and anguish.

Becket had excommunicated them. From strident voices we learnt Becket did not like them, declaring them "his bitter foes". These ordained high-ranking prelates appealed to Henry, begging him to petition the pope on their behalf. Becket's timing could not have been worse.

Instead of enjoying the final hours of such a holy day and our feasting, Henry was inflamed with rage. Nobody could console him. His disappointment that his old friendship with Becket had come to this was the last straw. The tenderness that had taken place between us was wasted in bitterness, with Becket's actions twisting a dagger of bile in Henry's guts.

***

Days progressed. Nothing I tried could comfort Henry, so I prepared to return to Poitiers, but the weather was sleety and blustery. I decided to wait till it cleared before riding from Rouen to Barfleur to sail to Bordeaux. Storms at sea, I thought, were preferable to another ambush.

Henry's state of mind and frustrations with Becket affected everyone. I could do naught, so I kept out of his way to spend time with Hal. He was enjoying his knighthood training, though he was disappointed and angry that his father failed to recognise his need for autonomy. I told him this was not the time to petition a distressed and fuming Henry. We were in this unhappy situation when chaos erupted in the bailey below. Horses skidded to a stop on the icy cobbles and raised, panic-stricken voices echoed around the castle walls.

Hal and I rushed down. There was something seriously wrong. Ashen-faced Henry was vomiting his breakfast, which lurched my stomach also.

Robert yelled, 'Becket has been murdered in Canterbury Cathedral!'

'Dear God, no! How?'

Horrified, we learned four of Henry's knights took his words on Christmas day literally. They had sailed across the channel, galloped to Canterbury, and stabbed Becket to death whilst he prayed in his Cathedral. The day, December 29, 1170, would forever be a nightmare for Henry.

Becket had been a thorn in our sides for years, but he did not deserve to die in this manner at the hands of Henry's men. What were they thinking? Why did they assume Henry's words were anything but bluster? Those of us close to him knew he was just being Henry when he fumed about being rid of Becket. He was exasperated he could not enjoy his Christmas court without the Archbishop of Canterbury disturbing the happy occasion with his family.

Henry was inconsolable. Instead of leaving Rouen as planned, I stayed.

Hal was stamping about and shouting, 'I know I should pray for Becket's soul, but I cannot. When I was under his guardianship, he always made me feel uncomfortable.'

'Hal, stop.' I beckoned and we walked outside his chamber.

'Darling, keep your voice down and thoughts to yourself. There are too many members of the clergy who were Becket's supporters, many within our own bishoprics, like Bishop Jean des Bellesmains. They are all capable of making our lives difficult.'

Hal's outburst prompted me to gather the older children together in my chamber, including Margaret.

'All of you listen to me. This is a challenging time for your father. He and Thomas Becket were close friends. Henry believed when he appointed him Archbishop of Canterbury, Becket would remain loyal. Instead, he turned on him, opposed English traditional law, and divided many within the church. I insist that all of you, particularly you, Geoffrey, keep your mouths shut.'

'All right! I will,' Geoffrey muttered.

'Becket has powerful friends, including, I am afraid, Margaret, your father.'

'Lady Eleanor, I will do what Hal wants.'

'Thank you, my dear.'

Hal agreed. 'Maman, you can rely on us. We will not talk or answer questions regarding Becket.'

'Your obedience is appreciated, Hal.'

'You sound like you are protecting Becket. I know you did not trust him, and he riled Papa beyond endurance,' Richard grumbled.

'Richard, I agree, and the feeling was mutual. Nevertheless, let me emphasise, your father is going to be sorely judged, accused of instigating Becket's murder. Let me repeat, this is not the time to air your opinions in public. Do you agree?'

'Yes, Maman.'

I thanked them and left to see what I could do for Henry.

Robert paced outside Henry's chapel looking dejected. He said Henry was in tears, begging God's forgiveness. I tiptoed into a fog of incense. Priests were chanting sotto voce. Henry was prostrate in front of the altar. I genuflected, knelt beside him, and reached for the hand nearest to me. It was freezing, colder than his usual extremities. I could see he had banged his head on the floor in his grief and guilt. I whispered in his ear that he should come to his bed chamber, warm himself, then come back to pray. It took me time to persuade him with the help of his chaplain.

We staggered down the gallery. I thought I would collapse under his weight. He had become heavy in his middle years. I sent a churl to fetch more wood. As close to his grate as possible I set about warming him. His manservant, Gerard, wrapped a thick fur-lined cloak around his shoulders. I sent him for some broth, bread and cheese and a flask of mulled wine.

I tended Henry like I would one of our children. He said naught, his eyes were hollow and haunted. A little colour returned to his cheeks after I fed him some broth. He looked like an old man, far older than his father was when he died. I poured him a goblet of the warm spicy wine and one for myself. Henry's hands were shaking so much I had to guide it to his lips. I whispered he should rest in his bed. The chamber was now toasty warm thanks to the churls who had heaped the fire. Henry allowed me to help him to bed. I massaged his freezing feet, then tucked the down-filled covers and furs around him.

'If I did not know better, I would think you loved me,' he croaked.

'Henry, this is not the time to discuss our feelings for each other. And I do.'

'What?'

'Love you.'

Instead of calming him, my words only distressed him.

'What am I to do?' His voice caught, 'What am I to do? How can I make time go back? I meant not to have Thomas murdered. Why did I utter those words? Why did my men not understand I meant no harm?'

What could I say? Henry, for as long as I had known him, was prone to impetuosity. How could I express I knew how he felt? How often had I wished to obliterate what I had spat out, to wake up and find it was just a horrible nightmare? But nothing I could say would change the consequences of his outburst or relieve the pain of his guilt.

All I could do was stroke his forehead and mop up his tears. I wondered if his adultery was much the same, brought on by an impulsive moment, unable to control his lust. Except for damn Rosamund. That conniving little witch was not as stupid as Robert painted her, knowingly flattering Henry, and batting her baby blue eyes at him. Well, she was taken early from this world—her just deserts as far as I was concerned. Vindictive or nay, I hoped she rotted in hell.

I could delay my departure no longer. I had to return to the Aquitaine. Only time would heal Henry's woes. His guilt would haunt him. All he could do was pray for God's forgiveness. To add more pain, I heard Becket was to be made a saint, the scene of his murder, a shrine. Heaven forbid!

'Eleanor, I need you,' Henry begged.

'I am sorry, but let me remind you, the last thing we want is for the Aquitaine to erupt into a volcano of violence, with the supporters of Becket spewing lava. I have no choice but to try to prevent that. And Henry, you have no option but to return to your duties in England…and to beg for the pope's mercy.'

He looked pathetic, but I knew I would be more help to him calming the clergy in the Aquitaine. I left John in his care. Such a strange little boy, but he seemed to like his Papa. I asked Robert to take care of Henry and to keep me informed.

Chapter 5 Aftermath

Clotilde was waiting for me when Richard, Geoffrey, the girls, and I arrived at L'Ombrière. After I sat down with her, I said, 'Clotilde, I think disaster is following me around like the grim reaper. I long for Peter and Jerome. I am haunted by their deaths, Lucille's and all the others. Now Becket's murder is another millstone around my neck.'

'Elea,' Clotilde answered. 'I sympathise, but stop wallowing in melancholy and self-pity. You have more important responsibilities to consider. Get on with it, Duchess of Aquitaine!'

She certainly had a knack of bringing one down to earth. I tried to relax after the drama of Becket and fulfil some family duties. Richard, Geoffrey, Lenore, Joanna, and I visited the family crypt to pay our respects to Renée, my mother Aenor and Dangerosa. We took bunches of flowers and sweet herbs. My children knew nothing of Aenor, their natural grandmother, and I was of little help because she died when my sister and I were just babies. I knew my Grandmother Dangerosa better. She lived to about my age.

Geoffrey was full of probing questions, having heard whispers of the family scandal between my mother's mother and my father's father. I told him this was not the time or place. But I knew he would store up his questions for a future interrogation.

Later, Clotilde and I talked about Renée and Jerome and reminisced about some of our childhood exploits, like the time we rearranged Renée's immaculately laid out herb beds by chasing a goat across them.

Jerome was going to demonstrate how to milk a goat because he had milked sheep when he was a young shepherd. But the goat would not comply. Nilla and I knew nothing about animal behaviour, Clotilde knew not much more. Jerome told Nilla and I to hold onto the animal's halter while he with his pale would extract the milk. All was going to plan till the goat started nibbling Nilla's smock. She let out a shriek, scaring the goat. It kicked over the bucket, and upended Jerome. Clotilde made a grab at the halter, missing it by leagues, while I was bowled over into the dirt.

There was much cursing in Langue d'Oc. Jerome yelled at us to catch the goat, so we bounded after it with yelps of glee. Unfortunately, the silly animal did not stay on the paths but galloped as a bird would fly across the herb beds followed by three over-excited little girls and a panic-stricken Jerome. We had a merry time. By now the terrified goat zigzagged from one end of the cherished plots to the other. Renée appeared and, in a voice that rang deeper than a cathedral bell, cried, 'Dear God and all the saints, what has happened to my garden?' We were a sad and sorry lot after the dressing down we received.

Clotilde and I were now in tears of laughter. 'Elea, you and I were covered in mud from our boots to the tops of our heads. Nilla had ripped her smock and Jerome was soaked in milk.'

'Yes, and by the time he had caught the goat it had eaten half a rosemary bush and most of the sage patch. Jerome ran away and hid till Renée found him and gave him a hug.'

'Yes, but she chided us—Lady Eleanor and Lady Petronilla, where is your decorum?'

We laughed and I took Clotilde's hand.

'Henry described Renée as a mother goose and how it was life-threatening to come between her and her goslings. Your Maman was an amazing woman, Clotilde.'

'Yes, I miss her. And what a dear little boy Jerome was, becoming a fine man.'

'Before he died, he told me he loved me.'

'You did not realise that Elea?'

'I sort of suspected, but I thought it was more brotherly love.'

'Poor darling, he was besotted from when we were about eleven. When you had to marry King Louis, he was so angry I thought he would do something foolish. We knew it would never work. You and King Louis were so unsuitable.'

Clotilde then asked the heavy question. 'Dare I enquire about you and Lord King Henry?'

I sighed. 'Clotilde, I love him one minute then hate him the next. I tried in England for Lenore's sake, but I cannot be a wife in name only or just a decorative queen. Henry and the oldest boys do not get on. He sees them as competition to his authority. And I know if I must choose between the boys and Henry, I must support my sons. I am, after all, their mother.'

***

The weather on our return to Poitiers was balmy and I was pleased to see the cathedral spires come into view after several days in the saddle. Later, as I sat with Uncle Ralph, he warned me.

'Eleanor, my dear, Bishop Jean desires to speak with you.'

'Oh, dear.'

'He is in a higher than mighty mood. He has been preaching that Lord Henry's and your opposition to Canon Law "is against all moral entitlements of the church." He said this was endorsed by Becket. Furthermore, men of the church, both lay and ordained, should be tried by Canon law, and that the Constitutions of Clarendon should be declared null and void immediately.'

'You jest.'

'No.' Uncle Ralph's reply was blunt. 'In a sermon he emphasised that Becket was so pure in his beliefs he was willing to die for his God and the rights of the church. He called him a martyr.'

'A MARTYR!' I could not believe my ears.

'Uncle Ralph, Henry had no more intention of having Becket murdered than a choir boy. I was standing next to him when in frustration he threw up his hands and uttered those fateful words. And now men of Jean's ilk are using this tragedy for political gain. The bishop needs to be careful. His See might suddenly become vacant if he continues to play that game. I think it is time I paid the bishop an unexpected visit.'

***

Bishop Jean was in his study writing and sipping wine when I was announced by a flustered archdeacon. He nearly fell off his chair when I entered. I dismissed the archdeacon who galloped out, almost tripping over his hem. 'Your Grace, I heard you urgently wished to speak to me. Not wishing to delay that meeting, I have come in all haste.'

'Milady, this is most unexpected. Had I been given warning, I would have been better prepared.' He flapped about to find me a chair.

'Your Grace, I am happy to stand. Please continue with your wine.'

He reluctantly returned to his seat. Before he could utter a word, I repeated what Uncle Ralph had said.

'I am amazed, Your Grace, that the late Archbishop of Canterbury is being called a martyr, hardly deserving.'

'Um…well…ah.' Jean flustered.

But I did not let him draw breath and said, 'After his ordination to the highest position in the English church, he flouted his authority, preached sedition against the laws of the land, then fled to France to avoid conviction.'

Before Bishop Jean could answer, I continued.

'Lord King Henry is devastated that four of his knights so misconstrued his words that they took it upon themselves to commit such a heinous crime. It is unbelievable! I was standing next to the king when he read the epistle received on Christmas day eve and witnessed the arrival of several distraught and eminent prelates. They had been excommunicated by Archbishop Becket. Not only was the king horrified by their plight, but the joyous occasion, the celebration of Christ's birth, was shattered. To know this was caused by the very man who had once been King Henry's dearest friend was disappointing.'

Bishop Jean harrumphed. 'Archbishop Becket was doing his duty by the church. A man of Becket's integrity would not have taken such measures if King Henry were not influenced by laws other than Canon Law.'

'Your Grace,' I replied, 'I beg to differ. As King of England, Lord Henry must judiciously uphold the Common Laws of his kingdom put in place by his grandfather and great-grandfather. It is his duty. He has over the years reformed and strengthened these laws, and might I add, he was aided, and advised, by Thomas Becket when he was chancellor.'

The bishop put down his wine, but before he could utter a word, I went on.

'Bishop Jean, you only met Thomas Becket briefly, before he became Archbishop of Canterbury.'

He muttered in his beard. 'Yes, it was unfortunate we had met but once.'

'Indeed, whereas King Henry's friendship with the late Archbishop went back more than ten years. Furthermore, Thomas Becket was invited to live within the Palace of Westminster for some time where he treated our regal residence very familiarly by inviting some undesirable elements to stay in his quarters.'

Jean squirmed in his seat.

'In fact, I had to request his removal from Westminster. After all, I had young and impressionable sons to protect. Even so, King Henry set Becket up on a fine estate across the Thames, far better than he deserved under the circumstances.'

I could see the bishop wished he could get rid of me without insulting his duchess.

'Nevertheless, to give Becket his due, he was clever, and Lord King Henry and the late Archbishop Theodore believed Thomas's skills in the law and other matters would make him a suitable Archbishop of Canterbury.'

'Indeed,' Jean muttered.

'Indeed, indeed! You cannot imagine how devastating it was to see that high office go to his head. To then misuse his powers, disobey the laws of the land, even those which he helped to draft, was shocking. Finally, he turned on the man who had promoted him and who had been his friend.'

I let Bishop Jean digest this before adding, 'Your Grace, I repeat, King Henry is inconsolable, distraught his words were misinterpreted, leading to Becket's murder. He was prostrate with grief when I had to leave Rouen. Nothing could give him solace.'

'Then, Milady, should not you as his wife have remained at his side?' Jean sneered down his sanctimonious nose.

'I think I have answered that question by standing here before you. Lord King Henry's words must not be distorted. We do not want the truth of what took place in Rouen Castle exaggerated by well-meaning clerics who could ferment trouble in my lands. It gives Lord King Henry peace of mind to have me here. Now, I have taken enough of your time. Before I take my leave, you might be interested in a vacancy in a bishopric on the border of Normandy and the Vexin. I hear it is a little bleak. If not, there is another See in central Ireland that could be more to your liking. I thank you for your time.'

I must admit I rode back to the palace feeling a little smug. Uncle Ralph's eyebrows shot up when I related what transpired between the bishop and myself. I told him I did not think any more Thomas the martyr sermons would be preached within or without his Cathedral. I went to the library and wrote to Henry to ask about vacant bishoprics that under Becket had not been filled. The red wax of my seal dried. Its imprint proclaimed me by the Grace of God Queen of England. Did I deserve it? In this case, yes!

***

I felt low. My lack of a personal confessor to whom I could unburden myself was gnawing at me. As I contemplated my predicament, there was a light tap on the library door. I was surprised to see Antoine.

'Pardon me for interrupting, Milady, but I have intercepted a rather ragged looking individual, I think a monk. I found him at the entrance of the courtyard when I was returning to the garrison. He said he was lost and certainly looked bewildered. He said he knew me, but I could not place him. He was most insistent he speak with her Ladyship.'

'Most odd. Did he give his name?'

'Yes, but I did not quite catch it, Milady.'

'Well, let us find out who he is and what he wants.'

I followed Antoine down to a small anteroom next to the main entry hall. There sat a dishevelled looking monk in a threadbare robe. As I walked through the door, he leapt to his feet, eyes twinkling with excitement. Joachim! Older, scrawnier, and grey around the edges of his tonsure, but who could miss those eyes. I let out a squeak of excitement, wrapping my arms around what was enveloped in the grubby habit two sizes too large for its occupant. Antoine apologised for not recognising him as he almost shook his skinny hand off his skinny arm.

I immediately escorted him to my sanctuary, my library, and instructed Antoine to have a page bring refreshments. Joachim's intake of breath when he entered was a joy to behold. Kindred spirits, he and I.

He looked over his shoulder for approval as he reverently

moved along the shelves of books, fingers caressing the spines like a lover.

'Oh, Milady. Now I can see where your love of books began. When, at that fateful time, God calls us from this earth, I hope this is what heaven will look like.'

We sat sipping lemon barley water and enjoying honey cake.

'Joachim, what has brought you so far from Paris?'

'I heard of your misfortune in an ambush which took the lives of your personal confessor Brother Peter and family mentor Brother Jerome. Whether their souls reached out to me I cannot say, but I had a vision where I was called to your side.'

'Really?'

'Yes Milady. So, I appealed to my abbot to release me from our monastery in your time of need.'

'Oh! Oh, I am overwhelmed. This is a miracle.' I could hardly speak. 'Please, Joachim, I beg you, stay within my household. But what of King Louis? He will not approve of you coming to Poitiers.'

'I do not think he knows of my existence anymore. After you left the French Kingdom there was no further use for me in the palace, so I returned to my monastery.'

This became the happiest day of my life for weeks. I organised for Joachim to be settled in our guest accommodation and provided him with whatever he needed, including new robes. In the meantime, churls prepared the quarters used by Peter and Jerome which had remained untouched since their deaths. I could not bear them to be entered. But I knew now their spirits would approve of their new inhabitant. Brother Bartholomew, our chaplain, also lived in that wing near our chapel. I was walking on air. A prayer had been answered.

With pride, I introduced him to Richard, Geoffrey, Lenore, and Joanna. I told him I had one of King Louis' and the late Queen Constance's daughters married into my family and one day I hoped he would meet Margaret and Hal. I explained John was with his father.

The children were pleased to meet Joachim. The girls were polite and Richard chivalrous. I sat close to Geoffrey, hoping I could stop him uttering something inappropriate. But not before he said, 'Brother Joachim, I am delighted to meet you.

Maman has mentioned you from time to time. I am mightily pleased you have agreed to become her confessor. I can assure you she has sins aplenty piled high which she needs to air into your ear. Ouch!'

I smiled simperingly at Joachim as Geoffrey rubbed his ankle. Richard punched his arm. Another ouch! I suggested through clenched teeth that they all return to their lessons. They scrambled out the door. A scuffle broke out in the gallery outside the chamber. I excused myself and speared them both with the eyes of a basilisk. Joanna and Lenore were tittering, so I glared at them too. I hissed at the four of them to move or else.

'He punched me.'

'You deserved it. Now all of you get out of my sight.'

Richard made another swing at Geoffrey who ducked and bolted. The girls scampered after him.

'Richard!' He reined to a stop. 'You are not helping. I suggest instead of your Latin tutorial you take yourself to Uncle Ralph for a lesson in jurisprudence.'

I returned to Joachim. 'I must apologise for Geoffrey's rudeness.'

He smiled in that sweet angelic way I remembered, which belied an impishness underneath. 'If I may be so bold, Lady Eleanor, the children seem to be as spirited as their mother who I can see has lost none of her clever wits, charm, or beauty.'

I blushed then brought up the sorry state of Becket.

'Joachim, on a more serious note, you must have heard the rumours about the late Archbishop of Canterbury. His murder has affected us all. Lord King Henry suffers greatly. Many of the clergy are divided over the man's behaviour and deeds. I am doing my best to keep the divisions within the Aquitaine under control. But there are as many thoughts on the matter as there are clerics.'

'I agree,' Joachim answered. 'It is a terrible to-do.'

I changed the subject and stood.

'Joachim, it is such a relief to have you here. A heavy burden has been lifted from my shoulders. Now, I will have you shown to our guest quarters till your permanent bedchamber is readied.'

'And thank you for my warm welcome.'

As we left the library he said with an impish grin, 'Maybe

sometime soon we should meet in your chapel so you can start ridding yourself of that pile of sins.'

Dear Geoffrey!

'Yes indeed! How is your chess by the way?'

'Ah!' he replied with sparkling eyes.

'I know just the opponent for you if you do not mind playing another precocious brat in the form of my son Geoffrey.'

For a man of the cloth Joachim was fiercely competitive. I hoped he would give my cheeky third son a good walloping.

***

I unburdened my soul the next day of the guilt I had carried since the ambush and explained why I had run from Henry. Joachim said naught. I wondered if the gap in our lives was too wide for him to understand why Henry and I had reached our stalemate. So, I poured out my life's history from when I married Henry. It flowed like a torrent, from the passionate love to the passionate arguments ending in recent times in violence.

'Joachim; I must always be right. I am unbending. I cannot bear sloppiness, from a tract of Latin to a rule of law, down to if Henry's beard needs trimming. I fear I have driven him into the arms of other women just as King Louis, and Île de France, drove me into the arms of other men. Deep down I think I still love Henry.'

'Milady, forgive me, but have you been unfaithful in your marriage to King Henry?'

'No, even when temptation stared me in the face. I had no need to look for love elsewhere.'

'And now?'

'I do not know. I am weak when it comes to searching for happiness and...um... fulfillment.'

My face was flaming. I hurriedly went on.

'So far, my duties keep me occupied as do my children, but they are growing and will soon be outside my care, like Hal. It saddens me that the boys do not have a good relationship with their father; and there is friction at times between them.'

Joachim sat quietly, then said, 'Let me think about what you have related, Milady...I am here to help. God has sent me to your side.'

Joachim made the sign of the cross over my head. I left the chapel relieved to have unburdened myself and to have left Joachim with my tangled emotions. I hoped he would not rush back to Paris for self-preservation.

***

Becket's murder was causing a furore in convents, monasteries, and houses of God from Normandy to Gascony. I knew I had silenced Bishop Jean for the time being, but I did not know of all his connections. I hoped I had enough esteem as Duchess of Aquitaine not to be judged like Henry, Richard, too. But there were dissenters in castles and abbeys on our borders who could cause trouble.

Uncle Ralph, Saldebreuil, and my most senior justiciars, urged I make a regal progress throughout the Aquitaine. My presence was needed to douse smouldering discontent. Alms would help, but the truth about what occurred in Rouen was imperative to calm others like Bishop Jean. I would take Richard.

The two weeks of preparation for Richard's and my progress were concluded. During this time, I decided Geoffrey was ready to move to Brittany. He needed responsibility to curb his over-enthusiastic energy, as well as exercising his mind. He was ahead in all his lessons and when left to his own devices he annoyed Richard. I was constantly arguing with him, and I thought I was pedantic!

I discovered Richard and Geoffrey were jousting, something I hated and could not watch. They were also pitting themselves against each other with broad swords. Neither would give an inch, and the last thing I wanted was them fighting to the death.

Their arguments were bad enough with Geoffrey doing the agitating. He knew just how far he could go to needle Richard who, like Henry, was easily riled.

I arranged with Uncle Ralph to escort Geoffrey to Brittany. I insisted his marriage to Constance not take place till I could attend, Henry too. We needed his permission as a matter of protocol after consultation with Duke Conan. Geoffrey, I thought, could be a stumbling block, accusing me of interfering in his life, but for once he was compliant.

'Maman, is Constance old enough to have children?', he asked.

I nearly fell off my chair.

'I do not know. Are you?'

Now that was a mistake.

'I have no idea,' he smirked, 'but I would not mind trying.'

I wanted to slap the lascivious grin off his face. He took off before I could clip his ear. In many ways I would miss him, but in others I would be happy to see the back of him.

I farewelled Geoffrey with mixed feelings, praying he would not disgrace himself. I warned him to keep his thoughts to himself and to be polite. Uncle Ralph raised an eyebrow. At least Lenore and Joanna were sorry to see him leave.

Richard muttered, 'God help all in Brittany,' but gave his brother a manly hug.

But I had to swallow the lump in my throat when Geoffrey rode away. My duplici, my Merlin, my brilliant, wickedly funny, disrespectful, and outspoken son was leaving me. I hoped Constance would appreciate what she was about to get in a husband, precocious brat that he was. I hoped they would be happy.

Chapter 6 Conflict

Richard and I travelled the length and breadth of our lands. I was proud of my son and heir. Even when he could have opposed his father, he respected Henry's position when it came to Becket. I was horrified when he related his own experiences as a young boy regarding Thomas's proclivities. It frightened me beyond belief. I had to be helped from the assembly at Mirabeau. Justiciars, who were ambivalent about the late Archbishop, changed their minds. Richard faced my panicked inquisition in private.

'For God's sake, tell me. What happened?'

'Let it go, Maman, I do not want to talk about it.'

'Does your father know?'

'No! But I never want to see Papa blamed for Becket's death. He had every right to run him through.'

'Richard, tell me please, I beg you!'

'Look, it was nothing. I handled it.'

'Handled what? Dear God, I cannot live without knowing!'

By now, I was roaring at Richard like a mad woman. My distress was too much for him.

'He tried to make me wear a gown. I refused. When he insisted because of the game we were playing, and tried to put it on me, I kicked him in the balls and ran away.'

'Were you alone with him?'

'No!'

'Who was with you?'

'Matilda, Geoffrey, and Hal...'

'And?'

'We were playing a game pretending to be Romans and troubadours, dressing up in linens and one of your old gowns, though it was Matilda who was wearing it. I was Julius Caesar. Matilda took off the robe and wanted to be Caesar. We were having a bit of a squabble. Then we saw Becket was watching our game. He said we should share, and I should wear the dress. I said no, they were for girls. But he kept insisting, saying it was fun. None of us felt comfortable. Geoffrey and Matilda ran away. Hal told him to leave me alone, but Becket pulled the sheet off me and tried to dress me in the gown. Hal ran off, saying he was going to get Millicent. I was only wearing my braies and shift. He was now sort of wrestling with me, trying to grab me, groping, so I kicked him as hard as I could and ran.'

'Did you find Millicent?'

'No, so we decided not to tell anyone because we thought Papa would be angry with us.'

To say I threw a mighty fit was an understatement. My voice rebounded off the walls.

'Maman, I did nothing. Are you blaming me?'

'No! Definitely not! Your father was a fool bringing that monster into our home; I told him at the time.'

I tried to work out whether the event with my children took place before or after the night Becket entertained us with his band of dubious mummers. It did not matter; I was incensed.

I stormed around the chamber, ranting, 'Richard, I cannot believe there are members of the church hierarchy who want Becket made a saint. Hell is too good for that sanctimonious bastard! Henry's health is being ruined at the whim of Rome. I should shove Canon Law down their bloody throats!'

Our voices were strident.

'Maman . . . God's Teeth. MAMAN!'

'To think that—that animal lived at Westminster, that your father placed Hal in Becket's household... How could he? Jesus, Mary, and Joseph! If he were not dead, I would kill him with my bare hands!'

'MAMAN! MAMAN! Calm down. There is nothing we can do. Like you say, he is dead. And please do not tell Papa! He will blame me.'

Richard wrapped his arms around me and practically threw me in a chair. I think I swallowed the goblet of wine he thrust in my hands in one gulp.

The rest of our progress was sullied by Richard's revelation. I worried about the reaction if his story started spreading throughout our lands. The Becket followers would accuse Richard of inciting him or whisper behind their hands that nothing less could be expected from the tainted French whore for spawning such a Prince... It was something I could never unburden to anyone. I needed to see Henry, though I could say naught to him about Richard. Time, I hoped, would heal. In the meantime, I had to keep my ears open for adverse gossip.

***

Uncle Ralph and Geoffrey arrived in Brittany after they spent some time with Hal and Margaret on William's estates in Normandy. Geoffrey, who seemed to be obsessed with procreation—I hoped it was just his age—confided to Uncle Ralph that there were no babies yet and asked if Maman or Papa had told Hal what he needed to do. Lord be praised he was many leagues out of my reach.

Duke Conan had made them welcome in Rennes, and much to Uncle Ralph's surprise, Geoffrey was quite shy in front of Constance. They were waiting to hear from Henry, so he and Conan could arrange the wedding date.

Richard and I rode back to Poitiers. Saldebreuil was heading the justiciars in my and Uncle Ralph's absence. I appointed him Regent till Uncle Ralph returned.

A letter from Henry caught up with me at Poitiers. I prepared to leave for Bordeaux then travel by sea as requested to Brittany. He said there were elements he did not trust in Poitou. *And whose fault would that be?* I thought. Anyway, I preferred travelling by ship as it was far more comfortable than interminable days in the saddle.

In Poitiers, I gathered Lenore and Joanna. Henry would bring John. Geoffrey wrote to me that Hal and Margaret would be attending his wedding. I was excited to have the family together. Hal had completed his knighthood and Richard was almost there along with Geoffrey, who surprised me often with his physical competence, being the leanest of the three oldest boys. John must be growing, too.

***

I was impatient for Hal's and Margaret's arrival in Rouen. At last, I heard horses' hooves ringing in the bailey. I rushed down to greet them. Henry and John were there, too, a surprise. I was not expecting them till the morrow. I hugged Hal even though his face looked dark. Something was amiss.

'What is wrong, Hal?'

'Ask him,' he growled, jutting his chin towards Henry, who strode off without a word.

I welcomed Margaret, who was looking worried, then turned to John, but he was following Henry.

I accompanied Hal and Margaret to their quarters, where Hal exploded.

'I am fed up with Papa, Maman. Did you know he plans to give land to that wimpy, snivelling, brat? I have nothing but a damn crown. It's not fair.'

'I am sorry.'

'He will not listen to me. He blames me for being impatient or walks out. Nor has he acknowledged my knighthood or any of my successes. I worked hard, got rewards from my tutors. I tried my best to please him to get some recognition, but no, nothing, not a bloody word!'

My gut churned; Margaret burst into tears. Lenore did her best to comfort her sister-in-law. Richard, Henry-like, was pacing and grinding his teeth. Joanna was bewildered. She had been looking forward to seeing her Papa.

It disappointed me that Henry had made no effort to acknowledge Hal's achievements. He would have known. William kept him informed like me, so why not praise him?

I walked to the door.

'I will speak to your father. I am displeased he did not greet me in the bailey. Not a word to any of us. Most uncivil.'

'I will come with you, Maman.'

'No, Richard.'

'I insist.'

'Then you will have to wait for me to dress.'

'You are dressed.'

'Wait with your brother. I will call you when I am ready.'

I had been careful with my appearance, but I was not expecting Henry. I needed a gown without a train so I could side-step him, if necessary.

I set off to Henry's chamber and sent a page to Richard. I arrived first. Robert ushered me in. He warned me Henry was not happy. I asked him to leave and to forestall Richard who would be close behind. John was nowhere in sight.

'You seemed to be in a hurry in the bailey. Not a word of acknowledgement.'

He turned. His flared nostrils took in my jasmine and rose perfume.

'Who are you trying to impress this time, me or yourself?'

'Maybe both of us.'

Henry was eyeing me up and down. Before he could advance, I confronted him, stupid in retrospect, but I was in no mood for small talk.

'Why could you not congratulate Hal's applauded knighthood? Especially as his success has been honoured throughout our lands... well?'

Henry stood like a post.

'What is wrong with you? You treat your vassals better than your eldest son. Everyone but you is praising Hal's accomplishments. For God's sake, show some pride in him,' I stormed on.

Henry glared. My voice was strident, 'Is a kind word too hard to push through your teeth? Hal should be rewarded. A bit of land would not go astray. But no, as usual, you overlook him. That is unacceptable.'

'And there you go again, Eleanor! Mother goose puts her goslings before her lord, to whom she refuses time and again to show allegiance.'

That gibe was the last straw.

'Henry, you have only yourself to blame by using your children as pawns on your chessboard of ambition. You have sacrificed your queen for other's beds, like foolish Ida de Tosney I hear, and caring little for her or your bastard brats. But you are only too happy to live off my wealth to support your fractious kingdom, which you cannot rule without my influence.'

Henry looked stunned, I presumed because I knew about the unfortunate Ida, but only for a second. In two steps, I was threatened by him as the door flew open. Richard, as lithe as a cat, sprang between us. His unsheathed broad sword was gripped in strong hands. Young, muscular power towered over his father.

My voice rose. 'Richard, put it down! Put that sword down!'

Plantagenet faced Plantagenet.

'I order you. Do as you are told!'

I pushed between them and shoved Henry with all my might. He staggered backwards. The sun through the window glinted off Richard's well-honed weapon. I turned on him.

'If you touch one hair of your father's head, you will be disinherited. Drop that sword at once!'

The sword clattered to the floor.

'Now get out!'

The door vibrated on its hinges. Henry had landed awkwardly, jarring his troublesome hip. I assisted him to a chair, shaking my head.

Henry grimaced. 'Why did you stop him?'

'Why do you think?'

On a nearby chest was a flask of wine with goblets. I poured us one each and paced as I drank. Henry's eyes bored into me. The day would come when I would not be able to protect him. Richard was already a half a head taller than him, and Hal nearly as tall as Richard. As for Geoffrey, same height now, but smarter than Nilla's old pet monkey Simian and twice as cunning. If it came to tactics, he would run rings around his father.

'I did not think you cared.'

'Henry, if you tried to understand your sons this would never have happened. Now I need to speak to Richard; his actions were excessive.'

I feared the day when the boys no longer heeded my words. I only hoped we could reach some sort of truce before we set out for Brittany. I picked up the heavy sword. Outside the chamber, Robert was propped looking like he had been winded.

'That boy is a battering ram.'

'And getting stronger, Robert.'

'Will you put this in my chamber please?'

Robert grunted. 'Nice weapon.'

***

Richard had returned to Hal's quarters. I was greeted by a smashed chair with bits of wood everywhere, testament to Richard's temper. He was raving I was as bad as their father. Hal was snarling like a dog, Margaret was sobbing. Lenore and little Joanna were trying to be peacemakers.

'Margaret, I am sorry for this despicable behaviour on behalf of the so-called noble Plantagenets. Hal, comfort your wife. Lenore, please take Joanna to your chambers. Richard, come with me and bring what is left of the chair. I presume it is your handiwork.'

Halfway down the gallery, we met a churl. Richard gave him the remainder of the chair.

'Maman…'

'Shut your mouth, Richard, and follow me.'

We strode across the bailey, then climbed the winding staircase to the battlements. I ordered the guards to one end out of earshot, before turning on Richard.

'How dare you take the law into your own hands. How dare you threaten your father! Have you forgotten the promise you made to me? Do you think I could go through the rest of my life knowing you harmed him or worse? What sort of animal are you?'

'I thought he was going to hurt you.'

'I am capable of defending myself, and I do not need you jumping to conclusions armed with a broad sword. Let me remind you we have a wedding to attend. We must put on a united front of family harmony. That goes for Hal, too. But first, you will apologise to your father.'

'Not on Satan's head!'

'Richard! You will do as I command. Do you understand?'

He towered over me, his Plantagenet blue eyes boring into mine, fury written on his rugged jaw. Dear God, he was handsome.

'Do you understand?'

'Yes!'

'Yes, what?'

'Yes, Maman.'

We retraced our footsteps. I had a page warn Henry of our approach. We entered as the page fled.

'Richard has something to say to you.'

I crossed my fingers that Henry would not retaliate, adding fuel to the raging bonfire towering beside me. My eyes burned into his, begging with all my might this meeting would end in peace.

'I am sorry, Papa,' Richard muttered.

Henry gave him a curt nod of acceptance, thank God. Perhaps Robert had calmed Henry in our absence.

'Thank you. Henry, I will be back shortly.'

I escorted Richard back to his quarters, then checked the others for peace and accord to find John with his sisters. At least they were being kind to their little brother. He stared at me in that perplexing way of his, like I was someone he had met once but could not place. I must try to relate to the child. Then how often do I say that? I suggested that we dine together after I had spoken to their father.

I found Henry limping worse than usual. By now my careful dressing was not as pristine. I was at a loss for words. To be honest I felt sick. I walked to the flask. There was some wine left. I poured it into my goblet which I gulped down then vomited. I was on my knees retching. Henry helped me up and wiped my mouth.

Churls quickly cleaned up. Henry helped me out of my gown, wrapping me in a cape. I was shivering. He assisted me to his bed and sent for Amaris and Clotilde. He found a cloth and poured some water from a ewer over it. Like old times, he, sponged my face then held my hand. All I could do was weep uncontrolledly. *Why, why, why!* Clotilde brought lavender oil for my temples. I fell asleep from emotional exhaustion.

Later, Clotilde told me when they dined together, they managed to remain civilised. She said she warned the boys to behave. Martin and Roger with their wives, and Robert also joined the family. Henry presided and managed to revert to his charming side. I was sorry I missed it. Joachim was also there. Poor man. God knows what he made of the Plantagenets. I would not be surprised if he preferred the French House of Capet.

The next day I felt disorientated. I called for Clotilde. I knew what the problem was but hated admitting it. I had reached the change, but I feared Henry finding out my childbearing days were over. God knows why. I did not live with him, nor did I want any more children. But I did not want him to know I was aging when he could spawn more brats to compete with our legitimate children.

'He is never going to find out from the women in your court, is he Amaris?' Clotilde said.

'Most definitely not, Milady.'

'Elea, your upset yester-morn was probably because of the arguments between your sons and King Henry, especially Prince Richard's over-reaction. That sent you into a shock.'

'Clotilde is right,' Amaris said. 'It has nothing to do with your…time of life, but an emotional reaction and the realisation that Prince Richard could have killed his father.'

Clotilde gave me a hug, reverted to her gruff self, and looked me in the eye. 'Eleanor of Aquitaine, this is a small stumbling block. Stop feeling sorry for yourself. Rise above it. You know your duty. Take a deep breath and follow your destiny for your people and those who love you.'

Like Renée, Clotilde understood me better than I did, and she was right. The only person who could prevail in my life was me. After all, she had witnessed my training as a child and had sat beside me in the schoolroom as Papa prepared me for my destiny.

Chapter 7 Geoffrey's Wedding

Geoffrey and Constance were to be married at Rennes. Lord Conan and Lady Marguerite welcomed us. Geoffrey had settled in, managing to charm his in-laws to be, and his betrothed.

They were impressed by his knowledge and intellect as well as his physical prowess as an up-and-coming knight. Richard and I looked at each other, wondering if they were talking about the same person. Henry was also sceptical, but he hardly knew Geoffrey and what he did know drove him to frustrated fury. I felt out of sorts—jealous, maybe. Was I sulking or was I lamenting losing my other self, my duplici?

I stared through my window to a pretty courtyard where Hal and Margaret were strolling. They were laughing together, comfortable in each other's company, and appeared over the family disharmony. I hoped they would remain so as I prayed to God for Geoffrey's happiness, although I found Constance unsettling. Perhaps she recognised that Geoffrey and I were too alike. If she imagined I had influence over him she could not be more wrong. Of my three oldest sons, Geoffrey was the least likely to take any notice of me. He would read my mind then do the exact opposite. Margaret, I knew, found me intimidating when I did not intend it, but I felt Constance saw me as competition.

***

The wedding was beautiful. Constance looked cherubic, which I did not believe she was. Geoffrey was the epitome of the heavenly knight from the Aquitaine, the chivalrous troubadour. With his honey-coloured curls, his large dark eyes, aristocratic nose, and sensual lips, he resembled an archangel who had alighted from heaven. I had tears in my eyes as they exited the cathedral together. Constance, I hoped, would tolerate his competitive tendencies to be right about everything. Even Henry was looking sentimental.

For once, our children behaved in a manner suitable to their status. So did their parents. After all the festivities were over, and I was alone with my quills and ink, the door between Henry's and my chamber opened.

'Are you still awake?'

'No, Henry, I am writing in my sleep. What do you want?'

He ignored my sarcasm.

'We need to talk about Richard. He is getting older, and we need to look to his future since Raymond-Berengar's daughter died. Another suitable betrothal must be considered.'

Henry had done nothing that I knew of to find another suitable pawn, and I had deliberately not prodded him to find a candidate. Now, I suspected he had sealed a match. I rose, slamming down my quill and almost pulling my fingers off as I cleaned them of ink. I faced Henry ready for a fight.

'Well, spit it out, what have you done? Who is she?'

'Alais, Louis' second daughter, Margaret's sister.'

'You mean Louis' fourth daughter.'

'All right, fourth, if you want to split hairs. Again, Louis refuses to have her under your roof, so I will place her in my court with Martin's wife's family.'

'Just like that. As usual, Henry, I have been left out of the discussion. Hal and Margaret are happy, luckily. Louis may now have a foot in England, but by God he is not getting one back into the Aquitaine.'

'Calm down, Eleanor, and look at the benefits if you are capable of impartial thought.'

'Benefits! Huh! Louis has schemed to get his grasping claws back into the Aquitaine and you have helped him achieve it. Not only do you not consult me about Richard's future bride, but you insult me as Duchess of Aquitaine by conniving with my ex-husband. Think, Henry, Louis' grandchild could be a future heir to my inheritance. That is unacceptable.'

'It is for all our benefits. We will gain potential dominion in France through Hal and Richard if something happens to Prince Phillip.'

'Well, you can tell that lily-livered worm from Île de France that I refuse to accept his fourth daughter's betrothal to Richard. If he thinks she will ever become Duchess of Aquitaine, he can think again, because I will do everything in my power to thwart that marriage. Now get out of my bed chamber.'

He did not move but loomed menacingly in front of me. I was at his mercy if he became physical. But what Henry said next had me open-mouthed.

'Today, seeing Geoffrey wed and Lenore standing at your side filled me with pride, Eleanor. It was as if the angels and cherubim had landed in my midst, a gilded trio of beauty. Now I wonder, where is my queen, where is that golden angel whom I wed, who gave birth to these beautiful children? All of them, as I looked about today; Hal, Richard, Joanna, and even little John are like Greek gods and goddesses who love their mother and who, like Medea, has turned them against their father.'

'I have not turned them against you. They have made up their own minds because of your neglect. What is more, Medea murdered her children to spite her adulterous Jason, something I would never contemplate. Nor, Henry, did you marry an angel. You married an intelligent woman with a mind of her own, someone you cannot manipulate. Just as your mother did not fit a mould, neither do I.'

Robert blundered through into my chamber.

'Could you two keep your voices down. Some people are trying to sleep.'

'De Lucy, shut your mouth. This has nothing to do with you.'

'Humph! For God's sake get into bed and sort out your differences the way you normally do!'

As if Henry needed encouragement! Robert retreated.

'Get out Henry!' I yelled as he grabbed me.

I fought with all my might, but that only aroused him further. He threw me onto the bed and got his way though he was left clawed and bitten. When I eventually pushed him out, I turned and wept into my pillow full of anger.

***

I had to leave. I contrived I had received an urgent letter from Poitiers, so I farewelled my hosts, my duplici and his new wife. By the smug look on his face, I did not believe she was still a virgin. I hoped they would be happy. Hal and Margaret, I invited to the Aquitaine. At least I could do something to train Hal for his future role if his father would not. I never got to say much to John who mostly looked at me open-mouthed.

Henry observed my preparations with a mistrustful glare, especially when he saw Hal and Margaret's entourages readying themselves as well. To make sure there was not an altercation, I had Richard leave at sunup with Joanna and Lenore.

He wanted to see the correspondence. 'Henry, the Aquitaine is none of your business. Now get out of the way of my horse.'

I mounted, nodded a farewell and left, astride, what-is-more. Once clear of the Palace at Rennes, I travelled at speed, hoping to catch Richard by nightfall. It was going to take three days to reach Nantes on the Brittany border. From there, I would cover the leagues to Fontevrault. This time I was travelling with Richard's and Hal's men as well as my Praetorian guard. It would take an army to ambush me on this journey.

The next day was pleasant. We were able to slow our progress. I rode alongside Richard. He was still none too pleased with the chastisement I gave him in Rouen.

'You did not have to humiliate me like that. After all, I was only thinking of protecting you, Maman.'

'You deserved what you got.'

'Yes! Well, it was excessive.'

I changed the subject.

'By the way, do you know about this betrothal connived for you by your father and that worm Louis Capet?'

'Yes.'

'Well, as far as I am concerned, Louis and Henry can plot in hell, but none of Louis' daughters, unless they are your half-sisters, are welcome in the Aquitaine.'

'And where does that leave Margaret?'

'She is not going to become its duchess.'

'Maman, you are fretting for no reason because I have no intention of marrying any time soon. Anyway, as far as I know, Alais is too young. She is five years younger than Margaret.'

'I am surprised you are so well informed.'

'Margaret told me. We were comparing little sisters. She said she was sad because she does not know her. She was sent to Normandy before Alais was born.'

I was amused. Knowing Louis, it was amazing they were conceived at all. My darling Marie and Alix were also five years apart.

'I hope one day, Maman, I can meet Marie and Alix.'

Richard's words were a jolt. Would I ever meet them, I wondered?

'Has Margaret met them. I have never asked her.'

Richard shrugged. 'I do not know.'

We rode on in silence as I pushed back that bitter, empty void.

Chapter 8 The Death of Pendragon

It was a relief to be back in Poitiers and to take up the reins of governance, rather than those of a horse. There were some petitions, charters, and writs demanding my exclusive attention, so the justiciars and Uncle Ralph left them for me to peruse. I showed them to Hal to study with Richard.

'As I have emphasised to your brother, Hal, it is necessary to read documents meticulously before signing them. Scribes make mistakes in transcription and their Latin is often appalling. Hal, you need to do your homework, to know the facts.'

'It does help, Hal,' Richard agreed.

I continued. 'Hours of dispute can be avoided by listening to both sides without prejudice. This way, most problems can be solved.'

Richard dug me in the ribs. 'Like your trip to the Limousin, hey, Maman?'

'We live and learn,' I replied.

***

Hal settled in and enjoyed sitting with Richard on the panel. It gave him valuable knowledge which he was craving. Occasionally, they argued. Richard complained that Hal was muscling in on his jurisdiction, trying to pull rank when he was not the future Duke of Aquitaine. Forced to be referee, I wanted to scream, hardly a good example. At least they just quarrelled rather than resorting to fisticuffs. Their rivalry, though, worried me.

To break up their tutorials, the boys hunted with some of the young squires and sons of my Praetorian guards; all young men who had finished their training for knighthood. Antoine's son had already been recruited into my personal bodyguard, as had dear Simeon's boy. It was time for some of the remaining guards to seek retirement, so it was beneficial to have young knights ready to join their ranks. Not that I think Antoine was keen to put his feet up, but he was enjoying preparing the younger men for their roles and the privilege of being personally responsible for my safety. I, too, was delighted to be surrounded by handsome young men.

Hawking was one of my pleasures. I joined in the hunt when I could. It was satisfying to arrive home with game for the table feeling pleasantly tired. We were disturbed by a weary courier early one evening after a successful outing. I thought of waiting till the following morn to attend to the letters he brought, and to enjoy my wine. But what sort of example would that set for the Young King and future duke? So, I excused myself and took them to the library.

The seals were from various sources, some familiar, some more obscure. All were carrying the same sad news regardless from whence they came. Owain Pendragon was ailing. The one from Brynn was the most sorrowful. She predicted he was not long for this world and begged me to return to England. His son, Prince Owain Gwynned, she wrote, was an astute young man of about eighteen years. Brynn believed he would make an excellent ruler, but he had no love of the English and less for King Henry. His father nonetheless had instructed his son to heed Queen Eleanor, and to keep the unwritten treaty between the two countries. Brynn asked me to come with all haste.

Malcolm of Scotland also feared war between the Welsh and the English. One seal I did not recognise was from Aeled. His father had died, and he was running their estates. He alarmed me. Skirmishes had broken out along the Welsh border, and he related the same news about King Owain. There was nothing from Henry, but he would have known what was happening.

My presence was needed, but if Henry would accept it I knew not. In all conscience, though, I could not allow war to break out between the two kingdoms if I could prevent it. I calculated how quickly I could have a ship readied to take me to England, then horses to Warwick or Gloucester, perhaps Shrewsbury. I was going to have to act like Henry. That was something for which I could thank him. His expertise in organising essential men, then moving swiftly, was unsurpassed.

I requested Hal accompany me. It would be useful for him to meet Owain Gwynedd. Margaret was not pleased she was not included. I explained to her the day would come when as

Queen of England, she would be alone and would have to travel without her husband. I told Hal to sort it out. I had no time for histrionics.

Before our arrival at Bordeaux, I had couriers dispatched to England. My entourage was reduced to my Praetorian guard, my maids, and only essential luggage. Horses would be waiting when we disembarked at Plymouth.

Neptune was in my favour, providing good seas and favourable winds. Swift mounts were bridled and saddled on the dock. We spent one night at the Palace of Winchester. By now, Henry should know of my arrival though he was nowhere in sight. There was a missive from him awaiting in Bordeaux, repeating what I already knew. He added should Owain meet his Maker, he hoped his son would honour the unwritten treaty. It had been sent from Warwick, so I aimed to travel to the castle, hoping he was still there. We left Winchester the next day before cockcrow.

The couriers I had dispatched were efficient. Fresh horses were ready for us at designated stables en route. I think determination kept me focused, so I did not tire. We stopped at a manor near Warwick, where we were able to rest, bathe, and prepare for our arrival at the castle. There was still nothing from Henry acknowledging my arrival in England. If I were an invading force, he would be caught unawares. I hoped he had not moved on, though by now my English informants would have alerted me.

Hal was withdrawn. When I questioned him, he said he was worried about Margaret. Since they married, they had never been apart. He also thought I was unreasonably peremptory with her when we left Poitiers. I reminded him why we were here. The last thing I wanted was for England and Wales to begin hostilities when peace, though shaky at times, had lasted all these years. I told him about the special rapport I had with Owain Pendragon, that peace between the kingdoms held because of it. I hoped I could convince his son to sign a treaty rather than rely on the present verbal agreement, which was about to go to a grave if it had not done so already. I still had no confirmation whether King Owain was alive or dead. I had to excuse myself. Hal was seeing a different side to his Maman, one who was single-minded.

***

I dressed in my black velvet gown for my arrival on Henry's drawbridge. I had couriered my arrival in England, but I was surprised he did not know how near I was. Too bad, I thought. As evening approached, I rode under the portcullis into Warwick Castle. His usual guards recognised me, or my sudden appearance could have been seriously questioned. Henry, I found, had been hunting all day, which perhaps explained why he did not know of my imminent arrival. *Damn his eyes*, I thought, I would enter unheralded just to see the expression on his face.

I strode along the familiar gallery to the Great Hall where I could hear minstrels playing, the odd laugh and a babble of voices. I had asked Hal to wait and to enter after I had been announced. I had no idea what my reception would be. Bored pages and trumpeters were leaning and chatting outside the closed doors. They did not immediately recognise who I was in the dim light of the flickering torches until an older individual suddenly jumped to attention as the flames glinted on the gold of my crown. My distinctive accented English had the doors flung open. The trumpeters blasted a fanfare over the top of whatever the minstrels were playing, not the most triumphant entry, but enough to announce my presence.

The minstrels wheezed to a stop as the whole assembly was alerted to their queen's unexpected arrival. Gasps circled the room as if I was some sort of spectral apparition. A voluptuous individual was draped over Henry. She objected to Henry trying to push her away, slow to notice why the hall had fallen silent. The gathered nobility dropped to one knee or curtsied deeply, except for Henry's putain who was objecting to his change of attitude.

With all the hauteur of my position, I asked, 'And who, my Lord, might this be?'

Henry had no choice in front of his guests but to behave, to show joy and surprise at my sudden appearance. He gave the woman a final shove. She staggered back, aware something was amiss as Hal followed the second fanfare. Henry, I knew, would be raging inside, embarrassed by my sudden appearance. By catching him unawares in front of barons, clergy, and other persons of rank, he could say naught.

I kept my demeanour, but not Hal, who bellowed at his father, 'How dare you insult the Queen of England, my mother, and your wife in this despicable manner by consorting with another woman in front of our subjects.'

The hall froze.

'To think my mother and I have travelled in all haste to be at your side for fear of an outbreak of war between England and Wales, only to find you with nary a care for your people and consorting with a whore.'

Hal's fist was around his sword hilt. Robert quickly stepped forward, but Hal shoved him away, with his sword halfway out of its scabbard. It was like Rouen all over again.

I grabbed his arm and spoke in Langue d'Oc, not raising my voice. 'Hal, enough. I can handle this. I appreciate you wanting to protect my honour, but this is not the time nor the place.' I stood in front of him.

'Sir Robert, will you be kind enough to escort the Young King to his quarters. Lord Henry we must speak.'

Hal backed out, fuming. Antoine hovered behind me. The putain was trying to slink from the scene as her predicament dawned. No-one was going to her aid, especially not Henry. As he was not forthcoming as to who she was, I commanded Antoine in Latin, so she could understand, to escort her out of the Great Hall. She started wailing hysterically, appealing to me. A ruddy-faced, corpulent individual lurched forward; her husband I presumed, and well in his cups. In Langue d'Oc, I told Antoine to arrest them both. Henry was grinding his teeth, unable to intervene. He excused us from the assembly. The rest of my guard were marshalled outside the door. I requested they accompany me to Henry's quarters. The last thing I wanted was to be alone with him. In his chamber he paced, demanding I send my guards to the garrison.

'So you can hurt me like you did the last time we were together? No, Henry, they are here to protect me. We can speak in Langue d'Oeil if you prefer, or English, then our conversation will be private.'

'Why did you not let me know of your arrival?'

'And allow you to get rid of your whore?'

'It was not what you think. She was drunk. I was trying to shake her off when you arrived.'

'And you expect me to believe that.'

'You can believe what you like.'

I decided not to pursue the matter before the whole reason I was in England ended in a screaming match. Henry was capable of twisting my good intentions into something from his imagination regarding Pendragon. Instead, I told him, 'I wrote from Bordeaux then Winchester announcing my arrival. Why you have not received the letters, I know not.'

'Well, yes, a courier delivered them, but I have only read the one from Bordeaux. I put the other aside because it arrived just before the hunt. When I returned, finalising the banquet arrangements took up my time.'

The thought of Henry having anything to do with banqueting arrangements was novel, but I said naught.

'Indeed, I am surprised you seem to have little concern about what is happening over the Welsh border. Is Owain Pendragon dead or alive?'

Henry eyed me, trying to read my face.

'I have no idea, but Owain must be alive, or I would have heard.' With a curled lip he sneered, 'You my dear, seem to be mightily fretful.'

To prevent a jealous outburst, I ignored his retort.

'I have brought all the missives I have received relating to the King of Wales' decline. You can read them now or on the morrow. My only concern has been to keep our tenuous peace treaty which Pendragon's son could easily ignore. That and only that is why I am here. As you keep reminding me, Henry, I am Queen of England.'

'Yes, when you want to be. I will read your correspondence after my breakfast on the morrow.'

'As you wish. Now I will go to my bed. I have been travelling non-stop for days fearing a Welsh attack. Furthermore, as I have emphasised in the past, it is imperative a document of peace be drawn up and signed either by the old king or his son to formalise our verbal agreement.'

My guards escorted me to my chamber where my maids had settled after I arrived, so all was ready for a good night's sleep. Before I could undress for bed, however, I had to speak to Hal.

As I approached his door, Robert was leaving him.

'He is still agitated, I am afraid.'

'Wait for me, Robert. I will try to calm him.' I closed the door. 'Hal, your father says that woman is of no consequence and was drunk.'

Hal scoffed.

'Hal, behave. I do not want any foolish behaviour on your part to snap the brittle peace between your father and me. Now, go to bed. I will see you on the morrow.' I kissed him and left.

As Robert accompanied me back to my bed chamber, I asked, 'Robert, what were that woman's intentions, and was Henry encouraging her?'

'No, she was just hopeful. Henry has no interest in her.'

In the dim light of the torches, Robert would not have noticed the sceptical look on my face. I thanked him at my door for his help with Hal and took myself to my bed and a fretful sleep.

Henry read the information I had received next morning. There was no disguising his jealousy that Malcolm of Scotland and that Welsh witch had appealed to me to keep the peace, and not Henry. Neither had Aeled consulted him. I could have gloated that my diplomacy was the more likely reason I was informed. His besiege and battle methods had many nobles and the Scottish King wary. They knew he could easily provoke the hostilities they were hoping to avoid. To calm him I stroked his ego by reminding Henry of Owain's respect for him as well.

Hal and I sat together with his father at a long table in his audience chamber the next day. I had him draft a peace treaty. Henry hated writing anything because he was impatient, preferring to dictate to scribes like Peter de Blois. I had to stop myself from snatching the quill as he scratched across the velum in his spidery hand.

With dripping sarcasm, he asked, 'Now Milady, does the perfectionist wish to correct my Latin?'

'Henry, it is a draft. Together we can improve the wording if you wish. But I think it is easily understood. Furthermore, there is nothing wrong with your Latin.'

He had learnt, though deep down I was sure he was determined not to give me a reason to criticise. He was chuffed by his effort.

'Mmm. My writing could be neater, though.'

'You could have a scribe re-write it if you are concerned.'

'Or you could do it, then Pendragon could have something of you to fondle, and on which to put his mark.'

Hal took a breath. I placed my hand on his knee; nor did I bite, but remarked, 'A scribe I am sure would do it adequately, should you choose.'

***

Henry, Hal and I set off to pay our respects to Owain and to wish him a speedy recovery. We met Brynn deep in Welsh territory. Henry muttered about Welsh witches appearing out of nowhere from bleak and wind-blown Snowden. I was wearing the whalebone talisman given to me by Pendragon. I had persuaded Henry that it was as a mark of respect, and for no other reason. We continued with Brynn towards Caernarfon Castle where Owain lay on his sick bed.

I wandered outside the quaint Celtic monastery, where we were staying early on our last day, to admire the spectacular scenery across a deep estuary. There I felt the most unusual sensation rush through my body. I was watching the sun rise over the wild terrain we had traversed the day before. I experienced a humming in my ears. A whisper of air fluttered my veil. The sun danced along the eastern ridge, forming an ethereal aura. Mesmerised, I could not move. A burning sensation seared my neck, then like a caress the talisman slid between my breasts, its leather thong no longer tied. I sank to my knees.

That was how Brynn found me. She helped me stand. I was bewildered, thinking I had contracted an ague. She helped me to a large, flat boulder where we sat.

When I described what had befallen me Brynn whispered, tears glistening, 'Lord King Owain has passed.'

My hand went to the etched whalebone; its loose leather thong scorched where the knot was tied. The sun had disappeared. The gentle zephyr was now a strong wind that whipped through the treetops. I put my arms around Brynn. We wept together.

Henry found us, perplexed by our tears. When I told him Owain was dead, he wanted to know how we had been informed because he had seen no courier or herald bearing news. Brynn stood, taking Henry's hands. In her musical lilt, she told him King Owain's spirit had flown though the ether and now enveloped all earthly and heavenly elements. Henry looked from Brynn to me and crossed himself. My body and mind registered that something outside our understanding had occurred where these dark Welsh valleys met the sea.

***

Owain's funeral was as awe-inspiring as his passing. He was not interred, but his body was taken to the sea where a magnificent long boat black with pitch gently rose on the swelling waters of Afon Menai between the distant island of Ynys Mon and Caernarfon. Clothed in a gown of white, King Owain Pendragon was laid to rest on the Oriflamme of Wales. He was surrounded by Celtic monks. Also swaying in similar robes was a choir of Druid priests. Their voices harmonised in their native tongue, a plaintive and beautiful dirge. Owain's sons carried aloft flaming torches. They pushed their father deep into Afon Menai, so his cradle of death was caught by the tide. The long craft was steadied as they set fire to the pitch. With one hefty shove and the tide gaining momentum, it swept the now flaming vessel into the strait.

Unashamedly, I wept on Henry's shoulder. Henry, and Hal too, were moved by the ceremony, a mixture of Christian and pagan and a remembrance of the ancient Vikings who once plied these shores. Slowly we followed the mourning party back to the castle where a wake was held. There we listened to some of the most beautiful music and singing we had ever heard.

We paid homage to the new young king as a mark of respect to his father. Henry gave a grand oration to an honourable man with whom, he said, he had occasionally crossed swords. He continued that for many years the two kingdoms had lived in peace. Henry then surprised me by declaring that this accord was mostly due to Queen Eleanor. As Queen of the Wood Sprites she had cast a spell over the late King Owain far stronger than any written and signed document. He said he sincerely hoped the now reigning monarch of Wales, Owain Gwynned, would honour his father's legacy, so goodwill between England and Wales would endure. Furthermore, he had a document they could both sign. But, personally, he said he would prefer they swore again on the honour of the Queen of the Wood Sprites and in memory of the late Owain Pendragon to keep the pledge. With that, the new Welsh King came to me and knelt, swearing to be my Liege Man of Life and Limb.

I was humbled. Henry's face flamed. For all his beautiful rhetoric he was furious but could say naught. He made the speech partly to honour young Owain, but mostly, knowing Henry, to get the young king's deference for himself when instead it came to me. Like Robert had written some time ago, my sovereignty when acting as Regent garnered more respect. The return ride to Warwick was going to be difficult. I would have to make sure I was never alone with Henry. I retied the talisman on its leather thong, and threaded it onto my girdle, where it could hang hidden in the folds of my gown.

***

When we arrived back at Warwick Castle, I remembered the duo still in detention. They were contrite. I emphasised the only way they would be freed was for the Baron, Lord Garth Bedwyche, to remove himself and his wife Lady Edith from King Henry's court. I found they had contrived to compromise Henry, so they, leeches both, could become part of his entourage. Sometimes I wondered about Henry's judgement of character, which brought me to the latest in the Becket saga.

No sooner had we returned to Warwick when Henry received an epistle from Pope Alexander III ordering him to attend a tribunal of powerful clerics in London. Henry rarely became agitated over such edicts. His temper could be riled, but this one upset his equilibrium. I had gone to his chamber to tell him about my plans to return to the Aquitaine where I found him alone with his head in his hands and thought he was unwell. I asked what ailed him. He thrust the crumpled parchment into my hands. Becket's ghost hovered over Henry. I sympathised with him over this matter, despite our differences. He was still troubled by his tragic outburst.

I could not leave him in this state, though I had good reason to do so. Henry's jealousy over young Owain's sworn allegiance to me was enough to paint Warwick Castle green from dungeons to keep. Hal and Henry were not getting on either, with almost daily arguments over Hal's ongoing frustrations.

His bellowing would have been audible in London, 'You do not give a damn about me, do you? Maman teaches me, lets me read documents, explains charters and laws of the land. But you do nothing but chase women. Then you spoil bloody John rotten.'

Hal pushed past me as I entered the chamber, slamming the door as he left.

'Henry, for God's sake, listen to Hal for once. You know what he needs.'

'Eleanor, keep your interfering nose out of my business.'

I turned on my heel. What was the point? Why Henry could not see that his intransigence was only causing trouble for himself I knew not. I went after Hal. He was on the limit of his patience. I think only my presence prevented a physical confrontation with his father.

I said, 'I am sorry, but I am going to have to accompany your father to London. I need to support Henry over this business with the pope and Becket's legacy.'

'Yes, Maman, go. I just want to return home. I miss Margaret.'

'Then leave, Hal, there is no need for you to stay. I will see you in Poitiers.'

I was pleased to see the back of his horse. I was tired of father and son arguing.

Chapter 9 Henry Cornered

London was stressful. Henry was a bundle of nerves. He had to face archbishops and bishops from, it appeared, every See in Christendom, with two cardinals as well. He returned to Westminster exhausted and in a foul temper after the first day. When I questioned him about proceedings, he refused to talk about what took place. He bit my head off when I insisted on knowing. In the end, it was not worth quarrelling about.

'Henry, why do I not accompany you to your next meeting?'

'No!'

'God's Teeth, Henry, think! I know as much about Becket as you do.'

'Eleanor, it is not Becket who is on trial; it is me. The panel is not interested in Becket's early life as advocate or chancellor, only as archbishop.' Then it came out in a rush.

'They want me to abolish what they call the "evil" laws and customs of England I have supposedly introduced, though most were established by my forebears. All I have done is insist the church uphold them. Worse, they want me to release the bishops from the oath they have sworn to obey the Constitutions of Clarendon.

Henry was right. It was out of my hands, so I prepared to leave England. I spoke to Brynn, who had come with me to London.

'I will miss you, Brynn. If you ever change your mind, you know your expertise would be highly respected in my court at Poitiers and beyond.'

'Milady, I thank you. But I will be of far greater use to you where I am.' Her eyes seemed to penetrate me and in her prophetic manner, she said, 'We will be together again in the future, where I will be invaluable to you.'

I felt a tingling run down my spine and my hand instinctively went to the talisman.

***

Henry was disappointed and ranted.

'Typical! Well, off you go. Leave your husband in his time of need for the bloody Aquitaine.'

'You said I cannot help with the council, so what need would that be, Henry? As a piece of gilded furniture to decorate your halls from time to time?'

Needless to say, my sarcasm did not go down well. Then out of the blue Henry said, 'By the way, I want you to take John back to Fontevrault.'

'Fatherhood too daunting for you, my dear Henry?'

He side-stepped that one.

'I am trying to arrange a betrothal for him.'

'Really? I would have thought he was too young.'

Henry was non-committal. I thought, *dear God, another pawn.* I supposed the trip might help me get to know John better. The little I saw of him did not impress. He demanded attention then abused what was given. He had a cruel streak, which I did not like. I was too distant, and we had never bonded. I wondered whether it was because I never suckled him. By the time I had healed from his birth he was no longer in my household and too many other events were overwhelming my life for me to take John into my care.

***

Henry did not see us off on the Thames's tide. I sailed to Barfleur, then rode to Nantes where Geoffrey had set up his court. I was looking forward to spending time with him. John would also enjoy seeing his older brother. Whether his brother reciprocated, though, could be another matter.

Geoffrey greeted us.

'Darling, it is so good to see you. Let me look at you. I think you have filled out. You no longer look like a willow branch. Marriage must suit you.'

'Indeed, it does, Maman. And you look as beautiful as ever.'

He escorted us to our quarters and gave John a half-friendly punch on his arm, 'And how are you, John, you snotty brat?'

'All right, Geoff,' said John, a little taken aback.

'Good. Well, off you run, I need to talk to Maman in private.'

John frowned but followed a page out the door.

'Maman, Richard, Hal, and I are not happy with Papa. The way he has treated you and all this business over Becket has affected us. It is upsetting.' Geoffrey did not mince words.

'Darling, only your father can atone for his sins regarding Becket. He was facing an investigation in London when I left. And do not let our disagreements affect you. I can handle Henry.'

'Maybe, but regardless of your bravado, your hurt is our hurt, Maman. You cannot expect us not to care. After all, where would Lord King Henry of England be without you?'

'Geoffrey, can we please change the subject?'

Geoffrey poured us some wine.

'Margaret's half-brother Phillip has also been talking to us.'

'What? I do not approve of contact with the French, you know that.'

'Well, Maman, it is better to have allies than foes.'

'Hmm! Maybe… just remember, they cannot be trusted.'

'Papa is driving us to despair, Maman. He is becoming more tyrannical, upsetting our vassals, and treating us, particularly Hal, with distain.'

I took a deep breath, 'I know… I know… But I might as well save my breath for all the notice your father takes of me regarding your brother.'

'What do you know about this betrothal he is negotiating for John, which would give that snivelling milksop more power than Hal?'

'No! Oh, dear God!' I was aghast. 'Geoffrey, I have scant knowledge. Your father only mentioned the betrothal in passing as I was leaving London.'

'Rich is not pleased either. We suspect Papa is going to endow John in some way but do not know how exactly.'

'Geoffrey, it is time for a family discussion. I will send John on to Fontevrault Abbey on the morrow. Can you return with me to Poitiers?'

'Yes, I will be happy to oblige.'

'Richard and Hal may have more information. Furthermore, if they can air their grievances, too, there is a chance that your father might listen.'

My influence over Henry was limited, but I could make sure he knew what was happening. Perhaps then he might try to communicate with his sons rather than disregarding them and treating them like troublesome vassals. If Henry respected them, he might receive respect in return. But I was sceptical.

The undercurrent of disenchantment between my oldest sons and Henry had worsened. I feared their alignment with Île de France. Hal was in an awkward position, Margaret being Louis' daughter. Although he had nothing to do with her upbringing, he still had a claim. She owed him her loyalty, which by rights our sons should owe to Henry. Worse, she was half-sister to the future King of France.

Chapter 10 Festering Rebellion

After a pleasant two weeks' ride to Poitiers, Geoffrey and I trotted into the courtyard, relieved to be home safely. We were welcomed by Uncle Ralph, Hal, Margaret and Richard. Later, we all met for a family repast. The three boys were eager to air their grievances. I told them that tonight I wanted to relax. I would listen after a good night's sleep. Also, I wanted them to prepare their arguments in a logical manner, so we could make sensible decisions.

I left the family to games and music and went to the library where a pile of sealed parchment awaited. Most were unimportant, but there were two from Henry and one, surprisingly, from Chancellor Ridel. He wrote that rumours were developing in some quarters and implied that nobles from England, Flanders and Normandy were concerned about the dissent between Henry and our sons. These vassals were supposed to be encouraging the three to rebel against him. Someone was stirring the pot. Could it be Louis? The information, however, was vague, so I put the letter to one side, deciding it was probably gossip.

Henry's first letter was full of grief and humility. He had managed to avoid excommunication and interdicts by the clerical panel in London and had made peace with the pope. Nevertheless, he had to negotiate a further settlement and was summoned to Averanches in Normandy. He commanded Hal and Margaret attend him there. There was no explanation why unless he intended at last to hand over some duties and land to Hal. One could but hope. I prayed his demand for Hal to meet him in Normandy would result in good news. Henry might finally have realised he could not treat his oldest son and heir like a two-year-old.

The second letter was about John and the inheritance Henry wished to bequeath him but mentioned no details. He vaguely hinted about the betrothal spoken of in London. What was the point? I threw the missive across the floor in disgust.

***

The cocks had barely stopped crowing when I had three eager young men hammering on the door of my audience chamber. I gave Hal the letter from Henry to read.

'I am damn well not going to be ordered around by that despot,' he exploded.

'Hal, ignore him.' Geoffrey clapped him on his shoulder.

Richard joined in. 'Geoff is right, Hal. What right has he got to demand what you do? He will only snub you again. Pay no attention to him.'

'I know, Rich. It will be the same old chant and he will do nothing.'

It was hard getting a word in edgewise. 'Will the three of you hold your tongues! Richard and Geoffrey, you are not helping. You all need to calm down. Yes, I agree your father's wording could have been more diplomatic...' I yelled over them.

Hal howled me down. 'I am fed up, Maman. Papa says one thing and does the exact opposite.'

'Hal, he could be feeling penitent. He has been absolved over Becket's murder; so, he could be in a conciliatory mood and therefore more likely to grant you some authority.'

'That will be the day!' Hal growled.

'Exactly, Hal,' said Richard. 'Do not let him gallop over the top of you. Take him on, do not let him push you around.'

'Richard, stop!' I took a breath. 'Do it for me, Hal dear, If he is not forthcoming, well, at least you will have tried. And you know I will always support you.'

'Maman, Hal...'

'Enough Geoffrey!'

'Jesus...'

'I said enough!'

The three glared at me.

'Well, Hal?' I said.

Hal glowered. I stared him down.

'All right! Only to please you, Maman, but this is the last time!'

Hal was on edge as he prepared to leave. Before he mounted, he had tears in his eyes and I, a lump in my throat. I kissed him on both cheeks. Margaret said she would look after him. I embraced her. Richard and Geoffrey muttered in the background.

I sent Geoffrey and Richard hunting the next day. They needed to be distracted and I had to meet with the justiciars.

Uncle Ralph asked to speak with me alone after we had finished discussions. We walked through the gardens.

'Eleanor, pardon me for being forthright, but I am concerned about how Lord Henry is treating your sons. They are no longer children.'

'Yes, Uncle Ralph, I know,' I sighed.

'And it is not only my nephews who are disgruntled, there is ongoing disharmony amongst members of your nobility in Poitou. Hugh de Saint-Maure, a powerful man as you know, is but one.'

Uncle Ralph waved a missive under my nose. Lord Hugh's words almost ignited the parchment.

'Oh dear, I knew there were still rumblings.'

'These are more than rumblings, Eleanor. Many of your vassals are looking towards the French King.'

'It makes me feel sick.'

'So, it should!' Uncle Ralph growled.

I gritted my teeth. 'Geoffrey also told me he and his brothers have thought of appealing to Louis through Margaret.'

'Dear God!'

'Uncle Ralph, I need your advice. But I warn you, regardless of what you say, I wish to have nothing to do with Île de France.'

'Elea, you must support your sons.'

'I most definitely will. They are of my body.'

Then I remembered Chancellor Ridel's letter.

'I also received some information from England that I dismissed as a rumour, but now I am not so sure. It implied that some in the Anglo-Norman empire are having thoughts similar to our vassals.'

'Tell me.'

'It hinted that there are English barons, nobles from Henry's Angevin lands, and counts from Flanders, who are encouraging Richard, Hal and Geoffrey to rebel against their father and side with Louis. If true, it is alarming.'

'Not good. Do you know who?'

'No. Which is why I dismissed it as hearsay.'

'You have not questioned your boys?'

'No.'

'Hmm... Let me see what I can discover. I will check with my... emissaries.' Uncle Ralph took my hand. 'If forearmed, we might be able to calm the situation before it gets out of hand.'

I hoped Uncle Ralph's web of informants could discover some truth.

***

My mind was full of conflicting thoughts. I left Uncle Ralph and walked from the gardens towards the river. On the bank, I picked up a fist-sized stone and threw it as hard as I could into the Clain, and then another and another, each one an unanswered question. My loyalty was being challenged every which way—to my sons as their mother, as Duchess of Aquitaine, Queen of England, and, infuriatingly, Henry's wife.

Over and over, I wrestled within myself regarding the laws of God. Surely, God could not expect me to honour my marriage vows if later in life they went against my conscience and obligations. When Henry's words and behaviour impacted on my duchy, I would rot in hell before I obeyed.

When it came to my sons, I believed it was imperative I stood by them to safeguard their lives and to guide their destinies. It was up to Henry to do the right thing, to set an example so they would respect him as their father and their king. Moreover, Henry should be supporting me instead of trying to drive a wedge between us.

***

I stomped back to the palace, ate my evening repast alone in my chamber and went to bed. The darkness worsened my worries. I tossed and turned, concerned about my three oldest boys and about what Henry had festering in his mind. I sometimes queried my wits, but Henry was becoming more erratic.

I hoped Hal would be patient though I understood his frustration. But Henry could only think of one thing at a time.

Until he came to terms with the consequences of his explosive, thoughtless words regarding Becket, Hal's wishes would be the last thing on his mind. I begged God they would find some equilibrium in their differences just as I prayed Henry's sins would be forgiven. I, too, wished he could take the words back. It made me sick to think the 'Holy Powers' were going to make Becket a saint. I heard that two of the knights who murdered Becket—Hugh de Morville and William de Tracy—had been forgiven. I knew not the fate of the other two, Reginald FitzUrse and Richard le Bret.

I prepared to ride to Limoges where Henry had arranged for us to meet. I sent Geoffrey and Richard ahead of me. They were to collect John, much to their disgust, from Fontevrault. They sarcastically asked if they could lose him along the way. I told them to behave, to try to get to know their little brother. I was to travel with the girls. Henry was making some grand proclamation regarding John, and I hoped Hal as well.

***

The time had come for Lenore to leave my household for Castile. She was now twelve. The father of her betrothed would be at Limoges. She was not happy, although I had been preparing her for this day since her reprieve five years ago.

'I do not want to go. I want to stay with you.'

'And I wish you could, too, but look on the bright side. You can speak Catalan and Spanish, and Sister Caterina has taught you about the customs and culture of Castile.'

I discovered Henry was trying to add my Duchy of Gascony to her dowry, of course without consulting me because he knew I would never agree. He was using Lenore as a pawn against me. But that game he could not win, unless he wanted a war. To place her in the middle was cruel. But I would protect her as I had done in the past, and I knew Henry was not so stupid as to take on the might of the Aquitaine. He had too much to lose.

Lenore was a bright happy child with a sunny personality. She was thoughtful and far more patient than I ever was. The rough and tumble of the Plantagenet clan had made her resilient and diplomatic. Like Matilda, she knew how to twist her brothers round her little finger. Even Monsieur Sabots Intelligents she could outsmart through common sense and a flash of those dark eyes. I reminded her how happy Matilda was with Henry of Saxony, Hal with Margaret, and Geoffrey with Constance.

'But not you and Papa, Maman.'

I ignored her comment. Nevertheless, although not consulted about any of Henry's choices, he had chosen well. I tucked her into her bed, kissed her goodnight, then in mine sobbed myself to sleep.

***

Limoges started off well enough. Henry was in a happier mood, having been forgiven by the church hierarchy and the pope for Becket's murder. But he had to pay dearly for it. Henry swore he had not wished or ordered Thomas Becket's death, that his angry words had been misconstrued. What Hal described was horrific.

'They flogged Papa, Maman, outside the Cathedral in Averanches. Papa removed his tunic. He had a hair shirt on underneath. Then monks beat him with birch rods on the steps in front of all these cardinals. I wept, Maman, so did the cardinals. It was cruel!'

Hal related this as we were about to move to the Great Hall. I had to sit, crushing all the silk I was swathed in. I swallowed, trying not to imagine Henry's pain and humiliation. Hal started pacing, the Plantagenet march.

'Hal, what you tell me is shocking. Do I detect there is more you wish to unburden?'

'Yes.'

'Can I beg your patience till the morrow. We must get through tonight with our many noble guests. I am duty bound this evening to be Queen of England, Duchess of Aquitaine, and royal wife, so, please my darling boy, can you wait?'

Hal sighed. 'Of course, Maman. You look beautiful, by the way.'

The pages arrived a little breathless. We were running late. I hoisted myself upright in what felt like a wagon load of embroidery and jewellery. Amaris arrived beside me to make the final adjustments. Apart from the scarlet gown, I was draped in an ermine-rimmed cape. The Crown of England was another weight to bear, in more ways than one.

At the door, Henry was performing another Plantagenet march. He stopped, head on one side and grunted. I presumed it was approval. Amaris removed my cape. The fanfares announced our arrival as I rested my hand on Henry's arm. With his chest out, and with practised hauteur, I accompanied my king through the throng, which was giving throat, 'Vivat Rex! Vivat Regina!'

There were the usual gasps of awe, the curtsies, and the kneeling in homage. Was it worth it? We hosted Alphonso of Aragon and Alphonso of Castile, both kings, Lord Humbert of Maurienne, whose daughter Alice had been betrothed to John, and the elderly King of Navarre. But Raymond V of Toulouse was a surprise. Years ago, he and Henry were at war with each other. Henry had tried to regain the county, which was my inheritance through my grandmother Phillipa, Papa's mother, and usurped by Raymond's grandfather. Henry unsuccessfully besieged Raymond V's castle. When I looked at Henry, my suspicions rose. What was he up to? And why was Raymond here in Limoges? Something was afoot.

The banquet was more lavish than usual because of all the royalty in attendance. The two main characters were missing, tucked up in their cots. Seven-year-old John, and four-year-old Alice were too young to be bothered that one day they were expected to be husband and wife. Lenore, too, was yawning and should have been in her bed. So was Joanna. Although the King of Sicily was not there, she was bound for his court. I gave birth to them, then Henry played chess with them.

I smiled and nodded. I was charming to the dribbling, fawning, gaping idiots in the room, those who could not keep their eyes off my pushed-up breasts to those who practically asphyxiated me with their wine-fumed breaths. Worse, Henry's hand was travelling up my inner thigh whilst we were seated at the table. Hitting it away did nothing as it returned with a vengeance. I could not do a damn thing without creating a to-do. The flaying he received had done nothing to quell his ardour.

The night seemed to drag on forever. My face was fixed in an insipid smile. One of the more intelligent prelates did remark he was pleased at last that the saga regarding Becket had been laid to rest. Tiredness had blunted my diplomacy, so I asked him what he thought of the canonisation of Thomas Becket. He caught my tone, answered it was to be expected, and left it at that.

It took forever to catch Henry's eye. The crown and everything I was wearing was burdensome and weighing me down. Before I collapsed, I needed to go to my bed. Lenore and Joanna had been spirited out by their nurses. I was wending my way towards Henry when Raymond of Toulouse barred my way. I had managed, except for our initial entry, to avoid him.

'Cousin, it has been many years since we have had the pleasure of each other's company.'

'Raymond, it is hardly a pleasure. Your family usurped my inheritance, and we became enemies.'

'Indeed, but now that I have conceded Toulouse as your ancestral right, I hope our differences can be put behind us.'

I gave him a penetrating look, not believing the veracity of his statement one jot. Something was going on. Raymond's sudden acknowledgement of my inheritance had every sceptical fibre in my body on alert. But this hour of the night was not the time for discreet investigations. Nor was I in the mood to make small talk with a man, cousin or no, whom I found repulsive. But I intended to make enquiries at the first opportunity, and I did not have to be a genius to guess Henry was behind it somewhere.

I excused myself and caught Henry's attention. I begged him to end the festivities. He made a charming goodnight speech then escorted me from the Great Hall. I bade him goodnight at my chamber door and said I would see him on the morrow. The pages manoeuvred me through the doorway, but Henry slipped in behind them. I had the crown off and was standing with arms outstretched to be unlaced when I saw him.

'And may I ask what you think you are doing invading my privacy?'

'Why do you think, my darling?'

'Henry, get out. I am exhausted and in no mood for what you are desiring.'

'Then I will be forced to find someone who is.'

What was I supposed to do? With all the esteemed guests

assembled and our children, the last thing I wanted was a scandal that the king had left the queen for another's bed.

'Thank you, ladies. You can go to your chambers.'

Amaris gave me a look as she closed the door.

'Well, Henry, you had better kiss me goodnight before you leave.'

I was too tired for a battle, so I gave in to his ardour. Except for there being no jousting scars on his body, he could have been his father Geoffrey, which was what I imagined to arouse my passion.

At cockcrow, he was still next to me. I saw the weals from the thrashing he received and the pimply abrasions on his shoulders from the hair shirt. I had not noticed them in the dark last night, having pushed my mind back to his father in my desire. What he saw in me now, I could hardly guess. He knew I could no longer bear children. Love, I thought not. Possession was more likely, something he could flaunt around like a well-bred horse, a wealthy piece of property. But I had him in a benign position, so I asked innocently, 'What on earth was Raymond of Toulouse doing at a Plantagenet gathering?'

'He owes me homage.'

Like hell he does, I thought. 'Why, Henry, unless he is using you in some way?'

Henry grunted and turned on his side, scrutinising me. 'No Eleanor, no-one uses me.'

His voice had a menacing edge. The only way I was going to get out of this situation, seeing I had aroused Henry's suspicions, was to arouse him in another way.

***

Bathed and dressed, I was ready to talk to Hal. He was breakfasting with Margaret and his sisters when I arrived. Geoffrey, Richard, their father and the large party of kings and nobles were hunting. Hal remained to talk to me. Henry would have noted his eldest son's absence. The girls and Margaret knew we needed to speak alone, so they left for other pursuits.

Before Hal said anything, I asked, 'What do you know about Raymond of Toulouse's attendance at the banquet last night?'

He turned scarlet.

'Well, spit it out!'

'Papa made him pay homage to us.'

'And you accepted?'

'I had no choice.'

My eyes narrowed. 'You are connected to Toulouse through me. Your father is not. The only reason Henry would be doing this behind my back is to undermine my claim to the county through your great-grandmother. He is signalling to Richard as my heir and future heirs of the Aquitaine that their only claim to Toulouse will be through an English monarch's rule. Very convenient for you, but not for your brother.'

'But Raymond has fallen out with King Louis, who is no longer inclined to support his claim on Toulouse.'

'Has he now?' My mind was racing. 'I imagine there will be some very disgruntled vassals from Poitou to Gascony over this deal, as well as Richard.'

'I am sorry, Maman.'

'So you should be. But I will put a stop to it. Now, what is it you need to tell me?'

Hal erupted like Vesuvius. 'Papa has bequeathed to John the castles of Chinon, Mirebeau, and Loudun, and estates in England around Coventry, Warwick, and near Oxford.'

'Oh, dear God!'

'Worse, he made me witness John's betrothal agreements to Alice of Maurienne as Papa pledged the castles and land to Count Humbert as part of the marriage settlement. It was humiliating, Maman. They are my inheritances. He has given away my lands to that snivelling brat and I had to endorse the transaction.'

'Hal, darling, what can I say?'

'I have had enough, so have Richard, and Geoffrey. Maman, we are fed up with Papa's meddling in our lives without consulting us and treating us like fools.'

'I can try again to make him see sense.'

'It is too late for that! He will not take any notice of you no matter how hard you try. We are throwing our lot in with Margaret's father. He is more concerned about our futures than our own father. King Louis has promised us redress, particularly me.'

Yes, I thought, *he would!* My mind was in turmoil. I arose and took Hal's hands.

'Hal, my darling, I need some time to digest what you have disclosed. I am shocked and not happy. I need to think it through. Can you wait?'

'If you insist.'

'I promise I will speak to you anon.'

I left for my quarters. I was now having to support my sons against my husband, something I had always hoped would never happen. Whatever I said or did the boys were going to rebel.

I paced. Henry's callous actions towards them was unconscionable. If they appealed to Louis for support—arms, troops maybe—how in God's name could I stop them... or did I want to?

When Geoffrey and Richard returned from hunting, I summoned them to my quarters. I went straight to the point.

'Your plans to ride to Île de France I find unacceptable, treasonous. I urge all of you to think very carefully about your actions.'

'Tell that to Papa,' Richard snarled. 'We are not taking it anymore. Nor the way he treats you.'

'Please calm down,' I begged. 'Consider the consequences.'

Geoffrey's laugh was harsh, 'We have! Papa has given us no choice, Maman.'

'You know I have always supported you and will continue to do so. But I insist you speak to your father again. Plead your cases, express your concerns before you act or do something you will regret. You are the future. That is your father's problem. He cannot face his mortality. He looks at the three of you and sees nothing but competition for his authority.'

They were reluctant, but I won out. Nevertheless, what transpired between them and Henry was a hullaballoo of shouted oaths, with the four almost coming to blows. Richard, Hal and Geoffrey stormed out and galloped to Île de France.

I avoided Henry. After all, what could I say to him that I had not said before. I prepared for my return journey to Poitiers, dejected because I could not prevent the three from rebelling and furious with Henry for making no effort to see their points of view. In this state, I had to farewell Lenore. I clung to her.

It was she, dear little girl, who consoled me.

'I will be all right, Maman. Please do not cry.'

***

I was in turmoil. Should I follow Hal, Richard and Geoffrey to Paris? Henry would erupt if I did. Louis' gloating would be nauseating, but I had sworn to fight for what was rightfully theirs. I had a mighty decision to make. I fell to my knees,

'Please God, give me strength. Please, I beg you, help me reconcile my boys with their father. Mother Mary and all the Saints, dear God I pray, sweet Jesus, help me guide my beloved sons.'

***

I pushed my horse and myself to exhaustion to reach Poitiers. I needed to discuss the situation with Uncle Ralph. He and my justiciars were unhappy with Henry's rule. The devastation he caused in my County of Poitou continued to fester, regardless that it happened before Joanna was born. Revenge teetered like an avalanche, then thundered into Poitiers in the form of Hugh de Saint-Maure. He was elected to represent the vengeful Poitivin nobles whose estates, like his, were still recovering from Henry's rampage. But Henry's collusion with Raymond of Toulouse tipped them over the edge.

Uncle Ralph met me as I dismounted. He was a sensible man, not prone to temperament, but he was furious. He demanded we talk immediately. Hugh de Saint-Maure, beside him, was almost foaming at the mouth.

I followed them to Uncle Ralph's solar, his cosy circular nest, his haven.

He paced and shouted that Henry had gone too far by driving the boys to Île de France.

'Eleanor, I demand you follow your sons. If they have refused to bend to Lord King Henry's more irrational demands, and who can blame them, your only option as Duchess of Aquitaine and their mother is to support them.'

'Milady, you owe it to us all as our duchess.' Hugh's voice was strident.

It was the hardest decision I ever had to make, to disobey Henry. But it was my duty—my duty as Duchess of Aquitaine and mother to my sons.

Chapter 11 Incarceration

I journeyed towards Chinon Castle, Henry's massive, forbidding fortress overlooking the Vienne River. My mind was in unrest. I stopped at Fontevrault below Chinon, hoping the good monks and sisters would pray for me. That was my undoing. My plans were discovered and disclosed to Henry. I suspected someone in the French clergy had found out I was riding to Paris. They had always hated me. I was given a letter of warning. In it was quoted, "Those whom God has joined... man must not put asunder... That woman who is not subject to her husband violates the condition of nature, the command of the Apostles and the law of the Gospel. For the man is the head of the woman."

The anonymous missive enraged me and fuelled my determination. I was angered that I was expected to return to my abusive, adulterous husband and to abandon my sons. I was not thinking logically as I galloped out of Fontevrault Abbey ahead of my guard who had to scramble to keep up.

But my movements were being monitored by Henry, and I was overtaken. My guards were faced by Henry's Normans, who threatened my life if my men refused to comply. I was taken to Chinon, where I was shoved, struggling and protesting, into my quarters. Amaris, Celeste and Marion were separated from me in fear for their lives.

Henry confronted me.

'So, Eleanor, you now add treason to your disobedience against your husband and king.'

'Treason! On what grounds? I am not the one who has committed treason. I have not waged war against MY people whom at MY coronation I swore to God to protect! Nor did I send men to murder Thomas Becket or fail my sons—'

'You black witch!'

'—sacrificed, to enhance your bloody empire which you cannot rule without brutality.'

Our voices overlapped.

Henry took a swing that I side-stepped as I unsheathed my stiletto.

My tirade echoed off the walls. 'I would never have considered breaking my wedding vows "to honour and obey" had you been a faithful husband. You accuse me of disobedience—what about you?'

'You turned our sons against me, and now you gallop off in their dust to Île de France whom you have railed against for years. For what reason, Eleanor? Certainly not to spend a few pleasant hours with your ex-husband—but to encourage your sons to wage war against their father—King of England—with the aid of Louis Capet.'

'Huh! Well, "King of the North", what do you expect, you thieving mongrel? You had no qualms about robbing Hal of his birthright, taking estates and castles belonging to him to bequeath to John. And, as for the others, Richard, you have never loved, and you cannot stand Geoffrey because he is clever and outsmarts your every move. Then you wonder why they have turned against you.'

'And who trained them to defy me? Whose skirts do they run to like babies when they cannot get their own way. "Maman, Papa will not let us do whatever we like, nor give us whatever we want." Then they gallop off to our enemy with your blessing and no doubt enough gold to help them on their way.'

'Had you not forced them through your betrayal of their love, they would not be seeking succour from our enemy. And to add fuel to the flames, you cosy up to Raymond V of Toulouse to gain control of my heirs' and my inheritance.'

I think Henry was surprised I had discovered his overtures to Cousin Raymond.

'People of the Aquitaine think you are nothing more than a foreign oppressor and if you believe they will allow you to align with Raymond, you are more fool than I think you are.'

That stunned him, and, for good measure, I added, 'And you think you are so good in bed. You are pathetic, paunchy. Do you have to use mandrake for the whores and pieces of brainless fluff, like Rosamund Clifford, to stiffen your manhood? You are not half the man your father was.'

The flood gates opened. I had never revealed my affair with

his late father while I was married to Louis, but I was out of control. My grip tightened on the honed blade.

We circled each other. Husky-voiced, dripping with sensuality, I purred, 'Geoffrey was beautiful, his body erotic, virile, sensual. His jousting scars against my naked breasts were an aphrodisiac. His dying words were for me and our love.'

Henry bellowed. Like an enraged bull he charged, at the last moment sidestepping my weapon. I missed his body but slashed his arm. Bloodied, he grabbed my wrist. I fought like a tigress against his bulk and strength. The knife was wrenched from my grip and clattered across the floor. I threw myself towards it hand outstretched as Henry's boot came down. My howl of agony brought everyone running regardless of the risk to their lives. He held his bleeding arm, bent over, gasping for breath, but I was a writhing heap, my right hand crushed.

Henry's wound was superficial, but rings had to be cut from my swelling fingers, more pain. When Henry refused to allow Matthias to tend me, Robert intervened. With a mighty punch, he knocked Henry to the ground, and threatened to pound his brains out unless I was treated immediately.

My hand was braced to a splint of wood and heavily bandaged. My fingers were also bound together, my thumb was separately strapped. My arm was secured upright to my body in a sort of sling. I whimpered like a kicked dog till I passed out.

After I gained my senses, the throbbing continued in my hand and wrist. My life was beyond my control, and I was fearful for the future. I was placed under arrest at Chinon. I ached. But my anguish for my sons was worse than any physical agony. My rational thought was then obliterated by a dwale Matthias prescribed. It rendered me senseless. My muddled recollections of those early months were a fog. I was taken to England, then transported within a closed carriage to Salisbury castle where I was held hostage to prevent our sons threatening their father. I would be kept alive so long as they obeyed.

I retreated within myself, curled into a ball in my bed, refusing to eat or drink. But Henry knew he had to keep me alive, for his threat worked the other way as well. If I died, the boys would go to war against him with the backing of the Aquitaine, Poitou, Gascony, even Toulouse, and worst of all, Île de France. It was a stalemate, our world on a knife-edge.

Marion and Celeste were sent back to Poitiers then to L'Ombrière. Only Amaris and Joachim were allowed to accompany me. My Praetorian guard was told I would be executed if they tried to intervene. Joachim said it hurt them to the core to have to leave me injured, not knowing my fate or where I would be sent. Robert requested to be my chaperone. Amaris said Henry goaded Robert to lay with me because it was what he had always desired. Robert replied he was above Henry's animal instincts. So, he lost his companion from childhood, his closest confidante, and loyal squire. Robert stayed by my side, preventing me from harming myself on one occasion.

I begged Robert, during one of my lucid moments, to return to Henry's service because he needed someone to keep him under control, and Robert was the only person I knew who could save Henry from himself. I begged him to bring news of my boys. I had no contact with them, not knowing if they were still in Paris or no.

***

As Henry's prisoner, I had no parchment or ink. I stole chunks of charcoal from the braziers. I scrawled on the walls a repetitive chant. Over and over, my words wailed, I wanted to die, to be rid of my never-ending nightmare. I tried to take my own life but was thwarted. I cared not if suicide were a mortal sin ending in hell. I was living in hell, so the real Hades could not be worse. I was befuddled by the haze of dwale, a concoction of opium, henbane and God knows what else. I often did not know my name or who I was.

Then a miracle occurred. Brynn re-appeared like a spectre, wisping through a cranny in the castle wall. As I was so heavily guarded, we wondered how she avoided my jailers. There was a whisper of Welsh intervention. Amaris said she was a joy to behold because she, Joachim, and Robert were battling with a woman they no longer recognised in wits or body. The little food they managed to get down my throat was just keeping me alive. The pain in my hand was excruciating. The dwale helped me sleep, but the opium and henbane were addictive. My brain was in an impenetrable fog, so I raved and sleepwalked. With my left hand I tried to stab myself in the neck with a fork, passing out before I did any damage.

Robert sat beside me day after day, imploring me to stay strong for my sons. Through the addled curtain of my despair, he begged me. He emphasised Henry's Anglo-Norman Empire from Scotland to the Pyrenees would erupt into war if I died. Robert stressed Toulouse and Île de France would retaliate also. Even if I hated Henry with all my being, the last thing I would want for him, or worse, our sons, was to lose their lives warring against each other.

Brynn worked her magic, and I climbed from my bed; though to begin with I could not walk without aid. My hand was useless. The swelling and bruising had subsided, but moving my fingers was painful. My little finger, despite the splinting, would not straighten properly.

Brynn started massaging my hand with lavender oil and other unguents. It hurt so much I cried. Agonising pains shot up my arm. She weaned me slowly off Matthias' physic. What I recall of that process was horrific. I hallucinated and shook as if with fever. In my lucid moments I walked in circles around and around the castle bailey, so thin a puff of wind could have blown me over. One sunny day, I climbed onto the wall surrounding the castle. I felt the breeze on my face ruffling my unveiled hair. Below was the cliff face Salisbury was perched on like an eagle's nest. It seemed to be drawing me to it. In my delusional state, I thought I could fly. My gown filled with the breeze ready to float me away. But a sharp tug pulled me backwards landing me on my derriere, knocking the wind out of me. The fog in my head cleared a little as I staggered to stand confronted by a small dirty face with a snotty nose. It was not one of my babies, I knew that. The grubby child had a voice that echoed through a tunnel, scolding me in English for being bloody daft.

'Ye could 'ave fallen off, Ma'am, ye coulda'ave. Wot was ye thinkin'?'

'Who are you?'

'I be Tom, Ma'am. Who be thee?'

Who was I? 'I... I am... am?' I mumbled through a maze of muddle. 'I think I am Eleanor.'

'Lord Jesus, do thee not know what thou art named?'

I shook my head not so much because I could not remember who I was, but where I was with these strangers. Behind the boy, I noticed two young girls holding hands, equally grimy.

'Who are they?' I enquired?

I pointed at them with my useless hand then realised for the first time in weeks, months, I could flex it. I proudly showed Tom.

'Look I can move my hand.'

The urchin looked perplexed.

'Ye art not the… mad queen, art ye?'

Tom took a step back towards the girls. I was not sure whether it was to be the young gallant, or because he was frightened. While I stood examining my hand, Amaris appeared with Joachim, both looking mightily relieved.

'Milady, with deep respect, what on earth did you think you were doing disappearing like that and causing us concern?' Amaris flapped about draping a cape around my shoulders.

Joachim smiled. 'I see you have found some friends.'

'This is Tom. I do not know the girls' names.'

Tom replied, Geoffrey-like, 'The tall girl be Frith and the little one be Agnes, and Ma'am is coo-coo climbing on the wall like that. She might 'ave fallen off. She knows not 'er name or 'ow many 'ands, she 'as got.'

I found this very funny. I laughed for the first time since…I could not recall.

I stopped writing with my left hand on the wall behind the tapestry where I had scratched with charcoal in every language I knew, "Please God, let me die. I want to die."

I longed for my journal, parchment and ink. I wanted to know if I could hold a quill and if my hand could function. I wished I could communicate with my boys. I begged Robert to find writing materials to smuggle to me. He was the only member of my little court who could come and go. He said he dared not because if Henry found out it would be disastrous for us both.

I found myself weeping again for no apparent reason. The day of laughter with those funny children turned again to despair. Joachim tried to distract me, but I was back to walking in circles in the bailey. Amaris, Brynn and Joachim took turns to keep watch. My charcoal scrawl had been discovered behind Salisbury's fading tapestries.

I walked and talked to myself—rambling. I had to regain my

wits because I was useless to my boys the way I was. I wondered if they knew of my whereabouts.

One day, while muttering in Greek, I heard a cheeky, 'Oi!' and Little Tom appeared. 'Ye still mumblin', Ma'am?'

'Yes, Tom.'

He shook his head. With the Wisdom of Solomon, he asked, 'Why do ye talk like the Tower of Babel? No-one can understand what ye are sayin'.'

I caught Joachim's eye, and saw he was smiling.

'How dost thou know about the Tower of Babel?'

'From church.'

'Ye speak Latin, Tom?'

'Nah, but ye get to hear the same words over and over, and Babel stuck in me 'ead, cos it sounds like babble.'

'Would thee like to learn Latin?'

'Yeah. But who is goin' to teach the likes of me, a churl to a mad queen?'

Is that me? I thought. So, I said, 'As the mad queen I think thou art speaking of Tom, I could teach thee Latin and to read and write.'

I did not think he was sure whether I was 'the mad queen' or some other crazy apparition, so I asked, 'Do ye know the mad queen's name?'

'Eleanor ye said so t'other day. 'Ave ye forgotten again? I know the king's name is 'enry. 'E 'ad to lock up the queen, cos she is mad.'

I shook my head at Tom's logic, but this innocent child's words did something. God's Teeth, I would prove I was not mad, starting with this boy, and I would include those little girls. I would teach them.

To begin with, I had Tom and the girls scrubbed. That was an experience to behold. They had never seen a tub before. I told them if they were going to be churls and kitchen maids in my household, they had to be clean. They screamed, yelling they were not witches to be ducked.

So, I had Amaris pour some precious perfume into the water to appeal to the girls' vanity. I asked would not they love to smell like roses. That worked. The girls told Tom to hide his eyes as they both timidly lowered themselves into the water. Soon they were squealing with delight. Amaris whispered to me they all had nits which had me scratching my severely plaited mane. Their heads had to be shaved. The three were less concerned about losing their hair than they were about bathing. They said it had happened before.

Clothing them was challenging. We had no cloth or looms. Henry had not left me bereft of gowns, so we cut some down to fit Agnes and Frith. Tom was more of a problem. So, Amaris altered one of Joachim's more ancient habits. It was a bit big, but Tom did not care. So, clean, strangely dressed and bald, I addressed my little class. I cleaned an area of the stone floored gallery outside my chamber where they sat cross-legged with pieces of charcoal shakily writing their first alphabet.

Tom was quick, as I expected. He was a bright child, Frith also. Agnes being younger was going to take more time, but she was meticulous, writing carefully. Nonetheless, I had no books, only scriptures. Henry looked after my soul but made sure I had no pleasure. Like Papa taught me, the three children had to learn their scriptures off by heart. I made up stories for them from Greek legends and old English tales.

The lessons filled me with an ambition to persevere. Each day brought me closer to normality. These funny little children reminded me of my own children. At last, I had a purpose to live and to release my frustrated maternal emotions. Their curiosity enthralled me. I became my Papa, and how he enveloped me into his world of knowledge. My mangled hand became stronger.

Robert Mauduit joined my household at about his time. He was appointed Constable of Salisbury. I did not trust him to begin with, suspecting he was there as Henry's spy. I discovered his family had served Henry's late mother.

***

I tried to find out if my sons were safe. I implored Joachim to ask if Robert the Constable had any knowledge of their whereabouts, but Joachim said, when he was fishing for clues, he either was not saying or did not know. I thought that unlikely, but what could I do. Henry pulled the strings after all.

One day, a lute arrived with Sir Robert. He said Henry could see no reason why I could not play. Robert managed to convince Henry it would help strengthen my hand. I think he must have been feeling guilty for injuring me. The lute looked familiar, though it was not Henry's. I realised it was one of Richard's; an old, battered instrument on which he had learnt to play as a child. I cradled it to me. As I did, something slid inside the bowl. Robert grinned and said he would leave me to enjoy what it had to offer. I shook the lute. Inside there was a letter. I needed a small hand to fetch it out. Frith obliged. I kissed the child, surprising her with this show of affection. With shaking hands, I ripped open the seal.

My Darling Maman,

How we miss your beautiful company. Hal remains in Paris, bored and frustrated. Even Margaret finds her father's home restricting. I am back with Uncle Ralph who is getting old and crochety, but helpful as usual with my learning regarding the Aquitaine. I am quite familiar with the laws now. The justiciars are instructive as well. Geoffrey is in Brittany. He seems to be doing a lot of jousting which I know I should not mention because you do not like the sport. But he is very adept. Remember how skilled he was when we had to practise on the quintain? And I think because he is so skinny, he presents a difficult target to hit.

You will be pleased to know Lenore is happy with Alphonso and he with her. I hear Papa is negotiating with King William II of Sicily for Joanna's hand. I have visited her at Fontevrault where she is contented, but like all of us misses your loving, graceful presence. She is becoming quite a beauty. I think we were always so overwhelmed by how much Lenore resembled you we forgot about Joanna who, I think, is a mixture of you and Grandmother Matilda. Her hair is as thick as yours, though a flaming red which looks like autumn leaves. King William will be agog.

As for Papa, he struggles with his barons. The young Welsh King now disobeys the peace treaty between

England and Wales. Informants report he swears his
allegiance to you, not to Papa. The clergy have calmed
down since Papa's mea culpa and reparations over
Becket. We are fortunate none of us were excommunicated. I know Hal wept when those monks flogged
Papa, but for what he has done to you Maman, I
think he deserves another whipping.

Hal, Geoffrey and I are afraid Papa will follow his
threat to have you tried for treason with dire consequences should we go against his wishes, so please do
not think we have deserted you. It is a fractious peace,
but he has us under his boot. When the three of us
were last together we agreed to curb our activities, to
obey Papa. We dare not stray for fear of what could
befall you. Your safety is paramount. Surely Papa,
one day, will realise he is being a stubborn fool.

As you can see, I have managed to have my old lute
sent to you by Sir Robert as a 'courier.' I will try
to send other missives in disguise when I can find a
chance. Papa has forbidden all contact; in fact, it took
time to discover your whereabouts. In the meantime,
know that we all love and miss you, humbled by the
sacrifice you have made on our behalf. We hope you
are well.

Your beloved son,
Richard

I read and reread the letter, smelling it for traces of his
familiar odour, kissing where he placed the letters caressed by
his hand. Tears, tears, tears! I filled an ocean. I longed to see
Richard. But this simple letter inspired me to keep fighting. At
last, I knew where the boys were, thankfully except for Hal, out
of Paris.

***

Joachim spent a lot of time exploring the nooks and crannies
of the castle, re-appearing rather smelly and apologising for his
appearance and odour. I wondered if he was looking for a way out.

I battled with despair. Unable to read or communicate

with the people I loved frustrated and angered me. Was Henry deliberately trying to drive me out of my wits? I started to see everyone in the castle as a potential spy, from stewards to tinkers and everyone in between, including poor Sir Robert.

My temper was on a knife-edge. Amaris and those three little mites all suffered. Joachim prayed, probably to keep me out of hell. Brynn was the only one unruffled regardless of how nasty I became.

One day she asked, 'Milady, where is Prince Richard's lute?'

'God's Teeth, how do I know? I could barely tune the damn thing. I cannot remember where I put it.'

Amaris knew and fetched it.

'Here it is. Good luck, Brynn!'

'Thank you, Amaris. Milady, I have a Welsh harp. How would you like to learn some Welsh music?'

I remembered the beautiful music played at Owain Pendragon's funeral and wake. Brynn cajoled and tempted me by playing and singing lilting music. It was hard and frustrating trying to strum the lute. My hand cramped when I attempted to stroke or pick the strings. My left hand fell back into finding the tune, but my right fumbled. Brynn could feel my disappointment. She would take my hand and straighten my cramped fingers.

'Now Milady, try again.'

We continued day after day. Every time my hand seized; Brynn would massage it till it relaxed again. At last, it looked normal, except for the little finger, but it ached. The process was slow. Brynn encouraged me to persevere. Her endless patience helped my hand become more flexible. The shooting pains up my arm eased. Music became the best physic of all. The children, too, learned to play.

***

Henry was losing faith amongst his people by his increasingly irrational actions, as reported by Robert. He worried that Henry was becoming like Stephen of Blois. I hoped and prayed this was not so. Robert said he needed my guiding hand. Even a tincture of my diplomacy would help. Ha!

Surely, Henry could not have forgotten what he fought for at his mother's side, or how he worked to restore law and order during the early years of our reign? I begged Robert to council him to keep him from slipping further into tyranny.

One day, during one of Robert's visits, he said, 'Milady I am so sorry, but I have learned that Lord Henry has stripped you of your rights.'

'Nothing would surprise me. Which ones?'

'Income and lands in England. He has used some to create royal foundations as part of the reparation he had to make regarding Becket's murder and built a priory for the Carthusians.'

'Well, at least it has been put to some good. Not that I received much of it the first place. It all went into Henry's exchequer.'

***

It was my third Christmas since I was arrested; the only one I could remember with any clarity. Salisbury was cold. After we attended the chapel, we gathered in my chamber, where the braziers burnt brightly. Our Christmas fare was served there, too, with goose and other fowl followed by sweetmeats, quite a feast after our daily frugality. There was mulled wine to keep our spirits up, and we had our little group of minstrels to make merry.

Before Christmas day, a loom arrived with skeins of linen thread to weave, and a spinning wheel with soft fleeces to be spun, which lit up Amaris' eyes. Sir Robert had worked hard to convince Henry that women's work was not going to enable me to escape, although weaving tested my stiff fingers.

For our simple Christmas festivities, we managed to find little treasures to give each other. I was spoiled. Amaris had saved the rings cut from my fingers at Chinon and had them re-joined by the castle tinker. Brynn recited a beautiful Welsh poem. The three children had composed a story about a princess rescued from an ogre (very apt), and Robert gave enough silk fabric to make a gown.

We were all enjoying our little gifts when lastly Joachim, grinning like a gargoyle, gave me a package wrapped in sackcloth. As I unwound the wrapping, the familiar aroma of leather and parchment filled my nostrils and overwhelmed me with joy.

There in my hands was a beautifully bound, pristine journal awaiting words. Ink and quills also appeared with a flourish.

Now I knew why Joachim was disappearing for extended periods, often returning a tad odoriferous. He had been scraping sheep's skin to make parchment, stretching it on frames which he then trimmed to size. Lord knows how he had managed to tool the leather cover or find the linen cord for the bindings. He obtained oak gall, iron filings, and vinegar to make the ink. The quills were the only easy items to find. There were plenty of goose feathers. I flung my arms around him. I could say naught as tears of happiness flowed down my face. During my life, I had received gold, pearls, precious gems, furs and riches, but never had I received such a splendid gift. Everyone was beaming. I think they all might have contributed in some way.

I had three lost years to drag from my memory. My life had experienced gut-wrenching pain and hurt, many triumphs, unbelievable passion, and this part of my journey held all those emotions. In front of my little court, I opened this gem of a gift. Its bindings squeaked with anticipation. Everyone watched as I dipped my quill in the ink. I had to concentrate with all my might on my right hand to will it to write. The quill felt awkward. But I managed, with my dear companions encouraging me, to write on the first page,

"This journal I dedicate to dear Brother Joachim. I will treasure it always as the most precious gift I have ever received."

Eleanor is back, Papa! I thought.

***

Joachim's magnificent journal boosted my confidence immeasurably. I nagged Amaris and all around me to jog my memory to record the last three years. I had to be dragged to dine and to bed. When my hand tired, I used it in different way like playing my lute. Amaris encouraged me to weave on our new loom, never a favourite pastime because I was impatient. Agnes, we discovered, was a natural. Her tiny hands flew across the warp. Her embroidery and tatting were as fine as that of the nuns who had made lace for my chemises.

***

I had passed my third year of incarceration when out of the blue a letter arrived from Henry. He wanted me to attend him at Winchester for the Easter Court. Could this be the end of my confined life? I looked around my prison in Salisbury Castle, as bleak as the fortress of Chinon and overall, not much smaller, though our quarters were cramped. The castle was built of forbidding granite. It overlooked Salisbury Plain. It was fortified to a depressing extent, impossible to breach with its inner and outer baileys, wide moat, narrow drawbridge, and a portcullis that could withstand Hannibal's elephants. If a force managed to breach its outer walls, soldiers would have to cross an expanse as bald as a monk's tonsure, exposing them to sentinel archers. On one side, it teetered on a cliff face. Did Henry think I was so dangerous that he had to incarcerate me in such an impenetrable fortress?

Sir Robert managed to purloin some rugs to cover the stone floors. We had little furniture and only braziers for heating, so we huddled together in one room. With the loom and a table on which I wrote, it was crowded. Joachim had a chamber the size of a closet next to the chapel, which he told me was luxurious compared to his cell in his old monastery in Paris. I think he exaggerated. Tom managed to squeeze in with him. Sir Robert took to the garrison with my gaolers when he visited. My bed chamber was next to where we all congregated. I learned to share it with my long-suffering women, little Agnes and Frith, who curled up together on a palliasse. Amaris shared my bed and Brynn slept on a narrow trundle. It was fortunate I was floating in dwale when we arrived, or I would not have been the most compliant of bedfellows. What the Queen of England had accustomed herself to was amazing. Should I be allowed to accommodate my old chambers at Winchester, I would need a scout to find my way from one side to the other. I faced the coming encounter with Henry with mixed feelings.

Chapter 12 A Loosening of the Shackles

I wished I could ride to Winchester, but I had to travel in an enclosed carriage heavily guarded. The carriage with its leather side curtains was airless, and the road was rutted after the winter thaw. I suffered the familiar symptoms of mal de chariot. I moaned to my guards that I needed fresh air, or I would be ill. Sir Robert, who was travelling with my entourage, convinced the guards I was not going to bolt, so they let me alight for a short period. It was most agreeable to see trees and grass after more than three years of granite walls.

We arrived after the noon-day bells. The familiar walls of the palace were a pleasure to behold as I alighted from the carriage. The honey-coloured sandstone and beautiful Gothic windows brought sadness and joy. I was met by the palace constable. His face registered deep sorrow as he bowed deeply. He made me feel honoured regardless of my predicament. Surrounded as I was by more guards than a common felon, he was unable to utter a word of welcome. I gave him an understanding smile as he led the way to my old quarters. There was no sign of Henry.

Before I left Salisbury, I was determined that no matter what occurred this Easter I would remain dignified. I was determined I would hold my head high and prove to the court that, regardless of how Henry treated me, I had not been cowed. I would be the woman my father trained me to be, the Duchess of Aquitaine firstly and, if needs be, Queen of England, and to hell with Henry.

***

I was nervous, despite my bravado. I wanted to see Henry to confront him, and to see, after three or more years, how he looked. I paced around my old familiar quarters, only now there were two guards outside my door. They allowed Robert to enter. He was grinning from ear to ear.

'Milady, the Young King is here with Lady Margaret, the Duke of Brittany with Lady Constance, Prince Richard of course, oh and Prince John too. A further surprise is Princess Joanna, whose betrothal to King William of Sicily is to be finalised. He is Henry's guest.'

So, I was allowed to meet the King of Sicily. My suspicions were raised as to why and I wondered what King William would make of my incarceration.

I put my dubious thoughts behind me though because of my eagerness to see my sons and daughter. Would I be able to speak with them? Alone, I doubted. Robert gave my hand a quick squeeze and handed me a written invitation to a banquet as he left. I noted it was not scribed by Henry.

While I paced and absorbed Robert's news my door opened again. It was Henry. I was not well dressed. But why should I want to look attractive for him! I remained aloof. We stared at each other. I drew myself up to my full height, standing rigid like a pikestaff. I was not going to be first to speak. I scanned his face. He looked haggard, I hoped, with guilt. A curtain of silence hung between us, broken by Henry.

'You look thin.'

No answer.

'Lost your viperish tongue, have you?'

He riled me. I turned my back on him and walked to a chest where my jewellery, looking glass, and hairbrush lay. Henry had not moved. I kept my voice as even as I could. 'I 'ava nothing to say to you, 'enri Plantagenet-a.'

'I 'ava no-thing-a to-a say to-a-you, 'enri Plantagenet-a.'

Henry's imitation of my Langue d'Oeil always infuriated me, but I took a deep breath, determined I was not going to be provoked. I picked up the brush. In Latin, which he could not mock, I replied.

'If you have said your piece and have nothing more to add, you can shut the door on your way out.'

'I have not finished, Eleanor. You will stay at Winchester after Easter instead of returning to Salisbury Castle. Furthermore, when you are feeling less abrupt there is a discussion we need to have.'

'Indeed.' I turned.

We stared at each other with eyes like basilisks. I did not request he enlighten me. Whatever was on his mind would not be pleasant. Nor did I want any pronouncements to spoil my meeting with my boys and daughter.

'It makes little difference where you incarcerate me, one prison is mightily like another. Now if you do not mind, I need to dress for tonight's banquet. Thank you for the invitation.'

I walked to the door, opened it, and stepped aside. Henry must have dismissed the guards when he entered, but I noticed three churls and two pages nearly fell over each other as they dragged their ears from the timber, disappointed there was not the fiery exchange their eavesdropping expected. Witnesses, such as they were, forced Henry to make a dignified exit.

My hairbrush bounced off the door. Amaris tiptoed from the wardrobe and collected it.

'Norman bastard!' I vented my frustrated fury in fruity Langue d'Oc.

My clenched fist made my hand cramp. Amaris waited for me to calm down.

'I have found a gown I think suitable for the banquet.'

'I do not give a damn what I wear for Henry, but I want to look attractive for my sons, and King William for Joanna's sake. Show me what you have found.' I followed Amaris into my wardrobe.

Amaris smiled with pride, 'It is this magnificent purple silk.'

'Good God! You would think I would remember it, but I do not. I suppose I wore it for some grand occasion here at Winchester.'

'Yes, I found it stored away in a chest.'

'Will it still fit?'

'Milady, I thought of that. With Agnes's help, we can adjust the lacings and with a stitch here and there, we can tighten it.'

'That is settled then. Thank you, Amaris.'

'Good. We will alter it and have it pressed ready for tonight, Milady.'

I wondered where my boys were within the palace. In the wing that housed their old chambers, I supposed. I was impatient to see them but feared if I poked my nose outside my door, I would be in trouble. I relaxed in a hot tub to regain my composure. My hair was lathered and scrubbed. The spring sunshine streamed through the diamond glass windows and dried my tresses.

The rest of the day moved at the speed of a tortoise. Amaris was able to confirm the whereabouts of Hal, Geoffrey and their wives, also Joanna and Richard. They were nearby; John, too. I wondered what they would be feeling and had they thought of breaking out to find me, or would they be threatened if they did?

Twilight had peeped through my windows, and the candelabras were lit by the time I was readied for the banquet. Time to dust the 'old' queen of her cobwebs. Amaris pulled two grey hairs out of my head while she was working on some elaborate style of plaits. After I had 'ouched,' wondering what on earth she thought she was doing, she muttered something about letting a pin stick into me.

I whirled on her. 'You are lying, Amaris, and not doing it very well.'

'Sorry, I pulled out a couple of grey hairs.'

'What! How many more are there?'

'None, honestly. I cannot see any more.'

Pathetically, I went into a panic. Was I losing my looks? I grabbed the glass, searching for lines, frowning at it.

Amaris said, 'If you scowl, you will get wrinkles. Lady Eleanor, Lord Henry has looked about ten years older than you for years. You have been blessed with striking features, beautiful eyes and alabaster skin. I do not believe you need to worry about two grey hairs. Though you are a little pale, from Salisbury. God in heaven, Milady! Stop frowning! I need to put the kohl around your eyes.'

Dressed, adorned with rouge and kohl enhancing my eyes, I concentrated on the joy of seeing Hal, Geoffrey and Richard, even John. The last time I was so arrayed had been at Limoges. I was reminded how heavy these elaborate gowns were. I left my quarters crowned as Duchess of Aquitaine. If Henry had a fit about my choice I cared not.

As I approached the Great Hall, my joy was overwhelming. There were my beloved sons looking so handsome, so regal. Even John looked like a prince instead of his sulky self. He had grown. The other three were heavenly. They knelt as the young knights they were, to pay homage. Then I was engulfed by giant hugs. Amaris was wringing her hands, begging them not to undo her hours of handiwork. They stepped back, and she bustled forward, tweaking here and there, and straightening my crown.

To one side Margaret and Constance were waiting. Both gave a little curtsy. I felt a little jealous lurch as Margaret stood as the Young Queen of England suitably crowned. Two grey hairs rankled. Constance looked at me with narrow eyes, envious, I think, of Geoffrey's show of affection for his mother. Hal grinned from ear to ear. Richard was beaming like a summer's day. Joanna gave me a lingering embrace and a kiss. She looked striking. John stared.

I took Richard's arm, asking him as my heir to escort me into the Great Hall, ignoring Henry. As far as I was concerned, he was superfluous. He fumed in the background, then grumbled we needed to enter before the trumpeters died of old age.

The doors opened. Henry alone led the way as the first fanfare echoed through the buttresses, followed by Hal and Margaret. Then, as Richard and I entered, the roof lifted from its ancient foundations.

'Vivat Regina.' Richard looked at me with pride.

How tall he was. Yes, he had Henry's blue eyes, auburn hair and chin but the height was all Aquitaine. I was so proud of him.

***

It was a night to behold. Just being able to talk to my sons was more than special. They were concerned about my health. The three older ones had begged Henry to release me, but he would not because he said he could not trust me or them. Yes, he had them where he wanted. While I was Henry's captive, they would not rebel against their father.

Richard gave me the good news that Matilda had made me a grandmother. At least I supposed it was good news or was it more proof that I was growing older. He repeated to me that Lenore was happy. But, so far, he had not set eyes on his betrothed. Princess Alais was somewhere in the depths of Henry's court. Hal and Geoffrey were happy in their marriages. As I looked at their beaming faces, I pushed my sorry situation to one side.

A sumptuous banquet was served. Fowl of many kinds, venison and wild boar were presented It was almost overwhelming after the meagre fare we were reduced to at Salisbury. But I was too excited to eat much.

Henry placed me next to the King of Sicily, which was a surprise. What King William knew of my circumstances I knew not. King William was older than I expected but was warm and friendly. It was obvious he was taken by Joanna, who had developed into a beauty. Tonight, she was dressed in a gown of peacock blue shot with green, which suited her flaming red hair and creamy skin.

'It is indeed a pleasure to make your acquaintance, Lord William. Many years ago, I had the pleasure of visiting your beautiful island on my return from the Holy Land.'

'It is a delight to meet you, also, Lady Eleanor, and I hope one day you might be able to return to Sicily.'

'One never knows. I hope you and Joanna will be happy together.'

'I am sure we will. She appears to be a vivacious girl.'

'Indeed. Might I ask your opinion on educated women? All my daughters are fluent in languages, can all read and write as I could as a girl, and they have been encouraged to speak their minds. They are all intelligent.' He looked at me closely I think, going past the glamour.

'I am sure an education is enhancing and seeing the passion in your eyes when you speak of learning, as a mere male, I am impressed. I hope Lady Joanna is as eloquent as her mother.'

He then turned to where Joanna was laughing and talking animatedly with her brothers. 'I can see, Your Ladyship, that Princess Joanna is more than a lovely face.'

Joanna caught his eye and blushed, managing to look a little demure. He turned back to me. 'If she is as charming as you, Milady, I cannot help but be enchanted.'

I beckoned to Joanna without consulting Henry, who was keeping his eye on proceedings. She approached shyly. She had grown and would be tall, but she was still a child. I was sure she was just as happy playing games than having to live in a strange household and to wed when she could bear children. Tonight, she was gowned like a beautiful doll. Joanna gave a little curtsy to William then snuggled into me as if for protection. She slipped her hand into mine. I wanted to hold her tight and not let her go, cursing Henry for separating us. The circumstances of John's birth and my months of recuperation affected her too. Like John, Henry sent Joanna to Fontevrault. She was only eleven months old when he was born. I had her returned to my court when she turned two.

Now she was back at the Abbey thanks to my imprisonment. Nevertheless, the nuns I knew would have diligently continued her education. I spoke to her in Greek, spoken throughout Sicily. She replied fluently. This broke the ice with her betrothed, who immediately started chatting to her.

'Are you interested in mathematics, Lady Joanna?'

'I can count, add and measure, but I think I am better at reading. I like the adventures of Odysseus and the plays of Euripides.'

'The reason I asked about mathematics is because Euclid, who is said to have founded geometry, lived in Syracuse.'

'Oh. I think Maman might have mentioned that, because she went there once, to Syracuse, that is.'

'Who taught you Greek? You speak it excellently.'

Joanna squeezed my hand and answered, 'Maman, mostly. We had Greek days, Latin days, English days, Langue d'Oc and Langue d'Oeil days, and the nuns at Fontevrault continue the tradition while Papa keeps Maman in — away.'

Now I thought she was going to cry. I saw her glance towards Henry scowling, as if to say, 'it is all your fault.' I could feel an awkward situation mounting.

'Joanna, my dear, I suggest you return to your brothers if Lord King William would be so kind.'

I gave him a weak smile. Although he said naught, he was too polite, I was certain he would know Henry's and my marriage was strained. Was he aware of my incarceration? Probably if the tattling grape vines of the various courts were active.

As Henry was striding towards us King William remarked, 'Lady Eleanor, you have a handsome family, and allow me to congratulate you on your sons' achievements. The princes' knighthoods are considered outstanding within and without your kingdom. It is obvious their mother's grace and charm has influenced their chivalry.'

'Thank you, Lord William, for your kind words. I am honoured.'

Henry would not have missed our exchange.

***

Henry had said little to me. I recognised he was jealous of the attention afforded to me by Hal, Richard, Geoffrey and Joanna. As usual, John looked at me like I was a distant relative. I tried to show interest in him.

'Hello, John, my dear, how are you?'

'All right.'

'Good. How are your lessons progressing?'

'All right.'

'And how are your languages coming along?'

'Well enough.'

'Do you like reading?'

'I suppose so.'

'I see... Do you have a favourite author?'

'No.'

It was heavy going. My questions bored him, and he showed no curiosity about me. I hoped one day we would find each other.

The Easter Court ended. My boys prepared to depart. For Geoffrey and Richard this was simple. They had lands to govern, duties to follow. Henry continued to dismiss poor Hal's approaches for recognition. His brothers understood his frustration but were tiring of being sympathetic, as was I. They had no influence over Henry.

Henry avoided me during the Easter Court. We sat down together, apart from the banquet, on only two other occasions. Because I could not trust myself to keep a civil tongue in my head, I let him talk and said little. This annoyed him more than if I had released my fury. But regardless of my hopes, I knew nothing was going to remove me from Henry's vindictive wrath. I did not dress to impress him; instead, I looked more like a nun. He grumbled about the boys not showing him respect. My smirk did not impress.

Winchester was a pleasant change of scenery. The discussion Henry wanted was a complete surprise.

I was expecting something dire and nasty, though he made one sour remark, 'Well Lady Eleanor, you cannot complain you had nothing to do with Joanna's betrothal arrangements having spent the banquet batting your eyelids at King William and speaking Greek.'

I did not bite. What was the point?

'I have decided while at Winchester you can help prepare Joanna's trousseau. She will be remaining here.'

I stared at him in disbelief. He had said little to me about Joanna.

'Thank you, I will enjoy her company.'

It would give me unbelievable pleasure to be in contact with one of my children, if only briefly. Henry was not skimping on her dowry, probably bestowing my English lands and purloined income to endow her. I thought with wry humour that the Aquitaine could adequately provide her with more than what was necessary. My duchy continued to maintain the English treasury.

***

Joanna's time with me ended too soon. It was a tearful parting. I had done my best to prepare her for her married life and as a young queen. I would miss her.

Henry decreed I could remain at Winchester after Joanna left. However, as time crawled by, I was allowed to move from palace to palace, castle to castle, or wherever Henry sent me, except London for some reason. I must admit I was more comfortable. Every now and then he trotted me out for Easter or Christmas courts when he required his queen.

Information trickled in my direction. Robert passed on whispers, as did Richard when he could. The barons in England were fractious, young Owain provoked Henry, and so did Malcolm's heirs. Ireland was a constant thorn in his side. Normandy did not give him too many problems, nor did Brittany. Geoffrey and his father-in-law kept control. It seemed Richard was serving the Aquitaine well. Hal despaired. Henry's promises to John were unacceptable, but of course I could do nothing to help, and I had to guard my sources. Not only would my secret informants be in trouble, but I could end up back in Salisbury, or worse.

Henry's health was deteriorating. He had to swear to the pope he would lead a crusade. He had to promise knights and men as part of the reparation for Becket's murder. But I did not believe he would last the many weeks of travel. To make matters worse, Robert told me Henry's horse had kicked him. Luckily, he had no broken bones, but his leg was badly bruised.

Becket was canonised. This was hard to reconcile, knowing him from old. A cult had developed, and The Knights of Saint Thomas of Acre was established in the Holy Land. There were even miracles attributed to him, which were laughable. What Henry made of that development, I knew not. New churches were built in Becket's memory, and the shrine dedicated to him at Canterbury grew rich with pilgrims. My thoughts I kept to myself, but he was one Saint I would not be appealing to in my prayers.

***

Scraps of news continued to reach me drip by drip regarding the kingdom and Henry's lands from Normandy and beyond. Snippets from the boys were a welcome distraction. I also managed from time to time to send letters to them about my boring existence. Hal was still frustrated and angry. I could not make Henry out. Did he think Hal wanted to usurp him? He was popular, liked by his peers, and well respected. Normandy would be excellent, then Henry would not have to be always rushing from one side of the channel to the other, ruining his health. Heaven forbid, I sounded like a parrot.

I winced at the knowledge the boys were jousting. If I were free, could I stop them? No! All I could do was pray that they would never be hurt. I chastised Richard in a smuggled letter that I did not give birth to them only for them to endanger their lives. I also reminded him to look at his father; constantly in pain from injuries he received after being dislodged from his horse. The reason Henry suffered from chronic headaches, which made him unbearable, was from his head hitting the ground, helmet or no. I threw up my hands when Richard replied that it would not happen to him because he was a better jouster than his father, as were Hal and Geoffrey. So much for motherly concern…

***

Henry deigned to tell me Joanna had arrived safely in Sicily, but I heard from Richard she was missing her home. King William's court was kind to her, for which I was grateful, but she was lonely.

Without disclosing anything, I asked, 'Henry, please allow me to write to Joanna. She is far from home and all that is familiar. I worry that she could be homesick.'

'She needs to grow up.'

'Typical! What would you know? Whereby I...'

'All right! And before you give me another lecture on your miserable life on Île de France... Yes! As long as you do not write in Greek or Langue d'Oc.'

'Why? Do you think I will disclose state secrets?'

'More like poison dripping from your pen.'

So, I wrote in Latin so Henry could censor it. I told her to be brave, to enjoy the splendours of Palermo and to continue her studies. I told her I loved her, and, like her brothers and sisters, that she was in my prayers. I hoped the contact would help, especially as she was so naive.

Henry nagged I should try to do more for John. Now that was interesting seeing he was supposed to be overseeing John's upbringing whilst keeping me under arrest. I broke my code of barely speaking to him.

With sarcasm pouring, I asked, 'And when are you sending me to Fontevrault so I can get to know John? Or do you intend to lock John up with me in some God-forsaken castle?'

He limped off with a backward sneer.

'Shut your mouth, Eleanor. You can rot in hell for all I care.'

Henry hit a sore point.

I yelled after him, 'I am a damn sight better preserved than you are when you talk of rotting. Have you looked in your glass of late? Your face is like a map of chasms and craters, and what is more, people think I am ten years younger than you.'

The stonework shuddered as he exited. For good measure, I yelled, 'CHECKMATE!'

Foolish Eleanor! The door was almost wrenched off its hinges as he hurtled back through it. But before he could rain fists down on me, Amaris was standing in front of me, arms outstretched. 'As God is my witness, you will have to slay me first, Lord Henry, before you lay one blow on her Ladyship.'

Amaris's raised voice brought a recruit. Joachim walked straight up to Henry with nothing but a wooden cross in his hand. 'Lord King Henry, your temper had Archbishop Becket martyred. Do you want to add regicide to your sins committed against your wife?'

Henry was breathing like a dragon but lowered his clenched fist. 'Milady, mayhap you could take back your words.'

With that, much to my shame, Joachim knelt and started to pray for both Henry and me, begging God to forgive us and to help us find a way to be reconciled.

We were deflated and glanced at each other. What could I do? The last thing I wanted to do was to apologise. I did not care one jot how much I hurt Henry's feelings, but in front of me was the saintly figure who had made me a journal to keep me sane and happy. For him, I would walk through fire. The words nearly choked me.

'I am sorry Henry?'

Henry glared. Silence divided us like a wall. I felt like screaming. He could at least thank me. Instead, I said I could massage his hip to ease the soreness. I told him about the unguent Brynn had used on my hand. Henry hesitated. But Amaris was through into the antechamber where such medicines were stored, coming back with a pot of the creamy mixture. Joachim rose, gave me a grin of satisfaction and rushed Amaris out the door. We were alone. He could still use his brutal force on me. My words were cruel, and I was expert at using my tongue to rile Henry. But he said naught, nor did he move.

I moved to the bedside, 'Lie here.'

Henry hesitated. For a moment, I thought he was going to walk out, but instead he limped over and hoisted himself with difficulty onto the mattress. I rolled back his gown and loosened his braies. The skin around his hip bone was swollen and inflamed. I winced. It was so much worse than when we were truly husband and wife. I took a scoop of the ointment. As gently as I could with my weak right hand, I started to massage Henry's damaged hip. He gritted his teeth.

'Tell me if I am hurting you.'

'I will live.'

I rotated my fingers over the damaged area, pressing and kneading just as Brynn did to my hand.

'Ahh! I think that is enough, Eleanor.'

'It will take several applications before you feel relief. If you wish, you can come back on the morrow.'

As he adjusted his braies, I noticed the horseshoe shaped scar on his leg. 'I see you have been kicked. Dear God, that must have hurt. You were lucky your leg was not broken?'

'Bloody horse. Do not know what got into him.' He limped out the door.

***

The unguent must have helped because he came again. It was odd attending to Henry's hip. My weak hand was strengthened as well as helping him. The next day I could see the redness had lessened. Neither of us said much, but I think the massaging might have released some tension between us.

That night, when I climbed into bed, I asked myself again why our lives had reached this unhappy impasse. While I was attending to Henry's sore hip, I felt a tenderness towards him. I wanted to stroke his head to take away his hurts. But realistically, I knew there was little chance of a way forward. He was not going to change, and neither would I, which was why I attacked him with all the vitriol I knew. It had gone beyond the pain and humiliation of his affairs. He had me where he wanted me, powerless...except for the Aquitaine, my remaining dominant piece on my chessboard of life.

I rolled onto my back and thought of our sons and daughters. Henry never understood why our children were my priority. Did Papa over-protect Nilla and me, the wealthy heiresses of a vast duchy? Henry would have attached us to someone before we could walk. Why did Papa jealously shield us? Well, I would never know. Nonetheless, what I did learn from Papa was a higher-than-normal expectation of fatherhood.

In our society, Henry's parents did what was usual. With Maud, baby Henry was sent to the de Lucy family. He only returned to his mother's side at ten years to ride with her to reclaim her inheritance of the English throne. When he was not going to war, he was educated by tutors in Angers. No wonder Henry had no idea of parenthood. But I followed Papa's example and educated my own. My father recognised I was clever and went out of his way to encourage my gift regardless of my sex. Did that make me a prodigium, a freak? Yes! Then I was called a witch. Was that what Henry feared — a supernatural power? Laughable!

Did my schooling of our heirs make them dangerous? Is that why my influence was curbed? I felt like a caged tigress trying to break out of the restrictions of my existence. Henry could not accept my intellect any more than Louis could. I used to think he did. Now I clawed and spat like the wild cat of frustration I had become. Abraham was the only man I knew who loved me because of my intelligence rather than what I looked like or my wealth and status.

I reduced myself to a blubbering mess. I had become a lonely, embittered woman. I would not beg Henry to release me. The consequences for my beloved boys would be too great. If only I could climb onto Beelzebub's back and ride with the wind in my hair, till we both dropped.

Chapter 13 A Stolen Inheritance

I was back at Salisbury. Henry had renovated my quarters, expanding them along one wall of the castle, which meant we were less cramped. I now had my own bed chamber. Amaris still wanted to be with me in case I had a bad night. I convinced her I could manage.

A large crate arrived. To my surprise, it contained gowns, furs and items of leather, including chamois slippers and beautiful riding boots. All very well, but where was the horse? Was Henry softening? Were my tender ministrations to his hip acknowledged, after all? He even rewarded Amaris with a scarlet gown and cape.

I spoke to Robert Mauduit about riding in the countryside around Salisbury. He said he could see no reason why not and to choose a horse from the stable. So, my wish to feel the breeze in my hair from horseback was fulfilled. We took part in some falconry as well.

But the latest news that the boys were fighting amongst themselves was distressing. I was slowly building up sources for information; people within my restricted community who I could trust to courier letters to my sons and to deliver replies. But most of what I learned did not make me happy. Henry granted more lands to John by robbing many women and girls of their inheritances. Female heirs had been granted equal shares of estates since his grandfather's day, but Henry violated this agreement. When his Uncle Reginald, Duke of Cornwall died, he disinherited Reginald's daughters, leaving them with only small portions. He then gave the bulk to John. Was this to spite me because I had equal control of the Aquitaine treasury? It upset Hal, Richard and Geoffrey, as usual, that John, let alone Reginald's heiresses, was favoured.

A smuggled missive from Uncle Ralph informed me that Henry had conferred the title of Count of Poitou on Richard without consulting me. He gave away my county just like that.

Richard did not dispute Henry's interference which really hurt. Poitou, like the Aquitaine, would become Richard's on my death. That I had been supplanted was no doubt another intention to weaken my position. I wrote to my son and heir expressing my disappointment, reminding him I might be physically restricted, but I was not dead yet!

Richard replied it was necessary to keep the warring nobles of Angoulême and Limousin under control. Moreover, he said, while I was complaining he had conducted a successful siege of the fortress of Taillebourg in the early spring of 1179. I suppose I was impressed but it smarted. I heard Henry was cock-a-hoop regarding Richard's success, the only time Henry had praised him, probably to get at me.

***

Henry ordered Richard to England. He demanded I attend him in London, where he wanted me to formally acknowledge Richard as Count of Poitou. The thought of being forced to hand over my title was humiliating. Richard would face my displeasure for accepting it.

It was with mixed emotions that I approached London. It was years since I had set foot in the capital. I was able to ride, albeit a dull bay mare instead of my prancing hispano, but brown horse or no I made sure I stood out. I wore the scarlet cloak Henry gave me and the crown of England for the people of London, not to appease Henry.

I had enough guards to create a stir, so it was not long before the good people were on the streets. Our progress slowed as Londoners flocked from their dwellings and marketplaces. I would have loved to have dismounted and walked among the good burghers and townsfolk as I had done in the past, but that joy was prevented by my guards. Nevertheless, they could not close the people's throats as a roar echoed from street to lane—'Vivat Regina'! The welcome made me swell with pride. I hoped with malicious glee that their loud spontaneous greetings were heard by Henry within the Palace of Westminster. It certainly caused a reaction amongst my guards, who spread from their tightly packed cordon to allow me to be better observed. The guards, I noticed, seemed to be more compassionate regarding my situation. Interesting!

We rode past Westminster Abbey where I was crowned with Henry, through the grand entrance of the palace to at last dismount. I was met by Richard and his father. Richard went down on his knee to pay homage. I growled at him not to bother, then gave a cursory nod to Henry. I strode with cloak billowing through the familiar doorway leading to my quarters, presuming that was where I would be housed and not the dungeons.

I paced and stormed about the dispossession I had to face. When Richard appeared, I let fly.

'How dare you embarrass me in this manner considering what I am forced to endure for you and your brothers! Have you no respect? Care you not for my honour? To go behind my back, to erode my heritage, knowing full well it would be yours one day, is despicable. How dare you, Richard!'

'Papa insisted that it was to prevent a Poitivin rebellion and attack from the north.'

'God's Teeth, and you believed him! You should have done what I trained you to do. You should have met with our vassals and made them see the error of their ways. And you should have emphasised they were letting me down as their imprisoned Countess of Poitou. Had you done that, there would have been no need to go into battle. Furthermore, a peace agreement could have then been signed without you overreacting with useless sieges.'

'I won, Maman.'

'At what price? This time maybe. But what about the next time and the next? All you are doing is following your father's bullying tactics and alienating the very people you want on your side. I am in no position to help you out of any mess you make. I know Henry from old. He is just making you do his dirty work. By stripping me of Poitou, he thinks he is winning. Again, Richard, you are being used as a pawn.'

Richard stood there in silence. He was fuming, but what could he say.

'I am sorry you consider me such a fool, Maman,' he muttered.

'I did not say that, but I know manipulation when I see it. I love you as I love all my children, but I am hurt, Richard. Now I must stand dishonoured in front of that panel your father has assembled and hand over part of my inheritance. It makes me sick. You are dismissed.'

He did not slam the door, but I knew he did not understand. He was elated by his victory, which I suppose he should be, but it was at my expense. Then I was expected to present myself like a penitent in front of Henry's chosen audience of church hierarchy and nobles. None would have any love for me and would be delighted to see me brought down. But be damned if I was going to be cowed. I would stand tall.

I dressed sombrely. The only jewellery I wore was the coronet of the county I was relinquishing. I would crown my son with it knowing it would be too small, proving it was as unfitting as the head on which it was to be placed.

I had to stand listening to the official litany that passed my County of Poitou to Richard. I knew he was feeling guilty, regardless of his bravado. After Henry's gilded speech, in a low voice, I requested Richard step forward and asked him to kneel. I took the crown from my head and placed it on his auburn curls. It looked ridiculous. So, it did not fall off, he had to hold it while he stood to kiss me on both cheeks. I thought, *if I were to be humiliated so will you, my son.* Red-faced Henry had to sit silent amongst his selected luminaries; my point not lost on him, or them. I asked to take my leave. Before I left, I made it clear that for such a momentous occasion it would have been honourable had I been consulted rather than being presented with a fait accompli.

Back in my quarters, I wept for my Papa, knowing how hurt he, too, would be. Henry did not speak to me. Within days, I was back on my horse to Winchester before Henry shuffled me off to another house of arrest.

***

I was lonely, longing for…love, comfort…a man's arms. I lost track of days in my boring existence. While I doodled away daydreaming about impossibilities, a letter arrived via a scruffy monk, another of Joachim's wandering hermits or pilgrims. It was from Uncle Ralph. It had taken weeks to reach me by the date. Nevertheless, any news was a joy till I read it. The new Count of Poitou was in trouble. Uncle Ralph wrote that there was some petty rebellion in the north of Poitou, where Richard tore in with unconsidered force and created havoc. He said there had been accusations of the rape of noble's wives and daughters by Richard himself. My uncle thought it unlikely, but who knew? Whether it was true or not, it was not something a mother wished to hear. I was devastated. Richard was behaving like his father. Henry had put him in a position where his inexperience had him floundering. Henry had to recruit Geoffrey and Hal to go to Richard's aid.

When the situation calmed, the Poitivins turned and appealed to Hal whom they considered more diplomatic. Hal listened to their grievances, which was what Richard should have done in the first place.

Uncle Ralph added that Richard had erected a castle at Clairvaux, a grey area on the border between Poitou and Anjou. Marginally, it was probably in Anjou, which Hal would consider his land if he had any. Furious with Richard over his thoughtless action, Hal had another reason to side with the Poitivin rebels. God knows what gleeful stirring Geoffrey was causing. He was well practised since childhood at playing one brother off against the other for his own amusement. Henry confiscated the castle.

I was filled with rage. Henry was creating more dissension between our sons. Hal was frustrated with his brothers. Richard and Geoffrey should be ignoring him, knowing what (and who) was driving him. John, too, was a nuisance, incapable of ruling anything. He lacked maturity from what I had seen of him.

As for Richard, he was given an undeserved responsibility to spite me. Regardless of how well trained he was as a tactician, it was short-sighted. Richard was still too immature to think logically. His one success had gone to his head. Uncle Ralph was getting too old to be forced into the difficult position of trying to council Richard. I crushed the missive. It bounced across the rug and into the door. My quills resembled feathers a dray had run over.

***

While I was storming around Winchester tearing my hair out, Henry arrived unannounced. I kept out of his sight. I could not trust myself to behave in a civilised manner. Then he charged into my bed chamber, bellowing, 'Eleanor, you are bloody well impossible! Why are you avoiding me, for God's sake?'

'Because you are wrenching doors off their hinges and snarling for a start,' I yelled back.

'What do you expect considering the way you treat me?'

I was dumbfounded. 'Now that is novel, Henry. I am the one who is mistreated, by your tyrannical behaviour. If you expect me to speak to you, stop acting like a bloody barbarian.' I was breathing fire.

'Why do you look so beautiful when you are angry?'

'Jesus, Mary, and Joseph! Will you ever damn well stop patronising me?'

'Eleanor please! I hurt…'

Though I felt like slapping him, I managed to contain my wrath — just. To be honest, he looked grey with pain.

'Wait here. I will send for Brynn's unguent.' I paused at the door. 'And for God's sake, Henry, stop pacing like a bear. Lie down and rest your hip.'

When I returned from instructing the page, to my surprise Henry knelt, with some effort, and buried his head in my waist, 'Please… please, calm your temper. I just want to be with you.'

His voice caught — almost a sob. God's Teeth, what was I meant to do? I had difficulty controlling my emotions. I was full of sadness. I wished I could go back to the time before John was born. I stood stiffly as his arms tightened around my waist. Feelings buried deep were surfacing. I stared down at Henry's unkempt curls, grey, each one. He needed his barber.

'Then free me.'

'I want you.'

His sorrowful expression was too much. I should have shoved him away except… except I was as lonely as he was. My yearning to have a man's arms about me took over from common sense. I knew Henry would not have been celibate during my incarceration, so why should I… He staggered up. I think if

I had pushed him away, he would have fallen over. Instead, I let him kiss me. His lips lingered on mine. His familiar smell of manhood and horse along with his scratchy beard were so familiar. Was there a corner in the depths of my being that still loved him—maybe. I knew he would not set me free any more than I would promise to obey him.

I gave in to desire, mine as strong as Henry's. It always had been. Then out of the blue he muttered as I lay across his body, 'Your affair with my father...'

I rolled off him onto my back. 'Oh, for God's sake, Henry, let Geoffrey rest in peace This is hardly the time...'

'William,' he whispered. 'What about William?'

'What about... what about William, Henry?'

He leant on his elbow and stared into my eyes, his face registering a thousand expressions, blurting, 'Was he...Was he, my brother?'

I took a deep breath, silently cursing my explosive confession at Chinon, which more than likely provoked Henry, along with everything else, to lock me up.

'No, Henry. Unless William was some sort of miracle. Had I conceived a child with your father, the birth would have taken place long before I met you.'

Henry swiped at a tear. He looked odd, as if he were about to either sob or cheer with relief.

'My affair with your father had ended long before we met. In fact, you were the reason he and I had fallen out. After I told him my divorce from Louis had been approved, Geoffrey insisted I remarry for my safety. Then he put you forward.'

Henry sniffed. 'You jest.'

'No. I was insulted. I felt I was being passed on like a tavern strumpet. We had a blazing row. I threw him out.'

'How do I know this is the truth?'

'God's Teeth, Henry! Why would I make it up? I did not see him again until months later when he acted as one of my escorts from Île de France because he was concerned for my safety. Before Orleans, I made it clear again that he was no longer welcome in my company. That was more than six months before your arrival at L'Ombrière... The next time I saw your father he was dying. Distressing for both of us... that is, you and me.'

He wiped his nose on his arm but said no more. He slumped back staring at the canopy above us.

'By the way, Louis has died. Phillip Augustus is now King of France, a quite different personality from your naïve monk. Far more cunning and manipulative.'

I was shocked, saddened no, but I did grieve for Marie, Alix, Margaret and Alais. I doubt they would have known their father that well, but Louis was their Papa, Phillip's, too. I asked Henry if I could send condolences to Margaret. He agreed. As for my French daughters…

After those few blissful hours, Henry was gone, and I was left with torn feelings and memories. One husband I had loved passionately, the other I loathed. I pushed the memories of Marie and Alix away. The echo of their newborn cries haunted me to this day… I then sent for Joachim to inform him about the new King of France.

***

Henry had left England to travel to Le Mans for the Christmas Court when I received a letter from Richard. He was fuming that his father wanted him to pay homage to Hal. This was another of Henry's crazy schemes to preserve his Plantagenet empire after his death. Geoffrey agreed, but then Brittany had always honoured Normandy. Richard refused, and rightly so, believing there was no need for this formality between brothers whilst their parents were still alive. Although it irritated me that Richard paid homage to the new French king, he was following protocol by showing respect for the new monarch. The kings of France were the Aquitaine's overlords, as galling as it was.

Another letter from Uncle Ralph arrived. He said that Henry, Richard and his brothers had a mighty disagreement, with Richard storming out. What was new! He also informed me that Geoffrey and Hal were supposed to hold talks with the Poitivin rebels, but instead they had joined a fracas of disgruntled Limousin nobles. I asked myself why my boys were behaving like rabbled idiots. They were galloping from disaster to disaster, much of their own making. To read they had raided religious shrines and monasteries reduced me to despair. But the intelligence I received was so old I needed confirmation.

Robert was visiting so I asked, 'What is happening? Every snippet of information I receive from Uncle Ralph I dread to read.' I showed him my last letter.

'Yes, it happened, I am afraid. Henry was forced to intervene when Richard looked like being defeated.'

'I suppose that is something of a consolation, Robert. Henry said young King Phillip Augustus is cunning.'

'Yes. He is forcing the Plantagenets onto the defensive. Nevertheless, because Hal is his brother-in-law, he aided him as did Raymond of Toulouse.'

'I know not what to make of that. I thought I had quashed that alliance before Henry imprisoned me.'

'It is all a bit messy I am afraid, Milady. Lord Henry denied Hal adequate funds so he could not pay his forces. Hal then sacked two religious bodies, Saint-Martial at Limousin and Rocamadour and its beautiful shrines, to support his troops.'

'Oh, Robert, no! What next?'

Chapter 14 Grief and a Joyous Reunion

I was back at Salisbury Castle. I was attempting to make sense of a dream—or was it a nightmare I had? I awoke suddenly, my heart pounding and in a sweat. The change maybe? I could not get back to sleep. Unlike most dreams, I could remember it vividly. Hal came to me in a vision wearing two crowns, one atop the other. The lower was as dull as lead. The one above was a golden halo gleaming as if hit by a beam of sunlight. Hal seemed ethereal, as if outside our sphere. He seemed happy but had a single tear rolling down his cheek. He was saying something I could not hear with his hand outstretched. I remembered trying to reach his hand, but he floated away in a vapour. I awoke sitting bolt upright, fighting tears.

I thought Joachim might be able to interpret my dream. I had this dread clawing my innards and I feared what was to come. Joachim thought it was just a dream. He smiled in that saintly way of his and said he was a monk, not a wizard. A jest? Except I did not see it that way.

Then the Merlin prophesy appeared on my desk. *The eagle of the third covenant shall rejoice in her third nesting.* I had not seen it in ages. Logic told me it was not that strange. It was amongst my belongings, and as I was always scratching around searching for parchment, I had probably brought it to light. But it unnerved me. Nor could I get that dream out of my head.

***

I sat alone in my quarters strumming Richard's old lute. I was not good company, and the thought of Agnes, Frith, Amaris and Brynn all gossiping around the loom or embroidering was too much for me to bear. I did not want to sour their happy labour. Melancholy had me softly singing Abraham's beautiful love song when I heard hooves echoing in the bailey below. My curiosity sent me into the gallery where I nearly fell over a page who summoned me to attend Archdeacon Thomas Earley of Wells. He had arrived with a party of nobles and clerics. I instructed the page to make them comfortable in my small audience chamber, and to have refreshments brought to them. I said I would be there directly.

Amaris and the others appeared in a flap. I needed to be more regally attired. I told Amaris not to fuss, but she was not going to lower her standards as to how I should appear. I opted to don the first gown she presented, a dark indigo brocade.

I apologised for keeping Archdeacon Thomas and his entourage waiting. I asked what had brought them from Normandy to England. By their demeanour, I knew something was amiss. My eyes flew from one to the other. A talon gripped me like an eagle gripped a hare.

'Milady, it is with deepest regret we bring sad tidings from Lord King Henry.'

Amaris was at my side with Joachim. I knew without Thomas of Earley uttering another word that it was Hal. My knees sagged and a reverberating 'NO!' howled from my throat. They assisted me to a chair where I was fanned. Someone gave me sips of brandy wine.

The Archdeacon's gentle words did nothing to console my anguish. My dream was not a hallucination. It was my dying son reaching out to his mother who could not save him. Like stones rattling in an empty barrel, their words of consolation bounced round my head.

Archdeacon Thomas produced a scrolled missive. I recognised Henry's seal. I shook my head. I did not want to read its contents. Joachim was doing his best to calm me. But I needed Henry. Why did he not come instead of sending a messenger? Maybe he was too grief-stricken to travel, perhaps his bad hip hindered him—or guilt?

***

Everyone was kind and sympathetic. Those who knew Hal within my little court were also bereft. He was much loved with his easy-going generous personality. Only his father goaded him to behave in ways not akin to his nature, and, latterly, it was Richard and Geoffrey, who should have known better. I cursed

Henry for locking me away; preventing me from guiding them as I did when they were young boys. My hands shook as I ripped through his seal.

Henry's epistle poured out his own anguish, and a mountain of guilt. Poor darling Hal knew he was dying. Henry said he could have drunk fouled water that produced a choler as described by Hippocrates. This was what caused my Papa's death in 1137.

Hal lived long enough, five days I was told, to make provisions for Margaret, and begged Henry to show me mercy. He made peace with enemies and provided restitution for the religious institutions he had plundered. He was buried in Rouen Cathedral with his Norman ancestors.

When I was strong enough to speak with the Archdeacon, I told him of my haunting dream, and how I had tried to interpret what it meant.

"What significance can be given to that upper crown if it is not eternal bliss that has neither beginning nor end? What is the significance of such an intense radiance, if not happiness on high?"

I tried to give myself comfort with words from the scriptures, attempted to understand God's will, knowing Hal was, deep down, a good person. *But why, God, why?* Through prayer, I endeavoured to accept my beloved boy's holy fate. But what tore through my head was anything but holy. Twenty-seven years ago, I gave birth to him. I could not accept he had gone and was in God's care and was far happier than within his father's earthly kingdom. My usual doubts were rampant. Hal should never have been barred from me. My anger tore prayer and common sense to shreds.

I needed to calm myself because I had to write to Margaret. What would her fate be, I wondered? Would she now, like all women of our status, become a pawn in a larger game, beholden to her half-brother? Phillip sounded like he could cause trouble.

Henry, I must reply to, then write to Hal's brothers and sisters.

I harangued poor Joachim with 'Why? Why is my life afflicted by God's wrath? Surely on this earth I have been punished enough. I am tormented by Henry and now God has taken my Hal.'

'Milady, I have not the answers you desire. I wish I did, but like you I am a mere mortal. But I know your son was a good person and he will be welcomed into God's Kingdom with God's love. Now let us pray for the Young King's immortal soul.'

I knelt and wept.

***

As I expected, Margaret became the next pawn to be sacrificed. Henry was not going to let Phillip get a toe in England through the dower-lands afforded to Margaret on her marriage to Hal. Instead, Henry gave them to me. That was curious, seeing he had robbed me of all my English estates since my incarceration. At least Hal's wish that Henry treat me with more respect had been honoured. I already had increased liberty within the English kingdom, and now I could travel to Normandy. But I was reminded I would still be heavily guarded. What was Henry worried about; that I would bolt to the Aquitaine, or worse, Île de France. That must terrify him, considering that my loathing was for Louis, not his son.

The Vexin was a problem. Margaret's dowry was a buffer between Normandy and France. It was now questionable. I heard from Robert that Phillip wanted it back, and, equally, Henry was determined not to return it. After much arguing, Henry retained it—quite a victory.

Not that everything was running smoothly. The stumbling block was Richard's betrothal to Margaret's sister, Alais. Phillip was demanding they wed. Richard was showing no desire to do so. I had no idea why he was reluctant. It was rumoured he had an illegitimate child. Was there a girl out there to whom he had pledged love? I knew not what to believe. Robert knew naught and I had not set eyes on Henry since Winchester, his last trip to England.

***

A letter arrived from Matilda that cheered me from my misery. She and her family were coming to England. There was rebellion in Saxony. Matilda's husband was in a dispute with the Holy Roman Emperor, Frederick. They were forced to flee their

163

home. Matilda was distraught because they were compelled to leave their third son behind as a hostage. They had arrived in Normandy with the rest of their children and were coming to Winchester. From there they would move to Windsor. Most importantly, I could be with them. I hoped I could be of some comfort to her without her little one.

Hal's death would be difficult for Matilda. She was close to her brother, deeply fond of him. Richard was always trying to interfere in their games and was jealous of their bond even after Geoffrey came along. But he was a thorn in all their sides being Monsieur Sabots Intelligents. We will have many memories to recall in our sadness.

Chapter 15 Matilda, Queen of Saxony

Matilda and her family were delayed. I was unaware she was close to giving birth. Henry allowed me to travel to Winchester to await them. I had refurnished much of the interior of the palace when I was briefly reunited with Henry years ago before my arrest. Henry completed the guest wing. The quarters, though, where I had met with the family last, felt desolate, echoing with the ghost of Hal's last visit.

For Matilda's sake, I pulled myself out of my melancholy. With my new allocation of moneys, I could at least get rid of the cobwebs. Every inch of the palace needed a good airing and cleaning. I assembled an army of churls to haul out rugs and tapestries to be beaten, and had the fireplaces cleaned, and chimneys swept. There was a flurry of activity so all would be in readiness when Matilda and her family arrived. Henry was to accompany them.

Day by day I became more impatient awaiting the sound of horses and carriages. I found myself scanning the horizon for tell-tale signs of dust, or a courier heralding that Matilda and family were nigh.

I was reading to calm my impatience when I was approached by a shy churl, Elric. He requested I accompany him to an attic room in a far wing where our retainers were housed. Joachim was with me, so together we followed this eager man scuttling along on busy legs. I would never have known this room existed without our guide. He unlocked a door and threw it wide with a flourish. I gave a gasp of joy. There in front of me was an array of cradles, cots, rocking horses and baby carriages. In a wooden box were Hal's and Richard's old carved soldiers with other long-forgotten toys like felt dolls and leather balls. It was as if the pope's jewels had been strewn before me. Elric explained they had been there for years, but it was not until my clean-up that they had been re-discovered. This dear man thought the contents of the room could be useful for Lady Matilda, whom all the palace retainers remembered from when she was a little girl.

I asked Elric to supervise reinstating the old nursery. Soon it looked so familiar it was as if my little children had never grown up and left. The only things I could not bear to re-use were the toys that had belonged to Hal. They were left as they were. Richard's soldiers were given another coat of paint, as were rocking horses, which my children had spent hours riding. Amaris, Agnes and Frith made new clothes for the dolls. I spent hours standing at the threshold inundated with memories, re-hearing the shouts and laughter from my growing children, no Joanna or John though. This was before they were born, when my marriage was full of love...

***

I was reminiscing in the nursery two days later when a page came to tell me that a vast cavalcade was approaching from the south. I flew down the gallery to the palace entrance as if my feet had grown wings. I was surprised Matilda was not on horseback, panicking she had not arrived from Barfleur. My fears were allayed as she stepped from the leading carriage.

'Maman, Maman!'

We flew into each other's arms.

'Darling, Let me look at you.' She stepped back. 'Matilda, it has been fourteen years. How grown up you look.'

'And you are as beautiful as I remember.'

We babbled in a mixture of Langue d'Oc and Latin till a light cough interrupted us. We were surrounded by children and nurses, as well as Henry the Lion of Saxony, Henry Plantagenet and, of course, their entourages. The fanfare that welcomed the regal family from Saxony was smothered by the maternal love of our reunion. We made our way inside, Matilda and I with our arms around each other's waists. Everyone else trailed along behind.

My priority was to have Matilda comfortably established in her quarters with her family. I then reluctantly left them to attend to myself. Also, I had not acknowledged Henry. He appeared in my chamber. But I was so happy I did not believe he could say or do anything to prick my joy.

I smiled. 'Thank you, Henry, for allowing me to enjoy our daughter's arrival and for honouring Hal's wishes to give me more freedom.'

His face clouded when I mentioned Hal. I could see Henry was deeply afflicted, and I hoped it was with remorse. I went to the chest by the window where a flask and goblets were laid out and poured wine.

'Thank you, a votre santé.'

We sat by the fire. My eyes raked over his time-ravished face. I wondered how he saw me since our last encounter. Because I had rushed to meet Matilda, I was dressed in a simple gown and tabard, hardly glamourous.

Our conversation was little more than small talk.

'How was your crossing from Barfleur?'

'The winds were in the right direction. Not too rough.'

'And your ride from Portsmouth?' I asked.

Henry grunted. I presumed—painful.

'How is your hip?'

He shrugged. 'About the same.'

We had yet to mention Hal. Henry rose and took our goblets to refill them.

'You are still limping. Do you have any of Brynn's unguent left?'

'It ran out.'

'I will get you some more.'

'Thank you.'

Henry sat with a heavy sigh.

'Eleanor, I ask myself, why not me? Why Hal?'

I wanted to yell 'hypocrite', but I let him continue.

'I have not felt so bad since William.'

His sincerity calmed me. Harsh words were not going to bring my darling boy back.

'Henry, I had a premonition, a dream. When Archdeacon Thomas Earley arrived, I knew.' I described it and cried, 'If only I could have grasped his outstretched hand, I believe I would have saved him.'

'You are not God, Eleanor.'

'No. Just Hal's maman.' Henry had no answer for that. We sat staring at the dancing flames in the fireplace, each in our own world. I broke the mood.

'It is such a joy to see Matilda and her family. She looks such a young lady now.'

'Indeed.' Henry continued. 'But I thought she looked a little tired.'

I smiled. 'Probably from the trip with all those little children. I can empathise.'

Henry nodded. 'The situation in Saxony is concerning, but Heinrich believes it will eventually be solved.'

'Heinrich. Well, that gets us around one of the three Henrys.'

Henry followed my train of thought.

'The little fellow they call Harry.'

'Ah! So, we have Heinrich and Harry of Saxony and you. How do you feel about being a grandparent?'

Henry grinned, his eyes twinkling. 'And you?'

'I know not,' I shrugged, 'It reminds me of my age, that I am no longer… desirable.'

Henry turned; his eyes bored into me. I was conscious I was not regally robed. No kohl or rouge enhanced my looks and my uncovered hair in a thick single plait fell over my left shoulder. I needed to change to become the queen I was supposed to be.

'I need to dress more appropriately.'

Henry put his hand on my arm. I stiffened.

'Eleanor, I like the way you look. I envy the freshness of your face and demeanour. A little older, yes, but glowing. You look ageless. You could put on a bit of weight, though.'

'I am not sure whether to be flattered or no. But I do need to change if you do not mind attending your own quarters. I will send for some of Brynn's balm.'

'I am too comfortable to move.'

I was not about to argue, so I left for my wardrobe where I could dress just as easily.

Amaris and I chatted. 'You and Lord Henry seem to be getting along … not yelling at each other.'

'Henry appears to have mellowed—at least for now.'

In the wardrobe closet, there were chests of gowns, some unworn for years. I had welcomed my daughter dressed more like a nun. Agnes and Frith were hopping from one foot to the other. They had taken to their role of dressing the doll with delight, regardless that the doll was aging. When Amaris carefully unfolded a gown of samite, its heavily embossed glory dripping with pearls, the little girls begged me to wear it.

'Pleeeease! Milady,' they chorused, looking like large-eyed spaniels.

'Agnes and Frith, not tonight, it is a family dinner, not a state banquet. I promise I will wear it on a more formal occasion. Oh, do not look like that, let us find something less burdensome. How about my favourite dark velvet?'

Amaris smiled, giving me a knowing look. Agnes and Frith gave in.

'All right, Milady.'

At least the red and gold-lined sleeves gave the little girls something to admire.

I organised a simple family welcome early enough to involve our grandchildren. I decided my chambers would be more suitable than the Great Hall. But before we gathered, I wanted a few moments alone with Matilda and her little ones. I arrived at the nursery door wondering how she found her old playground with its resurrected furniture and toys. Squeals of joy and fun greeted me. I paused to listen, letting memories swirl. When I entered, they all stopped and stared. Matilda had to extract herself. I was scrutinised by large penetrating eyes. Four thumbs popped into mouths like corks in jars. I smiled at the familiar gestures. But something was missing; there was no baby. I said naught as Matilda shepherded reluctant feet towards me. Did I look too grand and therefore terrified them?

I asked Matilda, 'In what language do I address them? I have no German.'

'They understand English and Langue d'Oc, Maman. And of course, Latin.'

One little boy was braver than the others. 'I am Otto.'

'I am pleased to meet you. I am your grandmaman.'

'Of course,' he replied.

'Dear God, Matilda, he looks so like Geoffrey.'

Matilda nodded. 'Behaves like him, too, I am afraid.'

The others soon realised I did not bite as Matilda coaxed them forward. Their shyness evaporated, and they returned to their games, ignoring the English queen in their midst. Matilda and I now had time to gossip and catch up. She had not mentioned the absent baby.

'Is the baby asleep?'

'He is dead, Maman. He did survive but an hour.' Matilda's voice was flat.

I enveloped her in my arms. Matilda changed the subject. She suggested we walk to the gardens before we gathered to dine.

We sat on a well-worn bench holding hands, Queens of England and Saxony. Although we sat in silence the noise in my head was cacophonous. But I could not contain my pent-up grief for Matilda's closest brother. I told her of my vision and how I knew Hal was no more even before the archdeacon uttered the fateful words.

'I find myself berating God for punishing me again as He did after William was taken.'

Matilda stared at me in disbelief as though I was a little crazy.

'Matilda, I have prayed till my knees have grown callouses. I have begged God to forgive my sins. I confess to Joachim daily; I have done penance and distributed alms to help the less fortunate. Why does God hate me so much? Am I Eve, the temptress?'

'Maman, you are not Eve, no matter how beautiful you are. I believe because you are so clever you think beyond what most accept. You always have. You play life and God out in your head like a game of chess, trying to use your superior intellect to win. Maman, I do not think you can checkmate God.'

How did my daughter get to be so wise? If her words had not been not so profound, I would have laughed. The thought of playing chess with God was quite amusing. But Matilda's loss was too sad for jesting.

'Darling, I am so sorry about your baby. I can empathise. You would have been too young to remember baby Phillip, who arrived too soon and died shortly after his birth.'

I omitted the screaming argument I had with Henry when I shook off his grasp and fell down a flight of stairs.

'Oh, Maman, I had no idea...' Matilda took a deep breath. 'It was a difficult pregnancy. The turmoil within Saxony did not help... having to leave little Johan behind as a hostage. I was worried, not eating properly and unwell. The baby, too, was born early...can we change the subject?'

We reminisced. Soon we were laughing about Geoffrey.

'Otto is so like him, Maman. He is smarter than his years, loves games that stimulate him, drives his sister and older brothers crazy and, I might add, his parents. I guarantee Otto and you will be of one mind.'

'No caterpillars, I hope.'

We laughed, then Matilda frowned. 'Maman, what has got into Papa? How are you managing?'

'I have good days and bad. The first three years of my imprisonment were the worst... best forgotten. But my life has improved. I have more freedom within the walls of wherever your father decrees I live.'

'I cannot believe he can be so cruel. Lenore, Joanna and the boys write, except John, I am afraid. Their discourses are disturbing. Also, the way my brothers are behaving is deplorable, Maman. Without you, they have no structure or purpose in their lives. Cannot Papa see that? You would never allow them to behave so badly or foolishly.'

I shook my head and changed the subject.

'Did you know King Louis had died?'

'Yes. I have met Phillip Capet. He is smart, but calculating and devious.'

'That is concerning. I thought relationships with Île de France might improve.'

'I doubt it.' We sat in silence. Matilda broke it. 'I pray constantly you and Papa can be reconciled, that you will forgive him, difficult I know. It tears me apart.'

In the folds of my gown, my hand ached in the late afternoon air. I suggested we return indoors. As we parted for our quarters, Matilda called after me.

'Maman.'

I stopped and turned to her.

'When Heinrich and I arrived in Rouen, I did not recognise Papa. I wondered who the old man was till he spoke. You have hardly changed. This morning when you ran to me, I saw what I thought was a young novice till you threw yourself into my arms.'

'You must be losing your sight. Amaris keeps pulling grey hairs out of my head.'

Matilda's face was serious.

'You and Papa must forgive each other, before it is too late.'

I gave her a weak smile, saying naught, then turned towards my quarters. How could I explain. Although Henry and I, when we occasionally met, were not arguing so heatedly, I could not foresee healing the past. The most I could consider would be a truce between warring parties.

***

It was a delightful reunion. It would have been wonderful if her brothers could have been with us, but that would have been like putting the Saracens and Christian Crusaders in the same room. Music was played, games as well. Matilda's children crawled and played at our feet. Little Otto decided I was his favourite grandmaman. He insisted on climbing onto my lap. He babbled away about his pony, how he came on a big ship and how naughty Emperor Frederick had stolen his brother. After a while, with thumb getting a good suck, he fell asleep in my arms. How reminiscent of my own children this felt. I stroked his silky hair, feeling almost teary. Henry was looking at me oddly. Was it envy or nostalgia? By now I was feeling like Otto. I handed the sleeping boy to his nurse, then bade them goodnight.

In my bedchamber, Amaris and I reminisced about my little children. My pillow was dampened. I mourned William and Hal and remembered the perfectly formed little mite, who lived but an hour. I questioned why Hal drank bad water and how had William been bitten by a flea or lice to give him typhus when I was so particular? Guilt reared for baby Phillip... had I not argued with Henry and pulled from his grip...

***

Amaris told me I had impressed Heinrich, who admitted he was terrified of me when we met in Rouen before he and Matilda left for Saxony. My reputation for being able to outsmart most men, and how I could handle myself as well as any knight in an ambush, was legendary. I was agog that the horror of that day had turned me into some sort of Boadicea. Heinrich said the troubadours sang not just of my beauty, but about the Amazon who led a crusade, and almost single-handedly dispatched an army of mercenaries and roustiers.

Later, I said to Amaris, 'I think Heinrich must have drunk too much brandy wine. I must take him to one side and persuade him I am not the woman of his imagination. What Henry Plantagenet makes of this mythical character; heaven knows. Perhaps Amaris, that is why he locked me up.'

'I do not think that is funny, Milady.'

'Neither do I, but the legend is so outrageous, it is laughable.'

***

I was returning to my quarters from playing with my grandchildren when I met Sir Robert.

'Ah Robert. You appear to be at a loose end.'

'Yes, Milady. Lady Matilda had something to discuss with his Lordship and I was ordered to make myself scarce. What I did glean as I shut the door though, was that it had something to do with "making peace" with you.'

'Indeed. That would have been an interesting conversation. I might need to do some detective work.'

Robert laughed and went on his way. I returned to Matilda's chambers. When I entered, I found her in a chair, head in hands. I could see she had been crying.

'Matilda, my darling, what is wrong?'

Matilda shook her head.

'Sir Robert told me you were speaking to your father. Has he upset you? If so, he will have me to deal with, even if he sends me back to Salisbury.'

'It is nothing, Maman. I am just a little frustrated...'

'Well?'

'Our conversation was private. I think you should mind your own business.'

'If he has hurt you in some way, it is my business.'

Matilda's obdurate expression ended my questioning. Matilda knew me too well. She would never add to my arsenal to attack Henry.

'Well, if that is all the thanks I get for my concerns, I will leave.' I stomped to the door.

'Honestly, Maman, you and Papa are as bad as each other!'

'Humph!'

True, except I lacked Henry's physical dominance. My tongue was my only weapon. I had forgotten what my stiletto looked like. These days I had to tear seals from parchment with my teeth, still strong and white, the Lord be praised.

***

I decided to keep to myself, but little Otto's nurse brought him to visit me in the library where I was reading. They found me curled up in a sunny corner deep in Virgil's The Eclogues and Georgics. I was deeply engrossed in the bucolic life and love of the Eclogues but was happy to put it to one side for Otto. He crawled onto my lap, wanting me to read it to him. Well, it tested his Latin, but he seemed not to care. He happily sucked his thumb listening to me. I bored his nurse, who nodded off in the sun. His eyes, too, began to droop, so I sang to him till he fell asleep. I managed to carry on reading with the child's head snuggled against my breast when I was disturbed by Henry. I hushed him not to wake Otto. He found another chair but roused the nurse who was embarrassed she had allowed the child to fall asleep in my arms.

The sudden activity woke Otto. Now grumpy, he did not want to leave grandmaman. I kissed his downy curls and told him he sounded like Grandfather Henry, who told Otto I exaggerated. Henry perused what I was reading.

'Very bucolic, my dear. Not your usual methinks.'

'What do you want Henry?'

'To let you know we will be travelling on to London in the following week.'

'I will miss your sunny disposition.'

'No, you will have to put up with me a little longer. I want you to attend me.'

'How novel.'

'But not looking like a nun. I am sure you have gowns more suitable to your station.'

'As you wish. But I have become used to a simpler life. Who do you want me to impress?'

'Myself, as my queen, if you can be bothered.'

I replaced the book on the shelf and said, 'Henry I am short-staffed. It will take Amaris longer than usual to ready me with the necessities for my role as Queen of England. If I had Celeste, Marion and Clotilde life would be easier. Agnes and Frith work hard, but they are young and have had no experience of what it takes to put my belongings together. If you want me to travel as before, instead of with the restrictions you have generously forced on me, I need more attendants.'

He glowered at my sarcasm.

'I am sure, Eleanor, if you put your superior intellect to it, you will manage.'

But I knew this was going to be an added burden for Amaris who, over the years of my incarceration, had been driven to exhaustion. Not once had she complained. As well as tending to my needs practically alone she had become nurse, physician and a shoulder to cry on. She, Joachim and Brynn had pulled me back from the brink of despair. Henry would never comprehend. Nor would I tell him Amaris was the reason I was alive, along with Robert and young Tom.

'Your generosity, as usual, Henry, is staggering. Now, you must excuse me so I can look suitably regal for tonight's banquet.'

Frith and Agnes were as excited as a kettle of frogs. I stood as patiently as my short temper allowed. Having my breasts bound to enhance them seemed a pointless exercise these days. Just who did they think I was going to impress? A chemise of silk and lace was followed by the under gown. Then I was trussed like a Christmas goose into the samite with its shimmering pearls and other gems. But whether it was Henry's edicts or the weight of the gown, my patience was exhausted. I managed to reduce Frith to tears when she caught my twisted little finger in the ornate sleeve. That brought a scolding from Amaris, who was close to dropping. I apologised though, and said that through no fault of her own, Frith had hurt me.

Finally, I was dressed, girdled and decorated in so much jewellery I could have been ransomed for that alone. Amaris was so tired she was shaking; Frith was still sniffing. Dextrous little Agnes offered to apply the kohl and rouge. Just looking at the crowns was enough to make my head throb. I chose the lighter circlet of the Aquitaine, spitefully knowing it would infuriate

Henry. A splash of my, and Henry's, favourite perfume finished the ritual. The bells rang out the hours during the process. All I wanted was my bed as the brigade of pages swooped on the train. But the drama was not fully over. I arrived at the door of the Great Hall (without murdering a page) to be confronted by Henry pacing and looking like a winter's day.

'You took your time.'

'Only to look beautiful for you, my dearest Henry.'

'God's Teeth, Eleanor, this is not the bloody Aquitaine. There are times you try a man's patience. That crown is not suitable for this occasion.'

'If you do not like it, I will return to my chamber, or you can escort Matilda and I will enter on Heinrich's arm.'

'As Queen of England, you will enter with me regardless of your inappropriate choice.'

Matilda by now had had enough and raised her voice. 'Maman and Papa, will you stop! For once keep civil tongues in your heads! If not, it will be me who will be leaving.'

A frosty silence ensued. The doors opened and we had to scramble to start the long promenade to our thrones as fanfares announced our arrival. I slapped my right hand down on Henry's arm, silly because all I did was jar it.

Everyone in the Great Hall was agog at my presence, knowing Henry and I were now husband and wife in name only. Many, I was sure, were surprised I still existed. By the time I was seated, or should I say arranged, I was boiling. Matilda sensed my humour. She glared at me from Henry's left. I turned my head away with as much hauteur as I could muster. Henry had dropped into his 'charming' Plantagenet role, conversing easily with Archbishop Baldwin of Canterbury to whom I was introduced for the first time. The banquet was like the saga of the Greek marathon. It went on and on. But I got through the evening and managed to impress the archbishop.

***

Henry found wives and daughters of some of his nobles to help Amaris ready me for London. I was sure they were instructed to report back to him. It took days for the gowns to be packed and those needing repair attended to, usually by clever little Agnes. But, regardless of the flurry of activity, the time for me to leave was galloping apace. My belongings were not going to be ready for Henry's departure.

'Henry, I cannot leave with you. There is too much to organise,' I said through gritted teeth.

'Eleanor, you will travel with me and my entourage.'

'That is impossible,' I retaliated, 'My wardrobe is nowhere near packed, and I will not leave without it.'

I stormed off, hissing, 'Frankly, I would prefer to return to Salisbury than be your pawn.'

'I am trying to honour Hal's wishes. At least, your Ladyship, you could try to comply.'

My anger was deflated. I wanted to enjoy my new freedoms, too, but at the back of my mind, I was sure Henry had an ulterior motive. He would just as likely have ignored Hal's deathbed wishes if it suited him, and I wondered what was really going on in his head. Neither of us had brought up Richard's succession. As he was now Henry's heir as well as mine, it must be gnawing at him. The son he had never seen eye to eye with would one day rule his empire.

Robert as usual was my only source of reliable information, so I asked him, 'Do you know what is really behind Henry's softening of my internment, because I do not believe it is totally due to Hal's wishes.'

'No, Milady. I am sorry. However, I do know there are disagreements between the princes, exactly about what I am not sure as yet. But you can guarantee the cunning new French King, Phillip Capet, will be fuelling the dissent.'

'Oh, Robert, that is disturbing. And I cannot do a damn thing! I am sure there is something going on. Can you send a letter to Richard for me?'

'Of course.'

'Thank you, yet again. Richard, at least, will reply. Geoffrey is hopeless, and John and I do not communicate.'

'It will be a pleasure. Do not despair; it could turn out to be nothing.'

I gave Robert a weak smile. I could but wish...

As discreetly as possible I excused myself early from the family gathering. I penned a hasty note to Richard and gave it to Robert. By now I was almost ready for London. Henry and I compromised. Some of my retinue would follow when my wardrobe was finally packed so I could travel with him.

He condescended to allow me to choose a horse more suitable to my status. It was one of Rebel's foals. She and Henry's old stallion had had a liaison. The mare was a beautiful, dappled grey; a cross between hispano and destrier. She was a little heavier than the hispano breed but had the characteristics of arched neck and prancing motion. Henry named her Penthicilea, with a twinkle in his eye, after the Queen of the Amazons. I had to smile despite myself.

Chapter 16 Amaris

The Palace of Westminster brought back too many memories. Hal's birth across the river at Bermondsey was one. I buried myself in the library. Henry said naught about my writing. He probably knew it would be fruitless trying to stop me. But it was going to be difficult to smuggle missives to Richard under his nose and receiving replies more so. Vigilance would be more than necessary.

I was disturbed in my musing by little Agnes, red-faced and babbling, 'I get mightily lost in this big palace. Milady, can you come quick?'

She raced ahead. I followed as swiftly as I could. In my quarters, Brynn was bathing Amaris's forehead with lavender water. She looked flushed, her breathing laboured.

'Lady Amaris fainted.' Agnes puffed.

I rushed to her side and placed my hand on her forehead.

'Darling Amaris… dear God, you are burning. Has someone called for Matthias?'

'Yes,' Brynn answered, 'Brother Joachim sent Tom to his chambers.'

I stood next to the bed gripping Amaris' hand and feeling useless.

'Stop fussing, I am…' Amaris' words ended in a fit of coughing.

'Oh, God,' I cried, 'What is wrong, Brynn?'

'Amaris developed an ague on the way to London; that cough has developed into a fever.'

'Please, Milady,' she said as she dashed to the door, 'can you keep bathing her forehead while I hasten to the herb garden? I will concoct a linctus to ease the symptoms. We need to prevent pneumonia.'

As I took the cloth, Matilda appeared, followed by Matthias and Tom. Joachim was quietly praying. The bed chamber was becoming crowded. We stood back while Matthias examined Amaris.

'Can I have more pillows, please, to prop Lady Amaris up to aid her breathing?' said Matthias. 'Her fever is too high for comfort. Milady, it would be better if you and Lady Matilda left. I do not want either of you catching her ague.'

'Matilda, go!' I commanded. 'You need to consider your new condition, but I am not going anywhere.'

Matthias rolled his eyes but said naught. I continued to bathe Amaris' forehead till Brynn reappeared with a liquor of liquorice, comfrey and horehound to ease the congestion. Gently she spooned the mixture into Amaris' mouth. At first, it made her gag and cough so badly I was sure she would die.

I was on my knees praying.

I grabbed Joachim's hand, gabbling, 'Joachim please, I beg you. Intervene with God. Please do not let my darling Amaris die. God hates me so much, He will ignore my pleas, but not yours.'

I clung to Joachim, my head buried in his robe, almost pulling him over as I rocked back and forth on my knees wailing.

'Lady Eleanor, I suggest you leave,' Matthias pleaded. 'You are upsetting the patient.'

Joachim said, 'Come, Milady, let us go to the chapel.'

'Nooo! Joachim, I cannot leave.'

He dealt with my panic as well as a gentle monk could, lifting me to my feet.

Henry arrived and was confronted by my hysteria. A sharp slap from him did nothing for my disposition. I hit him back. Pandemonium! Between Henry and Joachim, I was marched to Henry's chamber, protesting in fruity Langue d'Oc. He poured brandy wine down my throat, several goblets, I think, until I fell asleep on his bed.

I woke with a hangover beating a tabor in my head. Henry's grin did not help.

'Eleanor, you are a hopeless nursemaid, but you will be pleased to know Amaris is a little better. When you sober up, you can visit her.'

'Oh, God, my head!' I moaned, 'Henry, my mouth is full of sawdust.'

Henry called a page to bring me a tisane then went back to his reading. There was a pile of letters on his table by the window. My curiosity almost got the better of me till I tried to stand. The room did several revolutions of my head. I lay down again.

'Henry…dear God. How much wine did you give me?'

'Enough to shut you up. You were giving God a hounding. What is more, Joachim thought you were going to seduce him.'

'You are jesting?'

'No, the poor chap is prostrate in the chapel.'

A pause brought home that I was being teased. I threw a pillow at Henry. His sniggering was too much, so sore head or no I went to Amaris. She had improved but needed rest. Her breathing was easier and her fever not as severe. Brynn saw me approach, sensing she could soon have two patients.

'Milady, I beg you to sit. You look terrible. If you feel like vomiting, here is a bowl. Do not move. I need to concentrate on Amaris.'

'God's Teeth, do I look that bad?'

'Ghastly!' was Brynn's unsympathetic reply.

I fell asleep in my chair.

***

I faced Joachim red-faced with shame. I apologised, but the thought of losing Amaris was unbearable. My lack of control over life and death situations had bubbled to the surface. The old terrors were returning, like when William died and Hal—in fact, all whom I have loved whose deaths have torn me apart.

'What is the point of being intellectually superior if one cannot prevent God's wrath?' I declared.

'Amaris has improved. God has listened, Milady, to your prayers; He always does,' Joachim gently replied.

'Hmmf!'

'When we leave this earth, God, through His love, is helping a soul reach heaven away from its suffering.'

I wondered why Joachim always looked so sweet and ingenuous. For once I did not retaliate. But how could a three-year old innocent child's soul be suffering or a twenty-seven-year-old's, whose life's potential was cut down? Would it always be thus? Would I forever question? Was I really playing chess with God? Why could I not accept His will? My head thudded.

Amaris slowly recovered but was left with a persistent cough.

***

Henry was plotting something. He was in a dark mood, and it was not one of his headaches. I suspected it involved our sons. Robert knew naught but understood my suspicions. Matilda did not make a good spy. Henry would immediately suspect my interference if she started asking questions. Henry dictated that we move to Windsor. We had just arrived in London for God's sake! Once I took moving from castle to palace with Henry as a routine part of my life but now, I found it irritating. Henry might have loosened the chains of my internment, but I was still beholden to his whims.

My new maids were getting to know how meticulous I was. I instructed Amaris to supervise them. The new women could do the hard work of preparing and packing my garments, jewellery and linens for Windsor. I repaired to the library, leaving instructions should I find one item not attended to with the utmost care every chest would be repacked. Amaris gave me a conspiratorial look as I left for the library where Joachim interrupted me.

'Milady, a courier has arrived. Sir Robert is looking for you with some news.'

Robert and I almost collided in the gallery. I snatched the letter bearing Richard's seal from him, tearing at it in my impatience. Robert handed me his dagger. After I slid it under the hardened wax I raced back into the library and locked the door.

> *My Darling Maman,*
>
> *It is with deep regret I scribble these words to you. Papa is doing his best to unseat me in every way to promote John. He wants you to relinquish the Aquitaine in his favour, making him your heir. I am certain you will not agree. Since my succession after Hal's sad death, Papa now insists I forfeit my rights as Count of Poitou. I find his actions unacceptable. I know he hates me and favours John, who is the most conniving piece of dog's turd, please excuse my vitriol, in Christendom and cannot be trusted.*

*John, encouraged by Papa, and aided by Geoffrey,
whom I cannot fathom except that our father must
have promised him something, has attempted to invade
Poitou. I have thwarted both by successfully invading
Brittany. Geoffrey seems adrift like a broken-masted
barque in a storm. We both need your guidance. Geoffrey has no-one of intellect to challenge him. Although
he will never admit it, he is like a cannon ball shot
offline. He needs a good clip round the ears.*

*I received a letter from Papa ordering me to London.
I have little joy in meeting with him because I cannot
trust myself. It is only my promise to you that pre-
vents me challenging him. The treatment meted out
to us, his continuing attempt to drive a wedge between
Geoffrey and me, is intolerable. But of paramount
importance is your safety, so I must desist in thoughts
of violence against him—or John. Of course, I long to
see you, if it is possible, when in England.*

*Matilda keeps me informed regularly. She amazes
me how vehemently she wants you and Papa to be
re-united. I cannot consider the thought of you giving
in to him. His treatment of you is an abomination,
but we dare not break his iron declaration. Your safety
is up to Geoffrey and me now. John cares not a jot and
is only interested in promoting himself. I pen this with
the deepest pain but hope and pray to see you soon in
London.*

*Your beloved son,
Richard*

Richard's letter inflamed me. Yet I could do or say naught.
My knowledge would betray my tenuous link with Richard and
perhaps expose Robert as the source between us. The Aquitaine
to John, never! If I had Geoffrey within my reach, he would
receive more than a slap around his ears.

I re-folded the parchment and slipped it into my journal.
This was a burden I had to bear alone until Richard arrived. I
could not let Henry get a whiff of what I knew in case he sent
me back to Salisbury, and I missed contact with my beloved son.
I must bide my time and guard my fiery mouth.

***

I took my disposition out on my new maids, imperiously ordering them to repack my belongings down to the last ribbon. Amaris thought I was being excessive, but I cared not that my humour was foul. Matilda, too, was perplexed. I muttered I was out of sorts because my new maids were not accustomed to my precise ways and were aggravating. Not far wrong as it happened.

It distressed me I could not tell Matilda that Richard was coming to London. I presumed he would come on to Windsor, or was that another of Henry's schemes to keep us apart? I thought Matilda might have heard something when she and Richard corresponded, but she had not, and I could not probe too much.

Then Henry requested, 'Eleanor, I would like you to dine with me.'

'Really.' I tried not to appear too icy.

'Yes, if it is not too much trouble.'

'Thank you.' I added sarcastically, 'I do not seem to have any engagements tonight.'

We sat down together. I poked at the quail on my plate.

Henry growled, 'For God's sake woman, stop picking. I am not trying to poison you.'

'I am not hungry. But I would like some more wine if it is not too much trouble.'

He drained the flask into my goblet and ordered another.

'I thought you might be interested to know that your beloved Richard will be visiting.'

'That will be delightful. When?' I smiled, showing joy and surprise without over-acting.

'Soon enough.' Henry grunted.

We sat in silence. I finished my wine and stood.

'I think it is time I took my leave. Thank you for inviting me.'

Henry sneered, 'Well, be careful not to fall on your face getting back to your chamber.'

I ignored his retort. At least, I did not have to pretend I knew nothing of Richard's movements; nevertheless, the contents of his raging letter fermented like a barrel of ale.

***

As Henry and I rode together towards Windsor. I was itching to attack him about his scheming regarding the Aquitaine. I was surprised he had not taken into consideration my vassal's reactions. They would never accept John. While I was in charge, if nominally these days, they complied as they did for Richard to whom they had sworn allegiance.

Also, his latest whim to remove Poitou from Richard after he had bestowed it on him, without my authority in the first place, angered me. Though, I had to admit, it had allowed Richard to cut his teeth as a future ruler, mistakes and all.

Throughout the long silences between us, I mulled over how best to handle the situation. Henry would know I would not give in without a fight. Also, I knew him well enough to anticipate what he would put forward to soften my resolve. My total freedom would be offered. My rights as Queen of England would be restored as would my dower lands and estates. I could choose my maids. My Praetorian guards, now attending Richard, would be reinstated.

I also readied myself for his threats to my opposition. I could be tried for treason and executed, which I doubted. Because, if this happened, his Anglo-Norman Empire from Scotland to the Pyrenees would revolt, probably aided by the young French king. Henry was not such a fool to start a war he could not win. Worse, he would lose the Aquitaine completely because it would fall to Richard as my heir. Furthermore, Henry would find providing for his Anglo-Norman Empire difficult without its wealth.

He could threaten to send me back to Salisbury, remove Amaris and the rest of my loyal little court and throw me into the deepest darkest dungeon. But whatever his threats, never would I allow 'enri Plantagenet-a' to rob me of my inheritance bestowed on me by my father on my sixth birthday.

Finally, for my pièce de résistance, I would refuse to countersign any future treasury documents from the Aquitaine, which, even in my stricken state, I had continued to honour. Of course, Henry in retaliation would then withhold his signature, thus freezing our treasury.

But I had a final move on Henry's chessboard of lunacy. My legacy from Grandmother Dangerosa, unknown to Henry, had not been touched since my arrest. It would keep the Aquitaine solvent for at least two to three years. I would put Richard in charge of the distribution of my private inheritance with the aid of my loyal justiciars. And then there was the diamond! The Briolette's ninety carats could buy Henry's petty inheritances with change to spare.

With my thoughts in order, I was looking forward to the joust with the King of the North as much as I was to Richard's arrival.

***

Richard arrived much like Henry of old with his horse almost dropping underneath him. I was permitted to greet him. He had grown a beard—very manly. He knelt in homage then kissed me on both cheeks, his arms encircling me. Henry could not have been further from our thoughts though he stood a breath away.

Next, Matilda hugged her brother. Her new bulge caused a surprise. The rest of her children stood by, eyes agog. Heinrich shook Richard's hand. By now, Henry was rumbling. He was being ignored, not a good idea if we wanted to thwart his plans. I urged Richard to make a fuss of his father before we had an explosion of rage. Richard placed an arm around Henry's shoulder, asking if an ale was possible because his tongue was hanging out for a draft. Phew! I was not the only mummer in the family. They strode off together as the rest of us followed.

***

Our first dinner at Windsor was followed by a night of music, with Richard playing some new lyrical pieces he had penned. Henry and I managed to remain courteous to one another. I was determined to stay into the evening, hoping to have a word with Richard. But Henry rose saying, 'Well, I am off to my bed.'

'Good night,' I replied.

'Eleanor, you should also, so the younger members of the family can continue with their entertainment.'

It was the last thing I wanted to do.

'Henry, I am not ready for bed. I will see you on the morrow.'

'Did not you hear me? I insist you leave at once!'

He stood over my chair, his hands gripping my shoulders, making me wince. He brought his face close to my ear.

'If you want further engagement with Richard during his visit, you will do as I command.'

I pulled out of Henry's grip, stood and turned on him. The room fell silent.

'It has been some time since I have seen Richard. It is only natural I wish to spend his first night in our presence with him. I should be amazed you could be so selfish as to prevent me, but sadly I am not. Unless you have something to hide that you fear Richard might relate out of your hearing, I will remain in his company.'

Henry was in a bind. Every eye in the room was on us.

Matilda came between us, followed by Heinrich, apparently concerned for her condition.

'Maman, please wait for the morrow.' She turned to Henry, 'Papa surely you will allow Maman and Richard to walk in the gardens together in the morning. I would love to join them. There is much to reminisce about, do not you think?'

Intemperate words were on the tip of my tongue, but then I saw Richard reach for his dagger. Henry, too, was armed. A bloodbath could have happened in seconds.

I raised my hand. 'Richard, desist!'

My expression gave Richard no option but to obey. I turned and faced Henry.

'Very well. I will leave this chamber if you give me your word that I can spend time with Richard in the morning with Matilda.'

Henry gave a curt nod. Heinrich put his hand on his arm.

'Might I suggest to everyone we all leave for our bed chambers because it has been a long, exciting day, and Richard must be tired, too.'

I turned, snatched my cape from Amaris standing near the door, and strode off. Henry's footsteps followed behind me in the gallery. I quickened my pace, almost running by the time I entered my bed chamber. I slammed the door and locked it, rushing to bolt the adjoining one between us. My breath was coming in gulps more from fury than being out of breath.

Henry pounded on my door.

'Open the bloody door, Eleanor. I demand you let me in!'

'Go to hell!'

I removed my crown and jewellery, flinging my finery at the chests. Most missed the target. Then I heard Richard's voice, deep and menacing.

'Leave my mother alone or you will answer to me.'

I unbolted the door and pushed between them to prevent a confrontation. 'Richard, go to your bed.'

'Maman...'

'GO!'

Richard tramped off swearing in Langue d'Oc. I stomped back into my chamber, Henry following. I rounded on him.

'Surely you cannot expect me to lay with you after the way you have treated me.'

Henry sneered. 'I did not notice any reluctance on your part at Winchester.'

'True, but I was feeling lonely and miserable. So were you. I am amazed you can remember that out of all your other conquests.'

Henry harrumphed and my self-control evaporated.

'Henry, you have forced me to look to myself. I have had to become emotionally resilient to counter the mental anguish and despair you have caused me. I have had to suffer the humiliation of your adultery, the physical pain you have inflicted on me and your cruelty and barbarism towards my people. You are causing friction between Richard, John, and Geoffrey, inciting them to war against each other. Those actions leave me with little affection for you. If you think you can undo all that by making love to me which on this night fills me with revulsion, you are more deluded than I thought.'

I was greeted by silence. Did my words prick whatever conscience Henry might have or was he wondering from where I got my knowledge about the boys, I knew not. But he turned on his heel and left, almost knocking Amaris over as she was waiting to ready me for bed. I shut the door and locked it again. Amaris gave me a look that said, *well done* and set about unlacing my gown. I helped her collect my jewellery from the floor. As usual, she detected my heavy sadness. It was difficult keeping my demeanour.

I shook my head, whispering, 'I loved him so much.'

Amaris squeezed my hand. Over the years, we needed few words between us to reinforce our companionship. I thanked God for the day Amaris came into my life. Both of us were no longer young women. She had stood by my side through joy and travail throughout our years together. Her recent illness filled me with fear of the day we would be parted by death. Whoever God called first, the survivor would be devastated.

***

Richard, Matilda and I met as soon as we could the following day. We walked in the gardens that adjoined the Great Park to a suitable bench where Matilda could sit and rest. Richard was patient with his pregnant sister, not wanting to tire her. They recalled their happy childhood here where they rode their ponies, practised archery and played games of hide and seek. They revived memories of a joyous time in my life, now like a distant country I had once visited.

Matilda broke my revery and said, 'Maman, I know you want to speak to Richard in private, so I will leave you to talk.'

'Thank you, darling. But can you avoid your father for a while because he will not be happy if he knows Richard and I are alone.'

Matilda eyes were sorrowful.

'I will stay with the children.'

'Thank you, Sis.'

Richard went on to repeat much of what was in his letter.

'I know, Maman, you were furious with me when I accepted Poitou.'

'Yes,' I grimaced, 'it was humiliating. But that is in the past. I will not interfere with whatever decision you make regarding the County. It is up to you, Richard, whether you retain it or return the title to me.'

Richard turned to me.

'It is difficult. I realise my loyalty both as your son and heir is important to you.'

'It is, yes. But Richard, think it through, and do not make a rash emotional decision. I will accept what you decide.' I took his hand. 'But let me emphasise, I will never accept John as heir to the Aquitaine regardless of what your father might threaten. I will not change my father's succession to me and thence to you. I will die first.'

'Oh, Maman…'

My beautiful son rose from the bench and walked a little way from me in thought. He turned and said, 'I have much to consider, but the last thing I will do is hand over my succession to John; not only because it would dishonour you, but John is incapable of ruling anything.'

'Thank you,' I replied, 'I too have little faith in John's abilities.'

Richard came back and sat down again. I could feel his exasperation.

'Maman, John is weak and capricious; plays nobles off against each other, favouring those who grovel to him and alienating those who disagree. He causes trouble within the clergy and spends his time often with dubious people. The sad reality is, he is not stupid, but he lacks common sense. He has wasted his education.'

My guilt hovered. 'I am sorry to hear that.'

Richard went on. 'It is unfortunate, Maman, that he never had your guidance like the rest of us did.'

I hung my head.

'I feel partly to blame, Richard. I should have made more of an effort to bring John under my care when he was small. Instead, I took my vengeance of your father's infidelity out on him. I let others care for John.'

Richard turned and faced me.

'But you were dangerously ill after he was born. We were all scared you would die.'

'Yes, I feared it too. That I never knew my mother gave me the determination to recover… for all of you. The thought of…' I could not go on.

'Richard, I do not want to be reminded of his birth.' *Or*, I thought, *where your father was while John and I struggled to live?*

I continued, 'The few times in John's company have been awkward. We have nothing in common. Now I fear it is too late.

Also, your Papa does not set a good example.'

'No!' Richard's anger rose. 'He just indulges John and gives him whatever he wants.'

I put my hand on Richard's arm.

'I do love your young brother. But I have difficulty expressing it. I suppose because he seems to have little affection for me...I am also sure that he is never likely to heed any advice I could give him.'

'It is Papa's fault.' Richard kicked at a tuft of grass with his boot.

'Not entirely Richard.'

'Did you hear what happened in Ireland?'

'No.'

'Papa sent John there with the expectation he would become the Irish King.'

'Really!'

'Yes, more privilege. But, instead of uniting the warring clans with our Anglo-Norman nobles who have estates there, which he was sent to do, John alienated everyone. In the end, they all banded together and turned on him. It was a back-handed success in a weird way if a total failure for John. He was forced to flee when the combined armies attacked him. Papa had to mount a rescue.' Richard's voice was tense.

I exhaled in disgust.

'And now your father wants him to become Duke of Aquitaine? God's Teeth!'

***

Of course, nothing turns out the way one plays it through one's mind. Our confrontation hours later with Henry ended with no solution, only acrimony. Richard stormed out, and I had difficulty keeping my temper. I gave Henry the document I had prepared stating Richard was my chosen heir. It emphasised that his ordination had been blessed and sanctified in the Cathedral of St André at Bordeaux, accepted by the pope, nobles, and the people of the Aquitaine.

Henry jabbed it with a blunt finger and snorted, 'This does not take into consideration my position as your husband, whose rights overrule yours, Eleanor, if you want to be difficult.'

'Ha! Your rights have no credence whatsoever with my vassals. You destroyed that respect years ago by invading Poitou. The Aquitaine will erupt in rebellion aided by Phillip Capet for good measure if you try to revoke mine and Richard's inheritances by supplanting us with John.'

He was amazed I was so well-informed about Phillip's conniving from Île de France, but I had inadvertently exposed another snake pit. So, I continued to rub salt into the wounds as I leaned forward.

'Also, from what I hear about John's little escapade in Ireland, your favourite son could not control weeds in a herb garden let alone rule a duchy the size of the Aquitaine.'

I stood and left.

***

Richard rode off as swiftly as he had arrived. I wondered when I would see him again as I seethed about Henry's motives, and worried more about his state of mind. He was becoming more irrational by the day. His obsession with keeping his vassals in check and fretting about the future of his kingdom were taking their toll. Henry wanted to keep his vast empire within Plantagenet rule in equal proportions. But what he had created was as lopsided as a badly loaded cart. One son was now heir to the same lands Henry acquired when we married. He could hardly remove what Richard had inherited through Hal's tragic death. For the status quo, Henry had only himself to blame.

***

We were to return to London. Would Henry never stay still? My suspicions were raised. He had couriers galloping hither and yon. Of course, I would be the last to be informed. Matilda was getting closer to her confinement, my priority. I spoke to him.

'Henry, Matilda should stay at Windsor till after the birth of this baby. She should keep off a horse.'

'Well, you managed to ride many a time in the same condition, so why cannot Matilda?'

I threw up my hands, 'She lost her last baby, Henry, shortly after birth, if you remember. She and Heinrich have enough worries regarding Saxony without more strain on their lives. I will stay at Windsor with them. You can go on to London without me.'

He pushed back his chair. 'And allow you, my dear, to weave more webs of intrigue? No, Eleanor, you will attend me. Matilda can come or stay.'

Henry strode off. I threw up my hands in frustration.

Matilda returned to London. She wanted me to be with her when the baby was born, but she took the safety of a carriage rather than horseback. I rode alongside Henry. We were chasms apart with little to say to one another. To annoy him, I spurred my horse, knowing this would jar his hip if he kept apace.

I tried to put Richard's predicament out of my mind. I had to trust whatever decision he made would be satisfactory enough to keep Henry off our backs. I also had another thorny problem. I had to retire Amaris. She was becoming more and more tired performing her duties. I wanted her to be my companion without having to run my wardrobe, dress me and attend to the many tasks she undertook to serve me. I knew she would not be happy giving up her little "kingdom" to another who would have to be trained and learn to cope with my idiosyncrasies. Out of the women Henry had assigned to me, Sir Martin's wife Margaret, was the most dependable and likeable. Furthermore, I had known her for some years. More importantly, she would not carry tales back to Henry. Margaret did not like the way Henry treated me nor did she find me a monster. She was insulted that she was expected to relate everything I did to Henry. She liked and respected me as a person and did not grovel to titles, and that included the king.

***

I had to approach Amaris once we were settled after our arrival at Westminster to persuade her to be my companion and not my maid. It would be a gentle process while she trained her replacement. I was sure we would both be the beneficiaries of a better life, enjoying each other's company as our autumn years advanced.

I went to the library to keep out of everyone's way while my belongings were unpacked. I reluctantly left Amaris to supervise, but she would prevent an eruption should an item be placed not to my liking.

I think Amaris' suspicions were aroused as soon as I suggested she partake in a goblet of wine with me in my chamber, something we did at the end of a day, not mid-afternoon.

'Wine, Milady?'

'Just to relax. I have a few queries. Sit down, sit down, please. Who do you think among my new women are the most trustworthy, intelligent and capable?'

Amaris took a sip.

'Margaret for sure, a gem. Catherine, Beatrix and Mary are pleasant and diligent. Bella, I am dubious about. I cannot put my finger on it, but I feel uncomfortable in her presence. She seems a bit... sly.'

'Do you think any of these women will report my activities back to Henry?' I smiled wryly, adding, 'And, out of curiosity, I wonder who has lain with him.'

'Definitely not, Margaret.'

Amaris, I think, was indignant I would suggest her.

'No, I never suspected her. But those other young ladies are very pretty, Amaris.'

'Catherine, Beatrix and Mary, yes,' she replied, 'but they have determined minds, and I presume they are honourable.'

'Yes, well I know only too well how charming Henry can be when he chooses. So, Bella remains the only question mark.' I topped up Amaris' goblet.

She tilted her head to one side and eyed me in a curious manner.

'Thank you. But tell me Your Ladyship, what are you up to? With due respect, we do not usually drink wine at this time of the day.'

'Damnation! You know me too well.' I took a deep breath, 'Darling Amaris, I want you to become my full-time companion, not my maid. Neither of us is getting any younger and when you were ill recently, I was terrified I was going to lose you to God. The burden you have carried for all these years has been onerous. It is time for you to relax and to spoil yourself with the activities you enjoy which you have put aside for my care. Our friendship will continue as will our love and respect for each other. I will still be relying on you in many ways, but more as a sister if you agree.'

She smiled. 'As long as I can still be of use, and that you promise not to inter me in a nunnery, I will agree, Milady, with pleasure.'

I breathed a sigh of relief. 'The 'Milady' can go for a start. Eleanor, Elea or Elly is all I will answer to from your lips, and, no, I will not bury you in a nunnery unless I come with you.'

Amaris looked at me with tenderness. We embraced. It was easier than I expected. We returned to my new maids. Amaris was happy to train Margaret to take her place, Catherine, Mary and Beatrix would serve a probationary period. Bella would be watched. Should she step out of line or be seen to be disloyal, she would go no matter how much Henry protested.

Amaris took Margaret under her wing, schooling her in her duties and my likes and dislikes. They went through my wardrobe and official jewellery, learning what went with what on ceremonial occasions, not that I had many of them nowadays. I chose the crowns and other personal ornaments after gowns had been decided.

It was stressed I was most particular about cleanliness, bathing more often than most of my people thought was necessary. Also, my hair was washed regularly. Poor Margaret discovered life under the Queen of England was not going to be simple. Furthermore, it was emphasised that I expected my attendants to observe the same regime of cleanliness I did and that included their teeth. All would be supplied with coarse linen strips and a paste of ground salt or charcoal to rub across and between them. Personally, I preferred mine flavoured with mint leaves, but fennel, rosemary or sage could also be blended, depending on personal taste. If they did not like my rules about personal hygiene, or wished not to comply, they would be dismissed.

Margaret was amazed it took hours to dress me for grand occasions. Planning had to be meticulous to make certain I arrived at the allocated time. My hair took a long preparation depending on how it was dressed. It was fortunate deft little Agnes had become skilled in managing my waist length locks, enjoying the process.

The new maids diverted me for some time from Richard and the decision he had to make regarding Poitou. Then Henry suddenly informed me that Richard, Geoffrey and John were coming to London for discussions. Exactly what they were about, he refused to say. I suspected he still had the Aquitaine in mind for John. Huh!

I received a missive from Richard. He related that unless he returned my title as Countess of Poitou, Henry said I would descend on him with a garrison of troops. I almost fell over laughing. Where, in my present state, would I recruit an army? So, I curbed my impatience, bit my tongue, and waited for my three sons to arrive in London, sometime before Christmas, if Henry's vagueness was anything to go by. His sanity was becoming more and more questionable.

I returned to my quarters where I was interrupted by a knock on the door. Matilda had gone into labour.

***

Several bells had wrung and there was still no baby. As fast as the pains began, they stopped, leaving poor Matilda impatient and frustrated. Brynn, who I insisted attend her, said there was nothing amiss and that the baby was taking its time and would decide soon enough the hour of its arrival.

Matilda was so grumpy, I decided to leave her because there was little, I could do. I decided to play with the children for a while to take my mind off both Richard and Matilda. But, as I walked past the door of my bed chamber, I noticed it was slightly ajar. I knew, even in my haste to rush to Matilda's bedside, that I had closed it behind me and paused to listen. Someone was within. I knew it was not Henry snooping. He was in an audience with his justiciars and Archbishop Baldwin.

I pushed the door wide enough to allow me a better view of the room. One of my new maids was rifling through my possessions on a chest against the far wall where I kept my jewellery and other personal items. Although her back was to me, I recognised by her gown and small stature it was Bella.

'What in God's name do you think you are doing?'

She slid something up her sleeve muttering, 'Lady Margaret asked me to sort some jewellery.'

In two strides I stood in front of her, towering over her diminutive height. 'You lie! Lady Margaret knows nobody touches my personal possessions without my permission.'

Bella reddened, flustering and stammering. The Briolette diamond glinted in all its majesty in front of her. How did she find that? She dropped an earring of amethyst and pearls set in gold. The other hung from her left ear. My stinging blow knocked her off her feet. The earrings had belonged to my mother and had been given to her by her mother Dangerosa.

In terror, she babbled Lord Henry would hear about this outrage. I hauled her to her feet. I think she was astonished at my strength. I might be slender, but I have always been lithe and athletic. As Henry said all those years ago, I had muscled legs like a boy. My arms, too, were strong from years of managing a horse, archery, not to mention my crazy attempts with a broad sword.

I dragged her out the door. No matter how she struggled she could not free herself from my grip as I marched her to Henry's audience chamber. The guards on the door leapt to one side as I shouldered my way through the portal with my now screaming, hysterical captive. The men rose as one as I flung Henry's whore at his feet. Bella tried to stand but tripped on her gown, landing on her knees. I then grabbed her by a handful of her hair and ripped the earring from her ear.

Like a tiger-cat I spat. 'Lord King Henry, keep your chancred putain in your chamber. You can share syphilis with her for all I care, but her thieving hands and spying eyes are not welcomed in mine.'

In front of the stunned assembly, I ripped the tied sleeve from her robe to expose a golden cylinder used for holding precious missives. It clattered to the floor. Before I could grab it, it rolled to Henry's feet. He snatched it up and pulled it asunder to reveal its creamy parchment contents. Goosepimples raced down my spine; I had no recollection of what it contained. Bella must have thought it was worth hiding. Had she opened it or just shoved it out of sight when I descended on her in my bed chamber?

Henry unrolled the parchment with great drama to reveal its contents, so poignant they brought tears to my eyes and deflated my anger. It was a letter from Hal aged about five or six, with a spidery drawing of a horse and lopsided rider. He had written in scrawly Latin,

Mater Carissima

Traxi hanc imaginem tibi. Est mihi in mea mannulus. Meus soror nova potest eum aquitare cum maior est.

Te amo, Hal

(Dearest Maman,

I have drawn this picture for you. It is me on my pony. My new sister can ride him when she is bigger.

I love you, Hal)

I held out my hand. 'That letter is addressed to me. Might I have it back if you would be so kind.'

Reluctantly, Henry placed it back in the cylinder and handed it to me. Our eyes locked, reminded of the love for our beautiful son, Hal.

With that I acknowledged the embarrassed dignitaries with a brief nod, leaving Henry's thieving whore on the floor. At the door I turned. 'If I set eyes on that woman again, she will be sent to the Tower to rot!'

***

Matilda's baby eventually decided to enter the world in the early hours of the following morn. As I cradled my new grandson, I felt the overwhelming joy of his birth. I remembered my depth of maternal love for Henry's and my babies. Their gummy yawns, the wonder in their eyes when we first set eyes on each other, were etched in my mind like their baby odour, and newborn cries. All except John, who was whisked away, his life hanging by a thread.

Matilda was tired, but well. Brynn had worked her magic, bringing the little fellow into the world. He was strong and healthy. His lungs were lusty. Heinrich and Matilda named him

William, which was an honour and a sadness rolled into one.

This should have been a wonderous moment for Henry and me, but after yesterday's acrimonious events I was avoiding him. The new parents at least knew naught of what had happened.

Bella was banished from Westminster by Baldwin's decree, her reputation in tatters. Henry had been humiliated in front of his justiciars and the archbishop, who were all wondering what his relationship was with the woman he had sent to spy on me. But Bella's pilfering hands were her downfall, attracted as she was like a jackdaw to my jewellery. What else she thought she was going to find in my chest I knew not. If she was looking for my journal, it was well and truly under lock and key.

Matilda's baby was christened in the chapel by Archbishop Baldwin. It brought us together. When the family celebrated afterwards, Henry and I remained polite for Matilda's sake though Baldwin did have a quiet word in my ear to say Henry was feeling contrite. I let him know about the relationship Henry had with Bella and that she was one of many mistresses. I think the archbishop was more saddened than surprised by my frankness. Catherine, Mary and Beatrix I also dismissed.

Henry was in a bind.

'You can splutter as much as you like,' I told him, 'but how can I trust your other coquettes? Margaret, being Martin's wife whom I know, can stay. In the meantime, I will make do.'

***

Between Matilda's new baby son, and her other children, I had been able to keep my mind occupied and away from the repercussions of what could transpire when our sons arrived in London. I was eager to see them, but I dreaded the outcome. I was still amazed Henry would dare to contemplate I would relinquish my inheritance along with Richard's. I decided to confront him before the boys arrived, but first I rallied a recruit. I sent a message to Archbishop Baldwin requesting a private meeting.

We met while Henry and his close companions were hunting. I chose the gardens even though the weather was chilly.

'Your Grace, before I speak of my concerns, do I have your word that what I relate will remain confidential?'

He bowed his head and said, 'Of course, Milady.'

'Thank you.' I took a deep breath. 'I have learned Lord King Henry wishes to disinherit Prince Richard as my appointed heir to my Duchy of Aquitaine in favour of our youngest son, Prince John.'

'Is there a problem with the king's wishes,' he asked, 'seeing Prince Richard is now heir to the Anglo-Norman Empire?'

'Absolutely!' I gave my cape a determined tug.

'From my point of view, it is totally unacceptable. Prince Richard was ordained my heir when he was ten years old, approved by the pope and the people of the Aquitaine. That is how it will remain regardless of Richard's future duties. To put it bluntly, if my heritage is passed to John, the political situation in not only the Aquitaine but across the empire will disintegrate.'

'Are you certain of this, Milady?'

'I can assure you,' I answered. 'It will lead to a full-scale war from Scotland to the Pyrenees. Furthermore, King Phillip of France will gleefully join the fray.'

'Oh dear! That would be worrying, indeed. How reliable is your information?'

'My sources are impeccable, and I know my people, Your Grace. Here, let us sit.'

We made ourselves comfortable on a bench.

'Despite that I am no longer part of King Henry's court,' I went on, 'I am kept informed. As for the nobles of the Aquitaine, Lord Henry lost their respect many years ago. They also consider Prince John untrustworthy, whereas they honour Prince Richard more so now because of the position…I am in.'

Archbishop Baldwin was silent.

'You know about Poitou, I presume?' I continued.

'I hear the king wants Lord Richard to return it to you.'

'Yes.'

'And how do you feel about that?'

I sighed. 'I worry about Lord Henry. He told Richard if he did not comply regarding its return, I would attack the county. How? It is laughable. Honestly, I wonder at times about his sanity. I am not going to pressure my son one way or the other.

I have told him that. It is his decision.'

The archbishop nodded. 'Well, Milady, I certainly do not want to see rebellion erupt from one end of King Henry's domains to the other any more than you do. But how to convince him? I hate to say this, but from what I observe, your relationship with the king, being what it is, would achieve nothing but further bitterness.'

I raised an eyebrow. 'I am afraid you are right.'

We stood and walked in silence till the chill air drove us back in doors.

In my audience chamber with warming mulled wine, Baldwin said, 'I will broach the subject with Lord Henry before I leave London. Unfortunately, I must return to Canterbury before your sons arrive.'

'Thank you, Your Grace. I hope you can talk some sense into the king without divulging where your information came from. And I deeply appreciate you taking the time to allow me to convey my concerns to you.'

I walked to my door with Baldwin and bade him farewell. Whether the archbishop would be able to change Henry's mind, I could but hope. Henry would be highly suspicious as to where Baldwin gained his knowledge. So far, I did not think he would know it came from me. Nevertheless, I was pleased with the outcome and felt I had grown in stature in Baldwin's eyes. He had discovered I was not a fool or the mischievous scheming queen I had been painted. I believed we developed a friendly rapport.

***

Matilda's dear little William was now four weeks old. She and Heinrich were advised a truce had at long last been settled between Saxony and the Holy Roman Emperor, Frederick. Their eighteen months spent in England, although under trying circumstances, were a delight for me, but now they had to return home. To have Matilda's company, meet my little grandchildren and to enjoy their funny little ways, had been such a pleasure. Otto and I had become close. I had taught him chess. Already he was showing skill. I was able to help the others, too, with their learning. I would miss them.

Matilda was sad to leave but impatient to be reunited with the child held hostage. I was mightily surprised when she and Heinrich took me aside as if something was amiss.

'Lady Eleanor, Matilda and I have a request. Although the peace treaty has been successful, we do not trust the capricious nature of the Holy Roman Emperor. We fear he could create more trouble. To protect our family and heirs, we want to leave the children, except for William, with you.'

I smiled with joy.

Heinrich continued, 'We hope it will be only for a brief period, but until we return to Saxony to assess the situation, we want the children to be in safe hands.'

'I am honoured you trust me with Ricenza, Harry, Lothar and Otto. But I suggest you consult Lord Henry, also.'

Who could be as capricious as Frederick, I thought.

Out of politeness, I also spoke to him.

Henry replied, 'Yes, they requested the children stay, and I am happy for them to be left with you. It will keep you occupied rather than waging nefarious campaigns against me.'

'Really, perhaps you can enlighten me what they might be? Seeing you were the one who placed your thieving whore in my court to spy and report on my activities.'

With a curled lip he pushed a missive across the table in front of me. I recognised Richard's hand. His letter was succinct. He had notified his father he was returning Poitou to me; 'so I can devote and concentrate my time to duties on my mother's behalf in the Aquitaine,' he disclosed.

I had to contain my glee, not because of the return of my county and title, but for his emphasis as to where his loyalty lay.

'This is a surprise. I am pleased Richard acknowledges his obligations. Do you want me to go on a progress throughout my lands to ensure a smooth transition?'

'And deny you the pleasure of being granddame? I would not be so cruel.'

Oh, yes, you would, you son of Satan, I thought. *You would have no qualms at all to be as mean to me as possible, grandchildren or no.*

I ignored his sarcasm and asked, 'Are the boys still coming to London?'

'Yes.'

'When?'

'When they get here, Eleanor.'

'Will they arrive before Matilda leaves?'

'I doubt it. But there is a chance they might see their sister at Barfleur.'

That was as much knowledge he was going to impart. He stood and came round the table. As I went to leave his company, he grabbed my right hand, hurting it as he examined my fingers, but they were scrubbed clean of ink. I pulled from his grasp.

'Happy?' I snapped.

I did not slam the door. I smiled to myself. He had inadvertently given me an inkling as to when our sons would arrive. All I had to do was confirm Matilda's date of departure, add the time to sail to Barfleur, and for the boys to leave Normandy, then calculate how long it would take for them to arrive in London from Portsmouth. *You slipped on that tactic, 'enri Plantagenet-a.'*

***

Matilda took a break from organising their departure to walk with me in the gardens. The autumn leaves were brightening. Soon their branches would be bare, another reason for her and Heinrich to make haste across the channel before winter storms battered the coasts of England and Normandy.

Arm and arm, we talked about the children. Then on our favourite bench, she said, 'Maman, I am saddened there seems to be no resolution between you and Papa. I have begged him to mend the rift with you, but he says no matter what he does he cannot live up to your impossible expectations.'

'What rubbish!' My hackles were rising.

Matilda looked at me sceptically.

'He also says he cannot accept the way you turned Hal, Richard and Geoffrey against him.'

'That is not true, Matilda.'

'I know,' she sighed. 'And I know Papa caused the rift, but my brothers did run to your bosom like they did when they were little, and you happily accommodated them, taking their side even if they were partly to blame.'

'I object to your assumption. I did my best to make your father see he could not play one against the other. I begged him to give Hal the responsibilities he desired and needed. He just could not see what was as clear as a mountain stream. It was his attitude that exacerbated their rebellion, not any interference on my part.' I was indignant.

'But you took their side.'

'Not exactly.' I took a deep breath. 'In the end, Matilda, I gave up. Henry forced me by being intractable; driving me to protect my sons. I had no choice.'

'But why, Maman? How could you consider running to our enemy the French for protection?'

'Who told you that?'

She did not have to answer.

'Matilda, the last thing I wanted to do was to appeal to the French. Uncle Ralph and some powerful nobles in the Aquitaine were also furious with Henry and forced my hand. I was not seeking sanctuary. I hoped to bring your brothers home, by their ears if necessary. Your father never asked. He just jumped to conclusions, locked me up and accused me of treason.' I stood and walked away to control my emotions, then I turned back. 'I have paid over and over for my love of your brothers, and I will continue to do so. I also must daily suffer the humiliation of my restricted existence while your father continues to make enemies, and to ravish any woman he desires. Worse, I watch him destroy all we achieved in restoring England to peace and prosperity. I watch him erode the trust of the people of his Empire from England, Normandy and beyond. It frustrates beyond endurance because I am powerless to stop him.'

Matilda's face was forlorn. I knew she loved her father, and I was happy at least one of his children did. Probably so did Lenore and Joanna. He had no argument with his three daughters. They had served their purpose by providing Henry with alliances with Saxony, Castile and Sicily. Why he could not see his sons as allies instead of competitors, I knew not.

My lovely daughter and I hugged each other. 'I am sorry I disappoint you, but I cannot forgive your father for his treatment of me. Once maybe, but I have had to harden myself to survive.'

'Maman, yes it saddens me. But you know, despite his appalling behaviour, I believe Papa still loves you.'

I shook my head and wondered about that smouldering ember in the depths of my own heart.

***

Matilda, Heinrich and baby William departed. The children left in my custody were sorry their mother was leaving them behind. They did have their maids and nurses, of course, but their maman was their maman, after all, as was their papa. I did my best to comfort them, as did their attendants. I told them it would not be for long, and soon they would be home in Saxony, but their parents needed to make sure it was safe.

I spent hours with them teaching, playing and just loving. After a while, they settled into a routine. Even though the weather was cooling there were still many outdoor activities for them. We were returning from the gardens where the children had enjoyed an afternoon of diving into piles of autumn leaves when a page came to inform me that a large contingent of knights was approaching.

My boys! I handed my charges over and rushed to my quarters to ready myself for their arrival.

I waited with Henry as they rode into Westminster. Lithe as cats they leapt from their horses. Richard, I had seen more recently, Geoffrey, not for eons. He was tall, slender and elegant. They all knelt in homage, but John avoided my eyes.

After their welcome, they went to their quarters to change from travel-worn garments to bathe and to have some repast. We agreed we would all meet later to dine as a family, including Matilda and Heinrich's little ones. At least we would have one evening without dissent, I hoped.

When I returned to my chamber, I was surprised to find Amaris, Margaret, Frith and Agnes in a huddle. As I looked from one to the other, I noticed Margaret's eyes were red and swollen, despite her usual happy nature. Frith and Agnes excused themselves, collected linens and disappeared out the door. I raised my eyebrows to Amaris for an explanation, but she said it was nothing to fuss about. Margaret had received some news she did not want to worry me with, especially as my sons had just arrived. I was suspicious. Amaris busied herself with some embroidery, avoiding my eyes. It was puzzling because I noticed at the boys' arrival the usually jolly Martin looked quite dour. Had he and Margaret rowed? It was odd; they were such a devoted couple.

Later I caught Robert as he was bustling off on an errand. 'Ah, just the man, I need a word.'

'Of course, Milady.'

'I am concerned about Margaret. She has been crying. Do you think she and Martin could have had a row?'

He shrugged his shoulders. 'I am unaware of any disagreements. I have never heard a cross word between them since they married.'

'Well, something is amiss. Also, Martin seemed unhappy about something.'

'I am sorry, I have no idea…'

'Hmm.'

Robert, I felt was being as evasive as Amaris. I then tried Agnes. I hoped, in her innocence, she would let something slip. I found her alone busily restitching some loose pearls on one of my more opulent gowns.

'My word, Agnes, you are diligent. Beautiful work.'

'Thank you, Milady, a pleasure.'

'Did you notice Margaret was looking a little unwell.'

'Nah—no. Lady Margaret is all right, but she is just a bit worried about Princess Alais.'

No sooner were the words out of her mouth than Agnes froze mid-stitch and turned bright pink. I suspected she had spoken out of turn.

'Why would that be?' I asked.

Agnes gabbled, 'I think the princess has to go away for a while. And Milady, I know nothing more. Please do not tell Margaret I said anything because she said you must not be worried.'

I had never set eyes on Alais, thanks to Louis' edict. Henry agreed that I would have naught to do with her. She had grown up in the household of Margaret's family. Since Henry appointed Margaret to my retinue, I knew Alais lived at their country estate south of London. Alais must now be fifteen, maybe older. Why Richard had shown little interest in marrying her, I knew not. Could it be that he disliked for her for some reason which was causing Margaret and Martin's concern? Was Phillip demanding they wed?

I decided to question Richard. It was certainly time he was married. Of course, it could be because I did not want that girl as Duchess of Aquitaine. Though now she would be Queen of England.

***

We ate, for the most part, in humid silence. Henry could barely speak to his two oldest boys. I tried to keep things jolly for the sake of my grandchildren, but it was not easy. Geoffrey was his usual, know-it-all superior self. I was delighted to see him but felt uncomfortable in his proximity. I suspected he could still read my mind. Like Richard said, he was wasting his intellect on trivial activities. During dinner, he took vicious glee in playing John and Richard off one another, and Henry against each of them, too clever for his own good.

After our meal and the little ones retired with their maids to their cots, we adjourned to listen to the minstrels and other entertainment. Then Geoffrey challenged me to a game of chess.

'Will you stop nagging, Geoffrey? I replied. 'I need to speak to Richard.'

'Playing favourites again, Maman…ouch!'

Richard smirked. 'Geoff, you jolly well deserved that for being obnoxious.'

By now, I had lost my patience.

'As none of you can behave in a civilised manner I will leave for my bed.'

John was grinning with a slack-lipped curl to his mouth, so he got a whack for good measure as I blazed out of the hall.

Henry's sarcasm rang in my ears. 'Oh, what a tangled web the black spider weaves!'

I pushed two pages away and strode through the door.

My maids retired following my exit, leaving the Plantagenet clan to quaff ale with their entourages. I hoped it did not end in a drunken brawl. I believed Henry was hatching something. He was far too smug. His nasty retort not only raised my ire but continued to seed my suspicions about his motives. Furthermore, I wanted to pin Richard down regarding his reluctance to marry Alais. I suspected it was more than my disapproval. He did not know I was aware of his illegitimate child, and I wondered if he was in love with the mother. She could be of a status not suitable for him to wed, like Abraham and me, had I been free of Louis in Antioch.

Our next meeting was fraught with anxiety on my part and full of hostility and unfulfillment for our sons as well. Nothing was settled with the boys. As fast as they had arrived, they left. My very brief discussion with Richard regarding Alais was fruitless. He muttered something about not wishing to marry before fulfilling his ambition to carry the Cross to reclaim Jerusalem.

Why did I not believe him? Deep down, I felt that was an excuse, though secretly I was happy with the status quo.

Chapter 17 The Christmas from Hell

Henry decreed we would assemble for our Christmas court at Chinon Castle and insisted I attend. That depressing fortress filled me with dread as the memories of the beginning of my incarceration flooded back. It was the last place I wanted to spend Christmas, but what choice did I have? We arrived in Barfleur before the coming winter storms, though my innards were experiencing one of their own.

The leagues to Chinon were grim, and I could not enjoy the countryside of my lands which I had not seen for eight years. The closer we rode to Chinon, the more my anxiety increased. We stopped at Fontevrault for our last night on the road, where I poured my fear out in ink, hoping I could sleep the night. It was cold, though the community of monks and nuns were welcoming.

Amaris entered my small cell to spend the night with me. I had said little to her about my state of mind. I had been trying to keep my courage without giving into feelings of despair. But she knew. Without speaking she took my inky fingers in her hands. She did not have to speak. My breath came in ragged gasps as I fought my turmoil.

I took a lung full of air and blurted out, 'Amaris, I am afraid of the panic resurfacing. I am at the edge of wits. The last place on earth I want to enter is Chinon Castle.'

'You have overcome this in the past. Remain calm, do not give in. You will prevail.'

'My damn hand is cramping, with pains shooting up my arm. Logic tells me it is the cold, and I have been writing for too long, but the memory of Henry's boot crushing my outstretched hand is as raw as the bleak weather outside.'

'Breath slowly. You need to relax.'

She had some mulled wine which she poured into two goblets. I was shaking. She sprinkled the pounce across my words and closed the journal.

'Here, Eleanor.' Amaris guided the goblet to my mouth.

'I feel useless.'

'You are not useless.' She took my inky fingers in hers. 'Let me massage your hand.'

These simple gestures worked, and slowly I regained my composure. Amaris also massaged the tenseness from my shoulders and poured more wine, which I gulped down too quickly. By the third goblet, I was more relaxed. Then, on our narrow cots, tucked up in warming furs, we both fell asleep.

***

There had been a light sprinkling of snow overnight. The horses made their way tentatively on the icy ground as the land rose towards the bulk of the castle after we crossed the River Vienne. Richard rode on my sinistral side with his brothers behind their father on my dextral flank. Richard's presence kept me calm. Our breaths, like the horses, clouded the morning air. We clattered across the drawbridge, hooves echoing hollow over the moat, to dismount in the bailey. I prayed to God I would not vomit. Memories of pain, fear and total despair welled up in me as I stood beside my mount waiting to be escorted to my quarters.

I was carried out of here in the opposite direction as Henry's prisoner, although, thanks to Hal's dying wishes, my life was easier. Nevertheless, I suspected I was only invited because Henry had not given up on wresting the Aquitaine from Richard and me. To add to my concerns, I learned that the French court would be in attendance, too. Although Henry had said naught, maybe Richard's and Alais' marriage was to happen, a horror I dreaded for the Aquitaine. I had accepted Hal's wife Margaret, but she was never going to be duchess of my domains.

My teeth chattered as my maids rallied around. My chamber was warmed by the braziers, but my feet were numb. A page arrived with mulled wine and fresh bread and cheese. I did my best to put the bleakness of my early capture behind me.

My woollen clad feet were massaged back to life with care and attention. Little by little, I began to overcome the dread. Joachim knocked and entered. He had been told by Amaris I was battling past demons. He boosted my morale when he told me the three boys were housed in a nearby wing. Constance was reunited with Geoffrey, having arrived a week ago with their two daughters, whom I had yet to meet.

King Phillip of France was expected soon. His half-sister Alais was in our entourage somewhere, being escorted by Martin and his retinue. Henry was in his chambers next to mine. So far, the doors between us remained locked. Chinon was crowded with dignitaries. Archbishop Baldwin was also present. If I added up the attending courts it would put our numbers in the hundreds, but Chinon was vast.

***

Christmas day approached. We were to celebrate Christ's birth in the cathedral in the town below the castle on the other side of the Vienne, followed by a monumental banquet. Snow swirled in flurries around Chinon. Talk of a blizzard was on everyone's lips. The young French king had yet to arrive. Those who cared hoped he would beat the bad weather.

The women of our assembly gathered to chat and pursue womanly activities, while the men awaited Phillip. I had much on my mind, but at least my panic was controlled, for now. Nonetheless, I was never one to sit around idly gossiping. Besides, I think the women outside my immediate circle found me intimidating. In truth, I wanted to speak to Richard.

Constance came to my chambers and introduced me to my two granddaughters. Eleanor was three years old, and Alix nearly two. I was flattered the older one was named after me. Both were pretty children and bright. I enjoyed playing with them. They had a lot of Geoffrey's self-confidence, which was pleasing.

We were playing with some blocks on the floor when the door opened, and a slight wan-faced girl entered. I guessed immediately who she was. There was something of Louis about her eyes, and unfortunately, his beaky nose. Her hair was dark, though, from her Castilian mother, but it was lank and not braided in any way. Overall, she was not particularly attractive. To be honest, she looked sickly. Maybe it was the wintry weather giving her a pinched look. Margaret brought her to me. I had to disentangle myself from my granddaughters who, Geoffrey-like, did not want to have their game interrupted. Constance was annoyed by their manners, but I minded not. Alais, I think, found it strange that the Queen of England had no qualms about sitting on the floor with the little girls. Alais wore a most odd expression, almost as if she were about to burst into tears. Surely, I was not that terrifying, or did she know my feelings about the betrothal?

I disentangled myself from the clamouring children, and we sat together. I tried to draw her into conversation, thinking Louis would be rolling in his grave with her being in my presence. I questioned her about her likes and dislikes and whether she could read and write. She did mutter she liked to embroider, but apart from that seemed uncomfortable. Margaret was embarrassed for the girl. To be honest she impressed me not one jot. She did not have the warm friendliness of her older sister. I could not see her as a suitable wife for Richard or a future queen. Could this be why he was trying to postpone the marriage? If I saw no improvement in her attitude in the next few days, regardless that she might be shy, I was going to have to speak to Henry.

***

It was a relief when, at last, Phillip and his French court arrived before the oncoming storm. We met briefly. He was polite enough, but he made me feel uneasy—a woman's intuition perhaps or what Matilda had related after she had met him.

The next day, everyone rode to the cathedral under a dark and foreboding sky. The frozen grass between the cobblestones crunched underfoot. The Christmas ceremony conducted by Archbishop Baldwin and other clergy was moving. Beautiful voices soared through the Romanesque arches. The monks' plainsong was uplifting. Henry managed to look regal, though I knew the cold was playing havoc with his hip. My miniver-lined cloak kept out the icy draughts, though I felt the crown had frozen around my head.

During the ceremony, I was able to glance with pride at my handsome sons, who looked like they cared for each other. Henry was seated next to me. He squeezed my hand, his eyes glistened. He whispered I looked as beautiful as ever. Perhaps he was trying to soften me up. Nevertheless, I accepted the compliment. It was during this exchange I noticed Alais beside her half-brother King Phillip. Her expression was sour as she stared at me pouting. Such a strange one! I searched for Louis in her half-brother, but apart from his golden curls and slightly prominent nose, he must resemble his mother. He appeared to be a calculating man without the guileless naivety of his monkish father. The more I saw of Alais, the more my doubts grew. Her suitability to become Richard's wife and future queen worried me. It was not just that she was wishy-washy; she had no spark. She was sulky and seemed evasive, as if she had something to hide. I could understand Richard's reluctance to be her husband. He needed a woman with vivacity and intelligence.

Then I overheard a murmured conversation between Robert and Martin - something about a cover-up regarding an illegitimate babe. They mentioned Richard, and I thought surely not another one.

Martin said he and Margaret felt ashamed. They had no inkling about the affair till it was too late. They then had to send whoever it was away to have the child so that the father knew naught about it.

I hoped they were not talking about Richard. Perhaps one of the young squires in the household had had an affair with a maid, sadly nothing unusual.

***

After the Christmas service, we arrived back at Chinon, stamping the snow from our boots. We could not race to the Great Hall fast enough to thaw out our hands and toes. The first goblet of mulled wine was swiftly followed by another before any semblance of warmth thawed my extremities.

The Christmas banquet was a splendid affair with lots of wassailing and good cheer. By the time the day ended, we were all ready to fall into our beds nursing our distended stomachs. But before Richard, John, Geoffrey and I left for the night, Henry announced he wanted us to assemble the next day for a serious discussion. Included would be Phillip, Alais, the archbishop and our close attendants. Oh dear! What was so important it could not wait? It was Christmas and none of us were going anywhere. The blizzard had hit in monumental proportions. Snow had drifted halfway up Chinon's ramparts. Unless we wanted to freeze solid before we crossed the drawbridge, we were imprisoned.

***

The next day we gathered as requested by Henry in the Great Hall. The boys and I clustered together, wondering what he wanted. Richard, Geoffrey and John had no idea. Richard whispered in my ear it could be to do with his father's desire to alter the succession of the Aquitaine from himself to John. Soto voce, I reminded him if Henry tried such a stupid move there would be rebellion from one end of the Aquitaine to the other. So, we ruled that out. Henry addressed us all. Phillip was standing to one side with Alais, who looked whiter than the snow that had drifted in the bailey. And she looked like she had been crying.

Archbishop Baldwin was seated on the other side of Henry, who stood and addressed us all. I was not included in the group, unusual when it came to protocol. But I had scant knowledge as to what Henry was likely to do these days; after all, I had no formal function. I might squirm but could do little.

Henry had a scroll in his hand. He then announced to everyone's amazement he was seeking to have our marriage annulled on the grounds of consanguinity. His pronouncement was followed by a deathly hush. Colour drained from the top of my head through to my feet as I gasped in disbelief. Then a crescendo of voices rent the hall, broken by the full-volumed bellow of Baldwin, who silenced all. I was supported by Geoffrey and Richard.

Archbishop Baldwin turned on Henry.

'Lord King Henry, this is an abomination. I can only presume you have lost your wits.' Baldwin snatched the scroll from Henry's fist, reading its contents swiftly.

'And if you expect me, as Archbishop of Canterbury, to sign this document along with Lady Queen Eleanor, then you are truly mad. Nor will I allow this manuscript as Archbishop of Canterbury to be couriered to waste the pope's time on a frivolous whimsy because you cannot get your own way, I presume on the issue of her Ladyship's inheritance. You missed excommunication by a thread over Becket's murder, but this foolishness is of a new order. I suggest you think very carefully.'

'I want children who will love their father and rule my kingdom without bloodshed,' Henry cried.

By now, I had regained control. Why I was so calm when the maddest idea raced through my head?

'I will contest you for my marriage, 'enri Plantagenet-a. Geoffrey, a chess board, if you will.'

There was a collective intake of breath from the surrounding audience and cries of disbelief. Geoffrey obliged, and Richard brought a table. Two chairs were placed on opposite sides. What was going through my son's heads, only God knew. But I had to protect my legitimate progeny from Henry's bastards and my honour.

'If you win, our marriage will be over. If I win, we will remain as husband and wife.'

Henry's face drained of colour. If he refused to play me, he would suffer the humiliation of Baldwin's decree, excommunication, and other interdicts as well.

Henry and I had not played chess in years because I usually won. But, tonight, he had more to lose than his pride. Geoffrey took one pawn of each colour. He jiggled them behind his back then produced his crossed fists for Henry and me to choose. Henry selected white. I was happy with that because he would have to make the opening move.

Already, I had a plan to achieve my objectives. Henry was an impatient player who bored easily if the game was drawn out, but chess was one pursuit where I was as patient as a spider in its web. To add to the drama, Geoffrey produced a sandglass to limit the length of time we had per move. Henry started to complain but was silenced by a howl from the assembly. I breathed a sigh of relief because I did not want the game prolonged by Henry dithering.

Henry's first moves were standard openings. He was being careful. I had to play to his impulsive personality as well as his skill. Today, he would concentrate. We both lost pieces, but I could see he was protecting the centre squares, common enough manoeuvres. I could feel Geoffrey's mind drilling into mine. I changed tack and brought a rook into play. I had already placed a bishop and knight in positions that would force Henry to retreat if he made a hasty move. Now he could not move either of his pieces in the centre without exposing his king. I bided my time. Like the black spider he liked to call me, I was leading him into a trap.

'Check.'

To get out of check, he had to sacrifice his queen. Henry's face was turning crimson with fury as he realised I had him in a pincer movement he could not get out of without surrendering more of his pieces. I calculated I had checkmate in five more moves. Four, if his defence disintegrated.

The sandglass emptied. 'It is your move, Henry,' I said.

Henry's arm swept the pieces to the floor in a furious arc.

'Does that mean, you have conceded?'

Henry's fists opened and closed as I calmly collected the pieces from the floor and placed them back exactly where they were before Henry upset the game. This was a party trick, a gift encouraged by my father and inherited by Geoffrey, of picturing where each piece sat on the board. I knew it infuriated Henry. He would want to strangle me.

He started screaming, his face flamed to his hair-roots, 'I should never have married you, Eleanor of bloody Aquitaine! You were nothing but a whore. I want Alais.'

Shock hit me as Henry's revelation sunk in.

'So, it was you who was having the affair under Margaret and Martin's noses and the reason Alais was hastily removed from their household.'

Henry looked shocked that his secret was out.

'How dare you.'

My voice was low. 'I have never betrayed you, yet you have produced another bastard this time by that little harlot, your son's betrothed. No wonder Richard does not want to marry her. If anyone in this room is a whore, she is!' I pointed accusingly at Alais, now openly crying.

King Phillip's snide remark 'it takes one to know one,' catapulted my sons into action. Mayhem followed. I knew not who laid Phillip out, but he was crumpled on the floor. Next,

Henry was struck. Blood streamed from his nose. He staggered and fell. Out of the corner of my eye, I caught the glint of a broad sword. I threw myself over Henry as it slashed through mid-air, missing me by a whisker and catching a golden tip of my crown, sending it rolling across the floor. I covered Henry with my body as we were surrounded by a melee of roaring men. Grunts, punches and the clang of metal against metal rent the hall as Plantagenet fought Capet. Women screamed. Archbishop Baldwin's furious voice thundered over the ensuing battle, bringing these foolish, mostly young, men to a halt. Somewhere around my middle Henry's muffled voice begged me to loosen my grip.

'Eleanor you are suffocating me.'

I dragged him to his feet and managed to aid him limping from the room, leaving Baldwin, Martin, Robert and other more sensible knights to return the Great Hall to order. Women fled in all directions to their quarters.

Henry collapsed onto his bed after we staggered into his chamber and rolled onto his back. His injury was superficial, looking worse than it was. I ordered a churl to bring ice water to bathe his face and stem his nose bleed.

'God's Teeth! Eleanor, stop! That cloth is freezing my nose and face. You are torturing me.'

'Shut your mouth, or I will give you more than torture.'

He whimpered into silence.

'You might have a black eye, but your nose does not appear to be broken.'

I helped him remove his blood-stained robe with the aid of his man servant. We tucked the bedclothes around him.

'Thank you, Gerard. I will stay with his Lordship till he sleeps. You can go now.' Gerard gave a nod and left with the bowl of cold water.

My gown was a mess, Henry's blood had soaked through it.

'Can you take that off? It is making me feel sick.' He sat up as I was bending over him.

'Here, let me help.'

'What on earth do you think you are doing?' I tried to pull away. 'Surely, you cannot expect intimacy after the way you have just behaved. No, Henry...oh, for goodness' sake...'

'You won me back, remember. You are still my wife. Or am I just a chess trophy.'

'Honestly, Henry you are incorrigible.' I slapped his hands away, but they returned with determination, pulling the lacing from the front of my gown. It was becoming amusing. My under gown and shift were also soaked. Next, they were on the floor with Henry's braies. He had more tentacles than an octopus. Fighting him off was a lost cause. Henry's lips were on mine. I tried to pull away, but he held me with animal strength. I was not very heavy.

'Henry, no.' Resisting him was futile.

'No what?'

'Henry, let go. I am freezing. I need to dress into something warm.'

'I will warm you up. Just get into bed.'

For someone with a blackening eye, bad hip, and God knows what else, Henry had a grip like a vice, and I was freezing in only under garments. Gripping my bindings, he dragged me on top of him.

'Let go, damn you… You are a bloody opportunist!'

'Eleanor, shut up. I want you.'

'Why? After what occurred in the Great Hall, I thought you wanted Alais.'

He mumbled something into my neck about my now bare breasts ending the discussion. He hauled the bed covers over me. Henry's lips, tongue and hands were having an effect. I gave in to his sexual appetite—and mine. Triumphantly, I was still his wife. Yes, I had won him back whether he liked it or no, but he was showing every sign of liking it. Lust must conquer pain and, in my case, common sense!

I awoke in the early morn. By the vivid light filtering through the narrow window, I guessed snow must have fallen again during the night. I tried to ease myself from Henry's embrace. My neck was stiff from sleeping in the crook of his arm with my hair anchored under his shoulder. Gently, I pulled the plait away then swung my legs over the side of his bed. Henry snuffled but did not wake. The air was freezing. I searched around for my gowns and shift, but they were on the other side of the bed. I borrowed Henry's cape draped over a chair, then fetched my discarded garments and tiptoed from his bed chamber through to mine. Amaris was asleep in my bed. Margaret was on the trundle. I wanted to bathe but did not want to disturb my sleeping maids. What hour it was I had no idea. It was so freezing I dropped my bloodied clothes and retreated to the warmth of Henry's bed. My teeth were chattering. It was my turn to warm my feet on his legs. He did not wake.

***

Amaris came looking for me. It must have been the last place she searched. She let out a squeak of embarrassment before dashing back to my chamber. By now, both Henry and I were awake. I was reluctant to leave the warmth of his bed, but I needed to talk to our sons. Last night's debacle had to be discussed. Although not certain, I think it was Richard's sword that missed me by a whisker. Above all, I wanted to know what drove Henry to attempt to dissolve our marriage. Well, that could start now. I rolled away from his grasp.

'Why did you want to annul our marriage? If anyone should be applying to have it dissolved, it should be me.'

Henry's incoherent muttering into the bedclothes told me nothing so I continued.

'Our relationship to one another is of the fourth degree, yes, but that did not concern you in L'Ombrière or in the cathedral in Poitiers over thirty years ago, nor when William was born or all the others up until I was carrying John. You have been the one who has violated our marriage, not me.'

Henry popped his head out of the bedclothes. He looked terrible with one eye blackened, and his cheek swollen. Whoever hit him did a good job. He moaned as the pain raced around his face.

'I am aching, Eleanor. I do not want to be interrogated.'

I raised the bedclothes to climb out into the freezing air. 'You are letting in the draughts, Eleanor.'

I dropped back, cowardly dreading the chill myself.

***

Much later, when I tried to analyse my reaction to Henry's ardour, I had few answers except my own animal lust. Regardless of all our differences, we were practised lovers, skilled at giving each other pleasure. Which made me wonder why would he want to go to other women's beds? My appetite for him had always been as strong as his, which was why I lost control so often.

After I had bathed and dressed, with my maids' disapproval dripping like the icicles in the bailey, I went to speak to my boys. The archbishop had bottled them up with guards outside their doors. John, I chose as my first victim. He was reading quietly— Plutarch of all authors.

He greeted me with a sheepish grin as I sat beside him.

'Are you all right, Maman?'

'Yes. Though last night was not what I was expecting. A shock but…' I paused. 'Then for a horrible moment I thought there was going to be an all-out Capet/Plantagenet war.'

John gave a lopsided sneer. 'I am glad I floored that French bastard. Nobody insults our family, Maman.'

'It was you who punched Phillip?' John was looking pleased with himself. I was amazed.

'Thank you for defending my honour.'

He shrugged. 'It was nothing.'

'It is to me.' I was proud of John. His action was the last thing I would have expected.

He closed his book wearing a puzzled expression. He then took my breath away as he turned and scrutinised me.

'I am amazed you still love Papa.'

After last night in Henry's bed, I wondered that myself. John was amazingly patient.

'Maybe… maybe there is a corner in my heart that cares for the man I married, but the man he has become is a mystery to me.'

'Yet last night you played to remain our father's wife knowing you would win. Anyway, we did not want to be proclaimed illegitimate. We were willing you to checkmate Papa.'

'Thank you, John. I did not want that possibility either, which is why I challenged your father.'

John grunted. 'Good or we might have killed him.'

I stared at the young man seated relaxed in front of me, my understanding of him was as perplexed as ever. Time to change the subject.

'I did not know Plutarch was of interest to you.'

'Hardly a surprise. I mean, what would you know?'

My sigh was heavy. 'I agree… I see it is a Latin version. You should read it in Greek.'

'I am afraid I do not know Greek as well as my brothers and sisters.'

'Why not?'

'Because, Mother, you were not there to teach me.'

That punctured my feeling of 'getting closer to John'. His use of the formal 'Mother' grated. *So much for him protecting my honour*, I thought. I decided to go.

At the door, I said, 'Well, John, at least your English is excellent, far better than if I had tried to teach you.'

He shrugged and went back to his book. My earlier warmth had dampened.

Geoffrey was next on my list. It was unexpected not to find a guard outside his door, but on entering I found he was with Constance and the children. By the clutter around the table, I saw they had not long finished their repast. Geoffrey called for a churl to clear away the debris, but not before my sticky-fingered namesake climbed onto my lap. Little Eleanor grabbed for the bejewelled cross on its black silk ribbon around my neck. My fastidious nature had me stiffening. Geoffrey ordered Constance to ask Eleanor's nurse to wipe her fingers. The child screamed as she was snatched away by her mother, who glared at me with narrowed eyes. Geoffrey grumbled and said we should move to his chamber through the adjoining door.

I looked at my most attractive son. Richard was ruggedly handsome, but Geoffrey had an elegance of looks that turned people's heads. As usual, we both started to say the same thing together. He shook his head and asked me to go on, but I deferred to him.

'Your chess has not diminished, thank God, a masterclass in tactics. You had Papa after the sixth move, Maman, yet you prolonged his suffering. I was a little afraid you were going to let him win, making us all illegitimate.'

'John's concern, too. Yes, I could have ended the game earlier, but I had no wish to humiliate Henry in front of everyone.'

'I wanted to pound our father into the floor for the way he shamed you. If you had not thrown yourself over him, I would have reduced him to pulp.'

I then noticed Geoffrey's clenched knuckles were raw with broken skin.

'So, it was you who gave Henry his blackened eye and swollen face.'

'Quite frankly, I should have finished him off.'

I let that go. Geoffrey would have known what I was thinking anyway.

'Did you know about Alais?'

'No. But I think Rich was aware of something because he had been saying for some time, he was never going to marry her, regardless of how much Phillip insisted.'

Before I could say a word about him teaming up with John to attack Poitou, my Merlin got in before me.

'Papa told me I could have Anjou as well as Poitou. I had no intentions of handing it to John, who cannot find his cock, if you will excuse my vulgarity, but I underestimated crafty Richard. Anyway, you have it back now, so nothing is lost.'

I wanted to slap him, precocious brat, but instead, I asked him, 'What do you make of Phillip?'

'I would not trust him as far as I could toss him, but he and Richard are on good terms. That could be useful even if he refuses to marry Alais.'

'That will never happen,' I replied, 'I would rather die.'

'Maman, I think your imminent death will be safe in that respect.'

I was curious, hoping Geoffrey might have heard some whispers.

'What do you know about the child?'

'Nothing. By the way, can you still bear children?'

'Good God, no! Who do you think I am, Sarah, wife of Abraham?' Not a good analogy.

'Then why were you in Papa's bed?'

Does my Merlin know everything?

'That is none of your business.'

'You pair are like rutting deer. Quite frankly, I cannot understand what Papa sees in other women. If you were not my mother, I could quite fancy you myself.'

'Ouch! That hurt.'

I left. My face was still burning with embarrassment and disgust from Geoffrey's remarks when I knocked on Richard's door and was ushered in. At least his quarters were immaculate, unlike the piggery in Geoffrey's chambers. Tidiness was one aspect where Geoffrey did not resemble me one jot, whereas Richard was as fussy as I was about order and cleanliness.

Before I could open my mouth, Richard jumped in.

'Maman, about last night. I am so sorry. I have tossed and turned, knowing how close I came to hurting you, or worse. How dare Papa! I could not bear his hurtful insults regarding you any longer. The anguish you have had to suffer at his hands... I saw red. Wanting to marry Alais, to divorce you and to make all of us illegitimate because he cannot keep his hands off other women just makes me boil.'

My face reddened, knowing my self-control had flown off like migrating birds after the brawl.

'Richard, I do not know what to say.'

'What a mess, Maman... I broke my promise about never hurting Papa. After he had made his intentions known last night, I had every intention of killing him. Even now my hatred boils. I am sorry.'

He knelt, buried his head in my lap and wept. My tears flowed, too. The tragedy was that Richard and Henry were growing more alike in looks as well as in temperament. I had tried to teach Richard to think before he acted, to be thorough, to know the facts before making decisions. In that respect he was better than Henry, but when his temper was riled, he was just as impulsive.

'You knew about Alais,' I asked, 'and your father?'

Richard's face flushed.

'During my last visit to London I overheard two of Papa's churls who had seen them together. They were guffawing that "he could get his leg over such a filly." I stood in the shadows and listened to their lewd discourse before confronting them. I threatened to hang, draw and quarter them if they did not tell me the truth, so they spilled their guts in another way.'

I managed to remain dignified. But I wondered who had initiated the affair, Henry or Alais. Henry might not have the figure he once had, but in a craggy way he was still handsome. Also, he was adept at flattery and could easily sweep an innocent girl off her feet.

'I am never going marry Alais, Maman. I was told a child was conceived but not of its fate. I heard whispered it was ill formed. I also know Papa was unaware of Alais' pregnancy till recently.'

'What of Philip?'

'I think Alais has denied it to her brother, but Martin was going to tell him the truth whether he liked it or no.'

'She should be sent to a nunnery to contemplate her sins. Whatever transpired with Henry's help, she has ruined her life. She could have been Queen of England. Phillip must find her fall from grace embittering. Serve the damn French right.'

'Well, Papa has given me an out on a plate, Maman. I never wanted to marry her in the first place.'

'I suspected that, but might I recommend that you do a bit of praying on your own behalf and in future think before you act.'

He kissed me on both cheeks and gave me a hug that nearly broke my ribs.

'I will consider your words.'

'I should hope so.'

***

With the new year., snow was piled in high drifts around the castle. A cauldron of disparate beings, we were unable to leave, Archbishop Baldwin had my sons tethered to their quarters, the French to theirs. Henry's bad hip had him enveloped in furs surrounded by braziers. The churls were wearing ruts in the staircases to ply them with wood to keep us warm.

Margaret was next on my list. Questions required answers.

'I understand your desire to protect me from unpleasant information, but I should have been told about Alais.'

Margaret's face reddened. 'Lady Eleanor, I was so shocked when I discovered Alais was with child, I knew not what to do. My family had no idea who had lain with her except it could not have been Prince Richard who was across the channel. Alais eventually admitted to her condition but would not say who the father was. She was adamant she was not going to tell him.'

'Really?' I was sceptical.

Margaret soldiered on. 'Martin and Robert began their own investigations, with little success. Martin stressed Alais was going to have to be removed from the household and sent to sympathetic nuns before she started to change shape.'

'How did she react to that?'

'She was hysterical, but Martin was adamant. He told her there was a small chance she could still marry Prince Richard if the child was born elsewhere without King Henry or her brother knowing about her predicament.'

'And then?'

'We prepared her to leave, watching her like a hawk to see if she made any attempt to contact her lover. Martin confined her to her quarters. She was unable to leave without a chaperone. He had nuns from the abbey sleep in her bedchamber. The only person who tried to contact her—the poor woman studied her clenched hands—was King Henry. He was told by the good sisters he was not welcome. We assumed he could be the unknown lover and possible father. I am so sorry, Milady.'

I took a steadying breath. 'Did Martin question Alais after your discovery?'

'Yes. She tried to deny the fact, but she is not a good liar, so when we threatened her with your wrath, Prince Richard's, and King Phillip's, she confessed, begging the family not to tell the king about the child. Shortly afterwards, she was escorted by the nuns to their abbey.'

I shook my head. Sorrow consumed me, mixed with humiliation, but I continued regardless of my feelings.

'What happened to the child?'

'There was something wrong with it, a hand with missing fingers, a twisted spine. It was a boy. Alais was distraught. The nuns found the baby dead a few days after its birth... smothered.' Margaret swallowed. 'The nuns had no idea who the culprit was but suspected Alais, who said something about Lord Henry never accepting a crooked freak to lead his new dynasty. When she returned to the household, we made certain Alais' bedchamber was locked at night and a guard put on the door.'

Margaret was certain that Henry had no further contact with Alais. But I had my suspicions. Why did he prepare a document to have our marriage annulled, followed by his making a grandiose announcement? Was he trying to appease the girl? Or was the resulting melee all part of a plan to get out of a relationship in which he had become more embroiled than he intended? And the tender whisper, 'you are so beautiful' in the cathedral here on Christmas Day, why? But our game of chess was genuine enough. Henry hated to lose, but so did I. Whatever was going through his head damn near ended his life and caused further ructions with his sons and the French.

Had Alais told Henry about the child, saying it died at birth, so he felt sorry for her? Then, knowing she was capable of bearing children he had this insane idea about starting another dynasty. But what of our lovemaking later, as beautiful as any in our happy times together? I knew that was partly my doing, but Henry instigated it. I was curious.

***

Richard and Geoffrey were pacing and fuming. Archbishop Baldwin's decree that they would be excommunicated if they stuck their noses outside their quarters had them obeying the detention even if it was trying their patience. John, amazingly, was showing the most fortitude. Maybe all those years confined at Fontevrault had taught him to be self-contained, though from what I heard of his exploits, like his disaster in Ireland for instance, I doubted it.

Richard was pacing and grinding his teeth when I went to speak to him.

'Richard, calm yourself. Where can you go except to pick a fight with your brothers or father?'

'It is Phillip I need to talk to, Maman, not Papa, Geoffrey or John. I want to dissolve my betrothal to Alais as soon as possible.'

'I do not blame you. Is there someone else you wish to marry?'

'Hardly, but I am sure you and Papa will know of a suitable candidate.'

I ignored his sarcasm. 'Well, I am not in a position to find one. Meanwhile, I will try to arrange a meeting between you and Phillip.'

***

I scheduled to meet Archbishop Baldwin in his quarters. As it happened, we both wanted to speak to each other. He had ordered in honey cakes and mulled wine. He handed me a goblet.

'Milady you are a remarkable woman and carry yourself with great dignity considering the situation in which you have been placed. I admire your fortitude.'

'Thank you, Your Grace, but I assure you I have faults aplenty.'

'Ah, do not we all?' Archbishop Balwyn paused. 'I do not know, Lady Eleanor, how to put this delicately, but I must discuss concerns I have about the Lord King. When you said in London you were worried that he was at times… illogical, I was sceptical, but after his outrageous outburst after Christmas, I, too, fear his actions are becoming more irrational.'

'It was not one of his finest moments, I agree.'

'Milady, I believe you are the only one who can restrain him. He needs a strong woman by his side. Could you see your way forward if not to totally forgive him for his misdemeanours, but to be more attentive to his needs.'

I almost choked on my wine. Baldwin had to be the only person in the castle who did not know I had spent the night in Henry's bed after the brawl, if that was what he meant by *attending to his needs*.

I asked, 'Your Grace, have you spoken to the Lord King about this?'

'I am not sure how I could convey to King Henry that I am finding him more unreasonable.'

'Much of his behaviour is due to his inflamed hip,' I replied, 'which causes him considerable pain. He also suffers headaches that are unbearable. When King Henry is badly afflicted, he is almost impossible to deal with.'

'I see.'

'And regardless of any desire on my part to counsel him, I do not think he would appreciate my interference. In the past, he has found my advice confronting to his ego.'

'Milady, it is not just his actions the other night that worry me. I am concerned that the Lord King is struggling to maintain control over his empire. I fear some vassals are simmering. I know your power is limited, but is there anything you can do?'

'I am afraid Lord Henry objected to my methods of governance, Your Grace. He said I talked too much when action was necessary. He became jealous if my methods succeeded. Early in his reign, Lord Henry had a vision for his lands which he achieved through hard work and to some extent his charming personality. But he had no idea how to keep the peace he fought so valiantly to win, except by returning to the brutality he witnessed as a boy.'

The archbishop paused. 'And what if you had lost that chess game?'

'I knew I would not. I had to protect my sons' and daughters' legitimacy.'

'Ah. You are very cunning, Lady Eleanor.'

'Maybe… Lord King Henry did not think through his foolish notion about annulling our marriage. Had he freed himself, he would have freed me too. The Aquitaine and all my lands would have returned to my authority like they did when the late King Louis' and my marriage was dissolved. Our sons, regardless of their legitimacy, would still be my heirs, and if he attempted to disinherit Prince Richard's right to the Anglo-Norman Empire, he would have faced a rebellion of extreme proportions. My chess victory saved him from this. He plays chess in the same way, impulsively. But in triumph I also feel immense sadness.'

Archbishop Baldwin mulled over my words.

'So, Lady Eleanor, you feel you cannot help?'

'I would love to. But I am still Henry's hostage though he has given me more freedom. He will never allow me any meaningful contribution to the ruling of our kingdom. He would suspect me of treachery regardless of how genuinely I might wish to assist. The disagreements between our sons, the king and myself that led to my incarceration in this hideous castle and then in England, he will never admit to or forgive. Moreover, I would do it again to protect my boys.'

'It is a sorry situation, Milady, and a tragedy to see two intelligent people divided as you are.'

'You have witnessed that the king wants another wife and children to supersede the ones we have legitimately conceived because he has lost their respect and love.' I took a deep breath.

'My pride and spirit soars for the man I married, Your Grace, but that man I have lost. I occasionally see glimpses of him like an ignes fatui, a will-o-the-wisp in a misty wood, but when I reach out to him, he vanishes, and I am left with an ogre.'

Tears filled my eyes. Archbishop Baldwin handed me his handkerchief.

'I am so sorry, my dear Lady Eleanor, for re-igniting your sorrow.'

I shook my head.

'Prince Richard would like you to arrange a meeting between him and King Phillip. He can no longer marry Princess Alais for obvious reasons.'

'I will be happy to oblige.'

'Thank you.'

***

Richard wanted me to accompany him when he met with Phillip Capet. I told Richard I would never bend my knee to Île de France because I was his equal as Queen of England. Archbishop Baldwin came with us as adjudicator.

Phillip was royally housed and given the privilege he deserved. One of Phillip's clerical minions let us in, but I was not expecting to see Alais. She had a hide to show her face. The skin around Phillip's right eye was a purplish shade tinged in yellowish green. He moved gingerly although it was over a week since the brawl. I had a delicious feeling of satisfaction. Well done, John!

Richard gave him the required honour, which was sickening, but then he needed to follow protocol. Alais looked my handsome son up and down. Was it regret or hope that flitted across her pale face? God knew what Henry saw in her. She acknowledged me with an imperceptible bow of her head. Phillip looked at me expecting some reverence. I remained aloof. Baldwin looked suitably benign, disguising an iron resolve.

Phillip invited us to sit. He offered wine, but we declined. This was not a social occasion. I opened the proceedings.

'Lord King Phillip, you must be aware of the magnitude of this visit. It is necessary under the most unfortunate circumstances that my son Prince Richard of England and my heir to the Aquitaine must withdraw from his betrothal to Princess Alais of France. We have prepared a document that negates all that was previously written and agreed regarding Princess Alais' dowry and marriage contracts. It declares Prince Richard's and Princess Alais' betrothal null and void. All that is necessary is for the document to be signed. As witness, His Grace, the Archbishop Canterbury, will countersign.'

Phillip ignored the archbishop's presence. 'And what is the reason, Eleanor of Aquitaine, for this sudden withdrawal of a lawful obligation on Prince Richard's behalf?'

Richard answered, 'It has been brought to my attention that Princess Alais' has conducted an affair with — another. I also know she had borne the man a child. The baby was smothered in the Abbey of Saint Claire near London with the mother suspected of carrying out the atrocity. Under these circumstances, Lord King Phillip, you must acknowledge that Princess Alais is no longer suitable to be the future Queen of England.'

Alais let out a strangled cry, looking in fear at her brother whose eyes were as cold as the surrounds of Chinon. Phillip looked at me with distaste, perhaps ready to comment about my adulterous marriage to his father.

He was stopped, however, by our guardian angel, Archbishop Baldwin. 'Lord King Phillip, it saddens me to have to reiterate Prince Richard's concerns about the suitability of his future wife and queen. I, too, know your sister has lost her honour and therefore her betrothal to the future king of England must be annulled. What is more, this is conceded by his father Lord King Henry, who would be here petitioning you, too, Sire, should he not be unwell.'

Well, that was an unexpected embellishment. I struggled not to look smug, particularly as Henry had refused to have anything to do with these proceedings. We were happy with that. He could argue over the dowry at a future date, ironic considering what chaos and tragedy he had caused.

Alais started to babble hysterically. 'This is all your doing, Lady Eleanor. You are a jealous, treacherous witch who has ruined King Henry's life.'

Baldwin silenced her. 'Princess Alais, you should be on your knees, you should be contrite. Lord Phillip, let me emphasise that your sister would be best placed in a convent where she can spend her days in prayer begging God's forgiveness.'

With that she was dismissed, screaming hysterically at Phillip. The betrothal was declared null and void, the document signed and witnessed.

As we rose to leave, Phillip snarled at me, 'You broke my father's heart. God knows what he saw in you, you black witch!'

I stood my ground.

'Your father saw a mighty dowry with a beautiful face, but when it came to sex, I believe, he preferred men. It is a miracle you and your half-sisters were ever conceived. Was it seven years after Louis wed your mother that you were born? And I believe your half-sisters are years apart. Hardly a sign of connubial bliss!'

That left Phillip gasping like a landed fish. Richard hurried me out the door. Baldwin had missed the venomous exchange.

***

The weather improved, but everything was dripping as the snow melted. I had to speak to Henry.

Baldwin was not exaggerating when he said Henry was unwell. Like Phillip's, his blackened eye was changing colour, but his crashing to the floor after Geoffrey's assault, followed by his extra exercises with me, had done nothing for his hip. I swathed myself in furs and approached the lion's den.

Henry was a pile of silver fox and thick wool. His braziers needed wood. I think he terrified the churls, so they were only appearing when summoned. I chewed an ear or two, telling them they would be shovelling snow unless they kept wood supplied to the king's braziers.

'How are you feeling, Henry, any better?'

With a snarl, he replied, 'What do you want, Eleanor? I am sure you have not come for a convivial chat.'

I rolled my eyes. 'Richard and I met with Phillip Capet. Alais seemed to have some misguided idea she was still a suitable wife for Richard, but the betrothal has been successfully annulled.'

Henry was like a hibernating bear in his den of furs, so I rubbed it in. 'What a hide she had. To think, after bearing an illegitimate babe, then smothering the innocent mite, she believed she could still be queen of England. She must be mad!'

Henry grunted.

'I am surprised you were unaware she was with child.'

I could almost hear Henry's brain ticking as he contemplated his reply to my indignant revelations.

'What in God's name did you see in such a vapid wan-looking creature, or did she throw herself at you knowing you did not have the mental or physical fortitude to reject her advances?'

I was needling Henry, but his physical incapability was on my side for once. 'I hope it is guilt that is preventing your answer, or did you just use her, not caring one jot about the advantage you were taking over an innocent young girl to satisfy your lust? Disgusting, seeing the girl was entrusted to your care as your son's betrothed.'

At last, Henry answered. 'You amaze me, Eleanor. A week ago, you willingly laid with me, and you accuse me of lust.'

'Henry, I am your wife.'

'You were not all those years ago in L'Ombrière.'

'True, but I knew what I was doing. I was twenty-nine years old. I had borne two children to a husband of sorts and had had two lovers. I knew the difference between desire and lust. Furthermore, I knew what it was like to be married to a man who found my body repulsive. I did not want another husband with similar thoughts, who preferred men to women.'

'What! Are you saying Louis preferred men?'

'Think about it, Henry. It took nearly seven years of married life excluding a miscarriage to eventually conceive Marie. Louis eschewed my bed. When he was forced by Abbé Suger to do his duty it was a disaster. Five years later, I had Alix because, again, the church intervened, this time the pope. I never saw Louis naked, or he me. He rarely kissed me. He had never touched my breasts. He came to my bed, did what he had to do, then ran away to pray. Remember, he was brought up in a monastery Henry... When I discovered love, I was as a virgin. I had no idea sensual desire existed and, when I did, I grasped the sensation. That was what was missing from my marriage to Louis. In fact, when Richard and I met with Phillip, I told him I was amazed he had been conceived along with Margaret and Alais. Louis' incentive to enter his various wives' beds would have been prompted by the clerics of Île de France insisting he produce an heir.'

'So, that was why I had to past your test?'

'Partially. I had no desire to remarry, but I had no choice. I had avoided abduction by a whisker, thanks to the skill of my guards, with two men killed in front of me. Another made a determined effort with a force of five hundred men; then there was your brother and the Count of Champagne. I knew you were attracted to me. At least it was better to marry a man who could please me in bed than another Louis. Anyway, that is by the by because I fell in love with you. Now, you have destroyed that love.'

Deep in his pile of furs Henry was silent. Was he mulling over my conclusions regarding Louis or was he searching his conscience?

'Alais flirted with me — outrageously. I only lay with her thrice, and she was not a virgin. There was no certainty the child was mine. It could have been another's.'

I burst out laughing. 'Presuming, Henry, if she can count, she would have known who the father was. And if she was "entertaining" two men, that makes her even less suitable for the role for which she was betrothed. But I think she was in love with you and told you so.'

'Well, I am not in love with her.'

'Then why in God's name did you want to annul our marriage to marry her?'

'I want sons who love me, who do not run to Maman like babies when they do not get their own way.'

I rubbed it in with an ugly laugh. 'At least our sons are whole. Not like the deformed boy Alais gave birth to then smothered. Is that all your seed is capable of now, Henry — gammy-handed, twisted sons? Or is that all your putain can produce? I should have let you win that game of chess, so you and Alais could have conceived disfigured apes for your new dynasty. Then you could look at our strong, intelligent, handsome sons and rue what you had thrown away.'

A strangled groan issued from the bear in front of me. 'Witch!'

'Huh! You poisoned our sons' feelings for you by your adulterous treatment of me. You spurned their needs, especially poor Hal's. They wanted a father, Henry… love. Then you pitted one against the other till you created a snake-pit. And as for running to me, they begged me to ask you to listen, especially Hal. I tried but you disregarded my pleas. Hal wanted you to treat him like the Young King you had him crowned, and to be proud of him like when obtained his knighthood with distinction. But you favoured John and ignored him time and time again right up until he died.'

By now my anger was rising, my patience tried, so I left. Whenever I thought I was closing the gap between us, to form some sort of mutual understanding, I ended up frustrated and furious. I did not believe one jot what he said about his liaisons with Alais or that she was not a virgin. I was sure he had seduced her. That insipid pale-eyed child was no femme-fatale. As he said, he probably did not love her or give a jot about her. As for his new dynasty, more likely he thought she might be a useful alliance with the French. But a man of his age and status taking advantage of a foolish girl for his own gratification was abhorrent. Was the deformed child God's punishment?

Chapter 18 The End of An Era

The snow surrounding Chinon thawed into slushy piles. Those who had journeys to make left. Phillip and his entourage were the first. Alais went with her brother. What a wasted young life. A convent somewhere was going to enrol a new postulant unless Phillip could find a minor knight who did not mind how he was connected to Île de France.

I was eager to leave, too. I did not want to remain under Henry's roof, but, while my sons were there, I would stay. Of course, my movements were still at Henry's whim. Poitiers was not too distant. How I would have loved to visit my old home or return to Fontevrault to spend more time there.

While I was thinking of a way to persuade Henry to allow me to leave for England, if possible, via Bordeaux, he suddenly called a family conference. Whatever it was, I feared the outcome.

We met in Henry's chamber. Thank the Lord, Archbishop Baldwin had not left. At least we had a sane referee. John was looking smug. One did not have to be a scholar to realise the topic was going to be the Aquitaine.

Henry announced, 'Before he left Chinon, I spoke to the French King about the possibility of John marrying Princess Alais.'

Guffaws erupted from my two oldest sons. John, chords standing out on his neck, screamed, 'I am not marrying that pasty-faced whore, even if she were the last woman on earth!'

Henry bellowed over him. 'Calm down, John. You will get the Aquitaine if you do.'

Now, it was my turn. In a low voice, I stated, 'Let me remind you the Aquitaine is not yours to bestow on anyone. As its duchess, I have performed my duty, as had my father before me, to ordain who will be my heir. As you know, 'enri Plantagenet-a, the position is not vacant.'

'As your husband I have priority.'

'With whom may I ask? Certainly not with my vassals. You can offer me incentives, my freedom. You can throw me in the deepest dungeon in your kingdom, but I will never as God is my witness secede my inheritance to anyone other than my chosen heir, Richard.'

A quick glare at Richard had him keep his sword sheathed. Geoffrey slow-clapped my speech. I slapped him. John reddened with rage.

'Lord Henry, you cannot give away what is not yours to give, even as the Duchess of Aquitaine's husband.' Baldwin intervened.

'His Grace's explanation, I believe, ends this discussion,' I replied. 'Therefore, I will take my leave, return to England and to Matilda's children. But, before I do that, as my title to the County of Poitou had been restored to me, I should by rights make a regal progress through my lands.' I paused. 'I have another point to make.'

'And what would that be, my dear Eleanor?' Henry sneered.

'I suggest you desist in whatever schemes are hatching in your fevered brain regarding my duchy. I have no qualms whatsoever to withdraw my signature from Aquitaine treasury documents. Thus, you will be denied manpower, produce and other necessities for your Anglo-Norman Empire. Furthermore, should you continue down this path to upset my ordained succession, you must be prepared to put down a full-scale rebellion the likes of which you have never experienced, with Île de France joining in for good measure.'

The archbishop harrumphed, giving me a look that said, *do not push your luck*. So, I stood to leave, without being officially dismissed.

'You seem to forget your place, Eleanor,' Henry called, 'You have a charge of treason punishable by death against you, and I can bring the portcullis down on all of you now that I have you together. You can no longer run to France to incite your sons against their father.'

'And like I have just said, war will break out from Scotland to the Pyrenees. I do not have to run to France. Your defilement of Alais gives Phillip an excellent reason to go to war for her honour. Nor will my death solve your problems as you know, so keep your hollow threats.'

Richard's sword was halfway out of its scabbard.

'Enough, Richard!'

Archbishop Baldwin's patience had run dry. He dismissed John, Richard and Geoffrey, ordering them to their quarters. Robert and Martin, he asked to kindly leave us. They shot out the door as if released from a schoolroom. He rounded on Henry and me, glaring like we were naughty children.

'It disappoints me, that two people of your status can behave so despicably. I am within a hair's breadth of excommunicating you both. Although I knew you not in the early days of your marriage, I have been told there was love aplenty between you.'

Henry and I exchanged glances. Then Henry stared at his feet, and I sat twisting my wedding ring around my finger.

His Grace went on. 'You are both intelligent people, so why must you continue to feud into your latter years?'

I went to speak but was silenced. Baldwin knew the reasons our marriage had come to this. What of our conversation only days ago?

'Lord King Henry, you should show some respect for your wife and queen. To allow her to visit her lands will do no harm. Your Ladyship, a pilgrimage to your favourite religious houses to pray for your sharp tongue to be curbed would not go astray.'

'That will be the day,' Henry sniped.

Baldwin missed the remark, but I did not.

'Perhaps Henry, you should repeat yourself for His Grace's benefit.'

'The day you curb your tongue Eleanor, will be a miracle. Your Grace, Her Ladyship favoured our children and encouraged our sons to dishonour their father.'

I could not believe my ears. Did he not take in anything I had said regarding Hal and the others?

Baldwin held up his hand to allow Henry to continue.

'Eleanor, you questioned every move I made. You consider your intellect superior to every man in Christendom because you can read and write and have a fluency with languages. I am tired of not being able to live up to your impossible expectations.'

'Please, Your Grace, I should be allowed to speak in my defence.'

The archbishop nodded.

'My father taught me to question, to never accept mediocrity, to be meticulous. Lord Henry has accused me of searching documents for mistakes in Latin. I do not seek them; I discover them as I read. Too many important tracts are written most ill, enabling the interpretation of laws to be distorted by clever advocates. Yet if I point out these anomalies, I am condemned as an interfering witch. If such discoveries were found by Thomas Becket or Peter Abelard, even Lord Henry's scribe Peter de Blois or some other learned man, they would be applauded for their diligence.'

Both were silent, so I continued. 'I have been told that learning in one of my status and sex is unwomanly, even though my God-given talents were put to good use when acting as Lord Henry's Regent in England and when ruling the Aquitaine. I did what my father trained me to do. King Louis never accepted my intelligence, and I thought Lord King Henry did, but my present position proves I am wrong. Your Grace, I cannot change who I am, nor can I, as I once told the late Pope Eugenius, unlearn the knowledge I have gained over my lifetime any more than you can, or my Lord Henry.'

Archbishop Balwyn sighed deeply and said he would pray for us. He dismissed us with the sign of the cross. I helped Henry stand and we left the chamber.

***

Eventually, I was allowed by Henry to ride back to Fontevrault where I arranged more alms to be distributed for prayers for Hal's immortal soul. This time I was able to speak longer with the new Abbess Mother Magdalene, whom I met only briefly on our way to Chinon. I spent two weeks with the nuns and joined in their worship and simple way of living. My chess game with God, at least, had paused. I developed a rapport with the Mother Superior.

One day as we sat together and chatted, I said, 'Mother Magdalene, I constantly question God's will. I fear He does not like me very much.'

'Milady, I, too, sometimes have doubts and wrestle with my

faith regarding life matters I find cruel or alarming. I question why babies die or men war against each other and I often wonder why my prayers seem to go unanswered. But there is also so much good in the world that in the end I believe it balances out.'

'When I knew I loved Lord King Henry and he me, I thought my life was complete, but that has ended in bitterness, with the king jealous of me and those who pay me attention. My sons war against their father and each other. I ask why? Then I end up having another joust with God.'

'You must not despair. This is a path God has chosen for you, knowing one day you will prevail.'

I shook my head. 'Prevail? Maybe, but at what cost?'

***

I missed my boys. After I farewelled them at Chinon, I was left again with an empty hollow. The trip to Fontevrault had helped. Magdalene gave me strength to carry on, but news of Richard and Geoffrey aligning themselves with Phillip by following him to Île de France and embracing his court was distressing. Henry belched fire like a volcano. As far as possible, I avoided him. Matilda's children were brought to me on their journey home to Saxony. I stayed in Normandy for almost a year, a bitter-sweet experience. I must have wept an ocean beside Hal's tomb after an emotional visit to Le Mans and Henry's father's mausoleum before I rode to Rouen.

I discovered Henry had another mad idea to overlook Richard and make John his heir to England, which was why Richard was holed up in Paris. This, of course, bypassed Geoffrey as well. Never in history had a youngest son been so favoured, yet Henry wondered why his oldest were rebelling. Phillip, the cunning creature, would be rubbing his hands together and fuelling the divisions.

Neither had Henry given up on his desire to rid me of the Aquitaine. When his foolish notion to make John his heir to his Anglo-Norman empire failed, he went back to scheming to obtain my duchy, as well as Normandy, for John. Phillip made certain Richard was the rightful heir apparent to England. I was grateful for that though I also heard he was keeping Richard on tenterhooks by spreading rumours that Henry could change his mind which, knowing his father, had a lot of credence.

Eventually, Richard left Île de France and travelled back to Poitiers to thwart any attempt by his father to invade or cause disruption.

***

I was sent back to England and assigned to Salisbury Castle, not my first choice, but at least I had privacy from Henry's snooping.

The next I heard; Henry was preparing to sail back to Normandy to defend his lands. Before he left, he came to Salisbury. He spent a few days with me, looking grey with pain from his hip and headaches. How he endured, I knew not. I made up my mind under the circumstances to be courteous. Brynn was back within my household, so I massaged her creamy unguent into his hip.

We dined together, discussing our grandchildren, so many now. It kept us neutral and on an even keel. Matilda's little ones arrived safely back in Saxony. I missed them, especially Otto, who vowed he would return one day to be my knight. What a dear little fellow.

Before Henry left, he expressed his desire to spend his last night with me in a manner of our past. I was in two minds, but there was something about the way he took my hand and a poignancy in his eyes. Also, I thought it would be better to part from a sensual embrace than pouring vitriol on each other. Also, Archbishop Baldwin's final words to me before we left Chinon was 'to try again to bottle that will-o-the-wisp before I regretted it.' I said I would try if he told Henry to embrace the woman he once admired and married. Perhaps this was behind Henry's motive, too.

Before he mounted his horse to leave, Henry thanked me for being calm and pleasant. He said he looked forward to seeing me soon. He surprised me by kissing me tenderly. I told him to take care and begged him to think rationally before he acted. With gritted teeth, he hoisted himself onto his horse and rode out across the drawbridge without turning back. And I asked myself, could this be the same man who had acted the way he had?

***

I could have left Salisbury but decided to stay in one place for a while. One morning, I received a missive from Richard sent from Paris that did not thrill me. One minute, he and Phillip were fighting each other over the Counties of Toulouse or Berry, next they were allies again. I continued to read down the page in my chamber with my women, who were sewing and nattering. Richard's words, no matter how tenderly he couched them, wrenched my very essence apart. Geoffrey had been killed in a jousting accident. His death was too much; my crazy, funny, brilliantly gifted duplici, my Merlin. I fainted.

When I regained my senses, I could not speak but thrust Richard's letter into Amaris' hand. She, too, let out a moan of disbelief. Everyone was engulfed in grief. Quirky Geoffrey often infuriated all of us, family and retainers alike, but he was too endearingly funny for anyone to be angry with for long. His curiosity, his hunger for knowledge, even if he irritated us by showing it off, made us smile. He drove his tutors to tear their hair out. He would learn his Latin verbs in what seemed like seconds, then annoy his brothers and sisters. He was the only person I knew who could make calm, good-natured Jerome raise his voice, except, of course, myself.

Geoffrey would spend hours watching a butterfly emerge. I remember him capturing my imported silkworms to watch them spin their cocoons when I was trying to establish an industry for silk-making in the Aquitaine. I felt ashamed when I remembered the number of times I clouted him around his ears. Whereas Richard was my closest son as my heir, Geoffrey was me in a male body. We had this weird connection. We read each other's minds, ended each other's sentences. Together we would start saying the same things—laughing as to who should go first. He could beat me at chess and I him with each game becoming a marathon of minds and tactics. He rode like a Saracen to my aid during that fateful ambush, a little boy. We loved the same books, argued philosophy, and, in private, our sometimes heretical opinions of God's will! Again, I asked why He was taking my flesh and blood, Hal, and now Geoffrey?

I would have cheerfully taken their places. The potential lost was immeasurable. Even if Richard said Geoffrey was behaving like chaff, blowing every which way in the wind, I hoped he would settle, but was he too like me, always searching. Why did he joust? He knew I hated the sport. What now of his wife and daughters? Richard said another child was due. I had not bonded with Constance, but I knew she and Geoffrey were in love in a manic haphazard sort of way. It suited them. Constance, too, was bright though not as formally schooled as was Geoffrey. I knew he encouraged her to learn. She would miss him, poor girl, as would little Eleanor and Alix. Then there was the baby to come who would never know its father. *Why, oh why?*

I struggled with Geoffrey's death, angry he jousted and wasted his life. It was hard to come to terms with. I felt that part of me had been cleaved in two and one half thrown away.

***

I tried to continue with my life in a meaningful way. Amaris and Joachim watched my every move, which annoyed me. Joachim suggested chess. Not a good idea; too many memories of Geoffrey.

'Perhaps, Joachim, I should play God and try to win him back like I won back my marriage. I could try for William and Hal, tiny Phillip, too.'

My sarcasm did not impress my good kind confessor. He apologised for being thoughtless. I tried to embroider but ended up throwing what I had stitched across the room. It was a mess of ugly threads. Amaris said she would fix my efforts. Writing helped but was not its usual balm.

***

Almost three years passed at a snail's pace. Over time, I came to accept that Geoffrey was gone. Correspondence continued to trickle. Henry was not well. Richard and John continued to be divided.

One day, a courier arrived from Saxony. Not Matilda's seal, but an official looking one not known to me. It contained the soul-destroying news that Matilda had died in childbirth. My darling eldest daughter. Again, I begged God to tell me, to give me a sign as to why my beautiful children were being singled out to be taken away. Amaris, Margaret, everyone in my court, were trying to comfort me when they grieved themselves. Joachim sat with me holding my hands. He knew not to say she was in God's bosom, God's care, because all I could think of, as always, was that this was God's punishment for my sins. The thought of Matilda's large family left without their Maman tore me apart. My heart ached for Heinrich, too, because he and Matilda had loved one another.

I begged God on my knees to tell me why I must suffer this pain. Joachim said I should remember that most of humanity were far worse off than the Duchess of Aquitaine. That was blunt. He was right as usual, and I felt humbled.

In the end, it was Joachim's simple words that penetrated my grief. I thought of the bundle of rags who first greeted me on my arrival in England a lifetime ago, and of the beautiful woman Winifred who was prepared to give me her child because I had lost William; to me, so immeasurably privileged. I mourned, but, really, I was no better in the eyes of God than they were. I had allowed my arrogance to blind me. I had to accept. But could I?

I wondered what Henry was feeling. Matilda had loved her father, and he her. She tried so hard to encourage us to forgive each other, two of the most stubborn people in Christendom. Now I feel I should have made more of an effort for her benefit. Did not Christ say, 'turn the other cheek?' What sort of mother was I not to attempt to do what my daughter so desperately desired?

***

I needed to do something to drag my spirits out of the grim pit that had swallowed me. Although I was still guarded, my greater freedom allowed me to leave Salisbury Castle to explore my surroundings. I decided to venture to the nearby villages so I could learn more about Henry's and my people around Salisbury. I hoped I might salve my empty ache if I could do some good in Hal, Geoffrey and Matilda's names. I knew they would like that.

My guards and I rode off through fields and hedgerows into hamlets with poor housing, a few scrawny animals and little else. As I dismounted into the mud and animal excrement my stomach turned. The soft chamois boots I wore were destroyed after a few steps. Never had I seen such poverty. As Queen of

England, I had travelled through the larger villages and market towns, but never to where the serfs of local barons lived, if one could call it living. Swine were kept better.

I took Tom with me because my accented English was sometimes hard to understand; also, these people spoke a dialect. With Tom's help, I asked how the lives of these sad relics of humanity could be improved. Disease was rife. Joachim was concerned I could catch one of the illnesses that harried the folk with whom I tried to talk. Black death was common.

My faith in my fellow man was challenged. It was unbelievable how badly the feudal lords of this cluster of dwellings treated their serfs. They used them as beasts of burden, took most of the food they produced for themselves or for market. Most humbling were the little graveyards surrounding old stone Saxon churches where whole families were buried; too many of the graves held babies and children. My jousts with God over the deaths of my children felt like self-indulgence.

I discovered food was always short, even during good harvests. The living conditions forced on the serfs was lower than anything I had ever seen. I would not house a dog in the rude dwellings dug into the earth and covered by poor thatch. They were cold and damp. Mean cooking fires leaked smoke through the thatch in the centre of the only room of the poorly ventilated hut. The inhabitants suffered smarting eyes.

I was familiar with poaching because it occurred on Henry's lands and mine. It was a capital offence. But now I understood why risks were taken. If these peasants had one meal a day, they were lucky. Babies were born in fields then hitched onto their mother's back as she returned to her toil. If they died, they died. Their mothers had no privilege to grieve or have archbishops intone prayers.

Tom said the people to whom he spoke were full of disbelief when told who I was. They had never seen a queen before, not even the ladies of the manors whose land they worked. They were born, lived and died where they stood. Joachim met some Celtic monks, good men, but unschooled and as superstitious as pagans. They did their best to provide succour for their flocks.

When I returned to the castle, Joachim told Amaris to have my clothes burnt and that I be scrubbed from head to toe.

Clean, warm, pampered and privileged, I wondered how I could help these poor people. I would have to approach the barons who owned the lands, the nearby monasteries, and the clerical hierarchy to find a way to better the housing. More importantly, I needed to make certain the serfs had enough to eat. In my present position, though, I had no power to insist by Royal decree that the barons improve the conditions of their villains. I could write to Henry and plead with him to do something in our children's names. But how much notice he would take of my concerns I knew not. I could be told not to interfere.

***

With all the will in the world regarding the necessary help for the hamlets, I struggled. Hal, Geoffrey and Matilda's deaths dragged me into familiar darkness. I tried to pursue my project for the hamlets, but my usual determination was not there. I had spurts of energy, then depression would overwhelm me. Amaris begged Brynn for help. Joachim and Tom would not let me out of their sight as again I trudged the bailey in circles, muttering and cursing God's will in my topsy-turvy mind. Margaret contacted Martin, who was with Henry. How he felt I could only imagine. Matilda's birth had filled him with elation. He loved his eldest daughter with a passion. Geoffrey drove him crazy with his backchat and his Monsieur Sabots Intelligents ways. I remembered him telling Henry and me how caterpillars made armour and that men's big white caterpillars made babies. The wicked look on his face had me burying my head in my hands. Henry did not know whether to laugh or give him the toe of his boot. How often, to my fury, did Henry say, 'like mother like son'. Not that at ten or eleven I had any idea about the caterpillar analogy.

Martin and Robert told Henry I was not handling the deaths regardless of the time that had passed. Hal, 1183, Geoffrey, 1186 and Matilda, 1189. Henry ordered me back to London. In my agitated state of mind, I protested vehemently, citing I had not yet relieved the poor people of the district. Joachim, to my horror, told Brynn to knock me out with a physic before

I harmed myself. My memory of returning to London was therefore hazy.

Days and weeks passed, but Westminster, I think, gave me some relief. Archbishop Baldwin was also in London, so Joachim rallied his support to help me through my grief. The dear man cut short meetings to visit me. When he heard I was not eating well, he would arrive with oysters or he would find olives from the Aquitaine, cheeses from his own dairies and honey from his hives at Canterbury. He had discovered I loved oysters, something Henry had introduced me to years ago in Rouen from the coast of Normandy. These came from Dover, but it mattered not.

Baldwin would arrive before our evening repast, pour wine from Bordeaux and tempt me with different morsels he would tell me he was eager to try. Not wishing to hurt his feelings, I would nibble on freshly baked bread from our kitchens with the titbits brought by this good man. He became like a father coaxing a naughty girl, funny when I thought I might be older than him or at least the same age.

Agnes and Frith joined forces with Margaret to get me out of my nun-like garb and into more regal gowns, even if in mourning white. Eventually, I clawed my way back to whatever normality I inhabited. There were letters to attend to from my family. Even John wrote regarding Geoffrey and Matilda, as well as Joanna and Lenore. They expressed their grief and gave me their strength to drag myself out of the abyss into which I had plunged. Heinrich wrote me a tender letter asking if Otto and his older sister Ricenza could re-join my household. He said Matilda lived long enough to say how much she loved me and how much she owed me for her upbringing. Geoffrey was killed instantly, so no farewells from him—ironic because he always liked to get in the last word.

A letter from Henry arrived. It took more than courage to open it. I stared at the familiar seal. It took two swift gulping goblets of brandy wine before I could tear the seal from the parchment.

My dear Eleanor,

I can only imagine your grief if it is as excruciating as mine. Our gentle beautiful Matilda, whose last words to me were to stop deluding myself when it was obvious that your viperish tongue was hiding your love for me, and why could I not see through your cape of iron. I had too much respect for her earnestness to laugh in her face. But, yes, I know under that icy exterior is the most passionate woman I have ever known who, as you have pointed out in your highly articulate way, I do not understand. I know Matilda wanted us to mend our ways. Can we? Or have we drifted too far apart? Matilda said we were as bad as each other. So true.

I miss our darling daughter, her sunny nature, her goodness much, I know, my dear, due to you being her mother. I feel remiss. I feel guilty. I long for her.

Geoffrey's senseless death is unbearable. Whether he qualifies for heaven, I know not. If in hell, Satan will soon be rid of him to a higher place—too much competition. In heaven, no doubt he will be annoying God, all the angels and the saints. I sincerely hope he does not mention caterpillars. Geoffrey drove me to distraction arguing over minute details. But I miss his mental jousting. Not a good choice of words seeing it was the cause of his death.

But at least our beautiful children who have been taken from us will be together. They are in my prayers as you are also because I hear you have been deeply affected, which distresses me because we have not been together to comfort one another.

When I finish this campaign, I will return to England. I long to see your beautiful face.

Deepest love
Henry

The letter made me laugh and cry. As for his declaration of love, I knew not what to think. I showed it to Amaris who warned me, because he was unwell, he wanted me to be his nursemaid because I was the only woman who would tolerate the treatment he had meted out. I thought that was a bit harsh, but she had witnessed his capricious moods and knew how cruel he could be.

***

I spent grief-stricken days and nights pacing. I reread Henry's letter so many times, wet it so oft with my tears the parchment had almost fallen to pulp. Matilda wanted us to reconcile as well as Joachim, and His Grace, Archbishop Baldwin. I searched my soul for a glimmer of forgiveness. I tried to believe his words, 'deepest love', but I knew from old the moment I relaxed my guard Henry found a way to undermine my resolve to try again. I had given in to his sensuality, then locked my doors; agreed then argued, listened in horror to him wanting to annul our marriage and pitted my skills in chess to keep him as my husband regardless of Baldwin's threats. Moreover, I did not want Richard disinherited as England's next king or our children declared illegitimate.

In Antioch, a lifetime ago, Abraham's sister, the blind seer Judith, predicted my marriage would be turbulent, but did she mean it would be this bad? The love of my life became the hate of my life. Was I running in circles like a caged animal? Was this another lap of the cycle, or had I run so far off course I was lost to Henry and Henry lost to me? Amaris thought I was deluding myself. Henry would never change, nor would I for that matter. Archbishop Baldwin said, because Henry was unwell, the last thing I would want was for him to die unforgiven. He emphasised I would not want to carry that burden of guilt with me forever. I knew I wore my heart on my sleeve then encased it in armour when I was with Henry, the icy exterior he alluded to in his letter.

In the end, I penned Henry a letter that promised nothing, but I hoped gave him solace. I acknowledged how his letter had given me comfort. I looked forward to him returning to London, and that I was slowly coming to terms with Matilda's and Geoffrey's deaths. I told him the arrival of Ricenza and Otto was better than any physic. In many ways, I now had another small Matilda and a small Geoffrey. Their personalities were so akin to mother and uncle. I begged Henry to look after his health, telling him he was in my prayers.

I signed it saying, 'God knows the depth of my feelings for you,' which I knew could be interpreted however one wished.

Shortly after, Richard wrote that Constance had given birth to a baby boy whom she named Arthur. That was indeed good news. How proud Geoffrey would have been, but the news of my latest grandchild filled me with the wrenching sorrow that the child would never know his father. I wrote to Constance and sent the woollen shawl that was Nilla's and mine, used also for my babies.

***

Otto and Ricenza kept me busy. I found tutors for them, but I had no German, so I had to find someone to keep their native tongue alive. Joachim used his detective skills and found a monk from their country living near London. Brother Johannes joined my court, thrilled to be able to teach the children and to speak his native language.

I spent fruitless hours, mostly at night, jousting with God. I told Joachim I felt I was on a giant chess board. Around me there was a bishop, a knight and other pieces, mostly pawns. Of course, there was a king, but I was losing so many pieces I felt I was losing the game. I feared I could no longer protect what was left, and that I would be left a solitary queen.

Joachim shook his head at this analogy. He kept telling me my life was part of a giant plan, that I must accept the bad with the good. But why was it so lopsided? I sounded like Geoffrey or Otto.

'Because you are born to rule,' he said simply.

I nearly fell off my chair laughing. 'Joachim, Henry put paid to that over ten years ago.'

To change the subject, he asked, 'How are your plans going to help the hamlets we visited?'

'Frustrating. I no longer have the power to intervene with the nobles on whose estates the serfs are part and parcel. Are they, too, pawns in God's larger game, may I ask?'

I left the poor man shaking his head and probably praying for my wretched soul or re-mortaring that flimsy wall between me and Satan.

***

Agnes, who had decided my hair was her personal territory, had stopped, after my threats, from pulling grey hairs out of my head. I scanned for wrinkles. The frown line was becoming a rut. My pouty mouth was growing sour-looking, grim. I think I had almost forgotten how to smile, except for Otto, who could have me laughing till I cried. Though recently I nearly swatted him when I discovered one of my small jewellery chests in his bed chamber. Puzzled as to why it was there, I opened it. To my horror a mouse ran out. My screams echoed throughout Westminster. The whole palace guard almost became wedged in the doorway armed for battle, certain I was being abducted or murdered. I was standing on a chair with my skirts around my knees. I do not like mice.

Otto said, 'Grandmaman, the mouse is my pet, and I left all the earrings and bracelets in a neat pile on the big chest in your chamber. Because you have so many other boxes and the like I did not think you would miss one.'

Oh, Geoffrey, you have come back to haunt me.

'Otto, a puppy or a kitten would be a more appropriate pet.'

He replied with the seriousness of a biblical scholar, 'But Grandmaman, surely they would eat my mouse.'

I left him on his hands and knees searching every cranny in his chamber. After that, I needed a brandy wine to settle my pounding heart. I escaped to the library. On my desk were missives from a recent secret courier. I dreaded breaking the seals nowadays for fear of what the parchment might hold. Two were from Richard, one from Robert,

Robert told me Henry was most unwell. Moreover, Richard's alliance with Phillip Capet was not helping his health. I had mixed emotions. To be honest, Henry had forced this situation on himself. I had no sympathy for Henry's tyranny. His deteriorating health, though, saddened me. He did not think clearly when in pain. I hoped nothing foolish had occurred.

Robert had written his letter in two halves, which was strange. The first page revealed that Henry had a meeting with Richard that turned sour, with Henry ranting, 'My children will never do anything that is good. All they do is destroy me and themselves; they have done me harm and injury.'

Richard's homage to Phillip had all but broken Henry, with them invading Anjou and Maine. They had systematically driven a wedge between Normandy and the Aquitaine.

Oh, Henry, what have you let your stubborn militancy do?

I was powerless to rein Richard in. He could behave as badly as his father without a steadying hand. But Henry had never bonded with him. Richard was hurt by Henry's disapproval. His open preference for John filled him with resentment. It was no wonder he had aligned himself with Phillip when everything Richard had inherited his father tried to remove from him. Now growing old before his time and ill, Henry was paying for it.

He was too unwell to attend the peace negotiations and had fled to Chinon to recuperate. Then John inflicted the final blow by also siding with the Capets. Henry was devastated, forced to pay Phillip homage over lands disputed in the Auvergne and Berry; castles and gold were agreed upon as reparation. Worse, French clerics were braying like donkeys that Henry's downfall was due to his 'bigamous, incestuous marriage' to me. What that made Louis' second and third wives I knew not, or the legitimacy of the children born to the women. No doubt that had not entered their self-flagellating minds.

I sat there staring into space as the library darkened with the second page of Robert's letter on my lap. It fluttered to the floor. Ominous clouds shrouded the sun. I felt an unearthly chill as I sat twisting my wedding ring round and round my finger. Dread hovered over me like the Sword of Damocles. My quill was drying in a puddle of ink on a sheet of parchment as I eased the seal from Richard's second letter.

***

I remembered not how I walked from the library to my chamber after reading Richard's letter. One foot followed the other. My maids were retelling the mouse incident, laughing about my cheeky little grandson. When I entered one look told them something was amiss. Amaris arose and came to me as I fell into my chair staring at the ink stains on my gown and hands.

'Eleanor?'

'Henry is dead.'

'Agnes fetch Brother Joachim. Quickly, now.'

Agnes flew from the room. The rest gathered around. Margaret fetched me a goblet of wine. I shook my head bewildered. Brynn started a Welsh lament, haunting, beautiful. Silent tears slid down my cheeks.

Inside my head, like minstrels playing out of tune, a discordant voice echoed, 'You will marry the love of your life. You will bear him many sons. But your life will be tumultuous.'

I was free...

***

Richard had heard the news in Paris and wrote that they buried Henry at Fontevrault Abbey in a ceremony befitting a great king. Richard was on his way to England to be crowned.

I eventually read Robert's second page. He, Martin and Henry's bastard son were with him when he died. He said they clothed him in his royal garments and placed him on a bier for his final short journey from Chinon Castle. "With plain chant and fine service, the nuns received him as their master, as a mighty king ought to be received."

As it happened the heat of summer prevented Henry's body being transferred to Reading Abbey in England nor Le Manns to be interred with his father Geoffrey Plantagenet.

Of course, my detractors could not keep their vicious tongues still, describing beautiful Fontevrault as obscure and "unsuitable for great majesty" and insinuating that Henry strove to confine me there in a nun's habit. Untrue, but it hurt.

***

The mighty bells of Westminster Abbey tolled their lugubrious, sombre note, joined throughout the land by others for the king who reunited a broken realm, but lost his sons. Archbishop

Baldwin escorted me to prayers for Henry's immortal soul. The people of London reached out their hands to me, rich and poor, with "God bless Milady".

I tried not to weep. Joachim did his best to comfort me with gentle words. My mind was in turmoil. Grief I never believed I would experience for the man who so mistreated me in the later years of our marriage engulfed me. But overwhelming me was the vision of that russet, curly-haired boy with the piercing blue eyes, entrancing and charming, the witty, energetic man who made love to me with the passion of a lion — the love of my life.

www.ingramcontent.com/pod-product-compliance
Lightning Source LLC
Chambersburg PA
CBHW051523050726
47503CB00014B/1119